A LAMB
TO THE
SLAUGHTER

A LAMB
TO THE
SLAUGHTER

WILLIAM W. JOHNSTONE
AND J.A. JOHNSTONE

PINNACLE BOOKS
Kensington Publishing Corp.
www.kensingtonbooks.com

All Kensington titles, imprints, and distributed lines are available at special quantity discounts for bulk purchases for sales promotion, premiums, fund-raising, and educational or institutional use.

Special book excerpts or customized printings can also be created to fit specific needs. For details, write or phone the office of the Kensington Sales Manager: Kensington Publishing Corp., 900 Third Avenue, New York, NY 10022. Attn. Sales Department. Phone: 1-800-221-2647.

PINNACLE BOOKS, the Pinnacle logo, and the WWJ steer head logo Reg. U.S. Pat. & TM Off.

First Printing: June 2022
ISBN-13: 978-0-7860-5115-1
ISBN-13: 978-0-7860-4748-2 (eBook)

10 9 8 7 6 5 4 3 2

Printed in the United States of America

Chapter 1

"I ain't sure how much longer I can make it," Bart McCoy gasped when Roy Tate reached up to help him out of the saddle. "I'm bleedin' pretty bad."

"You just hang on," Roy told him. "We've gotta let these horses rest, or we're gonna be tryin' to make it to Tinhorn on foot. I'm gonna set you down under the trees. We'll let the horses drink some water and rest a little, and I'll see if I can tighten that bandage up some more. Accordin' to that feller back at that store at the crossroads to Athens, we can't be but about an hour's ride from Tinhorn. That was almost four hours ago, so don't cash in on me now. We've got plenty of time to get there before suppertime. Come on. Lean on over this way."

Although wounded, Bart reluctantly did as asked and leaned over to let Roy catch his weight on his shoulders.

"I believe we lost that posse," Roy said as he walked Bart over to settle him against a sweetgum tree while he took care of the horses. "I believe they went after Eli and the other boys. When I get back, I'll build a small fire big enough to boil us a cup of coffee. That'll buck you up a little."

"I 'preciate it, Roy," Bart forced out painfully. "You

coulda left me back there at the fork and gone with Eli and the others. I ain't never gonna forget that."

"I couldn'ta just rode off and left you with a bullet in your side, like Eli and them did," Roy declared.

"I wouldn'ta blamed you if you had gone with 'em, 'cause there ain't no tellin' if you'll ever get your share of that money. Eli ain't even gonna count it till they're somewhere safe tonight." Bart knew it wasn't like Roy Tate to trust anyone with his share of a holdup. He also knew Eli Curry well enough to know he would hardly go to the trouble of finding them to give them their share of that Wells Fargo cash shipment. Eli was a loser all the way around.

Instead of his share of the cash, Bart got a bullet in his side. He never was a lucky individual, so he wasn't surprised that of the six men, he was the only one the Wells Fargo guard shot before Eli shot down the guard. Bart's only hope for the present was that there might be a doctor in the little town of Tinhorn. He was still in a mild state of shock at Roy Tate volunteering to stay with him to find a doctor before the money was split. It just wasn't like him to let anybody ride off with his share of the money.

Almost as if he knew what Bart was thinking, Roy looked at him and smiled. "I wouldn't worry about it if I was you. You'll get your share of the money. We both will. See, when we was gettin' ready to leave that first place we stopped to rest the horses . . . you remember that, right? And Eli was tellin' you how sorry he was we was gonna have to leave you, 'cause we had to ride fast? Well, when he was tellin' you that, I noticed nobody was payin' any attention to those three money bags tied behind Eli's saddle. I told myself, 'them bags look uneven, one hangin' on one side, and two hangin' on the other'. So I thought it'd be a good idea to even 'em up a little. That black Morgan he rides oughta appreciate it, and this way, we don't lose our share of the job."

Bart was so shocked by Roy's bold statement he almost forgot his pain for a few moments. "I swear," he blurted. "Are you japin' me?"

Roy shook his head.

"You took one of those bags offa Eli's horse?"

Roy nodded, grinning all the while.

"You know he'll be comin' after us," Bart warned.

"He don't know where we went," Roy said. "He didn't ask me where I was gonna take you, so I didn't even have to tell him a lie. If he had any notion of comin' to find us and give us our share of the money, don't you reckon he mighta asked me where we was headed?"

"He's gonna be mad as hell when he stops for the night and finds out one of them bags is missin'," Bart said. "If he don't notice before that. When him and the other boys left us back on the other side of Tyler, and we started out, you cut back and changed directions so many times, I thought you were tryin' to lose a posse. Then I thought you were just tryin' to see if you could hurry me along, so I'd go ahead and bleed out, and you wouldn't have to fool with me no more."

Roy laughed. "No such a thing, partner. I was more concerned with not leavin' a trail for Eli to follow, in case he discovered he was missin' a bag before we got very far. I know he wanted to do the dividin' up hisself, but I don't figure we're cheatin' him or the other boys. There's four of 'em and they've got two bags. That's two shares to a bag. There's two of us and we've got one bag. Seems fair to me. I ain't never cheated a partner in this business." He decided not to explain one of the reasons he didn't want to leave a trail for Eli was because Bart's condition left some question about whether or not he would make it.

There was no sense in sharing Bart's share with the others, if he failed to survive his wound.

They sure as hell didn't offer any help to take care of him.

With Bart settled against a tree, Roy went to take care of the horses, and when he came back, he collected enough dry branches and limbs to build a fire. "You feel like you could drink a little coffee?"

"I reckon," Bart answered. "A little bit, anyway. I don't think I can eat anything right now."

"That's good 'cause I ain't got anything to eat. We oughta find something to eat in Tinhorn. You ever been there?"

"Nope." Bart gasped painfully when he tried to shift his position against the tree.

"Well, I hope they've got someplace to buy somethin' to eat, since me and you can afford to buy us anything we want," Roy boasted.

"How much you think is in that bag?" Bart asked, his curiosity stronger than his sense of pain at the moment.

"I don't know, but Eli said the total shipment was fifty thousand dollars, and they had it in three separate bags. Them bags looked pretty much equal, so what's three into fifty thousand?" He brushed the leaves away to expose some bare ground to use for a slate. "Too bad we ain't got Numbers here. He could do this in his head." Roy broke off a twig to use for a pencil and scratched his figures out on the ground. He worked for a while, trying to remember the little bit his mother had tried to teach him before she gave up. "Hell, I know that fifteen thousand doubled is thirty thousand, and another fifteen would make forty-five thousand. So that just leaves five thousand to split up three ways. Like I said, those three bags looked pretty much the same to me. So, we know we got at least fifteen thousand in that bag, plus a third of five thousand." He paused to work those figures in his mind. "I expect we've got sixteen thousand dollars, plus a little extra. That'll give us at least eight thousand apiece. Ain't bad for a day's work."

"How come nobody saw that bag after you took it off Eli's saddle?" Bart asked, still amazed Roy had gotten away with it.

"I dropped it under the creekbank, just in case he did notice it was gone," Roy said with a chuckle.

"Let's go ahead and count it now," Bart said. "It's gonna drive me crazy till we do."

Roy laughed. "It's workin' on my mind, too, so I'll empty it out here on the ground and we'll see how rich we are." They carefully counted all the money in the sack. When they came up with a total of twenty thousand dollars they figured they must have miscounted, and counted it again. When they reached the same total the second time, they realized that pure luck had given them a sack with ten thousand dollars each.

"Them other two sacks was just holdin' thirty thousand," Roy exclaimed. "Damned if we didn't skunk 'em on the money split, and we didn't even know it!" He threw his head back and issued a real horse laugh. "He's gonna be fit to be tied when he finds out we got ten thousand apiece."

After the horses were rested, Roy got Bart back in the saddle again. Feeling wealthier than when they had stopped, they continued on to the town of Tinhorn. Coming in from the north, the most critical question in Bart's mind was answered right away when Roy spotted the sign on the first house they saw. DOCTOR JOHN THOMAS BEARD it read.

"Well, danged if that ain't convenient," Roy declared. Looking up ahead, he could see the town was a little more than he had expected. The next building on the same side as the doctor's was a hotel. "That's convenient, too." Although he couldn't read nor write, he knew the word *hotel,* just like he knew *saloon* and *doctor.* "This place is bigger 'n I thought it was." He turned his horse onto the path that led up to the doc's office and living quarters.

"Looks like you got a patient coming in," Doc's wife, Birdie, informed him. "Two men on horseback. One of them bent over like he's hurt. Want me to go see?"

"No," Doc answered and put his coffee cup on the table. "I'll go see what they need." He got up from the kitchen table and walked to the front of the house, which served as his office. He arrived just as Roy was coming in through the front door.

"You the doctor?" Roy asked.

"I'm Dr. Beard. What can I do for you?"

"My partner's got a gunshot wound, and he's bleedin' pretty bad," Roy said. "Can you take a look at it?"

"Bring him on in here and we'll see how bad it is. Can he walk? Do you need help carrying him?"

"No, sir," Roy replied. "I can get him in here without no trouble. It was an accident. I was cleanin' my gun—"

"I don't care how he got shot," Doc interrupted. "That's between him and whoever shot him. Just bring him in and put him on that table in there." He pointed to the open door of his examining room. "Where is the wound?"

"In his side."

"Well, take him in there and get his shirt off him, and

we'll take a look." Doc went back to the kitchen to tell his petite Cherokee wife he would need her, while Roy went outside to help Bart get off his horse.

"What did you tell him about how I got shot?" Bart grunted painfully as he leaned on Roy for support.

"I started to tell him I was cleanin' my gun and it accidentally went off, but he didn't let me finish. Said he didn't care how you got shot, so I don't reckon we have to worry about him causin' us any trouble." Roy helped Bart inside the door, then took him to the examining room and helped him get his shirt off.

Doc went in followed by Birdie, carrying a pan of hot water. "This is my wife. She'll be helping me." To prevent any insult to his wife because she was an Indian, he always introduced her as his wife, especially when working on gunshot wounds and strangers who looked as if gunshot wounds were not unusual in their lives.

"Ma'am," Roy greeted her politely and Bart nodded his head.

After a careful examination, Doc informed Bart the bullet was deep in his side and would continue to cause him pain unless it was removed. "On surgery like this, I usually charge twenty-five dollars because I'll have to do a lot of cutting and stitching. It won't kill you if I just fix the hole, but it'll aggravate you for the rest of your life."

"Go ahead and fix me up right, Doc," Bart said without hesitation. "I've got the money to pay you. Don't worry about that."

"We'll get started right away." Doc motioned to Birdie to get the chloroform. "It's gonna take a good little while," he told Roy, "so you might want to get yourself something to eat, or a drink or two. But if you'd rather wait here, you can just make yourself comfortable in the parlor. He won't know whether you're here or not. I'm gonna put him to sleep."

Birdie came back then with a clean cotton cloth and a bottle of chloroform.

"I noticed a hotel right down the street there," Roy said. "I think I'll go see if we can get us a room. I don't think Bart's gonna be ready to travel right away. I reckon I'll have plenty of time to take care of the horses, too."

"Good idea. He might feel a little sick from the chloroform," Doc told him and watched him go out the door. *If he's thinking about staying in the hotel, maybe they do have enough money to pay my bill,* he was thinking. "You couldn't tell it by looking at him," he said aloud.

"What you say?" Birdie asked.

"Nothing. I was just talking to myself." Doc took the bottle of chloroform and the cotton pad from her and returned to his patient.

After he got Bart to lie back on the table in a comfortable position, he poured some of the chloroform on the cotton pad and held it under Bart's nose. "Just breathe in real deep," he instructed and continued the process until Bart passed out.

The surgery was quickly done, and the wound bandaged before Bart showed any signs of waking up, so he was still on the table when Roy returned.

"How's he doin', Doc?" Roy asked when he came back in the office to find Doc Beard sitting at his desk.

"He'll be ready to go in a few minutes," Doc answered. "He's just waking up right now. I'll tell you, since he might still be a little groggy from the chloroform, tell him to leave that bandage on for three days before he changes it. Tell him to keep it dry. And don't take a bath for three days."

Roy chuckled in response. "Won't be no trouble there. He can go three months, if you want him to. When can he ride?"

"To start with, it'd be best not to have him bouncing around on a horse for a couple of days," Doc advised. "After that, it's up to him. If it doesn't bother him, he can get on a horse then."

"Fine and dandy," Roy said. "'Preciate you takin' care of him. I'll settle up with you now, and he can pay me later. How much did you say it was?" Doc told him it was twenty-five dollars, same as he had quoted him.

"Twenty-five," Roy repeated. "That's a little steep, but I ain't complainin'. I'll tell Bart you charged fifty," he japed. "I rented us a room in the hotel, so I'll see if I can get him over there to rest up."

"You feel like eatin' some supper?" Roy asked after Bart had rested up a little and seemed to have recovered from his surgery.

"Yeah, I think so. I know I'm hungry enough to eat a horse."

"Well, let's go on over to the dinin' room and see if they've got a horse on the menu. Doc Beard told me they serve pretty good cookin'. Clara's Kitchen is what they call the dinin' room. We'll see if Clara cooks good enough to satisfy two rich gents like me and you."

They stepped into the hallway, Roy locked the door to their room and led the way down the hall to the inside door to the dining room. Bart walked carefully behind him. When they stepped inside the dining room, they automatically looked the room over before committing to a table.

Clara Rakestraw looked up when the door from the

hotel opened and the two strangers walked in. She watched to see if they read the sign by the weapons table and was not surprised when they paid it no attention. It was the usual occurrence with customers new to town.

"Good evening, gentlemen," Clara greeted them. "May I ask you to leave your weapons on the table, there, while you're our guests in the dining room?"

"Good evenin' to you, little lady," Roy answered her. "You certainly may ask us, but we ain't inclined to take 'em off. We like to keep 'em handy, especially when that big feller, settin' at the table by the kitchen door is wearin' his."

"He's also wearing a sheriff's badge," Clara politely told them. "Officers of the law are allowed to wear their weapons in the dining room." She pointed to the sign in the center of the table pertaining to the matter, then gave them a friendly smile. "Maybe I need to print a bigger sign."

"Ain't no problem," Roy said at once, but he was thinking she could make the sign ten feet tall if she wanted. He still wouldn't be able to read it. "We was just so anxious to try the food out that we didn't pay no mind to the sign." He unbuckled his gun belt at once. "Come on, Bart, peel that belt off. They ain't gonna feed us if you don't." When Bart winced suddenly in the process of removing his weapon, Roy asked, "You need help?"

"No, I got it," Bart answered and carefully pulled his gun belt off, then handed it to Roy.

Seeing Clara's inquisitive expression, Roy explained. "He just came from the doctor's office. Had to have a little surgery done on his side, and he ain't too frisky right now."

"Well, let's not make him stand here waiting," Clara said, and ushered them to the closest table. "Bonnie will be taking care of you. Do you want coffee?"

"Yes, ma'am, we sure do," Roy said.

Clara went at once to the kitchen to tell Bonnie. In less than a minute, Bonnie came to the table with two cups of coffee.

"Look here, Bart. They keep gettin' prettier and prettier," Roy declared. "Don't matter whether the food's fit to eat, or not, we'll just admire the scenery."

"You fellows *are* new in town, ain'tcha?" Bonnie asked.

"That's right," Roy answered. "And we could use some company to show us what there is to do here. Maybe you'd like to do that—show us a little of what we've been missin'."

"Well, now, I don't know," Bonnie replied. "I reckon I'd have to check with my husband about that."

"Hell, I won't tell him, if you don't," Roy chuckled.

"He'd know, anyway," Bonnie said. "He's sittin' right here. I'll go ask him." She pointed to Buck Jackson, sitting at the table by the kitchen door, and made a move to leave.

"Whoa! Wait a minute!" Roy exclaimed. "You're married to the sheriff?"

"Why, yes. You didn't know that? You are new in town."

"I sure am," Roy replied, "and I don't wanna get throwed in the jailhouse my first day in town. Why don't we just back up a little bit? You just bring me and my partner some supper, and we won't bother the sheriff."

"Good idea," she said. "What's it gonna be? Beef stew, or steak and potatoes?"

"I swear, I'm hungry enough to eat both of 'em. Because of Bart's surgery, we missed dinner, didn't we, Bart? I don't know." After a moment, Roy said, "I think I'll try the stew. That oughta be quicker, since you just dish that out. You'd have to fry a steak, right?"

Bonnie nodded, so Bart took the same.

When she went to the kitchen, Roy commented, "I'd

heard of Tinhorn, but I didn't think they were big enough to hire a sheriff."

"Well they've got one, and it looks like they wanted a big one," Bart said, taking another look at Buck Jackson sitting by the kitchen door.

Chapter 2

"You want some more coffee?" Mindy Moore asked. "I think that oughta do me for the night. Fix me up a plate for Ralph. I expect he'll think I forgot him, if I don't get back with his supper pretty soon."

"I'll tell Margaret to get it ready," Mindy said as she filled his coffee cup. "Is Flint coming to eat here tonight?"

"Yeah," Buck said, grinning broadly, for he knew it was more than a casual question. "He said he was plannin' to get back in time to get some supper here. That's the reason I've been settin' here so long, but I reckon I'd better take Ralph his supper."

"How long are you gonna keep that man in jail?" Mindy asked. "I thought he was supposed to go on trial two months ago."

Her question caused Buck to chuckle again. "He's servin' a life sentence. Me and Flint put him on trial. He's there for life, or until he walks out. His cell ain't locked. As his punishment, he has to keep the jail cleaned up and take care of any other prisoners we have in there. He's doin' a pretty good job, so far. I believe he's gonna stay with us for a good while."

"Who pays for the food you and Flint take him?" she wondered.

"Same deal as always," Buck said. "He's still a prisoner, so we still feed him. Same as it was for Roy Hawkins before he got killed. Ralph just took over Roy's job. Well, well," he said then, seeing his deputy, Flint Moran, walk in the door. "Here's Flint now." He was glad for the opportunity to change the subject. The topic of Ralph Cox was not one he was comfortable trying to explain. He was a former prisoner who had escaped from the jail before, but both Buck and Flint were convinced Ralph had just been unfortunate to have ridden with a real hardened killer. They'd become convinced he was no real threat to anyone, so they called off his trial and gave him the opportunity to stay in jail as a free man. With nothing legal about his pardon, they were reluctant to talk about it.

Seeing Buck still at the table, Flint said, "Good evenin'," to Clara and walked on back to join him. As Flint passed the table near the door, Roy Tate looked over at Clara and shrugged, his two hands spread up and out, his face a mask of confusion. She understood his confusion and answered with a gesture of her own. Pointing to her chest, she mouthed the word *badge*.

Roy slowly shook his head and said to Bart, "I swear, this little town is eat up with lawmen."

They both watched Flint as he pulled out a chair and sat down at the table with the sheriff. The other waitress had already gone to fetch his coffee by the time he was settled.

"I wonder if that other little gal is married to him," Roy mumbled after Bonnie placed their food on the table.

"Maybe we oughta take our meals at the saloon, if they've got a cook," Bart suggested.

"The desk clerk at the hotel said they had a cook at the saloon, but the cookin' was a lot better here," Roy said.

"Well, 'course he's gonna say that," Bart replied. "I reckon we'll have to decide that for ourselves. It's kinda crampin' my style to be settin' in here eatin' with the sheriff and his deputy."

"We ain't got nothin' to worry about," Roy assured him. "Even if they've heard about that Wells Fargo job, it was a robbery by a gang of six men."

"What if they've heard that one of that gang got shot, and me settin' here with a bullet hole in my side?"

"We'll tell 'em what I started to tell the doctor—that I shot you when I was cleanin' my gun. They ain't gonna arrest us for that. Even if they did, they'd just arrest me for shootin' you, so let's just eat this grub and get outta here." Roy attacked his plate of stew with serious intent. He had consumed a good portion of it when he noticed Bart wasn't eating at all. "Whaddaya waitin' for? Ain'tcha gonna eat? I thought you wanted to eat a horse."

"I thought I did," Bart answered. "But all of a sudden, I don't feel so good. I think maybe I shoulda stayed in that bed a little longer before I tried to set up here and eat."

Noticing what looked to be some problem at their table, Clara walked over to see if anything was wrong. When she looked at the two plates, one of them half-finished, the other one untouched, she enquired. "Is something wrong with the food?"

Looking as if in pain, Bart answered, "No, ma'am, ain't nothin' wrong with the food. It's me. The doctor knocked me out with some kinda medicine when he fixed my wound, and I think it must be makin' me kinda sick." He looked at Roy in distress. "I gotta go back to the room. Gimme the key." When Roy made motions as if about to get up, Bart quickly insisted. "I don't need no help. You stay here and take your time."

"All right. If you're sure." Roy handed him the room

key. "I'll pay for yours, too. You just go on back to the room."

Bart got to his feet and headed back to the hotel. He was in the hallway before he remembered to turn around, go back, and retrieve his gun from the table.

The little disturbance at their table did not go unnoticed at the table next to the kitchen door, especially when Bonnie returned to see if there was a problem. When Bart walked out the second time, Flint volunteered to go over to see if they needed any help.

"Is something wrong?" Flint asked when he arrived at the table. "Do you need some help, Clara?"

"No. This gentleman's friend just had some surgery done and I think he got sick from the medicine Doc used to put him to sleep." She looked back at Roy. "I'll put his plate in a paper bag and you can take it back with you. Maybe he'll feel more like eating later on."

"That would be mighty kind of you," Roy said, his eyes never leaving Flint's face, anxious to read his reactions.

"When did he have the surgery?" Flint asked.

Roy said he'd had it that morning.

Flint said, "I reckon he was pushin' it a little too soon at that. What kind of surgery did he have?"

"He had a wound in his side. The doctor had to put him to sleep because he had to go in him pretty far to fix it."

"What happened to him? What kind of wound did he have?"

"I shot him," Roy answered bluntly.

Flint's eyebrows lifted in surprise.

Roy smiled and explained. "We was settin' by the campfire last night. I hadn't cleaned my gun in a while, so I decided to clean it. I was loadin' it back up, and I thought I left an empty cylinder. *Bam!* The fool thing went off and caught Bart in the side." He shook his head as if unable to believe he had done it. "I ain't never done nothin' like that before in my whole life. I thought I had killed my partner." He chuckled then added, "We're still partners, but he won't let me clean my gun anywhere near him anymore."

Flint laughed with him. "Well, I couldn't say as how I blame him. You fellows in town for long, or just passin' through?"

"Just passin' through," Roy replied. "But we ain't in no particular hurry. I reckon we'll wait till Bart feels more like spendin' the day in the saddle again. The doctor said he oughta hold off for a day or two before gettin' back on a horse."

"Well, enjoy your stay in Tinhorn," Flint said, and returned to his table to find a plate of food waiting for him, a napkin placed over it to keep the heat from escaping.

"Mindy fixed that up for you so your supper wouldn't get cold," Buck said, unable to resist teasing his young deputy. When Flint didn't respond, Buck asked, "What was that about? Anything requiring the attention of the law?"

Flint told him what had happened that caused one of the men to leave and go back to the hotel.

"You say he shot the other fellow?" Buck asked.

"Yeah, said it was an accident. Said his gun went off while he was cleanin' it," Flint replied. "Nope," he answered when Buck asked him if he believed it. "He just doesn't look like the type to be careless with a gun."

"I reckon we better keep an eye on the two of 'em, but I don't expect they're up to anything in Tinhorn, with one of 'em shot in the side. Just came here to see the doctor, I figure, and they'll move on." Buck got to his feet when Mindy came back with a plate for Ralph. "I'd best take Ralph his supper before it gets cold," he said, and walked out the door, nodding briefly to Roy when he went past.

Mindy brought a plate with a couple more biscuits for

Flint, then she cleared Buck's dishes off the table. She came back with the coffeepot, and topped off his cup. "You almost waited too late to get any supper," she said, just to start a conversation.

"Yep, I reckon I did cut it a little close," he admitted.

"Clara will be putting up the closed sign in about fifteen minutes, and we'll start cleaning up. This coffee is still pretty fresh, and the pot is over half full. I think I'll pour myself a cup and sit down and enjoy it before I clean up these tables." She waited, making no move to get a clean cup until, finally, he responded.

"You might as well sit down right here and drink your coffee," he invited. "That is, if you ain't particular about the company you keep."

"Why, I'd be honored to sit and have coffee with one of our brave lawmen," she said, attempting to keep her tone casual. She hurried over to the sideboard to fetch a clean cup moments before Bonnie came to get the coffeepot.

"Mind if I borrow a little of that?" Bonnie teased. "Or is this a private party? My customer would like another cup."

"Take it," Mindy said. "I think there's about one cup left in it." She quickly looked back at Flint. "Did you want another cup? Because if you do, I'll make you a fresh pot." As soon as she said it, she flushed red, knowing how that must have sounded. She cringed when she looked at the grinning face of Bonnie Jones.

Oblivious to the teasing Mindy was the target of, Flint said, "No, thanks. I've had enough. Reckon I'd best get about the business I was hired for and take a look around town. Thanks for the company, Mindy. It sure beats eatin' with Buck." He walked to the register and settled up with Clara, nodded to Roy, who was the only customer left, and went out the door.

Flint took a walk up one side of the main street and

down the other before he returned to the sheriff's office to see if Buck was going to retire to his private quarters next to the office. The town council was still concerned about Buck's drinking problem, which was the main reason Flint was hired as a deputy. It had become well known that Buck retired every night right after supper to wrestle with his demons till daylight again. The town had no real problems with this arrangement due to Buck's reputation as a sheriff before alcohol sank its talons into the man. As the out-of-the-way little town began to attract more settlers, and consequently, more outlaws, however, the part-time law arrangement failed to protect the town. That was when Flint Moran had entered the scene.

He'd been Buck's personal pick to act as his deputy, and the town was soon to see the wisdom in his selection. As for Flint, he was ready to leave the family's small farm. Already burdened with the welfare of his two older brothers and their families, it promised a slim future if he decided to raise a family there, too. It was a bonus for Flint, Buck, and the town of Tinhorn as well when Flint turned out to be one hell of a lawman.

Satisfied that the town seemed quiet as usual for a weekday night, Flint returned to the jail to find Ralph in the office cleaning up the bench where he had eaten his supper.

"The sheriff's gone to his room," Ralph said. "He said to give him a holler, if you need him."

It was what Flint expected. Buck always said to give him a call if he was needed.

"Everything's pretty quiet right now," Flint told Ralph. "I doubt we'll have to disturb him tonight. You fixin' to go to bed?"

"Yep, soon as I finish cleanin' up a little here." Since

no prisoners currently resided in either of the two cells in the cell room, Ralph would sleep in one of them.

"You can suit yourself about the cell room door. I'll be here in the office for a little while, then I'll take another look around town. I'll lock the office door when I go. If everything stays as peaceful as it is right now, I'll go on to my room at the boardin' house, and I'll see you in the mornin'."

"Right," Ralph replied, "in the mornin'. But I'd like to empty my thunder mug before you lock the front door. I've already filled the coffeepot up with water for the sheriff's coffee in the mornin'."

"Go ahead," Flint said. "Be sure you walk it far enough over in those weeds, so a little breeze can't pick up the smell."

"I always do," Ralph replied.

Approximately one hundred yards of knee-high grass and weeds stood between the jail and the trees that lined the Neches River. After dark the area generally served as an outhouse for the jail and a place to empty waste receptacles during daylight hours. While Ralph took care of that, Flint opened Buck's desk drawer, took out a stack of wanted notices, and started leafing through them on the chance he might see something about a robbery by two men, one of them wounded.

Before Flint was halfway through the notices, Ralph returned, said goodnight, and retired to the cell room. Flint found nothing in the papers that would cast suspicion on the two strangers. *Maybe he did shoot his partner accidentally,* he thought, but he was still not convinced. Thinking more like Buck, he told himself he didn't care as long as they made no trouble in Tinhorn and were soon on their way. *Besides,* he told himself, *that fellow's wound is too fresh for us to have received a notice on it this soon.*

At nine o'clock, the town was shut down for the night. The only place open was the saloon, Jake's Place, and it was winding down when Flint took another walk around town. As he often did, he stopped in the saloon for a little conversation with Jake Rudolph, the owner, and Rudy Place, his bartender. He found Jake standing at the bar talking to one of the two strangers he had spoken to in Clara's Kitchen.

Seeing Flint, Roy gave him a cheerful greeting. "Howdy, Deputy. I didn't figure on seein' you again tonight. I was just havin' a little drink before I go to bed. I'd like to buy you one. Whaddaya favor?"

"Thanks just the same, Mister . . . I don't believe you ever told me your name."

"Tate," he replied at once. "Roy Tate."

"Flint Moran, Mr. Tate. Thank you for the offer, but I don't normally drink when I'm supposed to be workin'. How's your partner doin'?"

"When I left the room, he was sleepin' like a baby," Roy said. "So I snuck out to get a little drink before I turn in. I ate so much in that dinin' room I needed a little alcohol to burn some of it up. There's some nice folks in that place. We had the sheriff's wife waitin' on us, and she took care of us first class. I was afraid we mighta worried her when Bart took sick and didn't eat his." He paused then when he saw distinct expressions of astonishment on the faces of all three of the men at the bar.

"Sheriff Jackson ain't married." Jake was the first to remark.

Flint remembered then. "Bonnie waited on you and your partner, right?"

"That's right, Bonnie. She said she was the sheriff's wife." Roy looked from one face to another, realizing at the same time they did that he had been duped by the young woman. He struck a guilty grin and said, "She played me like a fiddle, didn't she? Well, it worked 'cause I sure didn't say anything disrespectful to her after she told me that." They all enjoyed a chuckle over that, then he went on. "Not that I said anything disrespectful before she said that." He paused to shake his head. "I sure painted a cockeyed picture of myself in this town. Shot my own partner while I was cleanin' my gun, then got played for a fool by the gal in the dinin' room. Just wait till I see that little Bonnie gal again."

Flint had a pretty good notion about what happened between Bonnie and Roy, and he had to laugh when he pictured it. Leave it to Bonnie to come up with a sure-fire way to quickly turn off a stranger's advances toward her, if she wasn't interested. As for Roy Tate, he seemed to be a rather good-natured fellow, who could laugh at himself. Flint could see no trouble for Tinhorn from him and his partner.

Still, Flint was a little curious about how his partner really got shot. "Where were you and your partner headed before you shot him?"

"Fort Worth," Roy answered without hesitation. "We work for a cattle buyer over there."

"I wouldn't have taken you two for cattle buyers," Flint said frankly.

Roy favored him with a knowing smile. "When you're carryin' a lot of money, it don't pay to look like it."

Flint nodded. "I reckon I can't argue with that." He hung around for a while longer, until Roy had a final shot of whiskey and bid them a good night. Flint walked outside with him and stood on the porch to watch him head up the street to the hotel.

In a few minutes, Jake walked out onto the porch to join him. "You reckon he's a big cattle buyer, like he says? He 'pears to have a sizable bankroll in his pocket, and he ain't shy about spendin' it."

"Maybe," Flint said. "It's hard to judge a man like that. And what he says is true about lookin' broke when you're carryin' a big roll of cash. Him and his partner look more like them that the ones with money have to watch out for." He said goodnight then and started toward the south end of the street, taking a quick look in the sheriff's office before continuing toward Hannah Green's boarding house. When he reached the house, only one lamp was burning low in the parlor, but he walked around to the back of the house as he usually did.

The small room he rented was actually an afterthought to the main house, it being a single room attached to the house by a covered walkway. It served his purposes, for he could come and go quietly at any hour without disturbing anyone in the main house. The town was quiet enough he decided to eat breakfast at the boarding house in the morning, instead of going to Clara's Kitchen.

Chapter 3

"How the hell could you not know it was gone?"
Swann wanted to know. "You got off that horse
and back on it two times since we left them behind, and
you didn't notice that 'stead of three bags of money, you
only had two? I swear, Eli, you threw your leg over them
bags twice and didn't know one of them was gone?"

"Well, you was ridin' right along with me," Eli shot back
at him. "Did you notice we was missin' a bag?" Swann
didn't answer, so Eli continued. "How 'bout you, Numbers?
You notice we was missing a sack? Junior, you notice one
gone?" He didn't wait for them to answer. Instead, he answered for them. "Hell, no. None of us noticed the sack
was gone, 'cause it didn't have no reason to be gone. None
of us thought ol' Roy would cheat on us and take money
that weren't his to take. I oughta knowed better. Him actin'
so holy and thoughtful and volunteerin' to stay with poor
Bart. I ain't never knowed Roy to wanna take care of anybody before. I wonder how far they got before Bart cashed
in his chips.

"Even if Bart ain't dead, they still cheated us. We
counted that money in them two bags twice. They packed
fifteen thousand dollars, even, in both of those bags. That

means there was twenty thousand in that bag he took 'cause the whole shipment was fifty thousand. Twenty thousand. If he ain't killed Bart, that's ten thousand apiece compared to the seventy-five hundred each of us is holdin' for the same piece of work. I don't know about you boys, but that galls my short hairs. And if Bart is dead, that leaves Roy holdin' twenty thousand. So I'm goin' after him. Am I ridin' by myself?"

"Hell, no!" Swann exclaimed. "I took my share of the risk. I want my share of the money!" His response was followed by similar outbursts of anger by Junior and Numbers Kelsey.

"I got a question," Junior said. "How the hell are we gonna find him? We left him and Bart settin' on the side of the river. You reckon he'll try to catch up with us at the hideout?"

"I ain't countin' on Roy showin' up there, especially if Bart don't make it," Eli said. "Roy's gonna wanna hold on to all twenty thousand. So, we go back to where we left him and try to cut his trail."

"What about the posse?" Kelsey asked.

"What about 'em?" Eli came back. "We lost them at the river. When it started gettin' close to suppertime, those brave citizens broke it off and headed for the house." He watched their faces, seeing a hint of caution on their part when it came to returning to the place where Roy and Bart split off. He stated bluntly, "I'll tell you this. I ain't sharin' any of that extra money with anybody who don't go with me to find 'em."

"I reckon I'm goin' with you," Swann said. Junior and Kelsey volunteered as well.

"We'll start back in the mornin'," Eli said.

* * *

They retraced their steps of the night before and found the spot beside the Neches River where they had left Roy and Bart. Thanks to Kelsey's skill as a tracker, they found their two partners' tracks where they crossed the river, then headed north.

"Reckon where he's headin' in that direction?" Junior asked.

"He ain't gonna go in that direction," Eli told him. "He just wants you to think he's headin' north. He'll be cuttin' back."

In less than a mile, Roy's trail led down into the water, and when Kelsey picked it up on the other side, it led back to the south. It crossed the river once more but continued south.

"He's ridin' around Tyler," Eli commented, "and it looks like Bart's still with him."

"How you know that?" Swann asked.

"'Cause there ain't no body layin' on the ground no-where," Eli answered, "and there ain't been no sign that he left the trail to hide a body. It looks like Bart weren't hurt as bad as we thought. The two of them musta planned to do this together." That thought was enough to generate a little more animosity toward the two double-crossers, making them more determined than ever to settle up with them.

"That don't make a lotta sense," Swann commented. "I mean, them cuttin' back to the south to go around Tyler. They was already north of Tyler. Why didn't they just head west and go around the north side of the town?"

"It don't make sense unless they're tryin' to throw us off their trail so we don't know which way they went," Eli replied. "I reckon they figured we'd come back to look for 'em."

So they stayed on a trail that was not that hard for

Kelsey to follow, even when it crossed back over the river once again. The trail continued to the south, however, until coming to a wagon road running east and west. The tracks were easily read, turning toward the west on a road they figured must be at least a couple of miles south of the town of Tyler. Less than an hour's ride brought them to a crossroads where a little general store stood.

"Let's pull up here and see if they saw Roy and Bart pass by here yesterday," Eli said.

Inside the store, Donald Stokely went to a window to watch the four riders approach. When they rode up to his hitching rail, he walked back behind the counter to wait for them, his hand resting on the double-barrel shotgun on the shelf under the counter. Something about the four strangers triggered a cautious response in Stokely's mind.

"Howdy," he greeted them when they filed in. "Somethin' I can help you fellows with?"

They just looked around the little store for a couple of minutes before Junior spoke. "I was hopin' you mighta had somethin' to eat."

"We don't serve no meals or anything like that," Stokely said, "but if you're wantin' something to hold you till dinnertime, we can fix you up with some coffee and cornbread my wife just pulled outta the oven. Couldn'ta been more 'n fifteen minutes ago."

"Well, now, that sounds to my likin'," Eli said. "I'll take you up on that. How 'bout it, boys?" He looked around at the others, received three confirmations, and gave Stokely a nod.

"Yes, sir," Stokely said. "Take a few minutes to make a new pot of coffee." He signaled his wife, who was standing in the doorway. "Sadie, you've got four customers for a cup of coffee and some cornbread."

"I heard you. The pot's already on the stove. How'd you fellows know I baked a cake of cornbread this morning?"

"It was Junior," Kelsey said. "He can smell cornbread bakin' five miles away."

"You fellows ain't ever been in the store before," Stokely commented. "You headed for Athens?" He assumed as much since he had seen them ride in on that road.

"Athens?" Eli repeated, having never heard of it. "Have they got a doctor in Athens?"

"No, there ain't no doctor there. Athens ain't hardly no town at all." Stokely paused to shake his head and smile. "I declare, you're the second stranger to ask me that question in two days. Couple of fellows yesterday asked me if there was a doctor in Athens." Had he been paying attention he might have noticed the immediate reaction on the faces of all four strangers.

"What did you tell 'em?" Eli asked casually.

"I told them the same as I just told you," Stokely answered. "I told 'em there might be one in Tinhorn, but I didn't know that for a fact. Tinhorn's a little bigger than Athens. There's a couple of doctors in Tyler, and it's a heck of a lot closer than ridin' down to Tinhorn, but they headed for Tinhorn."

"I never heard of a town named Tinhorn. How far is it?" Eli asked.

"'Bout twenty-five miles," Stokely said. "Maybe a little less than that."

"Down that road?" Eli pointed toward the road. At Stokely's nod Eli asked, "You say they was lookin' for a doctor, huh? Was one of 'em sick?"

"I think he mighta been shot or had some kinda accident," Stokely replied. "He never got off his horse, and he looked like he was hurtin'. They didn't buy nothin'. The one done the talkin' didn't come in the store. He just stood in the doorway. Got back on his horse and they took off for Tinhorn."

"Well, boys," Eli said, "better enjoy that coffee and cornbread, 'cause there won't be nothin' else till supper."

Anxious to get started again, the four outlaws polished off Sadie's cake of cornbread in short order. Much to Stokely's surprise, they offered no objections to his asking price of fifty cents apiece for the coffee and cornbread and were soon on their way. They left Stokely scratching his head over the two incidents with the strangers, and Sadie pleased with herself for earning two dollars.

"Lookee there," Junior announced as he pointed to the sign on Doc Beard's gatepost. "They got a doctor, all right. You wanna stop in there and see if he treated Bart?"

"I druther see if Bart's still in town," Eli answered. "And after I find that out, I wanna get some supper before that place over yonder closes for the night." He pointed toward Clara's Kitchen.

"Well, we'd best get to lookin'," Swann said, "'cause it's already gettin' pretty late. And this town's bigger 'n we thought it was."

"We'll just go to the hotel right next door to that dinin' room and see if Roy and Bart are checked in," Eli told him.

"What if they didn't check in the hotel?" Swann asked.

"You know Roy," Eli replied. "Think about it. With Roy carryin' ten thousand dollars, you think he's gonna sleep outside under a tree tonight? I ain't totin' that much, but I'm gonna sleep in the hotel tonight, if they've got a room." That made sense to all of them, so they pointed their horses toward the hotel.

Fred Johnson, desk clerk for the Tinhorn Hotel was just about to turn the desk over to the night clerk, J.C. White, when the four strangers walked in. "Can I help you gentlemen?" Fred asked.

"Yep, you sure can," Eli replied. "We're gonna need a couple of rooms for the night, and we're also lookin' for a couple of fellers we was supposed to meet here. They shoulda got here yesterday. One of 'em had to get here early, so he could see the doctor."

"You must be talking about Mr. Tate and Mr. McCoy," J.C. said. "Why don't you go on to supper, Fred? I'll check these gentlemen in." Turning back to Eli, he said, "Yes, sir, your friends are still here. Will you be wanting two rooms?"

"Two rooms will do." Eli turned to give Swann a surprised look after hearing Roy and Bart had given their real names. He thought about it and decided they might as well. Their names were not known in Texas. After calling off the four names, he asked if the hotel had a stable.

"No, sir, we don't," J.C. answered. "We have an arrangement with the stable down at the end of the street, so there's no charge for taking care of your horses. Mr. Lon Blake is the man to see down there, and he'll be open for a while yet tonight."

"What about that eatin' place next door?" Eli asked. "Are we too late to get supper tonight?"

"Clara's Kitchen," J.C. announced. "No, sir, Clara will be open for another hour, just to take care of folks like you who check in late."

"Fine and dandy." Eli turned to advise the others. "We've got time to throw our saddlebags in the rooms and take the horses to the stable, and still get back before the eatin' place closes. Let's get a move on and maybe we'll run into our friends before they finish supper." He was in no hurry now that they had definitely found Roy and Bart. "Ain't they gonna be surprised to see us?"

Grinning back at Eli, Swann said, "Come on. Let's get movin'." He took one of the room keys and hustled out to get his saddlebags and his rifle. He was followed immediately by the others and soon they were riding down the street to the stable. They found Lon Blake already bringing his horses in from the corral and leading them into their stalls. Spurred on by an eagerness to come face-to-face with Roy and Bart, they quickly pulled their saddles off the horses and headed back to the dining room.

"Good evening, gentlemen," Clara Rakestraw sang out cordially when the four strangers walked in the door.

Ignoring her greeting, Eli grinned when he spotted Roy and Bart sitting at a table, eating supper. "Yonder they are," he announced as his three companions stepped up beside him.

"Gentlemen!" Clara insisted. "I'll have to ask you to remove your weapons and leave them on the table here." She pointed to the sign on the table.

"Never mind that," Eli replied, his attention concentrated upon the two men not yet aware of their arrival. "We're gonna need our guns."

"Not in my dining room you don't!" Clara said forcefully and pushed between Eli and Swann to get in front of them. Like a stern schoolteacher, she pointed to the table and demanded, "Guns on the table."

Eli gave her a look of amusement. "Have they got their guns on?"

"Absolutely not!" Clara answered.

By this time, the two men in question became aware of the verbal altercation at the door and realizing they were helpless, they froze.

It was more than Eli could hope for. "Ha!" The exclamation fell out of his mouth. "We caught 'em settin' at the supper table without their guns. They don't look very glad to see us."

To get in front of them, Clara stepped around the four men standing in a broad line. "I'm gonna have to ask you to leave, or I'm going to call the sheriff."

"Woman, you're startin' to get on my nerves," Eli roared at her. "Now get the hell outta my way, or I'm gonna put another airhole in your face!"

"I warned you," Clara threatened. "I'm sending for the sheriff."

"You do that, and I'll put an airhole in his head, too," Swann threatened. "Then we'll clean this whole town out."

"Ain't no problem, Clara. I'm already here." The unmistakable voice of Buck Jackson came from behind them.

It caused the line of four men to freeze for a few moments, guns already drawn. It was a time of decision for all four.

"Toss those weapons aside, or I'm gonna start cuttin' you down," Buck warned.

There was hesitation on the part of all four, with no one dropping a weapon.

"Sheriff," Eli said, "you're challengin' four good gun hands here. You might shoot one of us, but that ain't gonna save your behind from gettin' shot down before you get off another shot."

"You might be right," Buck replied, "so I reckon I'm gonna pick you for my first target. And I'm pretty sure I'll get one more of you, maybe two."

"You take the one doin' all the talkin', then go to your right and take the one standin' next to him. I'll start with the one standin' beside the talker on your left and keep going." Shocking the outlaws for the second time, this voice came from the kitchen doorway as Flint Moran moved to position himself behind the table where Roy and Bart were sitting. "Clara, you and the other women go into the kitchen."

They did as he instructed.

Back to the four facing him, Flint said, "I reckon it's your move now. Are you gonna toss those guns aside, or are you gonna take your chances when we open fire? Buck, you ready?"

"I'm ready, partner," Buck answered. "I reckon I shoulda told 'em I'm holdin' a .44 in each hand. That don't seem fair, does it? But what the hell? Whatever it takes to keep the peace, right?"

Seeming much longer, a short standoff followed before Eli finally tossed his gun on the floor and cursed in anger. "The percentages are against us, boys. We shoulda took care of the law before we started. You're holdin' the cards this time," he said to the sheriff.

Swann, then Kelsey dropped their guns. Junior reluctantly held his gun out to drop it, but whipped it up suddenly to aim at Flint. He sank to his knees when Buck's bullet struck him between his shoulder blades. He remained in that position for only a few seconds before he keeled over to land on his side.

"Anybody else?" Buck asked.

No one moved.

When there were no volunteers, Flint walked over and kicked the dropped weapons up against the wall. He gave Roy and Bart a quick look to make sure they remained seated at the table. "Buck, you got 'em covered?"

Buck said that he did, and Flint holstered his Colt six-shooter. "Hold out your hand," he told Swann. He clamped one of his handcuffs around Swann's wrist and locked the other cuff around one of Eli's wrists, so the two were handcuffed together.

Buck saw what he was doing and tossed his handcuffs to Flint. He locked Swann's other wrist to one of Kelsey's wrists, leaving both Eli and Kelsey handcuffed to Swann with one arm free.

"Now we can all walk down to the jailhouse real peaceful-like," Flint said, causing Buck to chuckle in appreciation of his deputy's use of their handcuffs.

"Sorry about the disturbance, Clara," Buck said, then motioned to Fred Johnson, who had come into the dining room shortly before the four outlaws arrived. "Fred, I'm gonna need to help Flint put these prisoners away. Would you mind goin' to tell Walt Doolin we've got a body that needs to be moved?"

"Not at all, Sheriff," Fred replied. "You need to know these four men just checked into the hotel. Said they were here to meet Mr. Tate and Mr. McCoy."

"Is that so?" Buck replied. "It looked like they had some serious business to talk over, all right." He glanced over at the two men, still obviously in shock. "What about that? You know these men?"

"We know them," Bart answered nervously, "but we weren't supposed to meet them here."

"What he means is those four men have been tryin' to follow us ever since we left Arkansas, carryin' money from a cattle sale," Roy quickly added. "We don't know who they are or how they found out we were carryin' money. We thought we had lost 'em, and that's why we didn't say nothin' to you about it. And now, dad-gummit, they found us again." He shook his head as if perplexed.

"If we hadn'ta been so scared about defendin' ourselves, we wouldn'ta been foolin' around with our guns, and I wouldn't have shot Bart in the side."

"That's a damn lie," Eli blurted. "He's a damn liar. They ain't no cattle buyers. They ran off with some money that belongs to us, and we tracked 'em down."

Buck and Flint exchanged a quick look, both of them unsure of exactly what they were dealing with.

"Well, to start with, we're gonna march you three down to the jail until we get this all figured out." Buck nodded toward Roy and Bart. "You two ain't done nothin' to go to jail for, but I want you to stay in town till we're straight on this. All right?"

"Of course, Sheriff," Roy replied. "We'll be glad to help you any way we can."

"'Preciate it," Buck said.

"Wait a minute," Eli exclaimed. "You ain't gonna put them in jail? Then you ain't got no reason to put us in jail, neither. This matter is between them two and us. Ought not have nothin' to do with the law."

Buck gave Eli a patient look before giving his reasons for his decision. "Those two fellows have committed no crimes in this town, and they were settin' there minding their own business, eatin' their supper. That ain't no crime in Tinhorn. You, on the other hand, charged in here, guns drawn, and defied Mrs. Rakestraw's request to leave your guns on the table. And when she asked you to leave, you refused. Then one of your party," he nodded toward the body on the floor, "attempted to shoot my deputy. That *is* a crime in Tinhorn. Unfortunately, his actions forced me to kill him. Does that kinda clear it up for you?"

Eli hesitated for a moment before saying, "Junior started to shoot your deputy, and you shot him for it. So he's paid for it. You ought not arrest the rest of us for what he did."

"I forgot," Buck said. "There's another charge against you boys—disturbin' the peace—so let's get moving." He nodded toward Roy and Bart. "I'll be back to talk a little bit more with you."

"We'll be right here, Sheriff," Roy sang out. "Glad to see those bandits off our tail." Aside to Flint when he moved away from the table, Roy said, "We was mighty happy to see you and the sheriff show up."

"Right," Flint replied, but he was not completely convinced he could believe either side of the altercation. He saw Buck's logic in treating Roy and Bart as innocent victims in the matter, however, since they had done nothing to be arrested for.

Chapter 4

After they marched their three prisoners down to the jail, Buck and Flint decided to place all three of them in one cell. Consequently, they had to put Ralph to work moving one of the cots out of the small cell and setting it up in the larger one. Of course, Flint and Buck helped, and to do that, Buck got an extra set of handcuffs from his desk, and they cuffed each one of the prisoners to the bars of the cell. While Ralph fixed the big cell up with three cots, a water bucket, and two slop buckets, Buck and Flint searched the prisoners handcuffed to the cell wall. They were surprised to find all three were carrying a roll of paper money, each one of them with two or three hundred dollars.

"That's a lotta pocket money to be totin' around," Buck commented. "I wonder who's the poor soul who's missin' it."

"I expect we'd best go take a look at the hotel," Flint suggested. "Fred Johnson said they'd checked in a couple of rooms. It'd be a good idea to see what else they've got."

"Ain't you fellers forgettin' somethin'?" Ralph interrupted. When they both turned to give him a questioning look, he responded. "Supper. You didn't bring me no supper."

Buck had to laugh. "Well, we were kinda busy. I ain't had no supper, either. I forgot about that. I was on my way to eat when I walked in behind our prisoners. How 'bout you, Flint? Did you eat?"

"Nope," Flint answered. "I was on my way to Clara's when I almost walked right into your little party. Nobody saw me, so I went around to the back."

"I'm mighty glad you showed up when you did," Buck confessed. "My odds of not gettin' shot were slim and none."

"How 'bout us?" Eli blurted out. "You have to feed prisoners, and we ain't et, either."

Flint and Buck exchanged a quick glance and Flint volunteered. "I'll run up there and see if I can get us all something. Clara will be closin' up before long. You got everything under control here?"

"Yeah, get goin'," Buck answered. "Me and Ralph can handle things here. Our guests are all locked up."

Flint hurried out the door, realizing only then that he was hungry. He arrived at the dining room door just as Clara turned the CLOSED sign to face out. She opened the door and said, "I'm sorry, Flint, but we're closed. We've already started cleaning up. We've already thrown all the leftover food out." That was as far as she could carry on her charade without breaking up. "Come on in, Flint. We knew neither you nor Buck had eaten, so we fixed up a plate for both of you, and one for Ralph, too."

"Bless your heart, Clara. I shoulda known you wouldn't forget us."

She smiled sweetly in response but wondered if she shouldn't tell him that it was Mindy who worried he might miss his supper. Before she could confess, he asked a question she hadn't thought of.

"We've got three prisoners we need to feed, too. Any chance there's anything else left over to put together for them?" He could see by her twisted expression she had not given them any thought. "I wouldn't blame you one bit if you didn't wanna feed those three jaspers, but we have to feed prisoners."

"Let me go catch Margaret before she throws anything out." Clara hurried toward the kitchen. "Those two men your outlaws were trying to rob are still here," she added unnecessarily.

He could see them sitting at the table. He also saw Walt Doolin preparing to move Junior's body out of the dining room. "Did you check his pockets yet?" Flint asked as he walked by. "Was he carryin' a healthy roll of cash?"

"As a matter of fact, I did," Walt answered. "Am I gonna have to give that back? Is it some stolen money?"

"We ain't sure yet. Might be part of a robbery. Just count it, in case you have to return it. 'Course, you never know how much he's spent before he got shot." Flint followed Clara into the kitchen, leaving Walt to deduct his fee, according to his conscience.

When Mindy saw him walk in behind Clara, her face bloomed like a flower. "We saved you some supper," she said at once.

"Yeah, I appreciate it," Flint replied. "Clara told me at first that she'd thrown it all to the hogs."

"Oh, that was mean." Mindy frowned at Clara.

"Didn't fool him for a minute," Clara claimed then asked Margaret if she had thrown anything out. When Margaret said she was just about to, Clara said, "Let's see what we've got left. See if we can scrape up three plates of food for the three men he just put in jail."

While the women worked in the kitchen, Flint went back into the dining room to find Roy and Bart getting up from the table.

"I reckon we'd better get outta here before the boss-lady throws us out," Roy said when Flint walked up. "Like I told the sheriff, me and Bart are mighty glad you boys stepped in when you did. We'll stay around for a few days in case there's any questions you need to ask us . . . or anything we can help you with. You'd best be extra careful with those three fellers, though. They look awful dangerous to me. They looked like they was gonna rob us right here in the dinin' room." He shook his head slowly before adding, "I gotta give 'em credit for their imagination, though. Talkin' about us havin' money that belonged to them, they almost had me believin' it." He finished with a chuckle.

"We appreciate your cooperation," Flint told him. "We'll be checkin' back through the notices to see if there's anything they mighta had a part in, any descriptions or likenesses that might fit. In the meantime, we hope you enjoy your stay in Tinhorn."

Mindy came from the kitchen then to tell him they had six plates of food for him. "They might be too much for you to take by yourself. I'd better go with you and help you carry them." He said he'd manage somehow, but she insisted. "Nonsense. We can't scrape up anything more if you drop one of those plates. And like as not, if you dropped one of 'em, you'd probably drop two or three more, trying to catch the first one. Come on. You can carry yours and Buck's and Ralph's, and I'll carry the plates for the three prisoners."

By the time Flint and Mindy reached the jail, the street was already quite dark. The only place open was Jake's Place, and very little noise came from there. Everyone was hungry by that time, so the plates were well received. Buck carried the three plates into the cell room to give to the prisoners, along with some extra cups for the coffee Ralph had made. Standing in the office, Flint could hear the voice he had come to recognize as Eli's, attempting to convince Buck that Roy and Bart were actually members of their gang. His voice was getting louder and louder, so Flint decided it best to get Mindy out of the office before she might hear something come out of Eli's mouth a young lady shouldn't hear.

"Come on, Mindy. I'll walk you back to the dinin' room." She started to protest that his supper would get cold, but he told her he wasn't ready to eat. He'd warm it up on the stove and eat it later. "It's already pretty dark outside, so I'd best walk you back."

To Buck, he said, "I'll stay with Ralph and the prisoners tonight so you can get some sleep."

Normally, Buck would already have retired to his room, but he didn't seem to be too shaky and he hadn't mentioned a need for a drink. Maybe, Flint thought, the sheriff was starting to make progress in his battle with alcohol.

"It's mighty nice of you to walk me back," Mindy said as they walked along the dark street. "I know you've got more important things you need to be doing."

"Nothin' more important than makin' sure you get back to the dinin' room all right," Flint told her.

"What a nice thing to say. Thank you, sir."

Suddenly embarrassed, he sputtered, "Once in a while something just drops outta my mouth before I even know it's on my tongue."

"I still think it was a nice thing to say." That was the end of their conversation until they reached the dining room.

He thanked her again for saving supper for the sheriff's

department when he saw her safely inside the door to be greeted by three grinning women eagerly awaiting a report.

"Well?" Bonnie prodded.

"Well, what?" Mindy replied.

"You know what," Bonnie came back, and when Mindy offered nothing in the way of details, Bonnie said, "I declare, am I gonna have to tell him to come calling on you?"

"You do, and I'll hit you over the head with something," Mindy threatened. "Clara, tell her to mind her own business."

Clara laughed and replied, "I suppose that's good advice for everyone. If it's meant to happen, it'll happen."

"If it was me, I'd rather make it happen," Bonnie said.

With no notion he could be the topic of conversation in the dining room, Flint went next door to the hotel when he left Mindy at the door.

"Howdy, Flint," J.C. White greeted him when he walked up to the registration desk. "What can I do for you?"

"Hey, J.C.," Flint returned. "I need to take a look inside those rooms you put those four men in. I need to see what they're carryin' in their saddlebags."

"Oh," J.C. responded. "Well, I reckon that's all right when it's official sheriff's business."

"Yeah, it is. I'd like you to go with me, so you can witness it . . . if I do find anything suspicious."

"Whaddaya lookin' for?"

"Money," Flint answered. "All four of 'em was carryin' a lot of cash money in their pockets. I need to see if they have any more, then we'll try to find out where they got it."

J.C. picked up a lamp and led Flint upstairs to the first

room with two beds. A set of saddlebags was laying on each bed, and aside from some spare socks, underwear, and some personal items, the bags were stuffed with money.

"That's what I thought," Flint remarked.

It was the same story in the other room. He took possession of all four saddlebags and had J.C. write out a receipt of sorts and sign it. "Better give that to Mr. Smith to hold on to, just in case there's any question about where this money went." Gilbert Smith, the owner of the hotel would surely want to know about it.

"He don't like to be bothered about anything after supper, but he'll be in first thing in the morning before Fred comes in to take the desk. I'll give this to him as soon as he does, and I'll tell him what's goin' on."

"That oughta be good enough," Flint decided. "'Preciate it, J.C."

"I knew them four looked like they'd steal the shawl offa your poor old grandma," J.C. said.

"Bart! Come 'ere!" Roy Tate whispered loud enough to attract Bart's attention. Standing by the front window of Jake's Place, he kept his eyes on the street in front of the saloon. When Bart came over to stand beside him, he pointed and said, "Lookee yonder."

Bart squinted in an attempt to see the figure walking past the saloon in the dark street. "Who is it? Looks like he's carryin' a heavy load."

"It's that young deputy." Roy had been watching the figure longer and realized what was so odd about it. "He's comin' from the direction of the hotel and those are saddlebags he's loaded down with. He's totin' two saddlebags on each shoulder. You know who they belong to, and you know what's in 'em."

"Son of a—" Bart didn't finish, for it signaled the end of his and Roy's plans for the night.

With Eli, Swann, and Kelsey tucked safely away in the Tinhorn jail, they had planned to visit their hotel rooms in the wee hours of the morning to collect what he saw on the deputy's shoulders.

"Now what are we gonna do? We was gonna cut outta here first thing in the mornin'."

Roy was thinking about that, too. "We still better cut outta here in the mornin'. We can't count on that sheriff to keep believin' us, instead of them. And you know he'll be on the telegraph, tryin' to find out about any robberies. If they find out about that Wells Fargo holdup, they're gonna find out there was six of us, and not just them four."

"Hell, after the way this thing turned out, Eli's liable to tell 'em it's the Wells Fargo money they've got locked up in the jail. If they believe that, they'll likely believe there was six of us. They won't have to send no telegrams. Yeah, we gotta run."

"I swear, if our horses weren't locked up in that stable, I'd say leave tonight," Roy stated.

"Let's just make sure we get outta here before the sheriff gets up," Bart said. "I think if he believed what Eli was claimin', he woulda locked us up tonight. He thinks we're gonna lay around here for a few days, waitin' for my side to heal up."

"We might as well go on back to the hotel and go to bed," Roy decided. "We ain't gonna see that sheriff or his deputy tonight. We might as well head back to Shreveport and stay outta Texas for a spell. I'm gonna buy a bottle of whiskey to take with us. There ain't nowhere I know of to get a drink between this place and Shreveport."

Bart nodded his agreement, so they went back to the bar to buy a bottle. It wasn't until they returned to their room in the hotel that it occurred to Roy there was also no place between Tinhorn and Shreveport to buy food and other supplies.

"I swear, that is a fact," Bart remarked. "And we sure can't buy 'em here. The sheriff would find out we was fixin' to leave."

"Tell you what we can do," Roy said. "We can ride up to that little store this side of Tyler and get what we need there. Then we can just head east from there."

While Roy and Bart were making their plans to leave town, Flint and Buck were in the midst of counting the money they found in the four saddlebags. Just as a matter of record, they added up the amount in each saddlebag separately before totaling the four bags. They came up with a grand sum of twenty nine thousand, eight hundred dollars when they added in the money found in the individuals' pockets.

"I wonder how much they started out with." Buck had searched through the wanted notices for bank robbers, train robbers, and such without seeing anything related to a gang of four.

"Anything recent about a gang of six?" Flint asked, thinking about Eli's claims that Tate and McCoy were members of their gang.

"I didn't find anything," Buck replied, "but I ain't rulin' that possibility out. I sent a wire to the U.S. marshal and asked if there was any report about a robbery involving a gang of six men. I ain't heard back, but that was just a little while ago when you went up to the hotel."

"Whaddaya gonna do with all this money?" Flint asked.

"Well, tonight, I reckon I'll see if I can get it all in that little safe here in the office," Buck answered. "As soon as the bank opens in the mornin', I think it best to have Harvey Baxter put it in that big safe in the bank until we find out what we have to do with it. I reckon, just to be safe, we'd best guard it tonight."

"That's not a bad idea," Flint said. "I was plannin' to sleep here in the office tonight, anyway. Thought it'd be a good idea to be here for Eli and his two friends' first night in jail." Buck started to protest, but Flint added, "You've already stayed way beyond your usual time. Why don't you just leave it with Ralph and me? We'll keep an eye on things and maybe in the mornin' we can find out where this money came from."

"That's right, Sheriff," Ralph piped up. "Me and Flint'll keep an eye on that money. You need to go get your rest."

The expression on Buck's face told it pained him to hear Ralph suggest that he needed his rest. It had to be especially painful when he felt sure the sheriff badly needed his after-dinner drink of whiskey. Flint could imagine the strain Buck was feeling as he tried to maintain a solid front.

Finally, he gave in. "If you're still feelin' fresh, I'll turn in for a spell. You just bang on the wall if you need me."

"No problem," Flint replied. "I wanna make sure you're gonna be fresh in the mornin' when we've gotta find out about this money. You're better at things like that than I am."

Chapter 5

Just as they had planned to do, Roy and Bart left their hotel room with the first light of the new day. With their saddlebags on their shoulders, they walked behind the buildings on the main street, not wanting to risk being seen by the sheriff or his deputy. They arrived at the stable just as Lon Blake was starting his day.

"Well, good mornin', gents." Lon met them with a cheerful greeting. "Where you fellows headin' so early in the mornin'?"

"Mornin'," Roy replied, equally as cheerful. "There's a piece of land a feller was tellin' us about last night, not far outta town on the river. Said he was gonna sell it to somebody this mornin' at a real good price. We decided we'd get up there and take a look at the land, and if it's as prime as he claimed, make him a better offer. We oughta be back before supper, but in case we ain't, we'll take our packhorse with us, so we can at least have some coffee and some jerky to chew on for dinner."

"Thought you boys said you was on your way to Fort Worth," Lon said. "Didn't know you was interested in land around here."

"We are goin' to Fort Worth," Roy replied at once.

"But we're always interested in a good deal, and land close to Tinhorn might be valuable one day."

Lon helped them saddle up, then watched them ride off on the road to Tyler. "I don't know," he mumbled to himself. "Maybe they know what they're talkin' about but land up that way ain't good for much but farmin' or lumber. At least any that's close to Tinhorn." He looked Doc Beard's Morgan gelding in the eye and said, "I believe somebody was pullin' somebody's leg last night. Hope them boys don't get skint outta some of that money they appear to have."

Buck surprised Flint and Ralph when he walked into the office earlier than they expected. "I hope you and Ralph ain't drank all of that coffee.

"I wanted to finish it all up," Flint japed, "but Ralph said we had to save a little bit for you."

"Any problem with the prisoners?" Buck asked.

"Nope. They were doin' a lotta talkin' to each other, like they were tryin' to figure out a good story to explain all that money they were carryin'."

"I'll be interested to hear it when they come up with one," Buck said. "As soon as the bank opens, I'll take it up there. Why don't you go on up to Clara's and get some breakfast? You can bring the prisoners' grub back with you."

"And mine," Ralph added.

"I can wait, if you're ready to eat now," Flint offered. Ordinarily, they would have gone together, but with prisoners in the cell room, it was best not to leave Ralph with them.

Buck insisted he was not ready to eat yet. Flint assured him that he was and promptly went out the door.

He was met at the door of the dining room by a smiling Mindy Moore. "Good morning, Deputy Moran," she said sweetly. "You're not eating with Sheriff Jackson this morning?"

"No, with the three jaspers we've got locked up, we thought it best not to leave Ralph alone with 'em. They might talk him into some of his old ways." He said good morning to Clara and Bonnie as he sat down at a table, while Mindy went to fetch his coffee.

When she came back with it, she said, "Margaret's making pancakes this morning, if you're interested."

That sounded good to him. "I'll need to take four plates back with me," he reminded her. "But you're gonna have to trust me to manage 'em by myself. Clara won't want you runnin' off to the jail, right durin' your busy breakfast time."

"I thought about that," Mindy said. "Margaret saved me a big box that we can fit your four plates in without messing any of them up."

With Buck waiting, Flint did not linger over his breakfast. "Tell Margaret she makes prize-winnin' pancakes. Why don't we take some back to the jail?"

Mindy went back to give the order to Margaret, then returned to fill Flint's coffee cup. "You might as well have some more while Margaret's cooking the pancakes." She turned away to fill coffee cups at other tables.

In a short while, Margaret came from the kitchen, carrying the large box with the four breakfast plates inside. "I put a jar of maple syrup in there. Ralph can just bring it back when he brings the dirty dishes. Don't walk too slow, or they'll cool off."

He promised he wouldn't dawdle.

He arrived at the office steps at the same time Marvin

Williams' son, Mike, ran up with a telegram for the sheriff. "Papa said it was important."

Flint placed one foot on the first step so he could prop one end of his box on his knee while he dropped the telegram into a corner of the box. Then he fished in his pocket for a nickel to give Mike for delivering it.

"Thank you, sir!" the boy exclaimed, unaccustomed to gratuities.

Inside the office, Flint told Buck to take the telegram out of the box. "I'll go with Ralph to feed our guests. They're gettin' special treatment today, pancakes. Come on, Ralph. Let's get 'em served before these cakes cool off."

Ralph looked the four plates over for a few seconds before taking one out for himself. Then they took the other three into the cell room where Flint stood guard while Ralph carried the plates inside the cell.

Back in the office, Flint found Buck standing in the middle of the room waiting for him, the telegram in his hand. "Wells Fargo office north of Tyler, robbed three days ago by six men wearin' sacks on their heads. They killed a Wells Fargo guard and got away with fifty thousand dollars. The guard wounded one of 'em before they shot him."

"Damn," Flint swore. "How come they're just tellin' us now?"

"Damned if I know," Buck replied. "Maybe the robbers ran to the north after the robbery, and the marshal figured there wasn't no hurry to notify anybody down this way."

"Six of 'em, huh? I reckon we'd best go have another talk with Roy and Bart."

"I expect so," Buck said. "Ralph, we're leavin' you in charge. The prisoners oughta be all right for a while since they've got some breakfast. I'm gonna lock the office door, so nobody bothers you." He didn't tell him it was really because he had close to thirty thousand dollars in his small safe. "Don't unlock that cell for any reason, understand?"

"I understand," Ralph answered and repeated, "Don't unlock it for any reason."

Buck and Flint checked their weapons to be sure they were ready, and went out the door right away, heading for the hotel. "We'll check the dining room on the way, in case they came in after you left." When they got there, they took a quick look inside, and not seeing the two they were after, Buck asked Clara, "Were those two strangers, Roy and Bart, in this mornin' for breakfast?"

"Not so far," Clara answered and clearly wanted to know why he'd asked, but Buck closed the door and he and Flint went to the front desk of the hotel.

"Morning Buck, Flint," Fred Johnson greeted them.

"What room are Tate and McCoy in?" Buck asked.

"They're in room four at the end of the hall upstairs," Fred answered, aware that it was an official call.

"Have they come down this mornin'?" Buck asked.

"I haven't seen them," Fred replied. "But I just came on duty thirty minutes ago. J.C. would have been at the desk before that. He didn't say anything about them."

"Give us a key to that room," Buck said. "We might have to get 'em outta bed a little early this mornin'."

Fred didn't ask any questions. He just looked under the desk, found a key to room four and handed it to the sheriff.

Taking care not to make much noise, they climbed the stairs and walked down to the end of the hall to room four. Without saying a word, Buck looked at Flint to see if he was ready. Flint answered with a nod of his head. Buck inserted the key in the lock as quietly as he could manage before turning it, only to find the door was not locked. With gun in hand, he turned the knob. After another silent signal to Flint, he flung the door open, and they charged into the room. It was empty. Not only were Roy and Bart gone, but none of their possessions were in the room, either.

"They're runnin'," Buck announced and swore.

They went back to the registration desk where a very concerned desk clerk waited anxiously for some report.

"There's nothin' left in that room," Buck told him and tossed the room key on the counter, along with another key they found on the dresser. "They've gone."

"Gone?" Fred immediately looked alarmed. "They didn't check out. They said they would stay for a couple more days."

"We missed 'em," Buck told Flint. "The only chance we've got left is the stable. Maybe we can catch 'em there."

They turned and ran out of the hotel and into the street where they headed for the stable at a fast trot.

Buck made it as far as the barbershop before he had to pull up and walk. "You go on ahead, I'm plum winded. I'll be there in a minute."

Flint speeded up a little then and ran on to the stable, where he met Lon Blake coming from the barn. "Roy Tate and Bart McCoy?" Flint sang out as he pulled up before Lon.

"They was here early this mornin'," Lon replied. "But they ain't here now. What's the trouble?"

"We need to talk to 'em," Flint said. "I don't reckon they said anything about where they were goin', did they?"

"Matter of fact, they did," Lon answered, then paused when he saw Buck walking up to join them. "They said they was goin' to look at a piece of river property they was thinkin' about buyin'."

"Did they settle up with you?" Flint asked.

"No, they said they might not be back by suppertime," Lon replied, "so they took their packhorse with 'em."

"You hear all that, Buck?" Flint asked. "They took their packhorse with 'em." Buck said he heard, so Flint told Lon the bad news. "I'm afraid you just got left holdin' an empty sack. We figure they skipped out on you, and you ain't the only one. They skipped out on their hotel bill, too."

"Damn shame, too," Buck said. "If we got this figured right, they're carryin' somewhere in the neighborhood of twenty thousand dollars of Wells Fargo money between 'em." Thinking of the money in his office safe, he looked back at Flint. "That's something I've gotta do right now. I can't take a chance on something happening to that money while it's in my possession."

"After you do that, you might as well stop in to Clara's and get something to eat," Flint suggested. Turning back to Lon, he asked, "Did you see in which direction they rode outta town?"

Lon told him they rode out the north end of town, toward Tyler.

"That ain't a lot to go on," Flint said, "but maybe I can pick up a fresh trail of three horses. What are they ridin', anyway?"

"Roy's ridin' a dun geldin'," Lon said. "Bart's ridin' a sorrel, and the packhorse is a sorrel."

Buck spoke up then. "I don't know, Flint. You ain't got much chance of pickin' their trail outta everybody else's on that road. I'll let 'em know in Tyler that we've got four of 'em and the money they had with 'em. They can send some deputy marshals down here to get 'em."

"You're probably right, but it wouldn't hurt to take a look. I might get lucky. I'll saddle Buster and take a good look up that road. I might find a place where they turned off the road and went in some other direction." He was aware of the sheriff's feelings when it came to undesirables—if they moved on out of his town, they were no longer his concern. Flint, however, would like to prevent the two outlaws from getting away with their crimes.

Buck gave in. "All right, if you wanna test your luck, but any tracks they left are probably already too old to pick up. You be careful. Those two jaspers are big talkers, but I'd bet they are about as lowdown as you can get. If you ain't had any luck by dinnertime, come on back home."

Flint said he would. "If I don't find their trail by dinnertime, I ain't likely to find it at all." He slipped his bridle on Buster's head and led the big buckskin gelding over to the corral rail. He threw his saddle on the horse and slipped the 1864 Henry rifle in the saddle holster. All set, he climbed aboard, turned Buster's head toward the north end of town, and loped the length of the street to strike the Tyler road.

Once there, he dismounted to take a closer look at the tracks. Some looked fairly new, but they were left by riders coming to town. After a search of approximately ten minutes, he felt certain he had isolated the tracks of the two men he was interested in. He was further rewarded when he discovered that one of the shoes on one of the three horses had a small notch on one side, the result of a sharp rock in a stream bed perhaps. He decided they were the tracks he would follow and hoped they didn't lead him to some farmer and his son with a load of supplies on the back of a third horse.

Judging from the time Lon Blake said the two outlaws left his stable, Flint knew they had a two-hour head start on him. Hoping to shorten some of that time, he alternated Buster's pace between a walk and a lope, since that would give him the fastest pace the horse could maintain for any length of time without getting overly tired.

Their tracks never showed their horses ever breaking

from a steady walk, telling him he had to be gaining a little on them. All indications seemed to suggest the two men were simply taking the road to Tyler. To be sure he wasn't getting careless, Flint paused once in a while to take a closer look for the notched horseshoe to make sure he was still following the right set of tracks.

About two miles short of the spot he had planned to rest the horse, the buckskin showed signs of tiring, and he realized he might be working Buster a little too hard in his efforts to overtake the two outlaws. He was crossing a small stream that flowed into the creek he'd had in mind so decided to stop where he was. The creek ahead was a nicer place to camp, but he had no food to cook and no coffee to boil . . . and Buster had water right there. Climbing down out of the saddle, he led his horse about twenty yards along the stream to a small clearing. While his horse was drinking, Flint sat down on a log to watch him.

He thought about Buck's instructions not to track Roy and Bart very long. It seemed obvious he would not likely catch the two of them if they stayed on the road he was following. And when he reached Tyler, he expected it would be pretty hard to find their tracks among the many in town. He couldn't help questioning his certainty that he had picked out the right tracks to follow. It really didn't make sense they would return to Tyler.

Aside from Buck's instructions, he had not planned to track them for any distance. With no packhorse or supplies, and very little money, he wasn't prepared to do *any* tracking. "Damn," he swore, "I'm already hungry. I think we'll turn around and go home and wire the marshal that the outlaws are headin' their way. That all right with you, Buster?"

The buckskin raised his head from the water as if about to answer.

Flint saw the horse's ears pull back and flicker, like they did when he heard other horses. Immediately alert, his hand dropped automatically to rest on the handle of his Colt, while his eyes scanned back and forth along the stream. His gaze froze on a clump of bushes some thirty yards down the stream when he detected some movement among the leaves. He couldn't believe Roy and Bart would have doubled back on him. Why would they suspect he was on their trail?

His next thought was to find some cover, but then the leaves in the bushes parted to reveal an eight-point buck. He almost laughed aloud. *Now, that's more like it,* he thought. *If I can just get to my rifle before I scare him off, I won't miss dinner after all.* Moving in slow motion, he made it to his horse and slowly drew his rifle from the saddle sling. The deer finally realized his peril and jumped from the clump of bushes. But it was too late. Flint's bullet caught him just behind his front leg and brought him crashing to the ground.

Flint calmed Buster down after the big horse flinched when the rifle went off then took his reins and led him down the stream to the deer. "Now, I've got something to do while you finish resting up," he said to the horse.

He always carried in his saddlebags what he needed to butcher game. He took out his skinning knife and put the dying deer out of its misery. Taking his rope off his saddle, he used it to let Buster drag the deer to a tree of his choice. After he had the horse draw the carcass up to hang from a limb, he pulled off his vest and shirt before he went to work skinning the deer. He figured it wouldn't hurt if he got any blood on his undershirt. Nobody was going to see that. He removed the hide and gutted the deer in short order. Then he stopped long enough to gather some limbs and build a fire.

He cut some strips of meat off the carcass and soon had dinner roasting over the flames, while he continued to butcher the deer. "As soon as you've rested enough," he told the buckskin, "we're gonna hustle back to town and pass some of this venison around before it turns." He pulled a strip of roasted venison off the fire and sampled it. "Perfect. This day turned out a helluva lot better than I expected this mornin'."

Two miles from the scene of the unexpected venison dinner, there was some concern about the single shot just heard. Standing on the bank of the creek, Roy stood still and listened. It had been almost half an hour since hearing the sound of a rifle not too far away from the creek where they were resting their horses.

Finally, he said, "That shot ain't got nothin' to do with me and you. It was too far away. Whoever it was, they couldn't'ta been shootin' at us."

"Most likely somebody huntin' back in them woods behind us," Bart suggested.

"Right," Roy replied. "I bet that's exactly what it was." He thought about it for a few more moments, then said, "A deer or somethin' big 'cause he's usin' a rifle."

"Maybe so," Bart replied. "He musta hit it 'cause he didn't take but one shot. Some fresh deer meat would taste good right now, wouldn't it?" He nodded toward the pack-horse, carrying nothing at all to eat.

"It sure as hell would," Roy replied. "Maybe we oughta ride back that way and see if we can spot him. If he did get the deer, he'd still be in the process of butcherin' it."

"You think we oughta waste the time?" Bart wondered.

"It'd be worth it to me for the prospect of gettin' some

fresh deer meat," Roy said. "We ain't got no reason to think there's anybody tailin' us, have we?"

"No, I reckon not. We told that feller that owns the stable we'd be back."

"And we ain't checked out of the hotel," Roy reminded him. "Hell, I've got a cravin' for some venison."

Chapter 6

Roy pulled his horse to a stop where a stream crossed the road. When Bart pulled up beside him, he pointed down the stream.

"What?" Bart asked, seeing nothing in the trees. He looked again and saw what Roy had seen, a thin trail of smoke rising up through the leaves. "Well, I'll be. There's a camp down that stream, all right."

"It ain't that far back in the trees," Roy said. "Let's get our horses off the road and outta sight so they don't hear us coming. Then we'll walk back to that camp."

After the horses were secured, they made their way along the stream on foot until they got close enough to see the camp.

"Good," Roy whispered when he saw only one horse by the stream. "There ain't but one man, and danged if he didn't get him a deer."

They knelt where they were for a few minutes more, watching the man working on the deer carcass. His back was to them as he cut away portions of the carcass and placed them on the hide on the ground. A little shift in the breeze carried a hint of the aroma of roasting meat back to the two watching him.

Roy looked at Bart and grinned. "We might as well take all the meat and anything else he's got."

Flint paused for a few moments to take his bandana from the limb beside his shirt and vest. He started to wipe a little sweat from his face when he heard the call from behind him.

"Hello the camp!"

Startled, he froze for a few seconds.

"Didn't mean to slip up on you, but we couldn't help smellin' that deer meat you're cookin' on that fire."

Something about the voice sounded familiar. He knew he had heard it before.

"There's two of us, and we was hopin' you might feel like sharin' some of that deer."

Now he knew where he had heard it! He braced himself for the bullet he thought might come next. When it didn't come, he realized they didn't know it was him.

Taking the bandana in his left hand, Flint made an exaggerated motion of wiping his face as he turned halfway toward them. With an effort to disguise his voice as best he could, he called back to them. "Why, come on in. You're welcome to some fresh meat. There's some strips cookin' on the fire. Just help yourself." With his right hand down at his side and hidden from them, he eased his Colt out of the holster.

They walked into the little clearing and right up to the fire and pulled a couple of strips of meat from the limb rigged up as a spit.

"Yes, sir," Roy remarked. "There ain't nothin' better 'n the taste of fresh killed deer meat. Ain't that right, partner?" He grinned at Bart. "We could use some more of this."

Flint sidled over closer to the fire, still mopping his face until he was almost upon them. "I might let you have a little bit more of it if you don't give me any problems." He stuffed his bandana into his pocket and brought up his Colt .44 to bear on them. Shocked into a state of helpless disbelief, neither man could move for a moment as they suddenly recognized him.

"Deputy Moran," Roy finally found his voice. "What's goin' on? You know me and Bart. Why are you holdin' a gun on us?"

"That's the point. I do know you, and I mean who you really are."

Almost as an afterthought, Roy started to reach for his gun.

"Do it and you're dead," Flint promised.

Roy thought better of it. Bart, a strip of deer meat, dangling from his mouth could only stare dumbfounded caught in a trap of their own making as they were.

"All right," Flint told them. "I'm gonna try to do this without killin' anyone, but you make the slightest mistake and I'll shoot you down. Roy, you first, with your left hand, reach over and pull that six-gun outta the holster and drop it on the ground. Bart, don't you move."

With no choice, Roy reached over and pulled the weapon and let it drop. Then Flint had Bart do the same thing. With both handguns at their feet, Flint told them to step back three paces and stop.

"Now, get on your knees," he ordered.

When they did, he picked up their pistols, then whistled sharply. In a matter of seconds, the buckskin gelding trotted up from the stream. Flint took two pairs of handcuffs out of his saddlebags and proceeded to handcuff his prisoners with their hands behind their backs.

"This is all one big mistake," Roy tried again. "Have you started believin' that wild story those outlaws made up? We ain't got nothin' to do with those men."

"Roy, you might as well save your breath," Flint told

him. "We've got the straight story from the marshal's office in Tyler, and I'm bettin' I find about twenty thousand dollars in your saddlebags, or close to it, dependin' on how much you've already spent." He grabbed him by the arm and pulled him up to his feet. Selecting a small tree, he walked Roy over and unlocked one of the handcuffs, then pulled Roy's hands in front of him and locked them around the tree. He repeated the procedure with Bart at another tree.

"Just to show you I'm a compassionate man"—he gave each of them a couple of strips of venison—"I'm gonna feed you while I go find your horses." He walked back toward the road then, shaking his head in amazement at what had just taken place.

He found the three horses with no trouble at all, grabbed their reins, and led them back to the clearing, where he made a rough count of the money he found in their saddle bags.

"All right, ladies, you've enjoyed your little picnic. It's time to hurry back to Mother Eli. He's been worried about you."

They were not amused by his humor.

When he found nothing in the packs on their packhorse beyond a few pots and pans, plus a coffeepot, but no coffee, he was inspired to comment. "I reckon I owe you some thanks for bringing a horse to carry my deer back to town." The more he thought about the pure happenstance that brought about this unlikely arrest, the more he was amazed that something as crazy as this could happen. *Just don't get careless and let them turn the tables on you,* he told himself.

While he had their arms locked around the two trees, he searched their pockets for the money he figured they were carrying as pocket money. Like the other four, they both had a couple hundred dollars.

"I expect we'd best put this back with the rest of Wells Fargo's money." Flint put the money in the saddlebags with the major portion of the stolen bills. Then he released Roy and Bart from their trees, and with their wrists handcuffed behind their backs again, he helped each of them aboard their horses.

Ralph Cox got up from the chair he was sitting in on the porch of the sheriff's office and stuck his head in the doorway. "Sheriff, you oughta come look at this."

"Look at what?" Buck Jackson responded, not inclined to get up from his desk.

"Flint," was Ralph's simple answer. "You oughta come look."

"He oughta been back before now," Buck grumbled, but got up out of his chair and went to the door. "Well, I'll be go to hell," he exhaled. "How in the world—" He stopped, too astonished to finish. "Ralph, get your stuff outta that empty cell and get it ready to hold prisoners."

Buck hurried out the door to help Flint with Roy and Bart. "Well, howdy do, Flint," he sang out. "I reckon I don't need to ask you if you had any luck." He reached up and grabbed Roy by his arms and pulled him off his horse. "Mr. Tate, I believe. Welcome to the Tinhorn Jail." Noticing the packhorse then, he asked Flint, "What's in the deerskin on the packhorse?"

"Deer," Flint answered.

"Deer?" Buck echoed. "Whaddaya talkin' about? Was they deer huntin' when you caught 'em?"

"No," Flint answered, enjoying Buck's confusion. "I

was deer huntin' when they caught me." When Buck responded with a deep frown, Flint continued. "You see, my granddaddy taught me that you can catch most any kind of varmint, skunks like these two, if you bait a trap with deer meat. They'll come to it every time. So, I figured I'd rather draw these two skunks into my camp, instead of chasin' them all over Texas."

"Right," Buck said, too impatient to play along with Flint's silly story. "Let's get the two of 'em in the cell. Do they have the money?" Flint said it was in the saddle bags, so Buck continued. "After we get 'em locked up, you take that money up to the bank and have Harvey Baxter put it with the other money he's holdin' for us. While you're doin' that, I'll go to the telegraph office and send a wire to the U.S. marshal and tell him we've got all of his Wells Fargo robbers, and he needs to send a jail wagon to get 'em." He paused for a sign of confirmation from Flint before ending with, "Then you can tell me how the hell you captured these two."

"All right. But you ain't gonna believe it. I don't hardly believe it, myself. But I do have some mighty fine deer meat I need to do something with. It'd be a sin to let it go bad. I've got to do something with it today. I thought I'd take a nice piece of loin to give Hannah Green, but maybe you'd like to take that, instead."

"Why the hell would I wanna take it to her?" Buck responded. "You're the one who lives there."

"I don't know," Flint replied with a grin, knowing the sheriff was sweet on Hannah. "I just thought you might want to."

"Just take the money to the bank," Buck said. "We'll worry about your deer meat after we've got our new prisoners taken care of."

They led the two new prisoners into the cell room to a chorus of catcalls and insults from the current residents.

"Well, ain't this nice, boys?" Eli greeted them. "There's our old partners, come to visit us. Howdy, Roy, Bart. Have you got your memory back yet?"

"Go to hell, Eli," Roy shot back. "If you damn fools hadn'ta made that big scene in the dinin' room, none of us would be here in this jail right now."

"If you hadn'ta run off with one of those money bags, we wouldn't have had to come down here after you double-dealin' dogs," Swann charged.

Buck looked at Flint and remarked, "Kinda pulls at your heartstrings, don't it? It's like watchin' a big family reunion. Let's keep these two in the other cell. We'll have to tell Clara we'll need plates for five prisoners for supper tonight."

"And one for me," Ralph added. "That'll be six plates of supper."

Flint smiled. He suspected Buck intentionally left Ralph out every time he talked about ordering the meals, just to get his goat. As usual, Buck ignored his remarks, but never forgot to order food for Ralph.

"You boys might as well settle down and make up again because we already know the five of you and that one we had to shoot are the six men that robbed the Wells Fargo office. You'll get a fair trial and some time in prison, except the one that shot the Wells Fargo guard. I expect he'll hang."

"Junior was the one shot the bank guard," Eli was quick to declare.

"Anyway," Buck continued, "you might as well settle down and keep things between you peaceful. If you don't, it'll bother my memory. Sometime I forget to do little things like feedin' prisoners three times a day."

Once it appeared the initial verbal clash between the gang members had subsided, Buck locked the cell room door and told Ralph not to go in there until either he or Flint returned. Buck went to the telegraph office then, while Flint took the horses to the stable. After as brief a report of the arrest of Roy and Bart as he could manage, he left his, Roy's and Bart's horses with Lon. Then he led the packhorse with their saddle bags and his deer meat over to his boarding house and left a nice piece of loin with Hannah Green. She was delighted to receive it and said she and Myrna would cook it for supper.

After that, he took the rest of the meat and gave it to Clara, who looked it over very carefully before getting Margaret's opinion the venison was all right to cook if she did it today. He notified Clara they would need six supper plates now. Only then did he take the saddlebags with the Wells Fargo money up the street to the bank.

"There you go, Flint," Harvey Baxter said when he handed him a deposit receipt for the money in the saddlebags. "That's quite a piece of work you and Sheriff Jackson have done to corral the men who robbed the Wells Fargo office. According to what Buck told me, they had gotten away with fifty thousand dollars. So, with what you and Buck have deposited here, it appears the bandits didn't have time to spend much of the money. Wells Fargo didn't really lose much."

"No, sir, I reckon not," Flint responded, "unless you wanna count their guard who got killed durin' the robbery."

"Yes, I forgot about that," Baxter said. "That was unfortunate, but speaking as mayor of Tinhorn, I just want to tell you we appreciate the job you're doing."

"Well, thank you, sir. I'm glad to hear it," Flint replied.

When he got back to the jail, Buck and Ralph were sitting in the office waiting for him.

"I wired the marshal's office in Tyler," Buck said. "I told him we rounded up his Wells Fargo robbers and we'd appreciate it if he'd send a jail wagon down here and take 'em off our hands. I'm hopin' to hear something from him before supper. Did you get the money into the bank?"

"I did. Here's the deposit receipt." Flint handed the paper to Buck.

"Did Baxter count it?"

"Twice," Flint answered. "It says how much right there on that piece of paper."

Buck looked at it again. "Right. It was like we figured. They hadn't had no time to spend much." He settled back in his chair and exhaled a great volume of air. "Now, I'm ready to hear the real story about how you arrested those two jaspers."

Flint couldn't suppress a chuckle. "I told you the straight of it. I baited 'em with some deer meat, and they surrendered on their own, just to get some of that fresh killed venison."

Buck threatened to drown him in the water bucket if he didn't come out with the real story.

Flint finally gave up and admitted the arrest was nothing short of an unexpected piece of luck. "Yep, I was fixin' to head back here 'cause you told me not to go too far. My horse was about wore out, and it didn't look like I was gainin' any ground on 'em. Tell you the truth, I considered stayin' with it after Buster rested up, but I didn't have any supplies to start out on a long hunt."

"And that deer just come walkin' up the creek, yellin', 'shoot me, Deputy Moran!'" Buck japed.

"That was about the size of it," Flint replied. "So I shot him."

Buck kept after him with questions about how it actually happened until he finally got all the details of the

miraculous incident. He thoroughly enjoyed the whole
scene when he realized the absurdity of it. Flint knew it
was the kind of story that would not die mercifully. He
knew he was going to be stuck with it from now on. The
way Buck would look at him at odd moments and shake
his head in amazement made him sure of it.

Still living with the bitterness of the mistake he'd made
in underestimating the little town's sheriff department, Eli
Curry was prone to blame all his troubles on Roy and Bart.
Only days after scoring his biggest payday, and making a
clean getaway, he found himself not only in jail, but pos-
sibly facing a hanging. It would depend on a judge's decision whether or not to charge all of them for killing the
guard. It was because of Roy that he was in this mess.

Bart had been wounded and had little choice but to go
along with whatever Roy said. Eli felt no blame for leaving Bart behind when he was shot. Everyone in the gang
shared that risk. It was too bad, but that was just the hand
he was dealt. But Roy made the choice to steal the largest
portion of the money and run off with it.

The only thing that kept Eli from crushing the life out
of him with his bare hands was the wall of iron bars that
separated the two cells. Since that was not an option given
to him, he had to settle for the satisfaction of seeing Roy
and Bart arrested. That pleasure was increased even more
when he learned the circumstances of their arrest, information freely passed along to them by Ralph Cox.

As a result, Eli took great pleasure in loudly discussing
the fact that Roy and Bart had walked into the deputy's
camp and surrendered. Or as Eli preferred to refer to the

arrest, "Deputy Moran went deer huntin' and bagged a couple of skunks."

The story of Flint's deer hunt was not confined to the jailhouse, and Flint was sure he could give Buck the credit for that. Even the women in Clara's Kitchen were eager to question him about baiting Roy and Bart with deer meat.

Flint wasn't happy about it, and he wasn't sure why. It was no reflection on him. He'd promptly arrested the clowns in the incident—Roy and Bart. Still, it bothered him. He didn't want to be identified by any odd occurrence. He understood his role in the enforcement of the law in Tinhorn—do the things Buck couldn't do anymore. Flint was content with that role and preferred to let Buck have the reputation.

It was several days before Flint could walk in any door on the street without having to answer questions about the deer-bait arrests.

Interest in the five prisoners was rekindled again when two deputy marshals showed up in Tinhorn, riding beside a jail wagon driven by a cook named Smoky Jay. They pulled up in front of the sheriff's office and the two deputy marshals dismounted and went inside the office, where they encountered Ralph Cox sitting behind the desk.

"Sheriff Jackson?" one of the deputies enquired, obviously the elder of the two men.

"No, sir," Ralph replied. "Sheriff Jackson's gone to dinner. Deputy Moran's here, though."

Since the deputy marshal saw no one else in the office, he waited for Ralph to continue. He didn't.

"Where is Deputy Moran?"

"He's in the cell room," Ralph answered and pointed to the door.

"We'll go in there and take a look at the prisoners,"

said the gray-haired deputy marshal. He and his partner started toward the cell room door.

"Whoa! Hold on a minute!" Ralph responded. "Sheriff said not to let nobody in the cell room to look at the prisoners."

The gray-haired deputy paused to give Ralph a patient look. "I'm Deputy Marshal Arthur Page and this is Deputy Marshal Slim Jenkins. We're here to transport five prisoners to Tyler. I think your sheriff would tell you it's all right if we saw them."

"Oh." Ralph blurted but made no move to unlock the door.

"Who are you?" Page asked.

"I'm not nobody," Ralph answered. "I just help out."

"Well, you can help us out by unlockin' that door."

"It ain't locked," Ralph said, "'cause Flint's in there."

"Flint," Slim Jenkins repeated. That'll be Flint Moran, right?" When Ralph said that it was, Jenkins commented to Page, "That's a name we're startin' to hear now and again, ain't it?" He followed Page into the cell room.

In the process of constructing another bench to go into one of the cells, Flint looked up when the door opened. "I wondered who Ralph was talkin' to in the office. I thought maybe Buck had come back." Unlike Ralph, he noticed their badges right away. "We were wonderin' when you fellows would show up."

Anxious to show their defiance, the prisoners hooted and cursed the two marshals. "You sure you two can handle a bunch of wild broncs like us?" Eli taunted. Blaring at Slim, who was obviously younger, he asked, "They send you down here to get us? And you brought your daddy with ya. Ain't that nice, boys?"

"I advise you to keep your mouth shut, all of you," Flint said. "I ain't ordered any supper for you yet. If you don't behave yourselves, I'm not gonna bother bringing any food back." He turned to address Page. "I'm Deputy Moran. I hope you ain't gonna have to put up with much of that noise on your way back to Tyler."

"I ain't worried about it," Page responded, just loud enough for the prisoners to hear him. "I don't put up with any nonsense. If they don't behave, I'll put a bullet in the one that's causin' me problems. I'm ordered to bring 'em in, dead or alive, so it don't matter to me. I'll tell you one thing," he nodded toward Jenkins. "Slim'll back me up on this. It sure quiets 'em down after they ride a few hours chained to a dead man." He introduced his partner and himself and they shook hands with Flint.

"How you gonna transport 'em?" Flint asked. "Jail wagon?"

"Yep," Page answered at once. "We brought a jail wagon with a cook drivin' it. I know we ain't got far to take these buzzards, but it's the safest way for me and Slim to transport 'em. And in that jail wagon, it's gonna take eight hours at least to haul them to Tyler. That ain't countin' the time we have to stop for water and rest the mules and our horses. Besides, five is a large number of prisoners to transport on horseback with just two guards."

"Especially five like this bunch," Flint agreed. "You wanna load 'em up right now?"

"No. It's already later than I wanna start back. It's almost suppertime. Slim and I'll stay here tonight and load 'em up first thing in the mornin'." He grinned and added, "We'll let you feed 'em tonight, then we'll move 'em out of here before breakfast. Maybe you can recommend a good spot to park our wagon and camp for the night."

Flint pointed toward the back of the room. "The river's about one hundred yards behind us and there's good grass and firewood on the banks. Don't pay no mind to the open field between here and the river. It's nothin' but weeds, but there's decent campin' under the trees by the river."

"That sounds like what we're lookin' for," Page said. "Handy to the jail, too."

"Something I need to tell you about your prisoners," Flint said. "There's bad blood between the two locked in that cell"—he pointed to Roy and Bart—"and the three locked in the other one." He went on to tell the two deputy marshals about the split between the two groups.

Page and Jenkins had a pretty good picture of the problem by the time Buck returned.

Chapter 7

Flint and Buck went outside with the two deputy marshals to take a look at the jail wagon and say howdy to Smoky Jay. The wagon reminded Flint of a gunsmith's wagon he had seen in Tyler. It had a solid top, but instead of wooden sides, it had heavy gauge fencing all around, and a gate with a padlock at the end of the wagon bed. A long heavy chain was partially coiled in the back of the wagon, so it could be drawn out of the wagon when it was parked, and the prisoners could be chained to it.

"This here's my rollin' jailhouse," Smoky said. A stocky man with a large belly overhanging the heavy belt he wore to hold up his pants, Smoky appeared to like his own cooking. When Page told him where to look for his camping spot, Smoky asked if he was going to be cooking for him and Slim that night.

"No offense," Page answered, "but me and Slim were talkin' about takin' supper at that dinin' room up the street." He paused to ask Flint, "What was it?"

"Clara's Kitchen."

"Right, Clara's Kitchen." Back to Smoky then, Page said as a courtesy, "We was gonna ask you if you wanted to go with us." He caught Slim's surprised reaction when he heard that. They both knew Smoky would choose to not go, and for that they were grateful. His primitive eating manners were a little disgusting for polite company.

"Nope, thank you just the same," Smoky replied. "I'd best stay with my mules. Besides, I've got a little slab of deer meat I've been carryin' for a couple of days. Ain't hardly enough for one man. This'll be a good chance to cook it."

Buck spoke up then. "Flint just recently came up with a fresh supply of venison—"

"But that's all gone now," Flint interrupted, quick to cut him off before he went further. "You can't go wrong at Clara's. The sheriff and I eat there most of the time." He saw the mischievous look in Buck's eye, but Buck didn't continue with the story, showing his deputy some mercy.

"How many days have you had that deer meat?" Slim asked. "This time of year, you can't keep meat very long before it starts turnin'."

"Not more 'n two or three," Smoky answered. "Ain't nothin' wrong with it. I kept it wrapped up in a wet rag. Folks get too picky about fresh game. It don't go bad as quick as most folks think. Oh, sometimes it'll take on a little different flavor, but it don't hurt you to eat it. Hell, you're cookin' it. Besides, I had to brush some worms off of it this mornin'. And if the worms will eat it, then it's still all right to eat."

Nobody said anything for a few moments while they all formed that picture in their minds. Flint changed the subject, suggesting Buck should go on to supper with Page and Slim, and he would show Smoky where to set up his camp. That was agreeable with everyone, so they tied the marshals' horses onto the back of the jail wagon. Flint locked the office door, then he and Smoky drove out across the open field to the river. Once Smoky picked the spot he favored, Flint pulled the saddles off the marshals' horses and released them to go to the water, while Smoky unhitched his mules.

Saying he should get back to the jail because it would be a shame to lose the five prisoners after Smoky and the marshals went to the trouble to come down to get them, Flint left him. As he walked back through the weedy patch between the river and the jail, he thought again about Smoky's deer meat. He couldn't help wondering what the odds were they might find Smoky dead the next morning, or at the least, too sick to sit on the wagon seat.

Back in the sheriff's office, Flint found Ralph worried about whether or not Buck would remember to bring him some supper.

"He probably will," he told Ralph. "Least, I hope he does when he's got plenty of hands to carry six plates."

"Seven plates," Ralph promptly corrected him. "Don't forget my supper."

"I didn't. Five prisoners and your plate make six, not seven."

"Oh, that's right." Ralph made the mistake because he always had to correct Buck by adding one to the number.

Much to Ralph's relief, Buck and the visiting lawmen returned with a plate for each prisoner, plus one for Ralph. Both visitors expressed their compliments for the quality of the food at Clara's.

After they passed the plates to the prisoners, Slim had to ask, "Have these prisoners been gettin' meals this good every day? Or was this a special farewell supper the ladies fixed up for 'em?"

"No," Buck replied. "That's pretty much what they get every day, same as the payin' customers get."

Slim looked at Page and said, "We might have a fight

on our hands when it comes time to pull them outta that cell. The cookin' where they're goin' ain't nowhere near as good as this grub we had tonight."

Page laughed in appreciation of his partner's humor. "We might have to knock 'em out to get 'em outta there. But after they've had a couple of Smoky's meals, that grub in the Tyler jail will taste good." Changing the subject to business then, he said to Buck, "Sheriff, I've got some papers here that say I picked up five prisoners from you. I have to sign 'em, and you have to sign 'em. If you want to, we'll just sign 'em tonight, and I'll stick 'em in my saddlebags, and we won't have to worry with it in the mornin'. That all right with you?"

Buck said it was, so they signed the transfer papers to take custody of Roy Tate, Bart McCoy, and three prisoners who refused to give their names.

Flint began to worry about Buck's reaction if the two deputy marshals expressed a desire for a drink before turning in. Buck was already past the time when he typically became a little shaky. Ordinarily, he would retire to his room at this point.

Much to his relief, Page said, "If we didn't have ol' Smoky settin' over by the river, jumpin' every time he hears a cricket or the wind rustlin' the leaves in the trees, I might say let's go have a drink or two. But we're gonna wake you up pretty early in the mornin', so we'd best just go crawl in our sleepin' bags and bid you fellows a good night."

"That's quite all right," Buck said. "I wouldn't mind hittin' the sheets a little early, myself, and let Flint keep his eye on the town tonight. He's got younger eyes, anyway."

"All right, then," Page said. "We'll take possession of the prisoners about five o'clock. I figure we'll stop at a creek we saw about ten miles north of here and eat breakfast."

"That's a good spot to stop," Flint commented. "The water's good there." He could have told them that Roy and Bart should feel at home there, since that was where they were resting their horses when they'd decided to go deer hunting, but he didn't want to bring up the subject. He walked outside with the deputy marshals to give them a point of reference where to walk across the open patch. "Walk on that line and you'll bump into your wagon." He stood and watched them for a moment before turning around and going back into the office. Buck had already retired to his private quarters.

"You never got no supper," Ralph said. "And I expect it's too late now. I bet Buck didn't think about that, or he'da stayed here a little longer, so you could get you somethin' to eat."

"Yeah, I expect he would have," Flint said. "I'll take a little turn around town, and I can check Clara's when I go by. They might have some biscuits or something left." He went outside, locking the door behind him, and started up the street toward the hotel.

Everything was quiet in the little town, especially up toward the north end of the street. As he expected, the dining room was closed and he would normally have tapped on the glass, but not only was the CLOSED sign facing out, but the shade was pulled down as well. He figured there must be some reason to discourage any late comers for supper, so he didn't knock, and went next door.

J.C. White, the night clerk at the hotel, had already relieved Fred Johnson, and he greeted Flint cordially when he walked in. "Evenin' Flint. I heard you're gettin' rid of your guests."

"That's a fact," Flint replied. "First thing in the mornin'. I can't say as how I'll miss 'em." After a brief chuckle at that comment, Flint said, "I started to check by Clara's just now, but she's got the closed sign out and the shades pulled down. Kinda unusual. Anything goin' on?"

J.C. chuckled again. "If the shades are down and the door's locked, that usually means the dinin' room has gotten too much in need of a cleanin'. Clara gets those spells once in a while when the dinin' room and the kitchen ain't clean enough to suit her. I'm surprised you didn't know that, as long as you've been here now."

"I'm surprised myself," Flint admitted. "I reckon I never thought much of it before when the shade was down." This is the first time it's happened when I'm about to starve to *death,* he thought, *and that's the reason I noticed it tonight.*

He said goodnight to J.C. and continued his walk of the street. When he made his usual stop in Jake's Place, he was fortunate to find Rena had left some biscuits in the oven before she left for the night.

"She musta had a feelin' you were gonna miss your supper tonight," Rudy joked, "'cause she left a jar of molasses out on the table to go with 'em."

"The only thing better would be if she left the coffee on the stove," Flint said.

"Well, that ain't no problem. Jake just had me make a fresh pot of coffee not twenty minutes ago. I'll get you a cup."

"I reckon I could make myself some back at the jail, instead of drinkin' yours up. Where is Jake, anyway?" Flint was accustomed to seeing the saloon owner at a table in the back of the saloon.

"He took his coffee upstairs to have a business meetin' with Lucy," Rudy answered, unable to keep from grinning.

Flint grinned in response. "I reckon it's important to have meetings with your employees. I'm sure he has meetings with you and Rena, too."

"Not like the meetin's he has with Lucy," Rudy said, and they both laughed.

"How's that workin' out?" Flint asked. "I mean since Lucy's been workin' here. Has Jake had any more trouble from Baxter and the preacher about it?" He knew the mayor and Reverend Morehead had both registered protests when Jake decided to hire Lucy Tucker. Both were afraid Jake was on the verge of dragging Tinhorn down into the depths of sin. Jake maintained she was not a prostitute. She was hired to simply work the saloon, to encourage the sale of whiskey, and act as a hostess, so to speak. Jake argued that it was no different from Clara Rakestraw managing and hostessing Clara's Kitchen.

Mayor Baxter and Reverend Morehead were unsuccessful in saving Tinhorn's pristine reputation largely because they had no backing from any of the other members of the town council. So they accepted defeat, although Morehead still preached nearly every Sunday against Lucy's presence in their town.

Flint lingered long enough to finish off two biscuits with molasses and two cups of coffee while Jake was still in conference upstairs. "I guess I'd best see what's goin' on in the rest of town," he finally announced. "I'll tell Rena she saved my life again when I see her tomorrow. How much do I owe you for my supper?"

"Nary a cent. I ain't gonna charge you nothin' for them cold biscuits and coffee," Rudy replied.

"I expected to pay for 'em," Flint said. "You'd charge anybody else, wouldn't you?"

"Yes, I would," Rudy answered. "Tell you the truth, Flint, I know it's a policy that Jake started before he hired me. But I always feel a little guilty when we charge you for a drink of whiskey, and the sheriff's is on the house. So, I ain't chargin' you nothin' for the coffee and biscuits."

"Well, that's mighty generous of you, Rudy. I 'preciate it, and I won't expect it to be a regular thing in the future." Flint said goodnight and walked the rest of the town before returning to the sheriff's office where he found Ralph asleep on a mattress placed on the low bench he often used when prisoners were in the cells. After he went into the cell room to make sure the prisoners were all secure, he sat at the desk for about an hour before he rolled out his bedroll behind the desk and crawled into it.

He was awakened the next morning by Ralph shaking his shoulder and talking excitedly. "Flint, wake up. They're here! They're out front with the jail wagon."

"Well, unlock the door and let 'em in," he mumbled, still half asleep. "What time is it?" Sure it must still be in the middle of the night, he didn't feel like he had slept any time at all. Nevertheless, he crawled out of his blankets and pulled his boots on. He lit the lantern on Buck's desk and looked at the clock on the wall. They were early, but only by half an hour.

"You let them in," he told Ralph, "and I'll go get the ladies up. After you let 'em in, go see if you can get Buck up."

"You sure you want me to do that?" Ralph replied. "Buck's gonna be hard to wake up this time of mornin'."

"He's gonna be mad as hell if we let him sleep through it," Flint shot back. "Get him up. Tell him I made you do it." He went into the cell room then and lit a couple of lanterns. Banging on the cell bars with a tin water cup, he started yelling. "All right, gents, it's time to get movin' to your new home. Get outta those cots and get your business done in the slop buckets. It'll be a while before you get the next chance."

They were all off the cots and taking turns relieving themselves of the accumulated fluids of the day before, when the two deputy marshals walked into the cell room.

Flint gave the reins to Arthur Page and said, "I reckon you know how you wanna handle this. Just tell me what you want me to do and I'll try to help."

"We'll take 'em one at a time," Page told him. "That big one first. The one who did all the talkin'." He indicated Eli, who acknowledged his selection with a smirk. "Walk over here, and stick your hands between the bars," Page ordered.

"Why don't you come in here and get me?" Eli responded defiantly.

Page didn't hesitate. "I ain't got time to fool with you. Slim, shoot him!"

Slim didn't question the command, drew his Colt Peacemaker, and aimed it at Eli's head. He drew the hammer back.

"Wait! Damn it!" Eli blurted. "I'm comin'." He knew it might have been a bluff, but he wasn't sure. He couldn't risk calling Slim on it.

Still playing his part, Slim looked at Page as if he wanted the go-ahead. Page hesitated, but when Eli hurried to the bars and stuck his hands through to be handcuffed, Page accommodated him.

"Take him out and lock him on the chain," Page said, and Slim escorted him outside where Smoky was standing, holding a shotgun.

"You're next." Page pointed to Swann.

It was at this point the sheriff appeared, looking properly wasted.

"Mornin', Sheriff," Page greeted him. "We're doin' a little house cleanin' for ya."

Slim came in and took Swann outside to the jail wagon.

Buck stood there by Page until the last prisoner was chained up in the wagon. It happened to be Roy Tate. He and Bart McCoy were seated at the ends of the benches on either side of the wagon.

With no way to separate them from the other three, Page gave them a distinct picture of how he would handle any trouble between the two factions of the gang. "I will deliver a dead man, instead of a troublemaker. It's as simple as that. Any fights start, I'll end them permanently. You'd do well to take me seriously on that."

The deputy marshal was pretty convincing. Just as the five outlaws had obviously concluded, Flint was of the opinion Page was not bluffing.

With all the prisoners loaded, Page and Slim climbed up into their saddles and Smoky slapped the reins across his mules' rumps and started off up the street to strike the road to Tyler. The two deputy marshals lingered a moment to thank Buck and Flint for their cooperation. They, in turn, wished the marshals good luck on the way back. The whole transfer had been accomplished in a little over half an hour.

Still an early enough hour of the morning no spectators gawked at the jail wagon as it drove up the middle of the street. Flint, Buck, and Ralph were the only witnesses.

"I can't tell you how glad I am to see that crowd of visitors leavin' town," Buck remarked as they stood in the street, watching the exodus. "I took a headache from something I ate, I reckon. I'm gonna go back and lay down for another minute or two."

"Flint told me to get you up when they got here," Ralph was quick to inform him.

"Yeah, I'm the reason you've got a headache, I reckon," Flint confessed for Ralph. "It's too early to get breakfast, so I'm gonna go to the boardin' house. I feel like I need a bath and a shave. This time of day there won't be anybody else usin' the washroom. I'll probably be back here before Clara opens."

He decided he'd leave the option open for Buck—if he wanted to go to breakfast with him, or wait until later at Jake's Place. To Ralph, Flint said, "I guess you could use a little more shuteye. Well, you've got your pick of the cots. You can just lock the front door and I'll be back before you wake up, most likely."

Heading to the boarding house, he decided he could appreciate Buck's feeling of relief at being rid of the gang of five. He was surprised, however, the marshals had made no mention of the Wells Fargo money. Buck had told him there was nothing in those papers he'd signed that dealt with stolen money. It was a transfer of prisoners only. So, Flint supposed they'd send somebody else to get the money, a party of Wells Fargo officers perhaps. More than likely, they'd tell Buck to put it on the train. And if there wasn't a mail guard on the train, they'd request him to assign a man as guard.

Flint didn't have to guess who that guard would be. At any rate, Buck's part in the robbery was over, but his might not be. *Right now, what I want is a good hot bath,* he thought.

The house was still dark when he walked around to the back door. Not even a light was on in the kitchen, so Myrna was still in bed. She was always the first one up.

He climbed the four steps to the covered porch that connected his room to the rest of the house and went into his room to get clean underwear, shirt, and socks. Inside the washroom a handful of hot coals were still in the bottom of the stove. He took some kindling out of the box by the door and revived the fire, then added some wood from the stack on the porch. Pretty soon he had a bucket of water heating on the stove. Three more buckets and he had enough to give himself a quick bath and a shave in the round tub.

By the time he finished he could hear Myrna rustling around in the kitchen. After changing into his clean clothes, he picked up those he'd just taken off, threw them into the tub, and gave them a token scrubbing and wringing out. As an afterthought, he pumped another bucket full of water and rinsed his laundry in it. On his way back across the narrow porch to his room, he paused to hang his wet clothes over the handrail to dry.

He strapped on his gun belt again and walked back across the porch, through the washroom, and into the kitchen where he gave Myrna a start when he suddenly appeared.

"Flint!" she exclaimed when she turned to discover him standing in her kitchen. "So that was you I heard bumpin' around in the washroom. My hearin' ain't what it used to be, so I figured it mighta been a possum or somethin' crawled inside. I wasn't about to go in there to see."

"I'm sorry I gave you a fright," Flint said. "I had to sleep at the jail again last night. We had to load those prisoners up in a jail wagon, and I felt like I needed a little cleanin' up this mornin'."

"I expect it was a little chilly takin' a bath back there before you got that stove warmed up," Myrna said, "especially this time of mornin'."

"That sure is a fact. It's a lotta trouble, too. I woulda waited till it warmed up a little this afternoon and gone to the river. But I knew I might bump into you this mornin' and I didn't wanna offend you."

She responded with a throaty chuckle for his attempt at humor. "Is that so? Well, you didn't have to work that hard for a cup of coffee." Noticing him eyeballing the coffeepot sitting on the stove, she said, "It should be ready in another minute or two. Breakfast is gonna take a little bit longer than that. Are you gonna eat breakfast here?" she asked, knowing that more times than not, he ate at Clara's Kitchen. When he hesitated to answer, she said, "I gotta warn you. Hannah's gettin' excited about her niece comin' to visit in about a week."

Flint understood the warning. Hannah had already mentioned her niece's planned visit to him and had expressed her opinion Nancy and he would really hit it off together. Myrna suspected correctly he had no interest in meeting Hannah's niece. She walked over to the stove and poured a cup of coffee for him.

"Thank you. I can sure use that right now." He took a few cautious sips of the boiling hot coffee, then finally answered her question. "No, I probably won't eat breakfast here this mornin'. I won't know for sure till I get back to the jail. I know I've told you before, but I ain't ever lied to you, Myrna. I think your cookin' is better than Margaret's cookin' up at Clara's, but I always have to work around Buck's notions. It seems like he most of the time wants me to eat with him 'cause he wants strangers in town to see we've got lots of law enforcement in Tinhorn. Like I said, your cookin' is better and I ain't ever lied to you before."

This will be the first time, he said to himself.

"Don't worry yourself about it," Myrna told him. "I understand and just always know that we're glad to see you whenever you do show up."

"I wish I could eat here every meal. The cookin's good and it's included in my rent. I have to pay every time I eat at Clara's Kitchen." *That oughta convince her,* he thought.

That was actually the case. He paid for his meals at Clara's, but she did give him a discounted price. It had been his deal from the day the town hired him, even though they charged the sheriff nothing for his meals. It was unfortunate the food at Clara's was a little better than that at Hannah's boarding house.

He sat at the kitchen table and drank his coffee, talking to Myrna while she rolled out her dough for biscuits. He was tempted to stay and eat breakfast, but he had some concern about Buck. By the time the two deputy marshals escorted the jail wagon up the street, he'd thought Buck was a little shaky. Deciding it a good idea if he got back to town fairly quickly Flint finished his coffee. As payment for it, he filled her wood box, which was almost empty, then walked back up the street to the jail.

As he walked past the stable, Lon Blake called out to him. "I see you got your prisoners off this mornin'. That leaves some more horses to take care of. We need to ask Buck when we're gonna have another horse auction."

"I'll ask him," Flint said.

Chapter 8

By the time Flint walked back to the office, it was getting close to breakfast time. Clara usually flipped her WELCOME sign over to OPEN at six o'clock.

He found the office door still locked. Surprised, he unlocked it and went inside. Ralph wasn't in the office. He was still asleep on Roy Tate's cot in the small cell. Instead of disturbing him, Flint went back into the office, built a fire in the stove, then went to the pump and filled the coffeepot—all jobs Ralph normally did.

According to the clock on the wall, it was a quarter after six when Ralph came out of the cell room. He registered a genuine look of panic when he saw Flint sitting at Buck's desk. "I reckon I overslept," he blurted. "I'll fix us some coffee right away."

"It's already fixed. Get your cup and help yourself."

"Thank you, Flint. I could sure use a cup. I don't know why I slept so long. I hate it you had to make the coffee. That's my job." Ralph paused on his way to the stove and gave Flint another look. "You look like you went to the barbershop."

"I shaved and cleaned up a little. You don't have to tell

Buck you didn't make the coffee. I won't tell him. You ain't heard any word from him yet?"

"Nary a word," Ralph said and sipped his coffee. He grimaced as if in pain and commented. "You make coffee as good as mine."

"That's because I watched you to see how you made it," Flint lied. "I expect you'll be cleanin' up the cells today, so you'll need coffee and some food. I'll wait till I drink this cup of coffee to see if Buck's gonna stick his nose outta the covers anytime soon. If he doesn't, I'll go on up to Clara's and bring you some breakfast when I'm done eating." He took his time drinking the coffee.

With still no sign of life from the sheriff, Flint finally said, "If he comes in, you know where I'll be."

"Good morning, Deputy Moran," Clara greeted him formally. "Are you eating alone today?"

"Looks that way. Buck might be in later. We were up mighty early this mornin', so I think he might be makin' up for some of the sleep he lost."

"Why were you up so early?"

"We handed over those five outlaws to the deputy marshals this mornin', and they wanted to get started back to Tyler early." He gave her a grin. "So, I won't need but one plate of breakfast to take back with me this mornin'."

"Well, I know you're happy about that," Clara said. "Go sit down at a table so Mindy can set that cup of coffee down she's been standing there holding."

He went to Buck's favorite table in case he happened to show up. "Good mornin', Mindy," he greeted the young girl.

"Good morning, Flint," Mindy returned. "You didn't

come to supper last night. The sheriff came with those two lawmen from Tyler."

"That's right. As a matter of fact, I missed supper altogether last night. I ended up eatin' a couple of cold biscuits and some molasses at Jake's Place."

She almost seemed happy to hear he'd had to settle for cold biscuits rather than hearing him say he had decided to eat at Hannah Green's boarding house. "Well, you start on your coffee, and I'll make sure Margaret fixes you up a big breakfast to make up for missin' supper."

He took a sip of his coffee, realizing it was his third cup, beginning with the one he had with Myrna at the house.

"Morning, Flint," Bonnie Jones sang out when she came from the kitchen, holding a coffeepot. Unlike Mindy, who was too shy to make a forward comment, Bonnie paused to do a double take. "You look all spruced up this morning. All clean shaven, and it looks like you trimmed your hair some, too. What's the occasion? You ain't goin' courtin', are you?"

Flint had learned not to take Bonnie seriously. He just laughed and answered her. "I just had too many whiskers on my face. Decided to shave 'em all off and start over. While I was at it, I decided my hair was too long. I was afraid it would fall in my plate." He was surprised anyone would notice, but then he figured only Bonnie would think to exaggerate the smallest difference. Clara didn't. Mindy didn't.

Mindy came from the kitchen at that moment with Flint's breakfast, prompting Bonnie to comment. "Flint don't look bad at all when he's cleaned up. Ain't that right, Mindy? We better keep an eye on him. He might be up to something with one of these young gals that come into town on Saturdays."

"Go wait on your own tables," Mindy quickly advised

her. "Flint, pay her no mind. Half the time her mouth's running before her brain gets up in the mornings."

"Now you've hurt my feelings," Bonnie said, pretending to be offended as she walked away laughing. She filled a couple of cups for two of her customers, then went to the cash register stand when Clara signaled for a refill by holding up her cup. Still chuckling over her remarks to Flint and Mindy, she said, "I declare that man's as dumb as a stump. I guess I'm gonna have to tell him Mindy's waiting for him to take notice of her."

"Don't you dare," Clara told her at once. "If those two young people are supposed to get together, it'll happen when it's time. One thing I know about Flint Moran is that he is not dumb. I'm willing to bet he's aware of Mindy's attraction to him, but with the salary he gets as a deputy, he knows he can't support a wife."

"Why couldn't they both just keep working?" Bonnie asked.

"Now you're talking about a male thing. No respectable man wants his wife to have to work. And what about when she starts puttin' out young'uns? No, you'd best just let them be."

"All right," Bonnie said, "but it's a shame. I ain't ever seen two young people so right for each other as those two."

Flint did not dawdle with his breakfast, knowing Ralph was eagerly waiting for him to return with his plate. He was also aware Buck would likely be carrying a heavy dose of *medicine* and would need something solid in his stomach. When Mindy came again with the coffeepot, he told her to give him half a cup and get Ralph's plate ready to go.

Bringing the plate, she held it for a few moments while Flint fished in his pocket for money to pay for his breakfast.

She could not resist expressing an opinion. "It doesn't seem right for you to pay for your meals while the sheriff and the prisoners get theirs free."

Flint smiled. "Well, now you know how high deputies rank in this town, right behind the prisoners and way behind the sheriff. I reckon that's my own fault, though. That's what they offered, and that's what I accepted. I reckon I shoulda held out for a better deal, but I can't blame the town council. I didn't have any previous experience to bargain with, young as I was. I reckon I was lucky they took a chance on me." Tempted to tease her further, he said, "I think they were tryin' to decide between me and Louis Wheeler's son. But I got the job because Wheeler wouldn't let his son wear a gun."

She just shook her head in response to his nonsense, since the postmaster's son was not yet thirteen but bit her lip to keep from giving more of her opinion on the subject of his having to pay for his meals. Instead, she asked as casually as she could manage, "Will you be here for dinner?"

"Far as I know," he answered, smiling as he took the plate from her, then left to pay Clara on his way out.

He was happy to see Buck in the office when he got back, and still time to get breakfast at Clara's. He told Buck the ladies were expecting him, hoping it would influence him to go there instead of Jake's Place. Maybe it did.

Buck walked up to Clara's, ate, and returned in a little less than an hour. And looked a lot better than when he had left the jail. Flint hung around the office for a while, talking to Buck and Ralph, until he decided maybe it would be a good idea to see what was going on in the town.

"Think I'll take a walk around," he announced, plopped his hat on his head, and headed for the door. He walked out just in time to meet Raymond Chadwick about to come up the steps. "Howdy, Raymond," he greeted. "You lookin' for the sheriff?"

"The sheriff or you. I don't reckon it makes much difference," the blacksmith replied. "I just thought I oughta tell one of ya."

Flint stepped back into the office again while holding the door for Chadwick. "Well, come on inside and you can tell both of us."

Hearing Flint's side of the exchange of words, Buck looked up from his desk.

"Hey, Buck," Chadwick greeted him. "I just thought somebody oughta tell you two mules just came wanderin' into town a few minutes ago, pullin' a wagon."

Both lawmen reacted with puzzled expressions since that was nearly a daily occurrence in Tinhorn, and hardly worth reporting to the sheriff. "What I'm tellin' you is that there weren't nobody drivin' the wagon, and there weren't nothin' in it."

"Somebody's mules ran off," Buck replied. "Is that what you wanted to tell us?"

"Yeah, that and the fact that I know whose wagon it is," Chadwick answered. "It belongs to Bob Waldrop, and the mules are wore slap out. Bob lives seven or eight miles from here over near White Creek. And those mules look like they musta run most of the way."

"And you think the wagon belongs to Bob Waldrop?" Buck asked.

"I know it does," Chadwick replied. "I put a new axle on that wagon last month. I just wonder if somebody oughta see about it."

"Maybe somebody will show up pretty soon lookin' for it," Buck suggested. "Probably the best thing is to take 'em down to the stable and let Lon take care of 'em till Bob or somebody comes lookin' for 'em." Buck didn't see that as his responsibility and was not inclined to get excited about somebody's mules making a break for freedom.

"There was blood on the wagon seat," Chadwick said, almost as an afterthought.

Flint commented then. "Maybe I'd best take a ride out toward Waldrop's farm, just in case Bob's layin' hurt beside the road somewhere."

"That might be a good idea," Buck said, wondering why Chadwick hadn't started out by mentioning that. "Leave the wagon and the mules with Lon. I expect they're too wore out to turn around and go back right now, anyway." He turned to Chadwick and asked, "Where is the wagon?"

"At my forge," Chadwick answered. "I tied 'em there while I came to tell you. I can take 'em on down to Lon's stable for ya."

"Good. 'Preciate it," Flint said. "I'll go straight down to Lon's and get my horse." He grabbed his rifle and went out the door.

At the stable, he hurriedly told Lon about the driverless wagon and where he was going while he saddled Buster. Since he wasn't sure he would be back in time for supper, he got some beef jerky from his packs in the barn and put it in his saddlebags. He was riding down the street at a comfortable lope when Chadwick led the team of mules and the wagon in front of Lon Blake's barn.

Flint continued out the south end of town, past Hannah Green's boarding house, until he struck the trail to White Creek. He settled Buster down to a brisk walking pace, relieved to see the distinct wagon tracks on the trail, for that was a good sign the mules had come straight from Waldrop's farm. If there had been no wagon tracks on the trail, he would have been at a total loss as to where to search. The mules had evidently made the trip to Tinhorn so many times they just followed the trail right on into town. The fact that there was blood on the wagon seat told him that he was not looking to find where Bob Waldrop might have been somehow thrown from his wagon. Blood on the seat meant he was either shot out of the seat, or he was already wounded when he climbed into the wagon. It was difficult not to assume foul play was involved.

Flint continued along the narrow wagon trail, looking carefully left and right for any sign that might lead him to Waldrop. As he got closer and closer to White Creek, with no sign of Waldrop, another concern began to trouble him. He didn't know Bob Waldrop and had no idea where his farm was. White Creek was nothing more than a single store, more like a trading post. It was owned by a man named Luther Price who'd built it where the creek emptied into the Neches River. Not even certain it was still an operating store, Flint had never had reason to find out. And now he found himself counting on Price to tell him how to find Waldrop's farm.

Reaching a point where he felt sure the creek could not be more than half a mile or so, he came to a fork where another wagon trail joined the trail he was following. It had many wagon tracks on it as well, presenting a problem. Some of them turned in the direction of the store and added to the tracks he was already following. He had no course of action except to continue following the trail he had been following and hope the store was still in operation.

A mule with a saddle was tied to a corner of the porch as he approached the river and the White Creek store. He guided Buster to the corner post on the other side of the porch and dismounted. A sign over the door proclaimed the log building PRICE'S STORE. A smaller sign on the door said OPEN.

Flint opened the screen door and walked into the dark interior of the room, pausing a few moments to allow his eyes to adjust to the darkness. Refocused, he saw two men, one behind the counter, and one in front of the counter. Both were silently watching him.

"Afternoon," Flint greeted them. Looking toward the man behind the counter, he asked, "Mr. Price?"

Price nodded.

"My name's Flint Moran. I need to find Bob Waldrop's farm and I'm hopin' you might help me out."

Price didn't answer right away, but exchanged a look of suspicion with the other man at the counter.

"Well, Mister Moran," Price finally said, "a lot of little farmers come into the store now and again. I can't say as I know how to get to all of 'em. Can you, Tom?"

The other man shook his head in answer.

Flint realized they were reluctant to give out information on their neighbors to any stranger who walked in.

"Whaddaya lookin' for Bob for?" Price asked then.

"Look, fellows. I'm a deputy sheriff in Tinhorn." He pulled his vest aside so they could see his badge. "I'm looking for Waldrop because I think he might be hurt and needin' some help." He then told them about the wagon showing up in Tinhorn and his concern over the blood on the wagon seat. "I watched for signs of him all the way from town, but I didn't see anything on either side of the road." He saw the signs of concern in both their expressions upon hearing that.

"To get to Bob's place, you needed to take that fork you passed just before you got here," Price volunteered at once. "That trail follows the creek and his farm is about a quarter of a mile down that way."

"You'll know it when you get there," the other man offered. "A gate in the fence with a red rag tied on it marks the path that will lead you right up to the house."

"I hope Bob ain't in no trouble," Price said. "He was just here in the store this mornin'."

"I hope he's all right, too," Flint said. "And it might be nothin' at all, but I thought I'd best check to make sure. Thank you for your help. Now, I expect I'd best move along in case he's got himself hurt and needs some help fast." As he started for the door, Price came around from behind the counter, and he and Tom followed Flint outside.

Price felt the need to comment. "I heard Buck Jackson had a deputy, but this is the first time we've seen a lawman from Tinhorn down here at White Creek. We always figured the sheriff didn't give a damn about anything that happened outside the city limits."

Flint didn't want to take the time to have a discussion about that, especially when the possibility existed that Bob Waldrop might be in trouble. But he couldn't help thinking Price had figured Buck's attitude dead right. In Buck's defense, however, he could hardly cover the whole county by himself.

"I'll let you know what I find out," Flint told them as he climbed up into the saddle and wheeled Buster around toward the trail.

He held the buckskin gelding in a lope as he back-tracked to the fork. Turning onto the other trail, he asked for more speed since Price had said it was only a quarter of a mile to the gate.

The gate was wide open when he got there. He turned in, then pulled Buster to a sudden stop when he saw a body lying just inside the fence. He jerked his rifle from the saddle sling and took a quick look all around him before running to examine the body he assumed was Bob Waldrop. Of the two bullet holes in him, one was in the back, which no doubt accounted for the blood on the wagon seat.

Flint assumed the ridge of hard dirt between the two gate posts was formed there to prevent having a large gap between the bottom of the gate and the ground. He pictured Waldrop whipping his mules into a gallop as he tried to escape a pursuer. At that speed, the little ridge in the open gate could create quite a bounce, causing a fatally wounded man to be thrown from the wagon. The second shot was to the back of his head to hurry him along to his destiny.

Flint took another look around and noticed the column of black smoke climbing up through the thick stand of trees. It had not been visible from the store down on the creek bank. A rough guess told him whatever was burning—he feared it was a house—was about two hundred yards distant. He climbed back up into the saddle and followed the path until he could see the burning cabin—what was left of it—through the trees. The roof had already fallen in and was the major source of fuel for the flames. Since he saw no sign of anyone around the burning house or the yard, Flint dismounted and left his horse in the trees while he walked out into the clearing. Trying to see if there was anything or anybody inside the smoldering walls, he walked all the way around the house. Near the back steps, but outside on the ground, he found her.

Dead or alive? He couldn't tell at first. Her battered face and body made it difficult to determine if she was a woman or a girl. Lying with one arm twisted grotesquely behind her back, her clothes ripped and torn as if attacked by a wild animal, she was motionless. He felt sick inside as he gently pulled her broken arm out from under her, realizing only then that she was an older woman, probably Waldrop's wife. "I'm so sorry, Ma'am," he uttered softly. "I'm sorry I wasn't here to help you."

He was suddenly startled when her eyelids flickered weakly and her swollen and bloody lips tried to form words. He bent closer, trying to hear what she was straining to say.

"Able," was the sound she made. Then she repeated it over and over. "Able. Able." Each time it became weaker and weaker.

He didn't know what it meant. Didn't know if it was a name, but she was getting so much weaker he tried to tell her to rest. "Let me get you some water. You've been lyin' so close to this fire your skin's all red and hot." Then he realized she couldn't hear him. He was talking to a dead woman.

He frantically checked for a pulse, but there was none. "I'm so sorry, Ma'am." He felt miserable. The poor battered woman had desperately held on to those last moments of her life, just to impart those final words. And he couldn't understand what she was trying to say. "I'm sorry, Ma'am," he said again. "I'll see to it you and your husband are buried.

Flint got to his feet and shook his head sadly, then took another walk around the little house. The walls were burned down, and the roof burned up enough that he could see in each room of the simple cabin, allowing him to be sure no one else was inside. Whoever had done that horrible thing was long gone. Thinking to show some respect for the dead, he went back and picked up Waldrop's body and carried it over next to the barn. Then he carried Waldrop's wife's body over and laid it beside her husband. Flint looked inside the barn and found an old quilt. Having nothing better, he spread it over the bodies.

He climbed up into the saddle and as promised, headed back to the store to give them the news.

Chapter 9

At the store, he found Luther Price and his friend Tom waiting to hear if he had found Bob Waldrop all right.

"I'm afraid not," Flint told them. "Bob and his wife were both murdered, and the house burned down." He paused to let that sink in, and it obviously struck them both severely. "I reckon the wind must be goin' the other way. You sure woulda smelled the smoke if it hada been blowin' toward you. I would have thought you might have heard the shots, even if you didn't smell the smoke."

Luther's wife, Martha, rushed into the room from just outside the door where she had been listening. "Bob and Jane dead? Oh, merciful God! What about the girls? Are they all right?"

"What girls?" Flint asked. "There weren't any girls there, Just the man and woman."

"Do you know who did it?" Tom asked without thinking.

"I have no way in the world of knowin' who did it," Flint answered him. "I told you I just back-tracked a pair of runaway mules. I sure wasn't expectin' to find what I did. I reckon I need to borrow a shovel and dig a grave for those poor folks. Bob was dead a long time before I got there, but that poor lady died while I was tryin' to comfort her."

"Jane was still alive?" Martha asked, still shivering with the thought of the killing.

"Just barely," Flint said. "She was dyin' when I got there. There wasn't nothing I could do for her." He thought back, remembering her desperate attempt to tell him something, so he told them of her struggle to speak but she was evidently too far gone to put the words together. "All she could say was one word over and over. I couldn't make it out. It just sounded like she was sayin' able, ablc." He stopped then, for they suddenly reacted as if he had thrown a stick of dynamite in their midst.

"Abel!" Luther exclaimed. "Abel Crowe. That's what she was tryin' to tell you. It was him that killed her, him and those three sons of his."

"That animal has got those little girls," Martha uttered, trembling with rage. She turned to face Flint and pleaded, "You have to go get those girls."

"I'll go with you," Luther volunteered at once. "I feel awful bad to have to admit it, but I heard some shots from over that way. I didn't think much about it 'cause I hear shots around that creek lots of times, especially when Abel Crowe and his boys are back."

"You know where to find him?" Flint asked.

"He's got a shack two miles south of here on the creek, him and his boys," Luther said. "He's got a piece of land on the creek, but that sorry bunch don't work it. All they do is trap, and hunt, and steal anythin' that ain't nailed down. They were gone from here for a while, but they're back. One of 'em, his youngest, was in here last week tryin' to sell me a cowhide that still had a brand on it."

"How many are they?" Flint asked.

"Abel and the three boys," Martha answered him.

"Their mother's dead. That sorry crowd of worthless men worked her to death."

"You say there were supposed to be two daughters there at the Waldrop place?" Flint asked. "How old are they?"

Luther shrugged, so Martha answered. "Ellie's twelve and Ruthie's ten."

"We need to find them in a hurry." Flint turned his attention back to Luther again. "I need you to tell me how to get to their place, and I'll be glad to have you and Tom come with me, if you still want to. If you don't, I understand. Just tell me how to get there."

"I'm goin' with you," Luther said, "soon as I saddle my horse. You're gonna need some help. Abel's sons are all grown men."

"I'm goin' with you," Tom said, "but I'm gonna go on ahead so I can tell Sarah where I'm goin'. She's most likely wonderin' already when I'm comin' home. You and the deputy can pick me up on the way." He went out the door at once and jumped on his mule. Luther hurried to the barn to saddle his horse.

"You be careful, Luther," Martha called after him. Then back to Flint, who started for the door, she said, "Tom will tell Sarah about it, and she'll most likely have her son hitch her wagon up and come back here. We need to go over to take care of poor Jane Waldrop and get her ready to be buried, her and Bob, too. If you find those two girls, you bring 'em back here to me. I'll take care of them."

"That's mighty kind of you, Miz Price," Flint told her. "I just hope no harm's come to those little girls." He went out the door and climbed up into the saddle, then rode down to wait in front of the barn for Luther.

He led his horse out of the barn, climbed on, and led

Flint out of the barnyard at a lope, picking up a trail that followed the creek south.

They had ridden only about half a mile when they came upon Tom waiting beside the creek for them. His wife and young son were standing with him.

"It's a terrible thing people like that live in the world with honest folks," Sarah declared when they pulled up before them. "Bob and Jane don't deserve to die like that, nobody does. I hope you can catch those animals before they do real harm to those girls." She directed her warning toward her husband then. "You be careful. You're dealing with the devil's own kin." Then to Luther, she said, "Tim's gonna hitch up the wagon and we'll go by and pick Martha up. Then we'll go over to Waldrop's to fix those poor folks up for burying."

"Yessum, Sarah. Martha said you would," Luther replied. He led out along the creekbank again, following a trail that became more and more grown over in weeds the farther they rode. Finally, Luther pulled his horse to a halt and waited for Flint and Tom to pull up beside him.

They could see a shabby cabin close to the creekbank with a small barn and corral behind it.

"Don't appear to be anybody there," Luther said to Flint.

It was already getting dark in the trees along the creek, and if anyone was there, likely a fire, either inside or out, would be burning to cook supper.

Upon moving a little closer, Flint could see the corral was empty. He gave Buster a nudge with his heels and the buckskin entered the water and crossed over to the cabin. Dismounting, Flint walked up to the door and noticed a padlock on the hasp. He took a step backward to give himself room, then kicked the door open with one blow from his boot. "There's nobody here," he called back to

Luther and Tom, who had remained in their saddles on the other side of the creek. They promptly came across then.

The cabin proved to be little more than a crude shelter with a fireplace and a table with several wooden boxes that evidently served as chairs. Flint lit the lantern he found, then took a closer look inside the cabin. He saw nothing of any use or value left—no coffeepot, no frying pan, no bedrolls or blankets. All indications told him Abel Crowe and his sons were on the move and not coming back any-time soon. Over in a corner, Flint discovered a little pile of rags, still damp. Poking around in the pile with the toe of his boot, he saw what looked to be blood stains on the rags. To him, it was one more sign Abel Crowe had brutally murdered Bob and Jane Waldrop.

He was distracted by Tom calling to him. "Flint, take a look at this." He handed Flint a scrap of gingham cloth with a shred of white collar sewn to it. "Don't that look to you like it mighta been tore off a shirt or somethin' a woman or a little girl would wear?"

Flint took the scrap of cloth and held it close to the lantern. "I hate to say it, but it sure does. They brought those two little girls back here to this cabin, but they stayed just long enough to pack up everything and then left. Maybe that means they ain't plannin' to kill 'em. But those girls will be better off dead, if I don't catch up with 'em soon enough."

"You gonna try to track 'em?" Luther asked, knowing Flint had no responsibility or jurisdiction outside the town of Tinhorn.

"I sure as hell am," he answered. "I couldn't live with myself if I didn't."

His answer was unexpected, surprising Luther.

"I sure didn't come prepared to trail somebody, though. No packhorse, no supplies, nothin' to cook with. All I've got with me is a little bit of jerky I stuck in my saddlebags in case I didn't get back in time for supper tonight." He looked around. "And right now, it's too dark to pick up a trail to tell me which way they left this shack." He hated to spend the time it would take to go back to Tinhorn to get his packhorse and everything else he needed. Deciding he had little choice, he said, "I'll go back tonight and get what I need to track Abel and his boys. I can't track 'em till daylight, anyway, so I plan to be right back here when the sun comes up in the mornin'. I'd best get started back right now if I wanna catch Lon Blake before he closes up the stable."

"We'll take care of Bob and Jane Waldrop. Don't worry about them," Luther said as he and Tom followed Flint out the door.

"I expect Sarah and Martha are already preparin' 'em for buryin'," Tom said. "Luther and I will dig the graves."

Flint told them that was mighty thoughtful of them, and then pointed Buster in the direction of Tinhorn. He hesitated before giving the buckskin his heels to ask one more question. "Did Waldrop have any other mules or horses besides those two mules pullin' that wagon?" It would be helpful to have an idea how many horses he might be tracking. The more there were, the easier it would be to follow the trail.

"Yep," Luther and Tom answered simultaneously, then Luther finished the reply. "He had a dappled gray gelding, and he was mighty proud of that horse. Weren't he, Tom?"

Tom grinned. "He sure was."

That meant Abel Crowe had picked up only one extra horse at Bob Waldrop's place. Of course, Flint had no idea how many the Crowe men had when they struck the farm. But he could at least guess at a minimum number of horses he would be following.

Flint alternated the buckskin's pace between a lope and a walk back up the darkened ten-mile trail. Riding into Tinhorn, he managed to catch Lon Blake just as he was locking up, and Lon helped him load his pack saddle. It was too late to buy anything for cooking, but Flint had some coffee and a slab of bacon left in his packs and he knew he could live off that for a good while. If he had the opportunity, he'd pick up food somewhere. He planned to be back to White Creek before sunup, so he didn't expect to see Luther, but if he did, he could pick up some flour and lard, and maybe some dried apples or something from him.

Flint's next stop was the sheriff's office, where he found the door locked. Knowing that meant Buck had retired to his room, Flint unlocked the door and went inside.

"Flint!" Ralph exclaimed. "Buck went on to bed. Said he weren't feelin' so good after supper. I was just turning in for the night. We was wonderin' what happened to you. Did you find that feller?"

"Yeah, I found him. His body, anyway." Flint went on to tell Ralph about Waldrop's murdered wife and his missing daughters. "I want you to remember to tell Buck all this," he said, after he told Ralph everything. "Abel Crowe and his three sons have run off with those two little girls, and I've got to catch up with them as fast as I can. Buck ain't gonna like it. I don't like it, either, but I ain't got no choice. He'll understand that. We ain't got time to wait for the Rangers or the U.S. marshal. Those two little girls ain't got the time to wait. Can you remember to tell him all that?"

"I declare, that is sorry news. I'll remember to tell him. Are you goin' back in the mornin'?"

"I'm goin' back right now, tonight. I wanna be there as soon as it's light enough for me to see tracks. I'm leaving right after I make one quick stop to see if Rena left anything to eat in her oven." He started for the door, turned back, and said, "Tell Buck I'll be back as soon as I can."

Flint led his horses across the street to Jake's Place and went inside. He gave Rudy a quick howdy as he passed the bar and headed to Jake, sitting at his usual table near the kitchen. "Evenin', Jake. Did that angel you've got in the kitchen leave any biscuits or cornbread in her oven tonight?"

Jake chuckled. "Missed supper again, didja? Well, you're in luck. There's four or five biscuits in the oven on a plate, and Rudy just made a pot of coffee. Help yourself."

"Bless her heart," Flint said. "I wish you'd tell her when she comes in tomorrow she saved my life again. I wanna pay you something for the biscuits and a nickel for the coffee, unless you've raised your prices."

"Never mind the money," Jake insisted. "You can pay me next time."

Flint didn't spend much time at Jake's while he ate two of Rena's biscuits and two slices of cooked ham she'd also left in the oven. He washed them down with a couple cups of Rudy's coffee and was on his way in fifteen minutes.

At a leisurely pace, he rode Buster back down the White Creek trail, arriving at Abel Crowe's shack around midnight. Since it was not cold, and he was not going to fix anything to eat, he didn't bother with building a fire. He just rolled his bed out on a patch of grass a couple dozen yards from the cabin and went to sleep.

The next morning, Flint was awakened by Buster and his sorrel packhorse nibbling the grass around his boots. Rousing himself out of his blanket, he saw the first rays of light penetrating the leafy canopy overhead. His first order of business—check his boots before he stuck a toe inside—was to make sure no small critter had homesteaded them while he slept. He still didn't bother with a fire since he did not intend to eat any breakfast until he had to stop to rest his horses. As soon as he put his boots on and had his Colt riding on his hip, he saddled his horses. By that time, the sun had risen high enough to better light the creek bank, and he began a thorough inspection of the ground around the cabin. Supporting the kidnapping further, he found a red ribbon snagged on a laurel bush. The sight of it brought images to his mind of unpleasant scenes, increasing his anxiety to get moving.

But he cautioned himself to take a good look around to get an accurate idea of the right trail to follow.

Flint noticed tracks of boots and hooves all around the little cabin, many of them newly made. It was the same around the barn and the corral. He paid particular attention to the fresher tracks coming from the corral, thinking these more likely the tracks of the horses leaving the corral for the last time. He studied the tracks closely, hoping to find a nick or some mark in one of the shoes, but found none.

Next, he walked in a wide circle all the way around the cabin and barn, looking for fresh tracks of a number of horses leaving the place. He found tracks of that nature directly behind the barn, but they were leading toward the cabin. Evidently it was the way they had come back from Waldrop's place and explained why no one saw them on the trail following the creek. He continued on until he found the tracks he was looking for. He didn't know how many horses they had to begin with, but counted four sets of tracks, which meant four horses.

Remembering what Luther had said, Flint could bet they also had Waldrop's dappled gray. That made five. He moved to the edge of the creek to determine the number of packhorses. Looking at the tracks he could clearly see in the sand he would say three, which gave him a total guess of eight horses. He frowned. The two little girls could be on any of the horses, riding double with one of their captors, riding alone on one of the packhorses, or riding double on the dappled gray. The important part that worked in Flint's favor was the fact that eight horses traveling in a bunch should leave a trail easy to follow. That proved true enough when he came upon the tracks. All eight horses had left the yard of the cabin, entered the water, and climbed up the bank on the other side.

Flint climbed aboard Buster and followed. From there, the tracks started out toward the south. The trail never veered from its southerly direction until coming to a wide stream like White Creek, running east and west. Crossing the shallow stream, he found no tracks on the other side. They had turned, but which way? He looked east and west, then decided to go east, toward the river. He couldn't begin to guess where they were heading but thought maybe they might want to use the river to lose anyone on their trail.

In order to move a little faster and easier, he didn't enter the water, instead, riding along the bank beside the stream, keeping a constant eye on the sides. After a short distance his hunch was confirmed by a partial print of a hoof at the edge of the water. Having reached the point where the stream emptied into the river, their attempt to hide their trail was even more pathetic in Flint's mind, for they had torn up the bank, apparently in an effort to leave the stream without getting wet.

From there, they'd ridden along the river until crossing at a point where two small islands were formed in the middle of it. Once across, they continued eastward toward a long group of tree-covered hills.

Flint continued to follow the obvious trail into the hills where it struck what he assumed was an old logging trail. Ignoring the evidence of a long ago logging camp, he continued on the trail until he came to a busy stream and stopped to rest and water his horses. He built his breakfast fire and made some coffee to drink with his bacon and hardtack. It occurred to him he'd not found any evidence the party he followed had stopped to rest their horses. *Maybe,* he thought, *they don't have that much farther to go.* He thought about that possibility and the chance he might be close enough for his fire to be spotted. *The odds are against it,* he told himself, but he moved a little farther back from the fire and peered hard at the old logging road the tracks made leading deeper into the pines on the other side of the stream.

Taking another look at his fire, Flint decided it wasn't creating enough smoke to be easily seen through the thick growth of trees beyond the stream.

Chapter 10

Flint was accurate in his assumption he was not very far from Abel Crowe's destination. Less than half a mile up the old logging road on the stream where he ate his breakfast stood a roughly built, long-abandoned cabin of logs. Rough as it was, it was an improvement over the shabby quarters Abel had built on White Creek, and he counted himself mighty fortunate to have come across the camp when he and the boys were hunting deer.

The old drifter who'd taken possession of the cabin and had made some improvements on it was now lying in a shallow grave on the other side of the hill, a bullet hole in the back of his head.

On this sunny morning, Abel roused himself from his blanket beside the fireplace and stepped over the sleeping body of his youngest son, Billy, who was sprawled on the floor, his leg tied to the ankle of Ruthie, Bob Waldrop's ten-year-old daughter. Abel looked over in the corner of the cabin to see his eldest, Frank, still sleeping. Waldrop's twelve-year-old daughter, Ellie, was tied to his leg. Jasper, the middle brother, was sleeping on the other side of Ellie.

The two little girls were staring back at Abel with fearful eyes reflecting the terror that filled their minds.

"You're a mite younger than I'da liked to have," he said to them. "But I'll break ya and train ya just like any other animal. You might as well decide right now that's just the way it's gonna be, and it'll be a whole lot easier on you. You there"—he pointed to the older girl—"what's your name?" She didn't answer right away, so he threatened, "Answer me, if you don't want another whuppin'!"

"Ellie," she whimpered softly.

"Ellie?" It appeared to startle him for a few moments before he continued. "Well, that's my oldest boy, Frank, you're a-layin' beside. He's twenty-three years old and it's past time he got hisself a wife. You look like you're gittin' to childbearing age. Ain't that right?"

"No. No, sir!" Ellie cried. "I'm not that old yet!"

"You look it to me. Frank's mama weren't much older 'n you look when he popped outta her." Abel turned to Ruthie then, who had started crying again with Ellie. "Shut up that fuss or I'll smack you so hard your head'll get stuck lookin' at where you been." Back to Ellie, he said, "Frank ain't a bad-lookin' young man when he cleans up a little. You could do a lot worse. And we need some woman help around here."

He pointed at Ruthie again and told her, "You got a couple more years to grow. That there's Billy you're a-layin' with. He's already seventeen, if I remember right, so he'll be ready when you come in heat." Abel chuckled then. "We ain't got one for Jasper. Maybe Frank will share with his brother, just to keep peace in the family. We're gonna work on this place, fix it up like I want it. And we need women. You two might as well make up your minds to start learnin' how to please the men of the Crowe family." He paused to grin at the girls. "'Cause, if you don't, I'll kill you."

Realizing none of his sons were showing any signs of

waking up, he drew his pistol and fired a shot into the roof. It succeeded in getting the results he wanted. They all sprang out of their slumber, looking for cover.

Abel roared his delight when he saw the tangle that developed when the two boys forgot they were anchored to two little girls. "You gonna sleep the day away? Get up from there! We've got a corral to build and you ain't makin' much headway on it layin' around this cabin. And now you got a hole in the roof to patch."

When his sons were all up, Abel pulled Ellie up from the floor. Holding her by her shoulders, he locked his gaze on the innocent girl. "Now you're gonna show us what your mama taught you in the kitchen. We cleaned everything to cook outta your mama's pantry, so you oughta know what to do with it."

Hoping to bluff him, Ellie said, "I don't know how to cook. Mama done all the cookin'. She said I wasn't old enough to learn yet." She received a sharp rap across her chin for the remark.

"Don't you lie to me, you little weasel," Abel spat. "I know damn well you've been workin' in the kitchen since you was the age of your sister, there." He grabbed a handful of her blouse and drew back to deliver another blow.

"I'll cook! I'll cook!" Ellie cried out. "Don't hit me. I'll cook your breakfast."

He lowered his fist and released her blouse. "You're damn right you will, and that one is gonna help you. What's her name?"

"Her name's Ruthie," Ellie answered him. "We can fix you a good breakfast, but we need to go to the outhouse first. Neither one of us has gone to the outhouse since yesterday."

"We ain't got no outhouse," Abel told her.

Ellie looked desperate. "We've both got to pee real bad."

"Go outside and pee like the rest of us," Jasper suggested, laughing.

"Please, Mr. Crowe," Ellie pleaded. "We can't do that. There ain't no bushes to hide behind, and we can't go if there's somebody watchin'. Can we just go on the other side of the stream behind those bushes?"

"No you can't," Abel flatly replied. "I don't feel like chasin' you all over these hills before I've even et my breakfast."

"I'll take 'em, Pa," Jasper suggested. "I'll tie a rope on each one of 'em and take 'em as far in the bushes as they wanna go to let their water out."

His offer was met with jeers from his brother, who likewise volunteered to take the girls, but Abel thought it was fair for Jasper to get the job, since he didn't get to sleep with one of them.

"We can't go if he's gonna be watching us," Ellie said.

"I ain't gonna be lookin' at you," Jasper insisted. "You ain't got nothin' I wanna see. That's why I'm gonna put you on a long enough rope so you can get in behind a bush."

"You promise?" Ruthie spoke up for the first time.

"I promise," Jasper said, and winked at Billy.

"All right. If you promise, 'cause I'm 'bout to bust." Ellie planned to tell Ruthie she was going to untie the ropes once they were behind the bushes. Then they would run for their lives. Even if the Crowes killed them, it would be better than what the evil men planned for them. She would tell Ruthie that even if they did get shot, they would be with their mother and father. She was sure Ruthie would feel the same way.

"I swear, Pa," Frank complained. "Are you really gonna let him get away with that?"

"You'll get your turn," Abel replied. "I expect we all will by the time we're done."

With plenty of unwanted supervision from his brothers, Jasper took two coils of rope and tied one end of each around the waist of each girl. "All right, ladies, let's go drain your little bottoms."

Ellie led the way across the stream, heading for a thick stand of young pines. Afraid to go too far, for fear of Jasper catching onto what she was hoping to do, she stopped when she put the trees between them and the cabin.

"This is as good a place as any," Jasper said. "Just you go ahead and drop your drawers and do your business."

"Not with you standing there," Ellie protested. "You promised you weren't gonna look. You're just supposed to stay here and hold on to the ropes while we go behind those bushes over there." She pointed to a bank of laurel about fifteen yards away.

"Did I promise that?" Jasper smirked. "I musta still been half asleep." He was thinking how easily she had agreed to letting him go with them, and she wanted to go out of sight of the cabin to boot. "You picked the right Crowe to get it on with. Let's get to it." He started pulling the rope then, reeling her in like a fish in a pond.

Even fighting as hard as she could to keep from being pulled to him, Ellie was helpless to deny him. About four feet from him, he held onto the rope with one hand and started unbuckling his belt with the other. Unable to stand and watch, she closed her eyes tightly. She heard a shot, and the rope went slack. Quickly, she opened her eyes and saw a dark hole in the middle of Jasper's forehead.

He stood there for several seconds before he fell over backward to land on his back.

Ellie could not move as she stared down in shock at the fallen man. She jumped, startled when she felt a strong hand on her arm.

"Come, we've got to get away from here," the voice said.

Aware what had happened, Ellie felt her knees were going to give way, but he supported her with his hand on her elbow. Turning she saw Ruthie holding on to the man's arm, and became fully aware of the need to run.

"My name's Flint," he said. "I'm a deputy sheriff from Tinhorn. We've got to move fast and get away from this spot right now. They'll be comin' to see what that shot was about."

With eyes wide open in shock, Ellie could not speak, but she nodded her head frantically, and ran after him and Ruthie when he led them toward the laurel bushes she had sought before.

Flint had had no time for the luxury of making a plan to rescue the two little girls. He had been maybe a quarter of a mile away when he heard the shot Abel had fired through the roof of the cabin. Thinking it best to leave the logging road that led in the direction of the shot, he had led his horses up into the trees until he found a narrow ravine leading down to the stream. He'd tied the horses there and climbed up the slope until he came to a thick bank of laurel bushes, and quickly knelt down behind them when Jasper and the two girls suddenly appeared.

He remained hidden while thinking of a best way to rescue the girls. All of his sense of reasoning disappeared when he realized what Jasper had in mind. It was replaced with rage for any man who would force himself on innocent children. Flint's natural reaction was to rid the world of such a disgusting creature, just as he would a rabid wolf. Not taking time to think about the immediate results of his actions, he quickly set the sights of the Henry rifle on the sneering face of the girl's attacker and sent him to Hell.

As he ran with the girls, he gave thought to the best way to play the hand he had just dealt himself. Immediately, however, the important thing was to get the girls somewhere safe.

Since he hadn't said much to the girls other than telling them to run, he thought maybe he should say something to reassure them. "I promised Martha Price I'd find you and take you to her house. She wants to take care of you. Right now, I wanna find a good place for you to hide, till I can make sure those men aren't gonna bother you anymore. All right?"

Clearly recovered from her panic of before, twelve-year-old Ellie answered him calmly in spite of her heavy breathing from their flight through the woods. "Don't worry about Ruthie and me. We can run as far as it takes to get away from those men."

"Atta girl," Flint replied. "Miz Price said you two were smart little ladies. How good are you at hidin'?"

Ellie said they could hide where nobody could find them.

"Good." As they reached the narrow ravine where his horses were tied, Flint said, "I want you to find you a good place to hide where nobody can find you. I've got to go back up that way and lead the other three Crowes off away from you and my horses. Understand?"

Both girls nodded rapidly.

"But I want to make sure you two are hid just the same, and when everything's all right, I'll come back to the horses and let you know you can come out. All right?"

Again, they both nodded vigorously.

"Now, it might take a little time, so I've got some beef jerky in my saddlebags I'm gonna give you, so you won't get too hungry before I get everything taken care of. You might hear some gunshots, but they shouldn't be near your hidin' places." He looked at the two bright faces looking up at him. "Can you do all that?"

They answered once more with vigorous nods.

He went to his horse, got the jerky for them, then told them he would see them in a little while. He left them, hoping they lived up to their superior hiding claims.

Hurrying back up the hill at a trot, he wanted to draw the Crowes' attention away from the direction in which his horses and the girls were hiding. As he made his way closer to the place where he had killed Jasper, he thought about his act of execution without warning. As an officer of the law, he wondered if he should have given the man a chance to surrender and taken to trial.

Being honest with himself, Flint admitted that, given a second chance, he would do the same thing.

He questioned himself again when it came to the three remaining members of the Crowe family—straight-out execution again, or give them a chance to surrender? That was the question. For his own peace of mind, he decided to offer them the chance to come peacefully.

As he'd expected, the three men were already standing over the body of Jasper, talking frantically, looking all around them for the source of another attack. They were startled when Flint called out, "Abel Crowe!" from a position in the trees ninety degrees from the direction the girls were in.

"You and your two sons are under arrest for the murder of Bob and Jane Waldrop and the kidnapping of their daughters, Ellie and Ruthie. If you surrender peaceably, I'll take you back to Tinhorn to await trial."

All three reacted at once. With guns already drawn, they looked all around them, searching for the source of the command. Then they instinctively moved apart, looking for some form of cover, but little was to be found. They slowly began to back away from Jasper's body.

Thinking to keep Flint talking while they inched away, Abel yelled back. "Did you give my boy, Jasper, a chance to surrender before you shot him down?"

"He had to be stopped in the attempted assault of a minor," Flint answered. "He made a bad decision. I'm givin' you and your two sons the chance to make a wise decision and come in peacefully."

"Who the hell are you? How do I know you've got any right to arrest us? We ain't done nothin' in Tinhorn, anyway. What we do in the county ain't none of your business. Show yourself."

"That won't be necessary," Flint called out. "Just drop your weapons on the ground and take three steps backward."

"Like hell I will," Abel responded, certain now. "There ain't but one of you. He's in them bushes yonder, boys. Let's smoke him outta there. He killed your brother and stole those girls from us!" With that, Abel aimed at a bush he thought Flint was behind and took the top of it off with three rounds from his rifle.

Frank and Billy followed his example and peppered the bushes with a barrage of shots that lasted for a full minute, clipping limbs and branches and sending them flying.

Profound silence followed.

Having rolled over and over until several yards wide of his previous position, Flint took careful aim with his rifle. The front sight was resting squarely on the middle of Billy's chest. But Billy stepped sideways at the same time Flint pulled the trigger and scrambled on his hands and knees to a new spot a few yards away. He quickly fired another shot that barely missed Frank's head.

Billy grabbed his shoulder, stumbled backward, and fell against his brother. "Pa, I'm shot!" he cried out in shock.

Not sure where the shot came from that almost cashed in his chips, Frank panicked. "There's more 'n one of 'em! It's a damn posse!"

"Get to the cabin!" Abel bellowed and led the retreat back across the stream. He was not sure how many men were attacking—one man as he originally thought or a posse as Frank claimed. Since shots had come from different spots, he'd decided not to stand out in the open any longer until he found out for sure. "Let 'em come after us in the cabin. They'll find out it ain't easy to shoot up that log house."

Flint had an excellent opportunity to put a bullet between Abel Crowe's shoulder blades, but he hesitated to take the shot. He had already executed one of his sons. Moments later he regretted the decision. It was too late as the three men were running to the cabin. They had not only kidnapped the girls but had murdered their parents.

I should have taken every shot I could get, he scolded himself. *Maybe I'm getting like Buck. As long as it didn't happen inside the city limits, don't bother with it.*

Flint followed them to the cabin where they hurried inside and dropped a bar across the door to lock it. He looked at the solid log structure and had to agree with Abel. The log cabin was like a fortress. *Well, they've got to come out sometime.*

Then he remembered two frightened little girls, hiding somewhere, wondering if he would come back for them. "To hell with the Crowes. I need to take those little girls away from this place and take them home to Martha Price.

Abel Crowe and his two sons will get what they deserve somewhere down the line."

Flint got up from the ground at the side of the cabin where he had been watching and started to jog back to the girls and his horses when it occurred to him Crowe's horses were all grazing around loose. He'd seen no corral keeping them close. He stopped and turned around. Looking through the trees, one horse especially caught his attention, a dappled gray gelding. Someone had mentioned Bob Waldrop's favorite horse and Flint bemoaned the fact that it was in the hands of Abel Crowe.

Thinking it might be too risky to leave the cover of the trees, Flint ducked back down and realized one of the kidnappers would have to come out the front of the cabin to see him. The horses were behind the cabin. Looking closely, he saw no window on the back side. To remind them inside that he was still out there, he fired a couple of shots to imbed in the log wall.

Quietly he left his cover and approached the horse carefully, but the horse showed no tendency to bolt. *Bob must have spoiled the horse.* Flint took hold of the bridle someone had thoughtlessly left on the horse, stroked the gray's face and neck, and led him away from the cabin. As the other horses started to follow, he jumped on the gray and rode back across the stream. Soon he noticed the Crowe horses were beginning to tail off and linger at the stream.

Might as well make sure Abel is on foot, he thought.

He rode the gray around behind them and herded them down through the trees, driving the horses all the way down the gentle slope to the ravine where his own horses awaited him. He saw no sign of the two girls. He felt the need to hurry, even though it was unlikely Abel and his sons had ventured out of the cabin yet.

While Crowe's horses wandered about the narrow ravine, Flint tied the dappled gray with his horses and started searching for the girls along the ravine. "Ellie, Ruthie, it's me, Flint. It's time to go." He parted bushes as he walked, but found no sign of either child. Starting to worry, he was startled when a bank of bushes he had just passed parted, and Ellie popped up.

"I told you we could hide," she informed him. "Come on, Ruthie. It's time to leave here now." Ruthie crawled out of the small hole she had dug under a large laurel bush.

"You sure did," Flint said. "I thought I was gonna have to set the bushes on fire to find you. Are you ready to go? I brought you a special horse to carry you and Ruthie back to White Creek."

Just as he expected, both little girls recognized their late father's dappled gray horse and were excited to ride him back. He set them up on the horse's back, with Ruthie sitting behind her sister, and they assured him that they could stay on the gentle gelding without benefit of a saddle.

"We're gonna ride for a while till the horses need a rest, then we'll stop and cook some bacon, if you're hungry. White Creek ain't that far from here, so I wanna get you to Miz Price's house as quick as I can, all right?"

"All right," Ellie answered.

Chapter 11

"Martha!" Luther Price yelled. "Come quick!"

At once alarmed, Martha ran from the kitchen to see what he had done to himself, but he was not in the store.

"Martha!" he yelled again from the porch.

"I'm comin', I'm comin'," she yelled back, certain that he had somehow injured himself. Running out to the porch, she found him just standing there.

He turned toward her with a wide smile on his face. "Lookee yonder," he said, pointing toward the wagon road.

She released a little squeal of delight when she saw the horses coming down the path to the store with Flint Moran leading his packhorse and a dappled gray with two little girls on its back.

Barely able to contain her excitement, Martha stood beside her husband and hugged his arm with both of hers. "The Lord surely heard our prayers when he sent Flint Moran to save those girls." They stood together for a few moments longer before going down the steps to meet them.

Flint pulled Buster to a stop and quickly dismounted to

lift the two excited little girls off the gray so they could run to hug the beaming woman.

"Aunt Martha!" Ellie exclaimed. "Flint came to get us!"

"Well, he said he was gonna." Martha put her arms around the girls in a big hug. "Are you all right? They didn't hurt you nowhere?"

Ellie smiled. "No, ma'am, except for slappin' our faces."

"Well, come on in the house and you can help me fix some supper." Martha turned and all three started up the steps. "Then we're gonna get you settled in your new room."

They didn't get to the porch before Ruthie stopped and ran back down the steps to throw her arms around Flint's legs. "Thank you for savin' us, Flint."

Seeing her sister's gesture, Ellie realized she should do the same, so she did.

"You're both welcome," Flint replied. "I can't think of two pretty ladies I'd rather save."

They ran back up the steps again and went inside the store with Martha, leaving Luther to question Flint about the rescue.

"I didn't realize those girls were kin of yours," Flint commented.

"They ain't," Luther remarked, surprised Flint thought so, then understood. "Oh, those two have been callin' her Aunt Martha ever since Bob bought that piece of land four years ago." He chuckled. "No, we ain't no kin, but maybe we are now, seein' as how it looks like Martha has adopted 'em." He hesitated a moment, then decided to tell him. "Martha ain't never been able to have no kids of her own. And I hate like hell what happened to Bob and Jane Waldrop, but I think it's a lucky thing those girls have got someplace to go where they're wanted."

"I 'preciate you tellin' me that. Now I won't say no dumb-fool things that might embarrass somebody," Flint said.

Luther switched the conversation to a subject he and Martha should know. He fumbled with it for a few moments, but finally got it out.

Flint answered his question seriously. "No, I don't think so. I didn't ask either one of 'em directly, but they never talked about any harm other than gettin' their faces slapped. Although I heard them say Abel was plannin' for his eldest son to marry Ellie. Like I said, I think I got there just in time." Flint told Luther how he came to rescue the girls from Jasper Crowe.

"Do you think Abel will come here lookin' for the girls?" Luther asked, concerned.

"Well, I don't know why he would. He ain't got any idea where I took 'em. He doesn't know for sure who took 'em. There ain't no doubt he's as crazy as he is evil, but I can't believe even Abel's crazy enough to come back to a place where he murdered a mother and father and kidnapped their children. It's my opinion that he and his two remaining sons will be gettin' as far away from here as they can.

"If revenge is too big a thing for Abel to ignore, he might come after me for killin' his son. And that's only if he figures out it was me that done it. But the White Creek Tradin' Post, he ain't had no dealin's with you, has he?"

Luther nodded his head as he considered what Flint had said. "I reckon you're right. I ain't had much dealin's with that family a-tall. The young one tried to sell me a cowhide once. That's about it." He grinned. "Come on inside and have some supper with us. And like Ellie and Ruthie, I wanna thank you for bringin' those girls home."

"I thank you just the same, but I expect we'd better put the girls' horse away, and then I'd best get on to Tinhorn. I might not even have a job anymore, if I don't show up pretty soon."

"I'll put the girls' horse away, so you don't have to bother with that," Luther said and took the gray's reins. "He is a fancy horse, ain't he? Bob loved that horse. I never cared much for a dappled gray, myself."

Flint had only been gone from Tinhorn a couple of days, but it seemed like he had been away a lot longer. He held Buster to a steady pace in an effort to get back before Clara closed the dining room. If he was lucky, he might catch Buck there also. Flint was cutting it pretty close but didn't push his horses any harder. They had already had a full day of riding, and there was always Jake's Place and some leftover biscuits.

As it turned out, Clara's Kitchen was still open when he rode into town. Not willing to push his luck, he went there first. He tied Buster and the packhorse at the hitching rail and went into the dining room.

"Where have you been?" Mindy greeted him in a tone best suited for scolding naughty children. "I asked the sheriff when you were coming back to town, and he said he didn't have any idea. Said he didn't even know where you were." She motioned toward his table. "He's getting ready to leave. Just waiting for Ralph's plate."

Flint smiled at her. "I got here as quick as I could."

"Well, sit down and I'll get you some coffee," Mindy said.

He nodded and walked back to the sheriff's table and

sat down but didn't receive much better treatment from Buck.

"I've been tryin' to place you," Buck japed. "You kinda remind me of a deputy who worked for me one time. But you're a lot older than he was."

"I told Ralph what I was doin'," Flint said, ignoring the sarcastic humor. "I told him to tell you where I was, about Waldrop and his wife murdered, about their two little girls kidnapped, and that I was goin' after them. Did he tell you any of that?"

"Hell, he was so confused, he got it all mixed up," Buck replied. "I got pieces of all that, I reckon, but it didn't make much sense. Suppose you tell me what happened. Ralph can wait a little while for his supper." He raised his cup. "Bonnie, I changed my mind. I'll have one more cup of coffee."

Flint went through the whole thing for him.

Buck said, "Now you see why I say, if it happens outside Tinhorn town limits, it ain't none of my business."

Flint paused, thinking Buck was surely japing him again. "Buck, if I hadn't made it my business, those two innocent little girls would have been violated and ruined for life."

Buck took another gulp of coffee, wiped his mouth with the back of his hand, and said, "You're right, Flint. I wouldn'ta wanted that to happen. The only mistake you made is not killin' the other three men. The world would be a helluva lot better off without 'em, and you wouldn't have some revenge-huntin' lunatics out there somewhere waitin' for a chance to blow your brains out. That's somethin' I know about, and I wouldn't want it for you."

Flint didn't say anything for a few moments while he thought about what Buck just said. At the critical time, he had not been able to decide which was right and which was wrong. Now, he knew he should have taken all four of them out when he had the chance.

He truly didn't believe Abel Crowe would come looking for revenge. To begin with, Crowe didn't know who to look for. None of the Crowes had gotten even a glimpse of him, and he had not identified himself. The only mistake he made was telling them he would take them to Tinhorn for trial. If they did come to Tinhorn, he would deal with it when the time came. One thing he knew for sure, and he expressed it out loud to Buck. "Whatever trouble comes to me because of this, I don't regret it. I saved those two little girls and that's the important thing."

"You're right, partner," Buck said. "I can't argue with that. I'm gonna take Ralph his supper. You comin' into the office before you go home?"

"Yeah, I gotta do what I was hired for, watchin' the town at night. I've gotta take my horses to the stable when I leave here. Then I'll be in the office." Flint watched Buck as the bigger-than-life sheriff walked out the door, carrying a plate of hot food for Ralph. Then he was aware of a light touch on his shoulder and turned to see Mindy holding a cup of coffee.

"Mind if I sit down with you while I have my cup of coffee?" she asked.

"Not at all," he quickly replied. "Matter of fact, I'd be honored."

She placed her cup on the table and sat down. "Are you all right? You looked so serious when you were talking to Buck."

"Really? Just tired and hungry, I reckon. I'm a lot better now."

"Buck said you went to check on some mules and a

wagon running loose. That's all he said, but I don't think he liked havin' you gone."

"Reckon not." Flint gave her a big smile. "But I'm back now and everything's all right. How 'bout you? Is everything all right with you?"

"Yes, I reckon it is." She grinned, delighted. He had never asked her how she was before.

He lingered a little while longer while she drank her coffee before saying again that he should probably get out before Clara ordered him out. Mindy giggled in response and walked him to the door.

"Good night," he said to all three women, "and tell Margaret I enjoyed my supper."

Flint turned his horses over to Lon Blake, and as he expected, Lon wanted to know where he had been. After hearing a brief report, Lon wanted to know what he should do about the wagon and team of mules, since the owner was dead.

"I don't know," Flint admitted. "I really hadn't even thought about that. I expect they belong to Ellie and Ruthie Waldrop. I'll have to ask Buck what to do about that."

"I'll keep a record of my feed and other expenses, in case they decide to sell 'em," Lon said. "Or I'll just keep 'em if the little girls don't want 'em and won't charge them nothin' for takin' care of 'em."

"Like I said, I'll talk to Buck about it." Flint walked to the jail, went into the sheriff's office, and discovered Buck had already retired to his private quarters.

"He said he had a bad headache," Ralph reported. "Said he was gonna take it to his bed, and he'd see you for breakfast in the mornin'."

Flint was not surprised. His unexpected absence of a

couple of days might have caused Buck some worry. He might have been tempted to seek the confidence he kept in a bottle.

"Buck said you saved them two little girls before they was violated by them Crowe boys," Ralph said. "I'm glad of that."

"I was just lucky I got to the right place at the right time to stop it." Already weary of telling the story, Flint said, "I'd best get outside and take a little walk around town now. I may or may not be back in the office tonight, so I'll lock the door, and you can go on to bed."

"You tell me about it in the mornin', all right?"

"In the mornin'," Flint replied. "I'll tell you all about it. Right now, I'll go out and make sure ain't nobody tryin' to steal the town." He picked up his Henry rifle and went out the door.

Ralph listened to hear the bolt close and smiled. Buck didn't always remember to lock the door. Flint never forgot.

Outside, Flint took a deep breath of fresh air, then looked in both directions, north end of town where the hotel sat, then the south end, past the stables. No one on the street, and the only sign of life came from Jake's Place where a couple of horses were tied at the hitching rail. He could hear the sound of the piano Jake bought several months ago when Lucy Tucker talked him into it. She told him she could play the piano.

Flint had to smile when he heard the assortment of unrelated notes he heard coming out of the tortured instrument. No doubt they were coming from Lucy, or maybe Jake's cat walked across the keys. He decided to walk north, up to the hotel, then come back on the other side of the street.

He propped the Henry rifle on his shoulder and strode

casually up the street, checking the business establishments as he passed them. At the post office, he checked to see that the door was locked. Then he crossed over to the hotel, walked inside the doorway to say, "Good evenin'," to J.C. White, the night clerk.

"Howdy, Flint," J.C. returned. "Haven't seen you lately."

"I was outta town," Flint said, then continued his walk. He might have told J.C. that Buck had been keeping an eye on the town at night, but he doubted that was the case.

Flint walked back to the saloon and went inside. The piano was silent and Lucy was nowhere in sight, so he fig ured she must be upstairs with one of the men who rode in on one of the horses still tied at the hitching rail. He guessed the other one belonged to the man slumped over a table with his head resting on his folded arms.

"Evenin', Flint," Jake called out from his table in the back of the room. "Lookin' for a cup of coffee?" He knew the young deputy never drank whiskey when he was sup posed to be working.

"I could use a cup," Flint said and gave Rudy a "Howdy" as he walked past the bar.

The stranger slumped at the table, lifted up when he passed by and demanded drunkenly, "What the hell are you lookin' at?"

Flint ignored him, walked over to the sideboard, got himself a cup, then went into the kitchen and filled it from the pot sitting on the edge of the stove. He returned to the barroom and took a seat at Jake's table.

Jake started the conversation. "I heard you had a couple of rough days."

"Oh?" Flint responded. "Who told you that?"

"Buck was in here a little while ago to pick up a bottle of medicine to take back to his room," Jake said. Seeing

Flint's reaction, he quickly assured him. "You understand I wouldn't say anything about that to anybody else. I know you work with Buck and his problem all the time."

"If Buck's got a problem, it's his problem. I don't discuss it with him or anybody else," Flint stated flatly.

"All right, all right," Jake responded. "I didn't mean to rile you up about it. I just thought between us friends it was okay to talk about it."

"I ain't mad, Jake. I just don't wanna talk about anybody's problems right now."

"Fair enough, but you can tell me about that fellow you shot between the eyes yesterday," Jake pressed.

Flint shook his head impatiently, then said, "He was fixin' to do somethin' to a twelve-year-old girl I didn't wanna see happen." He finished his cup of coffee in several big gulps and got up from the table. "I expect I'd best go do the job I was hired to do." He headed toward the door.

As he passed the table where the drunk was sitting, the drunk stood up and stepped in front of him. "I asked you what the hell you're lookin' at?"

Using his rifle like a spear, Flint jabbed the barrel into the man's belly, causing him to double over in pain. Then he swung the rifle like a bat, delivering a solid strike to the man's cheekbone, dropping him like a rock.

"A no-good drunk," Flint said, finally answering the man's question. "That's what I'm lookin' at." He reached into his pocket and pulled out a nickel to place on the bar. "That's for my coffee," he said to Rudy, then walked out the door.

Scarcely able to believe what he had just seen, Jake walked over to look at the unconscious man. He looked at Rudy and said. "I've always thought Flint was one of the nicest fellows I've ever met, especially for a lawman. But I swear, it don't pay to rile him, does it?"

"I don't know, boss," Rudy answered. "Maybe we just got to see the real Flint Moran for the first time.

Flint walked on down to the stables to make sure nobody was fooling around there. He was disappointed with himself for his fit of anger back in the saloon and knew he needed to cool down. He honestly couldn't blame it on any one thing. It was more like a number of things going wrong, starting with Buck's refusal to stay away from whiskey, worsened by his attitude that nothing outside of town matters. Flint guessed it was made worse by the fact he felt Buck was a friend. And he was mad at himself for punishing a stranger for his drunkenness as if he was punishing Buck.

Deciding he'd best shake off this attitude that had so suddenly descended upon him, he also decided *I need a good night's sleep. But now, because I flew off the handle, I've got to stick around until those two drifters in the saloon leave town. Even though everything is peaceful in the town, I have to make sure they don't raise any hell wanting a piece of me.*

The two drifters were needless worry for him. When the belligerent drunk regained some of his senses, he wasn't quite sure what had happened to him. His partner came downstairs to find him heaving up the contents of his stomach with Rudy doing his best to hold a bucket to catch much of it.

"What the hell happened to you?" his partner asked. He looked at Jake and Rudy for help, but they both just shrugged. "What happened to knock a lump on the side of your face like that?"

"I don't know," the poor victim answered. "I reckon I got sick from all that whiskey I drank. Musta hit my face on the table when I fell down. I ain't feelin' so good. I don't think I want my turn upstairs. Not with the way I'm feelin'. Let's get outta here."

Lucy breathed a sigh of relief. "Thank goodness for that. I don't need the money that bad."

"Empty that bucket outside," Jake told Rudy. "We don't need to smell that all night."

"It's mostly whiskey," Rudy said. "I'll throw it out, and I'll throw some more sawdust on that spot on the floor. Reckon we oughta ask Deputy Moran if he'd like to help clean up after the mess he made?" Rudy japed.

"You ask him," Jake said, and they both laughed.

Across the street from the saloon, Flint sat on the steps of the sheriff's office and watched as the two cowhands climbed onto their horses and rode out of town. Apparently, the one he had put down was not of a notion to seek revenge. He remained sitting there for almost half an hour before he decided to pronounce the town peaceful, got up from the steps, and started toward the boarding house.

Chapter 12

I found 'em, Pa," Frank Crowe said when he came back to the cabin. "They was all bunched up together down at the bottom of the hill where the stream makes that little pond. Whoever it was that took them little girls wasn't after no horses, I reckon. They was all there but that gray we found at Waldrop's place. I expect the feller that took the little girls musta put 'em on that horse to carry 'em away."

"You didn't see no sign of the coward that shot your brother?" Abel asked.

"No, sir. Nary a sign. I saw where he was hidin' when he shot Jasper. But he didn't hang around after he got them two little girls. That's all he wanted. Soon as he chased us back in the cabin, he took off."

"He played us for a bunch of fools," Abel complained bitterly. "He weren't no lawman, and he weren't but one man all by hisself, just like I figured at first. He was jumpin' all around from one side to the other to make us think there was more 'n just him. And we let him get away with it. Shot Jasper right between the eyes."

"Jasper ain't the only one got shot," Billy complained. Sitting on the short stoop before the cabin door, he had a rough bandage on the wound in his shoulder and his arm was being supported by a crude sling. "Whadda we gonna do about my shoulder, Pa? It's hurtin' worse and worse. That bullet's in there deep and it ain't gittin' no better. I need to see the doctor. That's my gun hand. Why the hell couldn't he have shot me in my left shoulder?"

"Where the hell are we gonna go to the doctor?" Abel responded, tired of hearing his complaining. "Closest doctor is in Tinhorn, and I can't hardly take you there, since that's where the jasper that shot you is. We don't know if he was a lawman or not, but he did try to arrest us before he shot you. There's more 'n one doctor in Tyler but that's a ways up the road from Tinhorn. I ain't takin' a chance on goin' back to Tyler, anyway, since they've got reward signs up for us for robbing the train depot."

"We could take him over to see Aunt Minnie Brice," Billy's older brother, Frank, suggested. "That ain't as far from here as Tyler, and she's most likely treated as many gunshot wounds as a lot of bonified doctors has."

"That's still more 'n a half a day's ride from here," Abel said. "And we ain't goin' nowhere till we bury your brother." He asked Frank again, "You sure that damn jasper ain't hangin' around here waitin' to get another shot at one of us?"

"If he is, I reckon he don't think I'm worth shootin'. 'Cause I sure gave him plenty of chances when I was lookin for the horses. He's gone, Pa. He's got what he wants, and he's gone. We might as well get Jasper in the ground and take Billy to see Aunt Minnie Brice." Frank looked over at Billy then continued speaking to Abel. "His arm will most likely get a lot better after I get the grave dug." He didn't expect any help in the grave digging from his father, either. And he wouldn't be surprised if Billy had turned in the way of that bullet on purpose to get outta digging Jasper's grave. "That bullet in your right shoulder is gonna cramp your style a little bit, ain't it, Brother Billy?"

"Don't you worry yourself about that," Billy came back at him with equal sarcasm. "I'll still be faster than you with my arm in a sling."

"Maybe you oughta not take that sling off 'cause you've finally got an excuse for bein' so slow whippin' that six-shooter outta your holster." Frank couldn't help picking at his brother because he knew Billy's one desire in this world was to be the fastest gun in the state of Texas. Since childhood, the three Crowe brothers had competed against each other in every shooting contest they could think of. Much to Frank and Jasper's annoyance, Billy, even now only seventeen years of age, seemed to have been born with a natural knack for handling a handgun. He started beating his older brothers in quick-draw contests when he was thirteen. And he only seemed to get faster with each year that passed.

Abel Crowe always took credit for Billy's proficiency with a six-gun. When Billy was a baby, Abel put a Colt .45 Peacemaker in Billy's crib. And he wouldn't let his wife take it out. He wanted the baby to live with the gun until it became like a part of him. As the baby grew, it became accustomed to having the gun to play with and to hang on to. His brother, Frank, who was six years his elder, liked to torment Billy by pretending to take the gun away from him. The baby would hang on to the weapon so tightly Frank could lift him up and let him hang outside the crib, until his mother discovered his game and made him stay away from Billy.

When Billy began to walk at the age of twelve months, Abel insisted the pistol should be tied to the baby's waist by a piece of clothesline, so he could never walk away from it.

Abel Crowe was a cruel man. His wife, Ellen, was no stranger to his frequent violent moods, often times the victim of his wrath. One such occasion, nearly the day of her death, he came home from a night at the saloon and found Billy in his bed with no gun. So infuriated, Abel beat her until she was unconscious, even after she explained she had come into the room and found Billy asleep with the barrel of the gun in his mouth. The severity of that beating caused brain damage that took Ellen's life when Billy was still a child of seven years old. No one made a grander show of grief than Abel, who blamed fate for taking Ellen—his Ellie—away from him so early in her life.

That was ten years ago, but he was sure fate had sent her back to him. It had struck him like a bolt of lightning when he'd asked the twelve-year-old girl her name, and she'd answered, "Ellie." It was too late for him, but he'd decided immediately she had come back to them to be Frank's wife. It was a perfect match, Frank and Ellie, and it was too close a match to give up on.

And that's why he intended to find those two girls, Ellie at least. He didn't give a damn about the one called Ruthie, but Ellie would most likely be less trouble if her little sister was with her. Besides, it wouldn't be very long before Ruthie might grow enough to catch Billy's attention. Abel suddenly shook his head as if to clear it of those thoughts and concentrate on what to do about it.

As soon as Jasper was in the ground, Abel decided to ride over to the Angelina River to see Aunt Minnie. He needed Billy with both hands working to hunt down the jasper who'd walked right into their camp and stole the girls. Abel was sure he would find him in Tinhorn. He felt sure that was where the walking dead man must be, and that would surely be the place Ellie would be as well. Although he had avoided Tinhorn in the past because of the reputation of Sheriff Buck Jackson, Abel decided it was time he and his boys looked Tinhorn over. Buck Jackson ought to be getting a little long in the tooth and maybe not able to live up to his reputation any longer.

But first thing was to get that shoulder taken care of. "Frank, let's get that grave dug, and give your brother a proper sendoff. We're gonna strike out for the Angelina River in the mornin'."

"Right, let's get her dug," Frank responded. "You want the pick or the shovel?"

"Don't smart mouth me, boy," Abel threatened. "or I'll use that shovel across your backside. I wanna get Jasper buried so we can eat. Billy, go ahead and build up the fire. You don't need two hands to do that."

"I don't know. Pa, my shoulder's hurtin' pretty bad right now. Maybe I oughta stay here and keep Frank company while he works."

"I can dig it a little bit wider, Pa. Won't be that much more work to throw a lizard his size in there with Jasper," Frank suggested. "'Course Jasper might throw his scrawny ass back outta his grave."

"Show some respect for your brother," Abel ordered. "Go build that fire, Billy."

When the grave was deep enough to suit his father, Frank crawled out of it and he and Abel carried Jasper's body over and dropped it in. Frank immediately started shoveling the loose dirt back into the hole until Abel stopped him.

"Wait a damn minute! I need to say a few words before you cover him up."

"What for?" Frank asked. "He can't hear you."

"How do you know he can't?" Billy challenged.

"'Cause he'd be hollerin' 'get me outta this dang hole. It's dark down here,'" Frank said.

He and Billy both jumped when Abel's gun went off right between them.

"I swear, ain't you two never gonna grow up and act like men? There's your own brother layin' there shot in the head, and you two act like a couple of snot-nosed young'uns." Abel returned his pistol to the holster and walked over to the head of the grave, cleared his throat, and tried to think about something proper to say about his departed son. After a few moments when nothing inspirational came to him, he cleared his throat and spit into the grave. "I'm sendin' my second eldest boy to ya today. He's done some bad things, least what some folks would call bad things, but who ain't? You do what you have to do to get by in this world. He ain't never run from a fight and he usually gave as good as he got when he was in one. That's about the best thing you can say about any man."

He nodded at Frank. "Cover him up." Then he thought of something else, looked back at the grave and said, "Amen." Then he headed for the fire Billy had built and the coffeepot hanging on a metal rod bent over the fire.

Frank started filling in the grave and as soon as his father walked away, he looked down in it and said, "Yeah, amen, brother. Hope it don't get too warm where you're headin'.

Early the next morning, they rode out heading east, straight through the rolling hills until reaching the Neches River then followed the river south until striking a wagon track running east and west where it crossed the river. They stopped to rest the horses there before following the wagon track east for about fifteen or sixteen miles to reach the Angelina River. According to Abel's memory, it was only a distance of about three miles to Aunt Minnie Brice's cabin. After resting the horses only briefly at that crossing, they came to the simple log cabin sitting on the riverbank just past dinnertime and not close to suppertime. The door was standing wide open.

"Aunt Minnie Brice!" Abel called out when they reined their horses to a stop in front of her porch. "You boys let me do the talking."

When no answer to his summons came, he called out again, whereupon she suddenly appeared in the doorway. An old woman, with long stringy gray hair, she leaned against the door frame for support for her bony body.

Later that day, Frank would joke with Billy about her appearance in the door. "I thought she was a wet mop leanin' up against the door until she said somethin'."

"I heared-ja," Aunt Minnie said when Abel started to call again. "Whaddaya want?"

"We need some doctorin'," he answered. "My boy got shot, and the bullet's still in his shoulder."

She studied him closely while he was telling her. "Abel Crowe. I remember you. I pulled a tooth outta that young feller." She pointed to Frank. "You had three boys. Where's the other 'un?"

"He's dead. We buried him yesterday."

"That figures." She looked at Billy. "And this 'un got hisself a bullet wound."

"That's right."

"Where'd he get shot?"

"I told you, in the shoulder."

"I can see that," she said impatiently. "I mean, where was he at when he got shot? Am I gonna see a posse over here from Nacogdoches lookin' for the three of you?

Nacogdoches has got theirselves a sheriff since you was here last."

Abel shook his head. "Nah, we ain't been to Nacogdoches in a coon's age. You ain't gonna see no lawman showin' up here lookin' for us."

"Can you pay me?" she asked.

"I paid you last time we was here when you pulled Frank's tooth, didn't I?"

She shrugged. "I don't remember whether you did or not. Bring him on in the house and lemme take a look at him."

The three men dismounted.

Billy refused Frank when he offered to help him. "I don't need no help." He grabbed the saddle horn with his left hand, swung his leg over, and dropped to the ground.

"He don't need us," Frank said. "We might as well take care of the horses while she's workin' on him."

Abel agreed so they took the horses down close to the water, relieved them of their burdens, and released them to water and graze along the riverbank.

"Come on, let's go see what that old witch is doing to Billy." He walked back up the bank to the cabin, leaving Frank to follow at his leisure.

"Wipe your muddy feet," Aunt Minnie yelled when she heard Abel come across the porch.

"I ain't got muddy feet," Abel yelled back at her, thinking he was already tired of her coarse attitude. "I ain't been in the damn river." He walked on into the cabin where he found Billy sitting at the kitchen table, a pan of water on the table, and a fruit jar holding a clear liquid beside it.

The scrawny little woman was poking around the hole in his shoulder with something that looked like a knitting needle.

"Did you get it outta there?" Abel asked.

"Ain't no use to get it outta there," she answered. "He'll be better off just leavin' it be. It's buried itself deep in the muscle in his shoulder, and it ain't botherin' nothin' a-tall. Ain't no bones broke. The muscle is already tryin' to cover the bullet up." She demonstrated by taking hold of Billy's arm and moving it up and down, then sideways back and forth. "See that? It ain't gonna cause him no trouble, once the bullet hole heals up, and that ain't gonna be no time a-tall. If I go in there to get that piece of lead outta there, I'll have to cut a heap of that muscle out that's trappin' it, and that arm ain't gonna be good for nothin' for a long time. Leave it alone and he'll be back to robbin' banks and killin' innocent folks before you know it."

"You've got a sassy mouth on you, old woman," Abel couldn't help but remark.

"So I've been told," Aunt Minnie said. "I reckon a sassy mouth is about all I've got left." She turned back to Billy then. "How 'bout it, boy? You want me to cut that bullet outta there, or do you wanna let it be? It's your arm."

"I think she's right, Pa," Billy said at once, and moved his arm all around to show him. "It ain't keepin' me from usin' it a-tall."

"I told you that yesterday when I was diggin' that grave, Pa," Frank remarked, having come into the cabin in time to hear the last part of the discussion.

"I got a blame hole in my shoulder," Billy protested. "How the hell can you think that ain't painful?"

"You sure ain't gonna be the first feller walkin' around with a bullet in ya," Aunt Minnie told him. "I'll clean it up and kill any infection that's wantin' to start up in it. Then I'll put a clean bandage on it, and you'll be all fixed up. And it won't cost but my minimum charge of two dollars." She turned her attention to Abel again. "If I go in there with my knife, it's gonna cost you a whole lot more."

"Leave it in there," Abel said, "but make sure you clean it up good, so it'll heal up quick."

"I always do." Turning back to her patient, she cleaned around the bullet hole with soap and water. "Now, we'll put somethin' in that hole to keep it from gittin' infected." She took the lid off the fruit jar. "This might have a little bite to it," she warned, then poured some of the clear liquid directly into the wound.

Billy wasn't ready for the sting and let out a howl before he could help it.

She extended the bottle toward him. "Might not hurt to take a few swallows of it, too. It'll hold down the infection from the inside."

He took a shot from the jar and shook his head sharply, waiting for the fiery white lightning to subside. She took the jar back and took a shot of it herself, before screwing the lid back on and placing it back on the table.

"We're ready to bandage you up." Finished, she cautioned him to keep the wound clean to give it a chance to form some kind of scab. "It's hard to keep a bandage in place when the wound is on your shoulder, so take it easy on it for a couple of days." She held out her palm to Abel for payment.

"Two dollars," he said and peeled two from a roll he carried in his vest pocket. "How much for a jar of that infection medicine in the quart jar?"

"Another dollar," she told him, since that was what he had already peeled off his roll of money. She went to a cupboard in the back of the kitchen to fetch a full jar from her supply of a dozen.

As they collected the horses, Abel put his jar of moonshine into his saddlebag. "I bought this from that old hag, so we could have a little drink tonight when we camp. But I was thinkin' how close to Nacogdoches we are. We ain't been in that town for a long time. Whaddaya say we ride on over there and see what's goin' on? If we don't waste any more time here, we oughta make it there by supper-time."

"Suits me," Frank said, especially since they had not had any dinner. "Aunt Minnie said they've got a sheriff over there now, though."

"Well, that don't make no difference to us," Abel said. "We ain't wanted for nothing in that town."

"Don't worry, Frank. Me and Pa will take care of ya," Billy japed. "Won't we, Pa? And I ain't even got my arm in a sling no more."

"Don't even start with that noise," Abel replied, "or I'm gonna leave the two of you in camp while I go into town and eat supper." Without waiting for them to mount up, he rode off in the direction of the wagon track that crossed the river and led to Nacogdoches.

"It has growed a little bit since we was here, ain't it?" Abel remarked as they walked their horses down the middle of the street, looking right and left, pointing out the new shops and stores since the last time they were there. One of the newer buildings was the sheriff's office and jail. "Nice-lookin' buildin'," he declared in jest. "Wonder what it looks like on the inside?"

"Lookee yonder." Frank pointed down the street. "That weren't here before. What does the sign say?"

"Diamond Saloon," Abel pronounced slowly.

"I knew it was a saloon," Frank claimed. "I know that word. I just couldn't make out the name of it." He chortled. "The Diamond Saloon sounds like the place we oughta go to see if they serve any supper."

Abel and Billy agreed and all three guided the horses to

the saloon, hung their reins over to the hitching rail in front, and walked into the Diamond Saloon to find a busy crowd of customers eating supper.

"Go over there and get us that table before somebody beats us to it," Abel said to Frank. "I'll tell the bartender we're wantin' supper."

"Evenin', gents," Benny Brooks, the bartender, greeted Abel and Billy. "Whatcha gonna have?"

"We're wantin' to eat supper," Abel answered. "Who do we see about that?"

"I'll take care of that for ya," Benny said. "You boys are new in town, ain'tcha?"

"We've been here before, but it's been quite a spell since then. There's three of us."

Abel and Billy both turned and pointed at Frank sitting at a table.

"You just go on over there and set down," Benny said. "I'll tell Bessie you're lookin' to eat, and she'll take it from there. You want a drink of likker to take with you?"

"That ain't a bad idea," Abel said. "We'll do that."

The bartender poured three shots and they went over to join Frank. They were not there long before the cook came out of the kitchen and stood in the doorway until she got Benny's attention. He pointed out the table and she went right over to tell them what she had cooked for supper. Then she went back to prepare three plates for them.

"I don't remember when we ate this fancy before," Billy felt moved to comment. "How come we're havin' this fancy supper tonight? Ain't nobody's birthday, is it?"

"Nope," his father said. "We're celebratin' tonight in honor of your poor late brother. And we're makin' a promise that we're gonna find the buzzard bait that killed him."

"I reckon we'll all drink to that." Frank tossed down the rest of his shot.

"Amen," Billy said, just as Bessie brought three plates of beef stew and took forks from her apron pocket.

"Everybody want coffee?" She received three nods as they all dived into the stew.

Conversation between them stopped while they concentrated on the first real cooked meal in quite some time . . . until they heard a voice behind them.

"Abel Crowe?"

All three right hands dropped their forks and fell to rest on the butts of their six-guns. They turned to look at a chubby-cheeked man of about forty, his face wearing a question.

"Abel?" The man asked again. When Abel failed to respond, the man said, "I'm Bud Clackum, Huntsville Unit."

A light was suddenly turned on in Abel's brain and he exclaimed, "Bud Clackum! Well, I'll be go to hell . . . What are you doin' here?" He looked around the noisy saloon as if looking for lawmen. "I swear, I might notta knowed who you was if you hadn't told me your name."

"It's been a few years," Clackum said and scratched his head while he tried to recall. "Musta been four or five years since I saw you back at Huntsville."

"Four years. These are my sons"—he nodded toward each as he called his name—"Frank and Billy. Boys, this here is Bud Clackum. We was in the prison unit at Huntsville at the same time."

"Only thing is your pa left a couple of years before I did." He looked at Abel, who was grinning as he remembered. "I've been out for two years now, myself."

"You shoulda jumped on that wagon with Ike and me when we knocked that guard in the head," Abel said.

"Knowin' my luck, I'da most likely ended up like Ike and got caught before I got outta town. We was wonderin' how you slipped by without gittin' caught. Ike said he was so busy driving those horses he thought you fell outta the wagon. Said he looked around and you weren't there."

"Hell, I knew everybody in town would be lookin' for that wagon, so I jumped out as soon as we got away from the prison and passed a good spot to hide. I knew Ike weren't gonna outrun those guards on horses." Abel shook his head, still grinning over the chance meeting. "You say you been out two years?"

"Yep. Served my time," Clackum declared. "Boy, that seems like a long time ago. And you musta been outta the state for a while. But I thought you had three sons."

"I did, but my middle son, Jasper, was killed just a couple of days ago, over on the other side of Tinhorn."

"Well, forever more," Clackum replied. "I'm real sorry to hear that. How did it happen?"

"He was shot," Abel answered.

"By a lawman?" Clackum asked and took a look around the barroom when it occurred to him he might have put himself in harm's way.

"I don't know for sure. The shooter never showed his-self, even though he said we was under arrest." Abel went on to tell Clackum about the man slipping into their camp and shooting Jasper and Billy, then running away. During the entire telling of the story, no mention was made of two little kidnapped girls, nor the murder of their parents.

"I'm just thinkin' about one thing now, and that's to get the dog that shot my son. When he first sneaked up on us, he said we was under arrest, and if we surrendered, he'd take us back to Tinhorn to trial. That's why I think he musta been from Tinhorn, but he didn't sound like Sheriff Buck Jackson to me. I wish we coulda got a look at him, but he stayed hid, tryin' to make us think there was more 'n just him by hisself."

"Maybe you didn't know it, but Buck's got a deputy

now. He's supposed to be doin' most of the policin' around Tinhorn these days. Coulda been him. His name's Flint Moran."

Abel paused to consider that possibility. Still, he was not sure. "Our cabin is miles away from Tinhorn. That deputy ain't supposed to be workin' on anything outside of town, is he?"

"I wouldn't think so," Clackum replied. "But he's a young feller. Maybe he's tryin' to make a name for hisself."

"Maybe he is at that," Abel responded, speaking softly, mainly to himself as he considered what Clackum had just told him about a young gun in Tinhorn.

Suddenly he was certain he had been right. He would find Flint Moran in Tinhorn. The major problem was he could not recognize Flint Moran, while Moran had gotten a look at him and his sons.

But Moran would be wearing a deputy's badge.

Chapter 13

After a good night's sleep back in his comfortable bed at Hannah Green's boarding house, Flint woke early, and as he often did, decided to have that first cup of coffee with Hannah's cook, Myrna. Assured by sounds coming from the kitchen indicating Myrna was up and preparing to fix breakfast, he walked across the covered walkway between his room and the back kitchen door. Careful not to be too quiet so Myrna would not be startled when he suddenly appeared in the kitchen doorway, he checked the wood box outside the door as he went by to make sure she had plenty.

"Mornin'," he said when he opened the door.

Myrna returned his greeting cheerfully. "Good morning, Flint. I thought I heard you coming across the porch."

"Yes, ma'am. I thought I oughta make sure you were up and makin' breakfast for Hannah's guests," he joked.

She chuckled and answered in kind. "Lucky for you that you didn't bet against it. Are you gonna favor us with your presence this morning?"

"No, I'm afraid not. As much as I'd like to, my boss, Mr. Buck Jackson, left word for me to meet him for breakfast at Clara's. I've been gone for a couple of days so I expect I'd best be there. But I got up early so I could have the first cup of the day with you, just to make sure you ain't lost your touch."

"Well, it oughta be just about ready to pull back off the heat. Get yourself a cup."

"I 'preciate it. It'll give me the strength to walk to the jailhouse." He liked Myrna. She was always good company.

He poured himself a cup of coffee and made small talk with her for a little while before deciding he'd best get along to the office to see what kind of mood Buck was in. He hoped he had gotten over the little snit he appeared to have been in last night in the dining room. Nothing major had happened in town while he was gone, so he hoped a good night's sleep would have the same effect on Buck it had on himself.

Evidently it had.

At the office, Buck was already there and seemingly in good spirits. "I'm glad you showed up a little bit early," he greeted Flint when he walked in the door. "'Cause I'm hungry enough to eat for both of us."

"It's still fifteen or twenty minutes before Clara opens for breakfast," Flint declared. "Maybe I shoulda brought you one of Myrna's biscuits to hold you till Clara opens up." He looked around the office until he spotted his coffee cup.

"Don't even reach for it," Buck told him, "We're leavin' right now. Mindy will let us in early when she sees you with me."

"More likely make us wait till everybody else is seated," Flint japed in return. "Clara don't make much money offa me, and nothing offa you."

Just as Buck predicted, however, the door to Clara's Kitchen opened a few minutes before the hour when Buck rapped on it.

"Somebody must be extra hungry this morning," Clara said in greeting as she held the door open for the two lawmen.

They both said good morning in return as they filed by her, heading for Buck's usual table near the kitchen.

Bonnie saw them come in and started to go to the stove, but stopped to chuckle when she saw Mindy already filling two cups with coffee. As they walked past her, Bonnie said good morning to them then went over to comment to Clara. "I swear, she just senses it when he's close. She didn't see them coming up the street."

"I wouldn't be surprised," Clara said. "I might as well turn the sign around. It's not but a few minutes early, anyway."

While they ate, the lawmen spent the next fifteen minutes or so visiting with the staff of Clara's Kitchen. After the regular customers started coming in, Buck and Flint had to share Mindy and Bonnie's time and talk at their table naturally returned to the business of the sheriff's office.

"Why did you have to ruin my breakfast by bringin' up that subject again?" Buck asked. "To hell with Abel Crowe and his sons. Just let 'em move on to some other part of Texas and be glad they're gone."

"How do we know they'll move on?" Flint questioned.

"Because that kind always does," Buck insisted. "Why would he wanna stay around here? He's already lost one of his boys, and we know where their camp is. And it's—"

"Outside the town limits of Tinhorn," Flint interrupted. "I know, but doesn't it bother you that he got away with killin' Bob and Jane Waldrop and kidnappin' their daughters?"

Buck shrugged. "It ain't like he didn't get punished a-tall. It cost him the life of one of his sons."

"I know that's true," Flint allowed, "but doesn't that mean only one of 'em paid for what they did? The other two are still guilty. And Abel Crowe is the guiltiest of the lot of 'em because he's the boss of the whole thing. As long as he's alive and loose, I worry about those two little girls, especially after what they told me. Talkin' about marryin' that twelve-year-old girl to his oldest son, a grown man? That's crazy talk. You told me I made a mistake when I didn't shoot him, and I truly wish I had. It worries me that he and his two ruthless sons might still be hangin' around our town. It worries me that he might still be that close to White Creek. He's just crazy enough to go after those girls again, if he thinks nobody's gonna do anything about it."

Buck responded with an understanding smile, something that occurred rarely with the gruff lawman. "I reckon you're right, Flint. It bothers me, too, when I think about what they did. What do you wanna do about it?"

Surprised by Buck's reaction, Flint hesitated before he answered. "Well, for one thing, I'd like to see if they have moved on. I'd like to make sure they're not still in that cabin. And if they are, I wanna do what I shoulda done the first time."

Buck didn't respond at once, either. He gave serious thought to what Flint was proposing. "I understand this business has gotten ahold of you pretty bad, so here's what I say. In the first place, there's three of 'em, all killers. So I say you go ahead and scout that cabin and find out whether they're still there or not. If they're still there, you come back here, and I'll go with you to settle with 'em. Can you agree to that?"

Flint was astonished to hear Buck agree with his plan and quickly said, "Yep, I'll agree to that. I'll just find out if they're still there, but I'd like to take two days to do it."

"Why is that? You can ride down there and back in less than a day."

"Yes, but there are two cabins they've used. I need to make sure they didn't go back to that old one below White Creek. If I find 'em in the first place I look, that old loggin' camp, I'll be back in one day."

"All right. I'll agree to it, Flint, but you've got to promise me you'll be damn careful. I don't feel like breakin' in a new deputy right now. If anything happens to you, Mindy will never forgive me."

"I'll head up that way right after I finish eatin' breakfast, and be back tomorrow night at the latest," Flint assured him, ignoring the remark about Mindy.

Buck just shook his head.

Not wanting to be bothered with a packhorse on an overnight trip, Flint put his coffeepot and a few other things he couldn't do without in his war bag and hung it on his saddle. Figuring he could get an invitation to supper at Luther Price's store, he decided to go to White Creek first. It would give him time to set that old cabin on fire and wait it out until it was safe to leave it and not worry about setting the woods on fire.

Not wanting to be delayed in getting to the old cabin on the creek, he left the path and rode around Luther's trading post to avoid a possible lengthy visit with Luther and Martha. And learning how the girls were doing. Flint looked forward to that after checking the cabin.

He came back to the path with about a mile to go to reach the cabin.

Approaching the cabin within a distance of about a hundred yards, he became more cautious and alert . . . and reminded himself he was dealing with brainless idiots.

Riding close enough to see the cabin plainly, he watched. Seeing no signs of life of any kind, he continued on, splashing across the creek and up to the cabin.

It was just as he had left it before, the door still standing open as the result of his boot. A quick look around told him that no one had been back to the rundown shack, and he wondered if it was worth the trouble to burn it down. "What the hell. I need a cup of coffee."

He dismounted, broke up some boards from the siding, and built a fire in the middle of the floor. Once it was going good, he got his coffee and coffeepot from his war bag and filled it at the creek, counting it as fortunate the cabin was built in an open area and not under the trees. With no wind to create any disturbance of leaves in the closest trees, he felt confident it wouldn't get out of control.

Inside he placed his coffeepot on the fire but it wasn't long before he was forced to pick up the coffeepot and retreat from the cabin as the walls caught fire. Carrying some of the smaller pieces of the boards burning on one end, he created a smaller fire away from the fiery cabin, and set his coffeepot over it.

It took a good part of the afternoon before the cabin was reduced to a small pile of smoking timbers and Flint felt it safe to leave the site. He saddled Buster and climbed aboard for the short ride back up the river to Price's Store, where White Creek flowed into the river. He dismounted and walked into the store.

Luther Price's face lit up with a wide smile. "Flint! I was wonderin' if you was comin' back to see us!" He rushed to the end of the counter and the door to the kitchen. "Martha! It's Flint! Tell the girls Uncle Flint's here."

"Uncle Flint, huh? How you doin', Luther? Is everybody okay?"

"The girls will be tickled to see you. They talk about their Uncle Flint all the time. Martha told 'em you could be their uncle." He was about to say more but the two sisters ran into the store at that moment, followed by Luther's wife, Martha.

All were yelling his name, and he didn't know quite what to make of it. He'd never been welcomed like that before by anybody, anywhere. It made him suddenly think of his real nephews and nieces. His brothers Joe and Nate had boys and girls close to Ellie's age. They never got that excited whenever he visited the farm. But Ellie took one of his hands and Ruthie took the other one, rendering him helpless.

"How are you doin', Flint?" Martha asked. "These girls have been asking when is Uncle Flint coming to see us? I told them you have a very important job protecting the folks in Tinhorn, and it might be hard for you to get away."

Before he could answer Martha, Ellie interrupted. "Uncle Flint, you smell like smoke."

"That's right, I reckon I do. I didn't think about that." He looked at Luther and told him about burning the shack. "I didn't wanna take a chance on some other trash movin' into it."

"Glad to hear it," Luther said. "I'd thought about burnin' it down, myself."

"Can you stay for supper?" Martha asked the question he was counting on. "Or do you have to get back to Tinhorn?"

"No, I don't have to get back to Tinhorn tonight. Matter of fact I wasn't plannin' to. But I wouldn't wanna put you out none. You weren't expectin' another mouth to feed."

"Nonsense," she replied. "You'd be no trouble a-tall. I insist. You've gotta take supper with us. I was just startin' it. I'll peel a couple more potatoes and there's already more than enough chops. We killed a hog yesterday. You're staying!"

He looked at Luther and Luther grinned. "She's the boss. You gotta do what the boss says."

"Well, in that case, it'll be my pleasure to have supper with you and your lovely ladies," Flint accepted. It didn't occur to him he could never speak so eloquently to Mindy or Bonnie.

Martha blushed and Ellie and Ruthie giggled.

"You might as well unsaddle your horse and let him graze down by the creek," Luther said. "You can lay your bedroll down there or up here in the store if you rather be inside."

"I 'preciate it, Luther. I'll sleep down there with my horse. That way, I won't bother you folks when I leave in the mornin'."

"I'll expect you for breakfast in the mornin'," Martha said at once. "And I don't wanna hear no excuses. I'm gonna bake up a double batch of biscuits and I want somebody to eat 'em."

"I can't put you to that much trouble, Martha. You weren't expectin' me to pile in on you this evenin'. The supper is surely enough. I don't want to put you to so much trouble. The least I could do is pay you something for my food."

She put her hands on her hips and struck a pose. "Now you're insultin' me," she japed. She got serious then for a moment and said, "Luther and I can never repay you for what you did for us. You brought me my girls. I'll always be thankful for that. And you're welcome at my table anytime you're anywhere near here."

He was clearly choked up speechless.

She smiled at him and said, "You don't have to say

anything. Just go take care of your horse and come to the table hungry."

It was good advice. Certain anything he might come out with would sound foolish and he would regret saying it, he settled for a simple, "Yes, Ma'am." Then he went out the door and led Buster down beside the creek.

He took his saddle off and gave the big buckskin a little petting, then turned him loose to graze by the water. Still feeling a bit overwhelmed by the welcome he had received, he suddenly laughed—remembering how he was going to try to squeeze a supper invitation out of Martha so he wouldn't have to settle for beef jerky and some hardtack.

Oughta feel ashamed of yourself, he scolded silently.

Martha had not exaggerated when she said she was fixing plenty of food. Pork chops were always a treat to him whenever he got them, which wasn't very often. And he was pleased to discover Martha knew how to cook them just to his taste. In between bites, Flint watched the two girls and was pleased to see how happy they seemed to be, even at this short time after the violent deaths of their parents. He interpreted it as a sign of Martha's generous affection for them.

After supper, Flint and Luther retreated to the porch while Martha and the girls cleared the table and cleaned the dishes.

"She's spoilin' the hell out of 'em," Luther remarked, "but they're learnin' to help with the chores, too." He filled his pipe with tobacco and lit it, tamped it down and relit it. Satisfied it was burning like he wanted, he asked, "Hear anything more about those fellers that snatched Ellie and Ruthie?"

"No, I haven't," Flint answered. "That's where I'm headin' in the mornin', up to that loggin' camp where they were holed up before. I wanna make sure they didn't come back to that cabin. I don't expect to find them there, but they might be crazy enough to come back."

"I appreciate you takin' the time and trouble to check that camp out," Luther said. "I know it ain't the Tinhorn sheriff's responsibility to look after us folks outside of town. So I know you're goin' to extra trouble to look in on us."

"What kind of uncle would I be if I didn't pay a visit once in a while?" Flint chuckled when he said it, but he couldn't tell Luther how bad he felt for not completely eliminating the potential danger to Ellie and Ruthie, and to Luther and Martha as well.

After a breakfast the next morning, equally as big as the supper the night before, and a solemn promise he would come back to see them, Flint said goodbye. He rode down the river to pick up the same trail he'd followed to the logging camp and stopped to rest Buster at the same little stream he camped at before. Ordinarily, he would have taken that occasion to brew some coffee and cook some jerky. However, he did neither. Having eaten so much at Martha's table, he wasn't sure he would ever be hungry again.

Buster, on the other hand, had not been invited to join him at the table and was happy to help himself to the lush grass growing near the stream.

Thinking Buster was rested and watered enough, Flint climbed aboard and followed the old logging road up into the hills of pine. He reined the buckskin to a halt when he came to the spot where he shot Jasper Crowe and played the scene back in his mind briefly before riding on to the log cabin.

Stopping in the cover of the trees to look the place over before riding out in the open to cross the stream, no sign of life appeared anywhere around the cabin. He rode on across to the front door and dismounted. Since there was no lock on it, he walked inside. Looking around him, he saw no evidence that would suggest anyone was coming back to the cabin. That observation tended to make him feel a little more comfortable with the idea Abel Crowe and his two sons had vacated the cabin for good. Probably they were already far away from this territory.

Figuring he had found the evidence he needed to ease his mind a little, he went back outside and climbed up into the saddle. But instead of heading for Tinhorn right away, he sat there for a few minutes trying to decide whether he should burn this cabin down too.

It was a good, solidly built log cabin, and it was nowhere near Luther Price's store. It might be a real find for some poor soul in need of shelter.

Flint decided to leave it standing, wheeled Buster away from it, and set out for Tinhorn.

Chapter 14

The three men causing Flint Moran's concern had not left the territory as he had hoped. In fact, they were no more than about twenty miles east of Tinhorn, following a trail that ran beside the Angelina River.

"Yonder's some smoke comin' outta them trees up ahead," Frank Crowe called out to his father, who was riding ahead of him on the narrow path. He pointed to a grove of trees off to their right when Abel turned to look at him.

Spotting the thin column of smoke floating up from the treetops, Abel said, "Yeah, I see it. Might be a house or a campfire. Let's go see."

"I don't care which one it is," Billy declared. "I just hope they're cookin' somethin' to eat over it. I'm 'bout to starve to death."

They had left Nacogdoches after a skimpy breakfast of bacon and coffee and hadn't come upon any place to get dinner since. It was approaching suppertime and the column of smoke they all saw was the first possibility they might have stumbled over someone.

When Abel failed to make a move toward the smoke,

Billy complained. "Ain't we gonna ride over there and see what it is?"

"We'll just stay on this path till we get up even with it," Abel said. "I have an idea we'll find a creek right there. Then we can ride up a path to the fire."

They continued on the trail by the river and came to a creek at a point just about parallel to the direction of the fire. Abel turned his horse onto the path that led up the creek.

Frank turned in his saddle to call back to Billy, "See, that's the reason he's the papa and you're the baby."

Billy didn't respond, but when Frank turned back around, Billy drew his six-gun from his holster, aimed it at Frank's back, and whispered, "Pow!"

Only a little farther up the creek Abel raised his hand to signal them to stop. He dismounted and motioned for them to do the same, then walked back to give them his instructions. Speaking just above a whisper, he said, "That fire ain't but about another thirty yards. Leave the horses here and we'll walk on up there, take a look, then decide what we're gonna do."

Tying their horses there, they moved cautiously up the path until coming to a clearing with a small cabin near the bank of the creek. Constructed of long pine poles, a rough corral with one horse inside stood behind the cabin. The fire producing the smoke had been built between the cabin and the creek. Only one man was tending it, and at the same time butchering a carcass hanging from a limb of the only tree in the clearing.

"Look at that," Frank whispered. "There's our supper."

"What's he butcherin'," Billy asked. "A deer?"

"A deer?" Frank blurted. "You'd make a helluva cowboy. Wouldn't he, Pa? He's butcherin' a cow, cowboy."

"Shut up, Frank," Billy spat. "I couldn't see it that good with you standin' in the way."

"Shut up, both of ya," Abel scolded. "That feller's all by hisself. Ain't nobody else with him. We'll just walk on into his camp and see what's what. Be ready in case you need your guns."

Virgil Patch pulled a strip of fresh roasted beef off the spit he'd found inside the cabin, and took a bite. "Hot damn!" he murmured to himself. "That liked to blistered my tongue." He blew on the strip of meat a few seconds then stuffed the whole strip into his mouth at once. With his mouth too full to chew, he worked the meat around as best he could, swallowing the juice frantically to keep from choking to death.

"Evenin', friend."

The shock of the sudden word from Abel caused Virgil to cough the wad of beef out on the ground. When he turned around and saw the three grim-looking men walking up behind him, he was so startled, he backed into the fire. He rolled out of the fire, frantically trying to brush the live coals off the seat of his pants.

On his knees, his hands raised in surrender, he cried, "Hear me out! Hear me out! This ain't what it looks like.! This here poor cow had got hisself hung up in the creek. So, wantin' to do the right thing, I tried to help it outta the creek." He paused to determine if he was being believed or not.

The three men silently watching him gave him no indication. Interested to see how deep in it he could get himself, they said nothing. Just stood there watching him.

Desperate, Virgil continued. "Virgil Patch is my name. Most folks around here know me."

Still no reaction came from the three men staring at him.

"Like I said this poor critter got hisself so tangled up,

he musta somehow broke his legs 'cause he couldn't pull hisself out. I had to pull him out with that there rope he's hangin' on now. I knew I had to put him out of his misery 'cause he couldn't walk. I couldn't just leave him for the coyotes and buzzards to eat."

With the cow poacher assuming they represented the owner of the cow and the shack, the Crowe men enjoyed the fact they had full control of the situation and moved in closer around the fire.

Frank looked down at the cow's head, hide, and bones in a pile on one side of the fire. "Look at this, Pa. That cow healed himself. His legs ain't broke no more."

"Maybe this is one of them miracles they're always talkin' about in the Bible." Abel pointed a finger at Virgil. "Are you some kind of holy man? Did you make that cow's legs go back straight again?"

"No, sir. I ain't no holy man. I can't do no miracles. I'm a religious man, though, always believe in doin' the right thing. That's why I tried to save this poor cow. I knew most of your men was roundin' up cattle up on the north part of your range. And you wouldn't have nobody to come down here to help this poor stray." He looked from Frank to Billy, who were both grinning at him, then back to Abel. Misinterpreting their meaning, he grinned back and declared, "So, I stepped in and took care of the poor critter for ya."

"Virgil," Abel started, then paused to ask, "That was your name, Virgil?"

Virgil nodded vigorously, so Abel continued. "Virgil, you say you are a religious man."

Virgil nodded again.

"Do you believe in Jesus?"

"Oh, yes, sir, I surely do," Virgil answered.

"Well, tell him we said hello, if you run into him," Abel

said as he drew his .44 and fired a shot into the center of Virgil's chest.

That shot was followed by another a fraction of a second later. Both Abel and Frank turned to find Billy, still poised in a half crouch, his six-gun still aimed at Virgil Patch as he collapsed to the ground.

"Did you see that?" Billy exclaimed. "Quick as ever, wounded shoulder or not. I didn't know you was fixin' to shoot him. If I had, I coulda beat your shot when you drew. I damn-near tied you, anyway."

"Drag his butt away from the fire," Abel ordered. "Let's eat."

Frank and Billy each grabbed a boot and pulled Virgil away from the fire, then hurried back to put some more meat on Virgil's spit.

"Fill your bellies, then go get the horses and bring 'em up here. We might as well stay right here tonight. I reckon this is a line camp for some cattle outfit, but ol' Virgil knew wouldn't be nobody comin' to bother him. He said they was all up to the north part of their range. So he decided to have hisself some fresh beef. See if there's any coffee in that pot." Abel pointed to a small coffeepot sitting in the coals at the side of the fire.

"Half a cup," Frank said when he checked the pot. "And it's nasty-lookin' too. I'll go bring the horses up and make a big pot."

The mood was definitely lighter with all three of them. They had not only found a good spot to camp for the night, but fresh beef, butchered and already cooking, was awaiting their pleasure.

After everyone had eaten their fill, they wrapped up some of the cooked meat to take with them. Taking a good look at Virgil's horse, they decided it was in the same shape Virgil had been in before he passed, pulled a couple of poles out of the corral, and let the horse go free. They ransacked the shack, hoping to find something of value—hidden supplies or ammunition—but found nothing of real value. They carried better utensils in their packs than the small collection of pots and pans, and the little coffeepot Virgil had used so they were not tempted to take those found in the cabin.

The next morning, Frank revived the ashes of the fire and they had beef for breakfast before leaving the line cabin with Virgil's body lying where they had left it when they first dragged it away from the fire.

"Look at that, Pa," Frank remarked as they rode out of the clearing and pointed to Virgil's horse snuffling around the body. "He's sayin' git your lazy behind up from there and put my saddle on me."

Ignoring his brother's attempt at humor, Billy asked, "You still thinkin' about goin' to Tinhorn, Papa?" He wasn't bold enough to tell his father that going to Tinhorn seemed like the last place they would want to go.

"Hell, yeah, we're goin' to Tinhorn," Abel responded. "We've got business there with Flint Moran. He's got my Ellie and I intend to get her back. We was damn lucky to run into Bud Clackum, back in Nacogdoches. The coyote that killed your brother and took Ellie has to be Deputy Flint Moran. Else he wouldn'ta even thought about arrestin' us."

"We don't even know what he looks like," Billy pointed out. "And he's seen us."

"I expect it'll be easy enough to spot him." Abel then asked, "What's the matter with you? You talk like you ain't got the stomach to go after the dog that killed your brother."

"That ain't it, and you know it, Pa," Billy immediately replied. "I ain't a-scared of nothin'. I just wanna make sure we don't go paradin' around Tinhorn makin' big ol' targets outta ourselves. 'Cause he's seen us. And if he sees us before we see him, it'll be just like when he shot Jasper. Poor Jasper didn't know what hit him."

"How big a fool do you think I am?" Abel demanded. "We ain't gonna go paradin' down the main street. We'll slip into town nice and quietlike, get ourselves set up in the saloon or somewhere where we can see everybody who comes in the door. We'll find out quick enough who Deputy Moran is, and we'll pop him when he comes in."

Billy didn't comment further on the matter. He wasn't sure it would be as easy as his father said, but he held his tongue. He glanced at his brother and Frank shook his head slowly, indicating he had questions about the sensibility of riding into Tinhorn as well. Just as they always had since birth, the two brothers followed their father's lead. And he led them back down the path to the river trail, then turned north to strike an east-west trail that led to Tinhorn.

Flint made it back to Tinhorn in time to eat supper at Clara's with time to spare for taking care of Buster first. He rode on past the jail and climbed down from the saddle just as Lon Blake was coming out of the barn.

"Well, I see you got back all right," Lon said.

"Yep." Flint wondered if there was some reason Lon thought he might not.

"Buck came by here after supper last night," Lon said.

That alone was enough to surprise Flint.

"Said you was on a scoutin' trip back up in those pine hills where you shot that fellow."

"I was just checkin' to make sure the rest of the bunch hadn't come back. That's all there was to it." He pulled off

Buster's saddle. "They didn't." He wasted little time seeing to the buckskin's care before he told Lon he'd see him later. "I wanna catch Buck before he goes to supper."

"Here he is now," Ralph announced when Flint walked into the office. "Howdy, Flint, glad to see you back. Buck was just fixin' to go to supper."

Flint couldn't help noticing how relieved Ralph appeared to be.

"Well, I'm glad of that, because I know I'm ready to eat. Let's go, Buck." Flint opened the door and held it for him.

"What didja find?" Buck asked as he walked out the door. "Any trace of those jaspers?"

"Not a trace," Flint replied. "Looked like they left this part of Texas for good, or should I have said, for bad?" His remark was good for half a chuckle from the big sheriff, but still a sign Buck was feeling less tense.

Probably he had resorted to the bottle to get him through the previous night, which made Flint especially glad he had gotten back in time to go to supper with him. At the same time, it worried him that Buck was so dependent upon his presence on the scene.

As soon as they walked in the door at Clara's Kitchen, Buck announced. "Here he is! I finally ran him outta his hidin' place."

Flint could only imagine what tales Buck had come up with whenever Mindy, or one of the other women asked why he didn't come to the dining room to eat.

"Where have you been? I haven't seen you since breakfast yesterday," she asked Flint, giving Buck a scolding frown. "He told me yesterday at dinner you weren't coming here anymore. That you were going to eat all your meals at Hannah's boarding house."

Flint laughed. "I declare, Mindy, I sure thought you've known Buck Jackson long enough to know you can't believe half of what he says."

"I guess I do now." She made a face at Buck, much to his delight. Back to Flint then, she said, "I'm glad you're here for supper tonight. Margaret's brother killed a hog today and Clara bought some chops from him. I remember how you enjoyed pork chops the last time we had some. So tonight, you're gonna get some pork chops."

"Well, now, that is a nice surprise," Flint responded. "I sure woulda been disappointed if I had missed pork chops." He didn't tell her he had eaten pork chops last night at Martha Price's table. He would get the chance to see which women, Martha or Margaret, knew how to fix the best pork chops.

They took their time over the supper plates, even though Ralph was anxiously waiting for his supper. Both lawmen gnawed the bones until they were slick and shiny before declaring they were finished. As Flint had fully expected, it turned out both cooks knew how to serve tasty chops. Their enthusiasm even called for Margaret to come out of the kitchen and take a bow. She was carrying a plate of food for Ralph and she handed it to Flint, then returned to her kitchen.

"Don't ever lose that woman," Buck said to Clara after Margaret left the room. He turned to Flint then and said, "I reckon that's her way of tellin' us we've hung around too long."

Ralph was as enthusiastic over his pork chop as Buck and Flint had been with theirs.

Instead of going straight to his quarters for the night as soon as he got back from supper, Buck lingered in the office a while. He questioned Flint about his scouting trip to White Creek and the pine hills. He agreed it was a good idea to burn the cabin near White Creek and thought he might have burned the one at the logging camp as well. Flint admitted he had been undecided about that.

"From what you described, that cabin sounds like just what a gang of outlaws would be looking for."

Flint shrugged. "Well, I can always ride back down there and set it on fire," he suggested.

"Hell, no," Buck said at once. "You keep your butt in town where you're supposed to be." They talked a while longer before Buck announced he was going to bed. "I didn't sleep worth a flip last night. I'm gonna see if I can make up some of that sleep I lost."

"I'll make the rounds tonight as usual," Flint told him. "And I reckon I'll see you in the mornin' for breakfast."

"Looks like a heap of folks has camped on this spot," Frank Crowe commented. Looking for a place close to town to camp while they searched for the man who killed Jasper, they happened upon an oft-used little clearing on the Neches River. Plenty of trees surrounded the clearing for cover as well as firewood. And there was evidence of many campfires having been built there. By walking to the edge of the trees, it was possible to see the main street of Tinhorn.

"Lookee yonder," Frank called back to his pa. "That's the back of the jail. All we have to do to surrender to Deputy Flint Moran is walk about a hundred yards across that patch of weeds, and he can put us right in the jail."

"We gonna go into the town and look for some supper?" Billy asked. "It's about time to eat, ain't it?"

"Yeah, it's about time," Abel answered him. "But we'll build us a fire and cook the rest of that meat right here. We can't take a chance on the three of us ridin' into town. If that deputy spotted us, he'd just open fire, like he did before."

"Yeah, Pa, but there's three of us," Frank protested. "He's gonna come out on the short end of that deal. We could take care of him right quick and be done with him."

"Then we'd jump on our horses and ride like hell to keep Buck Jackson from gittin' on our tails," Abel said.

"Right," Frank agreed.

"You dang fool," Abel barked. "Moran would be dead, but I still wouldn't know where he's keepin' Ellie. And I mean to have her back. You oughta be thinkin' about that, yourself."

"Yeah," Frank said, "I didn't think about that." He turned and exchanged glances with Billy. They would just as soon their pa forgot his unrealistic passion for the two little girls. Back to his father again, Frank asked, "How we gonna find out where he's got 'em hid, if we don't jump his behind and beat it outta him?"

"Here's the way we're gonna do it," Abel said. "I'm goin' into town by myself tonight. He mighta told people about the three of us, so they might get suspicious if the three of us all show up at the same time. But they ain't gonna pay no attention to one old man stoppin' in the saloon to have a drink. I'm bound to see him somewhere. He's gotta go to bed sometime, and when he does, I'll follow him home and that's where I'll find them girls."

"What if they ain't where he stays?" Billy asked.

"They will be," Abel declared. "That's the reason he came after us in the first place. He's a deputy sheriff for the town of Tinhorn. This business happened in White

Creek. He ain't got no legal reason for doing anything about somethin' that happens outside of Tinhorn. I guarantee you he's got them girls somewhere he thinks he can keep an eye on 'em."

"I don't know, Pa," Frank questioned, not at all in favor of what Abel was planning.

"I know you don't," Abel told him. "That's the reason I call the shots." He grinned at him then and promised, "Don't worry. After I find Ellie and the other one, you boys will be in on the settlin' up with Flint Moran."

Knowing further discussion about the wisdom of voluntarily riding into a town where the sheriff and his deputy knew you were guilty of murder and kidnapping, Frank gave up. Their father's word had always been law, and neither son possessed the grit to go against that law. They started gathering wood for a fire, prepared to camp for the night, and took their time roasting the meat and drinking coffee. Abel was in no hurry to go to the saloon.

He purposely waited for it to get dark before he announced he was ready to go. And to further disguise himself, he swapped his Boss of the Plains hat for Frank's flat-crowned, narrow-brim model. "If Moran was to look right at me, he wouldn't recognize me. Might think he's seen me somewhere before but won't know where." Abel chuckled in appreciation of his cleverness. "You boys keep a sharp eye out. If I find out where he's keepin' them gals, we'll figure out how best to get 'em when I get back."

Chapter 15

"Evenin'," Rudy greeted Abel when he walked up to the bar. "What can I pour you?"

"I ain't had no rye likker in I don't know when. How much you charge for a bottle that size?" Abel pointed to a bottle he saw on a shelf behind the bar.

"That'll cost you a dollar and a half," Rudy answered.

"I'll take a bottle and a glass and set down at one of them tables and drink some of this likker." Abel figured he'd take at least half of it back to his sons. "Have you got any good cigars?"

"Sure have." Rudy produced a box from under the counter. "These come from Mexico, nickel apiece."

"I'll take two of 'em," Abel said. "Ain't nothin' like a good cigar and a drink of likker."

"Well, I hope you enjoy 'em." Rudy smiled at the odd-looking man, wearing a hat too big for him. "You must be just passin' through town. I don't recollect seein' you in here before."

"That's a fact," Abel said. "I've been ridin' all day, up from Nacogdoches. Made camp outside of town and decided I'd come in here, set down in a chair, and drink some likker. Just watch the customers comin' and goin'."

That caused Rudy to chuckle. "I hope you see a lot more comin' and goin'. This has been a slow night so far."

"Slow, huh? That oughta make the sheriff happy. Means he won't have much work to do."

"That's right, I reckon," Rudy said. "Wouldn't be any work for the sheriff in this town, though. He's got a deputy takes care of that."

"I didn't know Tinhorn had a deputy sheriff," Abel said.

"Yep, and he's a good 'un. Flint Moran's his name. He'll be showin' up here pretty soon, makin' his rounds."

"He stay up all night?" Abel asked. "He sleep in the daytime?"

"No, Flint don't stay up all night. He just keeps an eye on the town till everybody closes up. Then he goes home and he's right back on the job in the mornin'."

"Lives right here in town, does he?" Abel asked. "Him and his family?"

"Just him," Rudy said. "Flint's a young fellow. He ain't got a wife."

I expect he thinks he does now, Abel thought as he pictured a faceless deputy training little Ellie to take that role.

A couple of men at the other end of the bar called for another shot of whiskey. Rudy walked down to serve them, and Abel took his whiskey and cigars to an empty table and sat down. Facing the front door, he could see every man who walked in. He had a couple of drinks of rye from his bottle and lit one of his cigars. He was beginning to think the bartender might have been wrong in his prediction, then the deputy walked through the batwing doors. Abel knew he was Flint Moran by the way he carried himself and the easy way he moved. Abel could imagine the man he was looking at firing a rifle, then moving to a new position and firing again, like the gunman who shot Billy and almost hit Frank. Sure it was him, but if

Abel needed proof, it was in the badge Flint wore on his shirt.

The deputy went to the bar and began a conversation with Rudy. Abel strained in an effort to hear it, but there was too much noise in the barroom for him to make out anything they said. Concerned Flint would recognize him, he hesitated to move closer, but decided it would be unlikely with Frank's hat on. And the deputy surely wouldn't expect to see him in Tinhorn. He got up from the table and walked to the end of the bar as if to discard his cigar butt in the spittoon, keeping his back toward the deputy.

"You're okay here?" he heard Flint ask Rudy.

"Oh, yeah," Rudy answered. "It's the same old regulars that show up every night. It's even slower than the usual Wednesday night."

"All right," Flint told Rudy, "I'm gonna go home after I walk up to the hotel and back. It looks like everything is peaceful tonight. I'll see you tomorrow."

"Right. Good night, Flint," Rudy responded as Flint walked away. Then he noticed Abel was back at the end of the bar. "You need somethin' else?"

"Nope," Abel replied. "I think I'm ready to go turn in now. Got a busy day tomorrow." With his whiskey bottle in hand, he walked out the door and stood on the narrow porch while he lit his other cigar, watching the deputy walking toward the hotel. *Anxious to get home, are you? I bet I know why,* he thought.

Flint was walking on the same side of the street the saloon was on, so Abel figured he would probably come back on the other side of the street. With that in mind, he left his horse tied at the hitching rail in front of the saloon, stepped off the porch, and walked into the alley between the saloon and the barbershop, which was closed. He stood next to the corner of the saloon, so he could watch for Flint when he came back down the street.

Abel almost missed him, but suddenly he saw Flint walking past the jail across the street. Quickly moving into the darkness of the alley, Abel stood still as a statue and watched Flint when he was even with the alley and walking toward the south end of the street. It was tempting to pull his six-gun and avenge Jasper's death right then when there was no chance of a miss. But it would mean he might never find Ellie, and that was his purpose on this night.

So he waited until Flint had walked a little farther down the street before he threw his cigar away, eased out of the alley, then hustled across the street. When he thought he had a safe distance, Abel followed the deputy as he walked past the closed shops. Flint stopped at the door of the saddle shop to make sure it was locked, causing Abel to have to duck into another dark doorway to avoid being seen.

He saw no indication the deputy had seen him, for he continued walking past the last shop, which was the blacksmith's forge. The only building beyond that looked to be a boarding house.

A boarding house! That's where he lives. Abel dropped a little farther back since there were no more shops between the blacksmith and the house. He could feel his heart beating a little faster as Flint continued toward the house.

Abel was going to have to be careful about walking in behind him.

He would have to kill Flint before he could take Ellie away from there. And he had told Frank and Billy they would participate in the killing of Flint Moran. *Sorry boys, can't be helped,* he thought. *It's just the way it's working out.*

If he was lucky, Ellie might be in the parlor of the

house, which would make it a lot easier to walk in, shoot Moran down, and grab her before she knew what was happening. He was given pause, however, when the deputy did not go up the walk to the front door. He walked around the side of the house.

Abel waited until Flint disappeared around the corner at the back of the house. Then he hurried to get to that corner in time to see Flint walk up the back steps and cross a small porch to the door of a small addition to the main house. To Abel, that was even better. It meant the deputy was living apart from the rest of the boarders with his own little wife.

Abel drew his .44 and hurried toward the steps.

Flint walked into his room, closed the door, and went straight to the only window and lifted the sash. Holding on to it, he stuck his legs out the window and sat on the sill before launching himself out the window and dropping on the ground some five feet below. Without pausing, he ran around the back of his room addition to the porch steps again.

Ahead of him, Abel Crowe, his gun in hand, cautiously pushed the door open wide and saw no sign of life inside the dark room. He stood dumbfounded, unable to understand how Flint could have disappeared.

"Are you lookin' for me?"

The sudden voice behind him shocked Abel to the core. He swung around but not fast enough to prevent his pistol from dropping to the floor, the result of Flint's chopping blow with his rifle barrel across his forearm. Abel howled in pain, the force of the blow having broken the bone. He dropped to one knee, his left arm holding his injured right arm, still in shock.

Flint reached down and picked up Abel's pistol and stuck it in his belt. He got a match out of his pocket, struck it on his belt buckle, and held it in front of Abel's face. "I thought I recognized that ugly face of yours back in the saloon, but I wasn't sure. I am now. Where are those other two rodents you call your sons?"

"You broke my arm," Abel complained, obviously in great pain.

"That was an accident," Flint replied. "I missed your head."

He had felt a suspicion he was going to be followed when he left the saloon. It was confirmed when he came back down the other side of the street and happened to see the tiny red glow of a cigar in the dark alley between Jake's Place and the barbershop. Checking again when he stopped at the saddle shop, he was in fact being tailed. With every evil this man and his sons had done, Flint wondered if he was justified in simply shooting him in the head like any rabid animal.

Not in my room, though, he thought.

He gave thought to another problem he might be facing. Where were the other two coyotes? Papa was obviously alone, but could his cubs be far away?

Questioning his decision once again regarding Abel Crowe, Flint made a quick one. "In case you're wonderin', you're under arrest, so we'll be walkin' back to the jail now. Get up on your feet, and please give me an excuse to shoot you."

"I can't walk nowhere," Abel complained. "I'm hurtin' bad. I need the doctor."

"Right. That's why we're goin' to jail. We keep a resident doctor there all the time for emergencies like yours. Let's go get it fixed. We need to tell your sons about your accident and where they can come to see you. Where can I find them?"

"You go to hell," Abel replied. "Where's Ellie?"

"You go to hell," Flint answered. "Now get up from there."

"You're gonna have to carry me or drag me, 'cause I ain't walkin' a step to no damn jailhouse."

Flint paused for a moment to consider his options. He had no desire to carry Abel Crowe on his shoulder all the way to the jail. And it would be harder to drag him than it would be to carry him. It was a bad time to be caught without either Abel's horse or his own horse.

"There is one other option," Flint said, leveling his rifle at Abel. He changed his mind just as quickly when another option occurred to him. "Come on," he ordered as he grabbed the back of Abel's collar. Like an insolent child, Abel flopped lifelessly on the floor, refusing to move. Flint dragged him over to the steps, grabbing a coil of clothesline rope from a nail on a post as he went by. To the accompaniment of Abel's howls of pain, he dragged the outlaw down the steps and wrapped the clothesline around him, pinning Abel's arms to his sides.

He would have gone inside the house to get Hannah's permission to use her horse and buggy, but he was sure she had already gone to bed. And he didn't want to disturb her. Taking Hannah's mare out of her stall, he hitched her up to the buggy, took some more rope from the stall, tied it firmly under Abel's arms, and tied the other end to the back of the buggy.

Flint walked back to Abel. "All right, we're ready to go."

"You ain't gonna make me climb in that buggy," Abel declared. "I'm hurtin' too bad."

"Oh, I don't want you in the buggy with me. You've got two choices, walk or get dragged. It don't matter to me which one you pick." Flint tapped the mare lightly with the reins and she started off at a walking pace.

Unprepared for either option, Abel stood there confused

for a couple of seconds while the mare took the slack out of the rope.

Suddenly he was jerked off his feet. "Hey!" He yelped when he hit the ground on his broken arm. "Stop," he yelled, "my arm!"

Flint reined the mare to a stop and waited while Abel struggled to his feet.

"Wise decision." Flint tapped the mare again and they started out again.

Abel stayed on his feet and walked as Flint drove the buggy.

On his way back from Jake's Place after a few drinks with Jake Rudolph, Lon Blake was the only person on the street. Flint considered that a most fortunate coincidence and stopped the buggy even with him.

"Looks like you got you a new jail wagon there, Flint," Lon called out.

"Evenin', Lon. Wonder if I could get you to do me a favor?"

"Why, sure, Flint, whaddaya need?" Lon stared at the trussed-up man tied to the buggy.

"Abel, here, is checkin' into the jail tonight. That bay horse standin' at the hitchin' rail belongs to him. Can you take the horse back with you, and I'll talk to you about it in the mornin'?"

Lon said it would be no trouble and turned around to go back for the horse.

"'Preciate it, Lon." Flint took a good look up and down the street, a little uneasy about seeing no sign of the two Crowe boys. He found it hard to believe Abel came into town by himself. *I'll just count myself lucky,* he said to himself as he continued on to the jail, untied Abel from the buggy, and unlocked the office door. As he opened the door, Abel began to hang back, as if about to resist.

"Don't even think about it, Crowe. I'm tired of foolin' with you tonight. You give me any more trouble and I'm gonna show you what a rough arrest really looks like."

It caused Abel to think about it, but then Ralph walked into the office from the cell room where he had gone to bed. Looking at his broken arm, Abel figured he'd come out on the short end if he had to fight two of them.

"I thought you'd gone home, Flint. What you got there?" Ralph looked Abel up and down, marveling at how he was wrapped in clothesline.

"I did go home," Flint said. "But this piece of dung followed me home and broke into my room at the house. Which cell are you sleepin' in?"

Ralph said he was in the big cell, so Flint said, "All right. We'll put him in the other one." He started unwrapping the clothesline.

"You said you had a doctor here to fix my arm," Abel said.

"I do. You're lookin' at him." Flint looked at Ralph and announced, "This is Doctor Cox. Ralph, this slimy-lookin' jasper is none other than Abel Crowe, the man who, with the help of his three sons, murdered Bob and Jane Waldrop, then carried their two little girls off as prisoners. He's gonna stay with us for a while. For as long as he's in our jail, we know we're finally housin' something lower than a cockroach."

Ralph was astonished. He had never seen Flint spout off like that before.

"I promised Mr. Crowe you'd take a look at his broken arm. So take a look at it."

Puzzled by Flint's request, Ralph nevertheless looked at Abel's arm. "Sure looks broke."

"There you go, Crowe. Dr. Cox says it is broke, so I reckon we'll get the operatin' doctor to set it and put it in a splint in the mornin'." Ignoring Abel's immediate protests, Flint turned back to Ralph. "Put a water bucket and a slop bucket in the little cell and we'll untie him."

Once they got the complaining prisoner put away in his cell, Flint and Ralph went back into the office.

"Are you goin' home now?" Ralph asked, worried about staying alone with the protesting prisoner.

"Yeah," Flint answered. "I've gotta take Hannah Green's horse and buggy back to the house. I didn't even ask her if I could borrow them." Seeing Ralph's look of concern, he quickly assured him, "I'll be right back, though. I think it best if I sleep here tonight, since I don't have the foggiest notion where his two sons are. We'll lock the door while I go put Hannah's mare back where I found her."

"Don't take too long," Ralph pleaded. "That feller gives me the willies. I'm not sleepin' in there. I'm sleepin' in the office."

"Can't say as I blame you. He's got a mind that's turned to rot. I won't be long." Flint went out the door and Ralph locked it behind him.

Ralph went to the window to see if Flint really did bring the prisoner to the jailhouse with a buggy. He watched Flint climb into the buggy, but instead of heading straight back to the boarding house, he just drove the buggy across the street to the saloon.

"Doggone it," Ralph mumbled. "You said you was gonna take that buggy back and you just went to Jake's instead. You're gettin' bad as Buck." He looked back toward the cell room door as if expecting Abel to come through it any minute. "Dr. Cox," he snorted and remained at the window.

In a few minutes, Flint came out of the saloon, climbed back into the buggy, and started the mare toward home at a lope. He had thought to check with Rudy if there had been any sign of two younger men with Abel. Rudy told him the stranger had been alone, which only added to Flint's puzzle.

Flint was not the only one puzzling over the situation. Just a little over a hundred yards from the back of the jail, Frank and Billy Crowe sat by a campfire waiting for the return of their father.

"Whaddaya reckon he's doin'?" Billy wondered. "He's been gone a long time. What time is it?"

Frank pulled out his watch and held it close to the fire so he could see it. "Quarter to ten." He wound it before returning it to his vest pocket. "It's been longer than I thought. Maybe he ran into some trouble, but we ain't heard no gunshots or nothin'."

"You reckon we'd better go see if we can find him?"

Frank hesitated. "I don't know. He said for us to stay here 'cause they might know it was us if we all three hit town at the same time."

"Yeah, but he said he wouldn't be gone but a little while, too," Billy reminded him. "He mighta found out where that deputy is keepin' Ellie and Ruthie, and he's gone after 'em."

Frank swore. "Damn them two little girls. I wish they'da hid somewhere when we raided that farm. Pa's been actin' the fool ever since he got that Ellie in his head. Talkin' about marryin' me up with that young'un. If I wanted to get married, I'd take me a woman, not some little tadpole like Ellie."

"It's because her name's the same as Mama's," Billy said. "When he started tellin' that little gal that she was our mama come back to be with us, I thought he was japin' her. But I believe he got to believin' it, hisself."

"We better go find him," Frank decided. "If he's got to drinkin', there ain't no tellin' what he's liable to say to somebody."

"I reckon you're right," Billy said. "You wanna walk over there or ride the horses?"

"I'm gonna ride my horse," Frank answered. "I ain't gonna leave him here for somebody to find this camp. They might not be as honest as me and you. We're takin' a big enough chance leavin' our packhorses."

They saddled their horses again and Frank led the way across the open area of waist-high weeds to come out on the street, down a little from the jail, and directly even with the saloon.

"Pa's horse ain't here." Billy was the first to notice.

They looked up and down the deserted street, but saw no sign of their father's bay horse. The only lights still on were those shining through the saloon windows.

Billy shook his head. "I swear, this is about the deadest little town I've ever seen."

Frank got off his horse. "Come on. Let's get in there before they close up." Billy followed suit and they walked in the door of Jake's Place to find Jake, Rudy, and Lucy having a nightcap at the end of the bar. The rest of the saloon was empty.

"Looks like we got here a little too late," Frank commented.

"Come on in," Jake said. "You can still get a drink of likker, if that's what you're lookin' for."

"A drink of corn whiskey would taste pretty good right now," Frank declared. "Ain't that what you say, Billy?"

"Corn suits my taste," Billy replied.

"Rudy will fix you up." Jake nodded at Rudy. "You boys are ridin' late tonight. Your first time in Tinhorn?"

"That's right," Frank answered him. "We decided we'd ride till we got here. On our way to Tyler."

"Where'd you start out from?" Jake asked.

"Nacogdoches," Frank answered.

"Nacogdoches," Rudy repeated as he poured their whiskey. "There was another stranger in here this evenin' from Nacogdoches." He chuckled. "I ain't ever met anybody from Nacogdoches before, and now every stranger that comes in is from there."

"I swear, that is odd, ain't it?" Frank responded. "Did he say what his name was? Maybe we know him."

"No, he didn't give me his name. He was an older fella." Rudy chuckled again. "If you wanna ask him, I reckon you could. He's settin' right across the street in the jail."

"Well, I'll be—" Frank almost spilled his drink. He tossed it back and locked eyes with his brother. "What did he do to get put in jail? Try to rob ya?"

"No, he was in here a little while," Rudy said. "Bought a bottle of whiskey and a couple of cigars. I don't know what he was thinkin', but he sure made a dumb mistake when he decided to follow a man home and break into his house. The trouble with that is the man he picked to rob is the deputy sheriff, Flint Moran."

"No, sir," Jake commented. "The evenin' didn't turn out so well for that poor fellow. Lon Blake, he owns the stable, said Flint took that fellow to jail walkin' behind a buggy. Told Lon to come back here and get the fellow's horse."

Dumbfounded, Billy could not get a clear understanding of what Jake was describing, but he finally calmed himself enough to ask a question. "What do you mean, he was walkin' behind a buggy?"

Jake painted a picture for them, just as Lon Blake had done for him. "Well, Flint's settin' up there, drivin' Hannah Green's horse and buggy. He's got this fellow all wrapped up in a clothesline and tied to the buggy with a rope, walkin' to the jail."

With that picture in his mind, Billy was rendered speechless. He couldn't believe anyone could do that to his father. He looked to Frank to know what to do, and Frank was lost for their next move as well. His first impulse was to punish these people for laughing at his father's expense. When he thought about it for a moment, however, he realized they had nothing to do with Abel's shame. His vengeance should be directed at Flint Moran, who'd made his father an object of scorn.

"Nope, that don't sound like anybody we know," he finally managed. "Come on, Billy, we've gotta get back to camp. Early start in the mornin'."

"Right," Billy managed.

They each dropped a couple of coins on the bar and walked out.

"Well, they didn't make much of a visit," Jake said. "Didn't even notice you, Lucy."

"I'm glad they didn't. I didn't like their looks, either one of 'em."

"You know," Rudy wondered, "Flint was askin' if two younger fellows were with that old guy. All three of 'em said they came from Nacogdoches. I think maybe I oughta mention that to him when I see him tomorrow."

Chapter 16

"What the hell are we gonna do?" Billy asked when they walked back outside and untied their horses. He turned and looked across the street at the jail. "Pa's locked up right there. We're gonna play hell tryin' to break in there to get him out."

"Let's get outta here before those people in the bar start gittin' suspicious of us," Frank said. "We'll go back to our camp and decide what to do."

"Maybe we better ride around that big field of weeds, instead goin' back the way we came," Billy suggested. "We'll have a path beat down if we don't, and it'll lead right to where we're campin'."

"Good idea," Frank said.

They climbed on their horses and rode down the street until coming to the end of town. and rode through the trees till they reached the river. Turning north, they headed back to their camp and dismounted but left the saddles on the horses, unsure if it was too dangerous to camp so close to the jail. Their father had always made all the plans and decisions, telling them what and when, and if it wasn't done to his satisfaction, he took it out of their hides.

"Maybe Pa can tell us what to do," Billy suggested.

"Well, how in the world is he gonna do that?" Frank responded. "He's in jail. Ain't you been payin' attention?"

"I know he's in jail, but maybe there's a window in his cell and we could talk to him through the window."

Frank shook his head. "Dummy. They don't put windows in jail cells. They'd have prisoners jumpin' out of 'em."

"I ain't talkin' about a regular sized window big enough to jump through. I'm talkin' about them little windows next to the ceilin's that lets light and air in."

"That's right. I weren't thinkin' about them kind of windows. If his cell has an outside wall, he might have a little window." Frank turned his head to look across the weed field at the back of the jail. "We can sure ride across that field and get up to the back and see if there's any windows or not. We oughta wait a little bit longer and make sure everybody's asleep, though."

The minutes on Frank's watch ticked by slowly, but finally, they agreed it was late enough to find out if there were windows in the outside wall of the cells. Once again, they climbed on their horses but rode around the open field of weeds in the opposite direction than before.

Riding up to the back of the jail, they discovered a window was just as they had speculated—too small for even a child to squeeze through, and high up near the ceiling. It was, however, a window. While Billy held the reins of Frank's horse to keep him still, Frank got to his feet and stood on his saddle, which brought his head up level with the window.

"Can you see anything?" Billy whispered up to him.

"No," Frank whispered back. "I can't see a blame thing. It's darker in there than it is out here. And there's some kinda screen or somethin' in this window making it harder to see," he added, referring to the grille to make it impossible to pass a gun through the window.

"Who's up there?" The question came from the dark jail cell, startling Frank so he almost lost his balance.

Recovering, but not sure who the question came from, Frank answered with a question of his own. "Who wants to know?"

"Frank, is that you?"

"Pa?"

"Yeah, it's me. I got bushwhacked by that damn deputy. He broke my arm and throwed me in here. I ain't found out where he's keepin' Ellie yet."

"What do you want us to do?" Frank asked. "You want me and Billy to come in there and get you?"

"You'd just get yourselves shot, and I'd still be in jail," Abel said. "They gotta fix my broke arm in the mornin'. I ain't sure if the doctor's comin' here, or they're takin' me to his office. That might be the best chance to spring me. Best thing for you and Billy is to stay right where you're camped. You oughta be able to see anybody comin' or goin' at the jail from there.

"If they take me to the doctor, that'll be the easiest place to jump 'em. If the doctor comes here to treat me, maybe you can grab him and make a swap with 'em— him for me. But you and Billy have gotta keep your eyes on this jail and make sure you see what's goin' on."

"All right, Pa. We'll keep an eye on this place," Frank said, although he was thinking it might be easier said than done.

"Better go on back and get a few hours sleep now, so you'll be ready to watch this place in the mornin'," Abel said.

Frank lowered himself to a sitting position in the saddle. "Let's go back to the camp," he said to Billy, who wanted to hear what his father had said. "I'll tell you then."

Back around the field they rode, still conscious of not

making an obvious trail by cutting straight across then
Frank told Billy everything their father had told him,
which didn't help their feelings of incompetence.

"He said not to just walk in that jail and break him outta
there?" Billy asked.

"He said we'd just get ourselves killed. We should
watch for the doctor and see if there's a good chance
then."

Why there would be, neither brother had an answer for,
so they crawled into their blankets and tried to go to sleep.

When Buck came into the office the next morning, he
found Flint and Ralph sitting there drinking coffee. "You
got here early this mornin'," he said to Flint, as he picked
up his cup and blew into it in case it had collected any dust
since he last used it.

"He ain't here early," Ralph informed the sheriff. "He
slept here last night."

"You did?" Buck reacted. "How come? Hannah lock
you outta your room?"

Ralph spoke again for Flint. "We got a new boarder last
night. He followed Flint home and got himself arrested."

Buck looked to Flint then for an explanation.

"We've got Abel Crowe in a cell back there," Flint said,
then told him the circumstances that led to Crowe's arrest.
"He's crazy as a bedbug. He came to town lookin' for me
'cause he thinks I've got those two little Waldrop girls
hid away somewhere." He didn't tell Buck the part about
bringing Crowe in walking behind Hannah Green's buggy,
but Ralph was quick to cover that phase of the arrest.

"What about the two sons?" Buck wanted to know.

"I don't know," Flint answered. "They weren't with
him. That's the reason I decided I'd best stay here last

night, in case they tried to break him outta here. I know they've gotta be around here close."

"You say we need Doc Beard to look at his arm?" Buck asked then. "What happened to his arm?"

"He broke it," Flint said.

"How'd he do that?" Buck asked.

"He was fixin' to shoot me, so I had to make him drop the gun. I reckon I hit him a little too hard with my rifle. Anyway, he ain't lyin'. It's broke all right. I figured we'd get Doc to come take a look at it. Or maybe I oughta take Crowe up to Doc's office 'cause I know he's gonna have to set that bone." Flint paused to let Buck mull that over before giving his opinion.

When he didn't offer one right away, Flint posed another question. "You think we need to telegraph Tyler to schedule Judge Dodge down here for a trial?"

"I reckon," Buck answered that right away. "Tell you the truth, though, I'd rather have a public hangin' for that monster after what he did to that family. And he's still tryin' to get those poor little girls. I'd like to hang all three of 'em."

Back to the issue of the prisoner's broken arm, Buck said, "I expect it's a good idea for one of us to be in the office as long as we've got Abel Crowe locked up, at least till we catch the two boys. You're probably about ready for some breakfast, so why don't you go on up to Clara's first? You can bring Ralph's and Crowe's breakfast back. Doc oughta be open by the time I finish breakfast, so I'll go tell him about Crowe, and he can decide if he'll come down here, or we need to take Crowe up there."

"That works for me," Flint said. "You sure you wanna wait, though? I could go later."

"No, you go on ahead. I ain't that hungry this mornin'. Besides, I'd like to visit with our prisoner a little bit. In all the years I've been in the law business, I don't believe I've ever run into a man with a mind as sick as his."

"Well, don't get too close. That kind of evil can rub off on you," Flint japed and headed for the door.

"Is that him?" Billy asked when he saw Flint walk out of the door of the sheriff's office. They had left their horses in the trees where they camped and gone just far enough to be able to see the office door.

"I don't know," Frank answered. "It could be. Ain't nobody else gone in this mornin' but that big feller a little while ago. That feller just come out musta been in there all night. I wonder where he's goin'. Maybe he's gone to get the doctor to fix Pa's arm."

"Maybe," Billy agreed. "We could follow him and see. Whaddaya think?"

"Might as well," Frank said. "I'm startin' to get the itch from somethin' in this bush. Let's get outta here."

They walked on out of the field and paused at the edge of the street to watch Flint as he approached the hotel.

"Looks like he's headed for the hotel. Maybe that's where he's keepin' them two little gals."

"Yeah, maybe," Billy responded. "Pa would really like to know that when we get him outta that jail."

But Flint turned to go into Clara's Kitchen just before reaching the hotel.

"Where's he goin'?" Billy asked.

"To breakfast, I reckon. That's an eatin' place. I wish to hell we was goin' to breakfast. I'm hungry."

"Me, too," Billy responded. "Shoot! We could go in there and eat. We ain't ever seen him before, so he don't know us."

"I swear, Billy, Pa's right. You're dumb as a stump. We

ain't ever seen him, but he put a bullet in your shoulder and almost shot me in the head. He'd know who we are."

"Oh. That's right. I forgot about that."

"We'll just wait him out," Frank said. "Then we'll jump him when he comes outta there."

Inside Clara's Kitchen, Mindy Moore stood at a window on the side wall of the dining room. Setting the small tables for breakfast, she had happened to glance out the window as she passed by it. Something caught her eye, causing her to stop and fix her gaze on a sight very special to her, the powerfully graceful stride of Flint Moran. *Like a mountain lion,* she thought as she watched him walking up the street until her sight of him was blocked when he reached the front of the dining room. Something concerned her, however, and she went to the door to meet him. She waited a moment while Clara greeted him and he returned her greeting.

Mindy smiled when he said good morning to her. "Good morning, Flint. May I show you something?" Curious, he said yes and followed her to the window from which she had watched his arrival. "Do you recognize those two men standing at the corner of the post office?"

He peered through the windowpane at the two men she had pointed out and he couldn't be sure at that distance. "I'm not sure. I might have seen them somewhere before. Why?"

"I just happened to be looking out the window and I saw you coming up the street. Those two men looked like they were following you. They looked like they were being careful to stay the same distance behind you. And when you came in here, they stopped at the post office, but they didn't go in. They just stayed there by the corner of the building."

He knew then who they were and wanted to kick himself for not knowing as soon as he saw them. Finally, the two sons had come to light and were stalking him. Flint looked at Mindy and wanted to give her a big hug but gave her a gracious smile instead. "Bless your heart. I do know who they are, and I owe you a lot for being so sharp. Those two are wanted men, and thanks to you, I just might have missed gettin' shot. I'll take care of them first and be back to eat later."

"Oh, have I caused you some danger?" Mindy was at once alarmed.

"No, ma'am. You most likely saved my life. I'm gonna go out the back door and see if I can take care of this. I'll be back to eat later. Don't be upset," he said when he saw the frown of concern on her face. "You did the right thing." He ran through the kitchen, much to the surprise of Clara, Bonnie, and Margaret, on his way out the back door.

"Mornin', Flint," Bonnie said sarcastically as he rushed by. "If he's runnin' for the outhouse, I hope he makes it," she remarked as he went out the door.

At the back corner of Clara's Kitchen, Flint held up to make sure the two Crowe men were still standing by the front corner of the post office. Then, hunkering down in a crouch in an effort not to cast a profile that would attract attention, he moved quickly over the alleyway between Clara's and Harper's Feed and Supply. On the other side of Harper's, he ran along the side of the long warehouse until reaching the street. It was the point of his most concern.

Thinking that running would attract the attention of the two men watching the dining room, he crossed the street in a slow, casual walk. He appeared to be right, for both of them continued to watch the dining room, never turning to look in the street behind them. He went behind the fabric shop to the back of the post office. Billy and Frank were talking, but never taking their eyes off the front door of Clara's Kitchen. Flint drew his Colt Frontier Six-Shooter and walked quietly toward them.

About fifteen feet behind them, he said, "I was won-derin' when you boys were gonna show up." It had the effect of a stick of dynamite exploding in their midst.

Both brothers turned at the same time, Billy with his gun already in hand. He dropped it before turning fully around when the bullet from Flint's six-gun slammed into his shoulder, close to the spot where his original wound was still healing. Frank started to reach for his pistol, but upon seeing Flint's gun already cocked and waiting for his reaction, he raised his hands instead.

"You can take your left hand and unbuckle that gun belt and let it drop to the ground," Flint told him. "I said your left hand," he added when Frank started to reach down with his right. "You know your left from your right?"

Frank immediately used his left hand. "Are you Flint Moran?" he asked while fumbling with the buckle on his gun belt.

"That's right. Were you lookin' for me? I was hopin' we were done after our business back in the pine hills. You boys coulda been gone to Kansas by now. Well, your pappy will be proud to see you found me. He's waitin' for you." Flint pointed to the ground. "Step back away from your gun belt."

Frank did as instructed, and Flint stepped forward, picked it up, and put it on his shoulder.

"You two finished your visitin' yet?" an angry Billy blurted as he stood with his right arm hanging straight down and holding it with his left hand. "I'm bleedin' to death while you're talkin'. You shot me in the same shoulder, you lowdown dog!"

"Well, I am sorry about that," Flint responded sarcastically. "If you'll start drawin' your gun with your other hand, I'll shoot you in that shoulder next time. We'll get the doctor to take a look at your shoulder. He's gonna have to fix your pappy's broken arm, anyway." He quickly bent over and picked up Billy's six-gun. "We'll take a little walk down the street to the jail now and you can have a family reunion."

"I'm hurtin' too bad to walk anywhere," Billy protested, trying to come up with any excuse to delay getting locked up.

"What if we say we ain't gonna walk down to no jailhouse?" Frank asked, thinking the same as his brother.

The thought of Abel Crowe refusing to walk to the jail returned to Flint's mind and he had to ask, "What is it? Something in the blood of you Crowes? I'll tell you what's gonna happen if you don't start walkin' to that jail. You see that big son of a gun hustlin' up the street? That's Sheriff Buck Jackson, and if you refuse to move, he'll just hold your trial right here. He'll find you guilty of murderin' Bob and Jane Waldrop and kidnappin' their children. The penalty's gonna be death by a shot to the head and he and I will carry on with the execution immediately. Is that clear enough for you? You can look at it this way, though. It'll save you a walk down to the jail."

"You're real funny, ain't you?" Frank spat out.

"It always helps to enjoy what you do for a livin'. How's your occupation workin' for you?" Flint looked at Buck, who was almost up to them. "I thought you mighta heard that shot."

"Figured maybe you might need some help," Buck

replied. "I wish to hell these pains in the butts wouldn't show up at mealtimes."

They marched the two new prisoners to the jail and Buck told Ralph to get any of his stuff out of the large cell. "We'll put these two in with their papa till you get the large cell ready, then we'll put 'em all in the large one." Back to Flint, Buck said, "I already told Lon to saddle my horse, since he ain't gettin' enough exercise. I might as well ride up to Doc's house and get him set up to take care of two prisoners now. If you'll stay here, I'll come right back and you can go to breakfast again."

Chapter 17

"I told you, Pa," Frank explained. "He sneaked up on us. Me and Billy followed him to that eatin' place next to the hotel. He never saw us. I know he didn't. And we saw him go in the door. I don't know how he knew we was waitin' for him to come outta there, or how he ended up right behind us. Just like he did at the camp when he shot Jasper and run off with them two gals."

Abel was almost sick with frustration over the realization his two sons had allowed themselves to be arrested and thrown in the jail with him, especially when he had purposefully told them to wait and watch. He looked at Billy sitting on the floor in a corner of the cell, holding his right wrist with his left hand, and rocking back and forth with the pain. Then a stab of pain reminded Abel, as it had all during the night, that he had a broken arm.

As miserable as he had ever been in his life, he looked at Frank again and repeated what he had told him several times already. "Wait and watch, I told you, until you knew who was comin' and goin'. If you done that, you mighta seen when the doctor was takin' care of me, and you coulda jumped Moran, or maybe if the sheriff and his deputy was both gone at the same time. You just had to wait and watch."

"We thought that was what we was doin', Pa," Frank pleaded. "When that feller came out of the jail, we knew he had to be Moran. And when he headed toward the hotel, we thought maybe that was where Ellie and Ruthie were."

The door between the cell room and the office opened, and Buck walked into the cell room, followed by Doc Beard. "You can use that cell for your examining room, Doc"—he pointed to the smaller cell—"and I'll bring 'em in there one at a time."

Doc asked for the broken arm patient first and went into the empty cell.

"All right, Abel," Buck called out, unlocking the cell door. "Dr. Beard is ready to take a look at that arm."

"When you gonna feed us some breakfast?" Abel asked gruffly as Buck let him out of the cell.

"In a little bit," Buck told him. "After we find out if Doc's gonna cut that arm off or not." He received a scowl in response.

Flint was standing by in case he was needed.

Buck told him to go on back to Clara's and eat breakfast. "I told Clara about the extra plates for the prisoners, so you can bring 'em back with you."

Standing not far away and listening, as was his usual habit, Ralph asked, "How many plates did you tell her to fix?"

"Three." Buck winked at Flint.

"Three?" Ralph questioned as usual. "We need four, Flint. Don't forget one for me."

"Have I ever?" Flint replied. He looked back at Buck then. "You sure you don't want me to stay here till Doc's finished?"

"No point in it," Buck said. "If you don't hang around

Clara's talkin' to Mindy, you'll likely get back in time for me to go. If you don't, Rena will cook me some breakfast over at Jake's."

Flint hustled up to Clara's and told her he was in a hurry to eat and take the prisoners' breakfasts back with him, so Buck could make it to breakfast before the dining room closed. Then he told Mindy the same thing.

"I'm so relieved to see you back here for breakfast," she said. "The way you ran out of here, I was afraid I might have put you in danger. And then we heard a gunshot."

"Not at all, Mindy. Those two fellows you saw are sittin' in the Tinhorn jail right now, and it's all because of you bein' alert when something didn't look right."

"Are they really bad men?" she asked childishly.

"The worst kind. They are Frank and Billy Crowe, the sons of Abel Crowe, the fellow I locked up last night. The three of them, along with another son, who's dead now, are the men who murdered Bob and Jane Waldrop and kidnapped their two little girls."

Mindy made a disgusted face then, and Flint said, "See what a big thing you did when you spotted those two?"

"I'm just glad you're all right."

"Well, thank you, ma'am. I reckon I'd best get busy on this food, or I'm gonna make Buck miss his breakfast."

Returning to the jail, Flint found Abel Crowe's broken arm had already been treated. With Buck holding on to Abel's elbow and Doc holding his wrist, they'd forced the two broken ends of the broken bone far enough apart for Doc to guide them back into the proper place. By the time Flint placed the breakfast plates into the large cell, Abel's arm was wrapped in a splint, and he was ready to eat.

Billy was another story.

As Doc examined Billy's shoulder, he discovered Flint's shot that morning had driven deep into the muscle and very close to the first bullet. Looking up, he asked Billy, "Who worked on this older wound?"

"Aunt Minnie Brice." When Doc obviously didn't recognize the name, Billy explained. "She's an old medicine woman over near Nacogdoches."

"I see," Doc said. "That bullet shoulda been cut outta there."

"Aunt Minnie said it was all right to leave it where it was. Said it weren't hurtin' nothin', and before long, I wouldn't even remember it was there."

Doc shook his head as if impatient. "She told you that because, if she had tried to cut it outta there, she'da likely messed your shoulder up so bad, you'da lost your arm. Did she make you a poultice to put on it?"

"Nah," Billy answered, not realizing Doc was just debunking the woman's farce. "She was goin' to but said she didn't have no gooseberries to chop up, and that was what I needed."

"There's a lot of men walking around with a bullet or rifle ball or something still in 'em. But they're in places that don't affect the operation of the muscle and the veins. You've got two chunks of lead in places that ain't good in the long run." Doc called out to Flint then. "Deputy, I'm gonna need to cut both those bullets out of his shoulder, or they're eventually gonna shut down the full movement of his arm and shoulder. I can't do that here. I'll have to do that in my surgery." To Billy again, he said, "You go ahead and eat your breakfast. The sheriff and I will have to work out a time to repair that shoulder."

He picked up his medical bag and went into the office and waited while Flint put Billy back in the cell with his brother and father.

When Flint came back into the office, Doc walked over and closed the cell room door. "I expect I better talk to you and Buck about that boy's shoulder. I guess you heard what I told him. Both those bullets should be cut outta there. But it's kind of pointless to do it, if you're fixing to hang the three of them right away."

"There ain't any doubt that Abel Crowe and his three sons did that dirty business down at White Creek, so there will be a hangin'," Flint told him. "As much as Buck and I would like to string 'em up right now and be done with 'em, we'll wait till the judge gets down here, and gives 'em their day in court. Then we'll hang 'em." He paused briefly when a thought struck him. "Unless the judge finds them not guilty. Then I reckon we'll hang the judge, too. I'll wait to talk to Buck about Billy Crowe's shoulder. Like you say, he might not want to bother with the surgery."

"Bring him up to my office after you decide and I'll clean that wound up," Doc said. "I might be able to get that last shot out of there without too much trouble. Make it a little bit more comfortable for him while he's waiting for his trial." *No sense in passing up a surgical fee,* he thought to himself.

After Doc left, Flint went back into the cell room to make sure everything was all right. Everybody but Billy had finished their breakfast, including Ralph, and Billy was complaining his had gotten cold while Doc examined his shoulder.

"Sorry we don't run the place to suit you," Flint remarked. "When you're all finished, put your plates and cups and forks in that box I left by the cell door." He figured that would make it a lot easier for Ralph to open the door and pull the box out with all the dirty dishes in it while he stood guard.

"My plate's right here on the floor by my bed," Abel

Crowe protested. "You might have us locked up in your damn jail, but we ain't gonna do your housework for you. You want my dirty plate, you come and get it yourself."

"That's right," Frank Crowe blurted, thinking to back his father's protest. "You can't make us do your house-keepin' chores for you."

Flint looked at one and then the other, a smile on his face. "No trouble a-tall. We ain't gonna force you to do any little chores like that, if you don't want to do 'em. It actually makes a little less trouble for us, and saves the town money, too. You see, that's the system we use to order the number of meals from Clara's Kitchen. It's pretty simple. The number of dirty plates that come back to the box is the number of plates we order for the next meal. You just had a sample of the cookin'. You get the same food the sheriff and I get, and you've gotta admit, it's pretty good food. Hell, we're certainly not gonna try to force you to eat, if you don't want to."

Neither prisoner made any reply, but Frank got up from his cot, picked up his and his father's plates, and took them immediately to the box by the cell door.

"I reckon it's only fair to tell you to be careful when you put 'em in the box. 'Cause a broken plate counts the same as no plate a-tall." Flint was grinning as he left the cell room.

Buck returned to the office a few minutes after the "system" was explained to the prisoners.

"Did you get to Clara's in time to eat?" Flint asked. "You've been gone a while. I was afraid I took so long with my breakfast you mighta had to go to Jake's."

"No, I ate at Clara's," Buck answered. "I've been at the telegraph office. I sent a wire to Tyler to see about a trial date for the Crowes. I waited for a reply and got one right away. Judge Dodge is scheduled to come down on

Monday for a trial on Tuesday. Today's Thursday, so I'd best let Gilbert Smith know the judge is gonna want his regular room ready for him Monday night."

"I need to talk to you about Billy Crowe's shoulder. Doc wants to know what we decide we're gonna do about it." Flint told Buck everything Doc had said about the seriousness of the shoulder wound, and what he had to do to fix it. "The question Doc wants an answer to, is whether or not we want to fix Billy's shoulder completely, or just make him more comfortable for the five days before his trial."

The sheriff didn't respond right away while he gave it some thought.

Flint said, "Buck, you know those three are gonna get the death penalty. If that young man has accepted it, you know he don't give a damn if his shoulder is fixed or not."

Buck still didn't say anything, but Flint could see the big lawman was really working on it in his head.

Impatient to wait any longer, Flint said, "Be the most humane thing to just take 'em outta that cell and hang 'em today, wouldn't it? But it wouldn't look too good for the city of Tinhorn's sheriff department. And it would be the main topic of Reverend Rance Morehead's Sunday sermons for the rest of the year."

Buck finally spoke. "All right. You can quit playin' your little brain games with me. I ain't gonna string 'em up. I just told you I contacted Judge Dodge. We ain't gonna smear the town of Tinhorn's image. We'll take the young one up to Doc's and let him work on that shoulder."

"I never thought you'd do anything different," Flint claimed. "Now, another thing we need to do is find out where those three jaspers left their horses. Maybe they're ready to tell us that."

Buck agreed. He walked to the cell door and asked bluntly where their horses were.

Still hoping for a chance to escape from the jail, Abel refused to tell them where the horses were tied. Not even humane requests to save their horses from dying of starvation and dehydration seemed to soften his resolve. Finally Buck gave up and returned to the office.

Only then did Ralph, who had been listening to the questioning, remark casually, "I know where their horses are."

That got Flint and Buck's attention right away.

"They left 'em over by the river where everybody else has camped. On the other side of the weed patch."

"Do you know that for a fact, or are you just takin' a guess?" Buck asked.

"I know it for a fact," Ralph insisted. "I saw 'em in the trees when I walked halfway out in the weed patch to empty the slop buckets. There was two saddle horses and two packhorses, but there weren't nobody in the camp."

Flint laughed. "Thank you, Detective Cox. I'll go over there and take 'em to the stable right now." Afraid they were tied and couldn't get to the water, he didn't waste any time heading out across the weed patch.

Horses were there, just as Ralph had said, but Flint had been a little concerned the horses belonged to someone else. No one was anywhere about, the fire had long since burned out, and the horses were tied to a rope stretched between two trees. The first thing he did was untie the horses and let them go to the water. He rolled up two bedrolls and stuffed everything he saw into bags evidently there for that purpose. When the horses were watered, he saddled the two he deemed the riding horses, loaded the other two with the packsaddles, and rode one horse as he led the others to Lon Blake's stable.

When he got back to the jail, Buck had cuffed Billy's

hands behind his back, and was ready to take him to Doc Beard's office. "You found 'em where Ralph said, I reckon?"

"Yep, they were right there, tied between two trees," Flint answered. "I had to wait a little while to let 'em get some water."

"That don't surprise me none." Buck gave Billy a hard look. "Makes me wanna dig that slug outta your shoulder, instead of takin' you to Doc's."

"Want me to take him?" Flint asked.

"No, I'll take him." Buck started toward the door. It opened before he got to it, and Mayor Harvey Baxter, along with Reverend Rance Morehead and Postmaster Louis Wheeler, walked in.

"Sheriff Jackson," Baxter announced, "We need to talk to you in our official capacity as representatives of the Tinhorn town council, on a matter we feel is of grave importance to the reputation of our town."

"Official, huh?" Buck responded. "That sounds kinda serious." His first thought was the council had finally decided to no longer pretend they didn't know about his drinking problem. "Does this official meetin' need to have Deputy Moran in attendance, too?"

"No," Baxter said, then turned to look at the preacher and the postmaster in case they had a different opinion. "No," he repeated. "That's not necessary."

"All right. Flint, take Billy on up to see Doc Beard." Turning back to Baxter, Buck said, "Come on in, gentlemen. What's on your mind?"

Sharing the same concern Buck had felt when the delegation from the town council requested a meeting, Flint sat just outside the door of Doc's surgery where he could keep a constant eye on his patient through the whole operation. Billy had offered no resistance during the procedure, and at the present, he was sleeping peacefully under the effect of the chloroform Doc had administered.

"Won't be long now," Birdie, Doc's Cherokee wife, told Flint when she came to pick up his empty coffee cup.

"Will he be able to walk back to the jail?" Flint asked.

"He walk," Birdie said. "Pretty soon."

Just as she predicted, Billy began to stir and Doc said to her, "Fan him."

She took a wide fan and began to wave it vigorously in Billy's face in an effort to rid his lungs of the chloroform fumes.

In a few minutes he seemed to be coming out of the fog he had been in. He was aware of being awake when he suddenly felt the pain in his shoulder. "Damn! What did you do to my shoulder? It's on fire!"

Doc didn't answer him. Instead, he told Flint, "I cut a little more of the muscle in his shoulder than I thought I'd have to. He's gonna hurt like hell for a couple of days, so I'm asking you. Do you want me to give him something he can take for that pain?"

"I expect he's gonna be pretty noisy if you don't," Flint said. "Rather have him quiet if you've got something that'll do the job."

"I'll give him some laudanum and that oughta help him out." Doc waited for Flint to say okay then gave Billy some instructions. "It doesn't take but a little sip of this to ease that pain, no more than a teaspoon. This stuff will kill you if you take too much of it at one time. Listen to what I'm telling you. There's enough in this bottle to kill you, so take a little sip a couple times a day and you'll have enough to last you four or five days. After that, you probably won't need it. You understand?"

Billy nodded and took a little sip from the bottle.

"That's about all you'll need for several hours. All right, Flint. He's all yours. I'll send my bill to Harvey Baxter."

"Much obliged, Doc." Flint then turned his attention to Billy. "You'd best keep that bottle in your pocket when we get back to the jail."

"You didn't have to tell me that," Billy said.

"I know your shoulder is pretty tender right now, so I won't handcuff your hands behind your back. You can just walk in front of me and if you try to make a run for it, I'll just shoot you down. Understand?"

Billy didn't answer but started walking.

The delegation from the town council was gone when Flint and Billy returned to the jail. Flint didn't waste any time putting Billy back in the cell then he was pressing Buck about his meeting.

"There ain't gonna be no public hangin'," Buck said. "At least not in Tinhorn. Don't want to have that on record in their fine little city. I had to go to the telegraph office and request the marshal service to send a couple of deputies and a jail wagon with Judge Dodge. I reckon they'll hang 'em in Tyler. They could stop and hang 'em on the road somewhere, for all I care. Just get 'em outta our hair."

"Is the trial still set for Tuesday?" At Buck's nod, Flint said, "So we'll still get to entertain 'em for five days."

"And we won't even get the pleasure of seein' 'em swing," Buck said, thinking about the evil the Crowes had brought down on the Waldrop family. He glanced up at the clock on the wall. "It's gettin' along toward dinnertime. I reckon we'd best go one at a time for as long as we've got those three in there. You wanna go first?"

"I ain't especially hungry yet," Flint confessed. "Birdie Beard gave me a cup of coffee and a slice of apple pie while ol' Billy was knocked out on the table."

"Why, you dog. I'll go first then," Buck declared. "I've got a good mind to tell the gals at Clara's you've been havin' coffee with the doctor's wife. That'll give Mindy something to ask you about." With that, he got up from his desk and started for the door. "I'll have Clara fix three plates for the prisoners," he called back over his shoulder and waited for the familiar refrain.

"Four plates, Buck," Ralph called after him. "You need to tell 'em four plates."

Buck didn't reply, just kept going. Ralph looked at Flint and shook his head, exasperated.

"Ralph," Flint said to him, "I'm gonna tell you a little secret. Buck does that every time just to stir your puddin'. He ain't gonna forget to bring a plate for you. Even if he did forget, Clara and the other women would remind him."

"You swear?" Ralph asked, not sure Flint was telling him straight.

"I swear."

As Flint had sworn, Buck came back with the correct number of dinner plates. Ralph took his pick of the four and looked at Flint, who winked in return. He waited until the plates had been put inside the cell and the cell locked, then he went to Clara's. When he walked into the dining room, he received his usual friendly welcome and Mindy was immediately at his table with a cup of coffee. No remarks were made about his coffee and pie at the doctor's office, so he knew Buck had been japing when he'd threatened to tell Mindy.

As she often did when Flint was there close to closing time, Mindy sat down with a cup of coffee and visited with him.

"I reckon I'd best get back to the jail," he finally declared and said he'd be back for supper.

Back in the office, he told Buck he'd take a walk around town just to make sure everything was as peaceful as it appeared. Buck mentioned Billy didn't seem to be handling the pain from his little bit of surgery very well.

"He's complainin' a lot. I'm thinkin' about puttin' him outta his pain," he joked.

"You don't wanna cheat the hangman," Flint said and left to do his walk.

The rest of the day passed without anything of any consequence requiring the services of the sheriff's department. Suppertime came and Flint and Buck repeated the same schedule for their supper as they had at dinnertime. Billy didn't show any improvement, but he quit groaning and complaining about his pain. He lay on his cot, half asleep. Since he showed no interest in his food, his father and brother were happy to divide it between them.

Buck retired to his quarters as soon as Flint returned from Clara's. Flint and Ralph slept in the office.

To Flint's surprise, Buck arrived at the office early the next morning and offered to let him go to breakfast first.

"That suits me. I'm hungry this mornin'. Your prisoners are all accounted for and except for Billy, are already up. I won't kill a lotta time at Clara's, so they won't be waitin' long for their breakfast."

"I don't have to say nothin', right?" Ralph asked, unable to help himself in spite of what Flint had told him before.

Flint just shook his head and chuckled. "No, you don't have to say anything."

He enjoyed his breakfast as usual and answered the women's questions about the three Crowe men. He told them that, in spite of the cruel crimes they had committed, they were treated just like prisoners of lesser crimes.

"They oughta beat 'em to death," Bonnie commented. "Killing those poor people and making orphans outta those little girls."

"I know how you feel," Flint told her. "At least I can tell you those two little girls are with a woman who is the next best thing to their mother." He took the box Margaret brought him with four plates in it and went back to the jail.

Walking back down the street to the jail, Flint saw Ralph come out of the sheriff's office and run across the street toward the barbershop. "Hey! I've got your breakfast here," he yelled.

Ralph stopped, paused for a second, then yelled, "I'll be right back!" Then he ran to the barbershop.

Thinking it unusual to see Ralph run anywhere, Flint walked into a scene of minor chaos inside the cell room. "What the hell?" he blurted, for Buck had put Abel and Frank Crowe into the smaller cell, leaving only Billy in the larger one, and he was still in bed.

Buck was standing over him. Hearing Flint, he turned and said, "He never woke up this mornin'. His heart ain't beatin', either."

"Did you send for Doc?" Flint asked.

"No, I just sent Ralph to fetch Walt Doolin." When Flint

asked why he sent for the undertaker, Buck said, "'Cause he's dead. Listen to his chest. See if you hear anything."

Flint looked at Abel and Frank standing at the bars dividing the two cells. At that moment, they didn't look especially interested in what he had in the box, so he set it on the bench where Ralph ate, went into the cell, and laid his ear on Billy's chest. Like Buck and Abel before him, he heard nothing. He had to agree.

Then a thought struck him, and he searched through Billy's pockets until he found what he was looking for. He held it up for Buck to see, an empty bottle. "He drank the whole bottle at one time."

"What was in it?" Buck asked.

"Laudanum," Flint answered. "Doc gave it to him for the pain, but it was supposed to last him till after the trial. Just a little sip, two, three, times a day. He told him the stuff could kill him if he overdosed on it."

"He never said nothin' about it," Abel said. "Wonder why he didn't say he had that stuff?"

"'Cause he didn't wanna share it with me and you," Frank answered.

"That's the second one of my sons you've killed," Abel Crowe cried out.

"The hell it is," Flint declared. "He killed himself. Doc warned him not to take more than a teaspoon at a time. Told him it'd kill him. He committed suicide to keep from bein' hanged."

"Sure looks that way to me," Buck agreed.

Walt Doolin came in then. "Ralph says you've got a body to pick up. I brought my handcart. If one of you will gimme a hand, I'll take him right outta here. I'm kinda in a hurry. I left Lon Blake settin' in my barber chair. But I'll get this body outta your way and put it in my mortuary."

Since Ralph had followed him in, together they picked up the body, carried it outside, and placed it on his handcart.

Doolin frowned. "He musta just died 'cause he ain't got stiff yet."

"Well, that's one less to worry about," Buck commented. "Maybe we oughta ask Doc if he's got enough of that stuff to kill the other two."

The two lawmen expected to hear a great deal of mournful complaining after Billy's death. But if anything, the two remaining prisoners acted as if Billy had somehow cheated them by avoiding the rope.

"He never got the chance to prove he's faster with a gun than anybody else," Abel said.

"I expect there's plenty of gunslingers waitin' to try him out where he's headin'," Frank remarked. "Hey, Sheriff, how 'bout stickin' them breakfast plates in here. They oughta be cold enough by now."

Chapter 18

The unexpected death of Billy Crowe turned out to be only the second most mysterious incident to take place before suppertime on that particular Thursday. The most mysterious one occurred after Lon Blake's shave.

"I don't know, Buck. All I can tell you is what I know," Walt Doolin tried to explain to Buck and Flint. "I finished up with Lon and went right back to my mortuary. And Billy was gone. He walked out, or somebody took him. All I know for sure is, he ain't there no more, and the lock is still on the door."

"One of us better stay here," Flint said. "Want me to go see if I can find him?"

"Yeah," Buck replied. "I reckon that would be best. I don't know how he done it, but I swear, his heart wasn't beatin' when I listened for it. And he was white as a sheet."

"Come on, Walt," Flint said. "Let's go to your place and see what we can find."

Back to the mortuary, Walt unlocked the barn-type door and pointed to his hand cart. "That's right where I left it, and he was layin' on it."

"Let's look around and see if we can find where he

got out," Flint said. "If we can't, then he's still in here somewhere."

"Well, I don't know if I like the thought of that," Walt said.

"Where's that door go?" Flint pointed to a door with two steps before it.

"That's the door to the barbershop. He wouldn't hardly have gone out that door 'cause I was in the shop shavin' Lon Blake and trimmin' his mustache."

That rang a bell in Flint's mind. "Is there a back door from the barbershop to the outside?"

Walt said there was.

Flint hurried through the door they were looking at and found himself in a storeroom for barber supplies with a door to the outside. "This is how he got out. You had Lon Blake in your chair up front," he reminded Walt. He didn't say anything else, and took off running to the stables.

At the stables, he found Lon standing in the middle of the tack room, looking dejected. He turned when he heard Flint come in behind him and confirmed what Flint already suspected. He was too late.

"I'm missin' two horses that belong to John Harper, an almost new saddle, and a Winchester rifle. Whoever took 'em musta known I was gone. He took John's horses right outta the stall. I'm gonna have to make all that good to John, but he ain't gonna like it."

"It was Billy Crowe that stole the horses," Flint said. "Now, I'd like to see which way he went with 'em."

"Billy Crowe?" Lon asked, surprised. "I thought he was dead."

"So did I." Flint went outside to see any tracks that looked recent enough to be Billy's. Every track that looked new headed out into the street to join a host of tracks going in both directions. Forced to admit he had no idea where

Billy went, he did have a feeling that Billy's only thought was to get away from Tinhorn.

Flint reported his findings to Buck and told him he figured Billy would not likely make a try to break his father and brother out of jail, but they would have to prepare for the possibility he might.

Buck agreed with him. "That young rabbit is headin' for the high brush. Just like he didn't share the bottle of laudanum with Abel and Frank, he ain't gonna share his chance of freedom, either."

That was the state of alert they planned to maintain until the trial was over, and their two prisoners were loaded on a jail wagon and transported to Tyler. For the first two days, sheriff and deputy were constantly watching for any sign of Billy. By the time the weekend had passed with nothing out of the ordinary to distract from the peaceful state of the town, Flint and Buck were convinced that, wherever Billy was, his stolen horses were always pointed directly away from Tinhorn.

On Monday, Judge Graham Dodge arrived on the train, and two deputy marshals showed up with a jail wagon, thinking that a safer way to transport two prisoners of the Crowes' reputation.

Buck and Flint went back on their highest stage of alert during the trial on Tuesday, thinking if Billy was as deranged as his father, that might be the time he would strike. But the trial went as they expected, with death sentences for both Abel and his son. They were loaded into the jail wagon as soon as the trial was over, and the deputies started back immediately.

"I reckon tonight we can both go to Clara's for supper as soon as she opens." Buck chuckled and added, "And bring back one plate for Ralph."

As for Flint, he was looking forward to sleeping in his bed at the boarding house. He was really proud of Buck's efforts to pull his share of the load during the past five days but knew he must be smoldering inside for a drink of whiskey. Expecting Buck would be sleeping late in the morning, after supper Flint said he would be in on time in the morning. With no prisoners, Buck didn't need to get there early.

Just as he'd promised, Flint was on time the next morning. As Buck was not there yet, Flint left Ralph in charge and went to Clara's to eat and bring back Ralph's breakfast. He was greeted warmly by Clara and Bonnie, who were standing by the door talking. It seemed to him the greeting was a little warmer than usual.

"Come on, Flint," Bonnie said. "Set yourself down and I'll get you some coffee." She seemed in a hurry. "I'll be right back with your coffee." Indeed, she hurried away and returned with his coffee the moment Mindy came out of the kitchen. "Oh, there you are, Mindy. He's all taken care of."

Mindy did an immediate about-face and went back into the kitchen. When she returned, she had a plate of food for Flint. She gave him a cheerful, "Good morning!" then went straight to the front door where Clara and Bonnie were in conversation. "Did Bonnie tell him where I was?" she asked Clara.

"Yep," Bonnie answered for her. "I told him you were occupied at the moment."

"She did not," Clara said. "She's just after your goat. I expect Flint knows that women have to poop, just like men do, anyway. You don't have to worry, Honey, he's not thinking about anything but bacon and eggs right now. Go talk to him."

Ralph met Flint at the door of the jail.

He had such an anxious expression on his face Flint was prompted to comment. "I wasn't gone that long, was I? See any sign of Buck?"

"He's already come in the office and now he's gone," Ralph replied.

"Gone where?" Flint asked.

"Jake's Place," Ralph answered and shook his head slowly. "He said to tell you he'd be back after a while."

"What is it, Ralph?' Flint pressed. "Spit it out."

"He's got into the bottle pretty heavy," Ralph reported reluctantly. "I don't think he went to bed a-tall. He wasn't even tryin' to hide it, you know, like he usually does when he's had a couple of snorts. He'd had enough he didn't give a damn anymore. I know 'cause he just threw the empty bottle into the trash can."

That wasn't news Flint wanted to hear. He'd thought Buck was making some solid progress in his battle with alcohol, and he found it surprising after the piece of business with the six Wells Fargo bandits, that dealing with the Crowes could have driven him up the wall.

A thought occurred to Flint. "Ralph, how long was Buck here before he went to Jake's?"

"'Bout half hour or more," Ralph said between bites of sausage and eggs. "He came in right after you left." He tilted his head in the direction of the desk. "He hit that bottle he thinks we don't know about pretty hard before he went to Jakes'."

That was another surprise to Flint. What could have caused Buck to fall off the wagon so drastically and so suddenly? At this early hour of the morning, it seemed unlikely, but he asked anyway. "Did anybody come in here while Buck was here?"

"Yeah, I was gonna mention that," Ralph replied. "Marvin Williams' boy, Mike, came in. Said he saw Buck comin' in, and his daddy told him to give Buck a telegram, soon as he saw him. Said it was important."

"Well, for Pete's sake. Did he take it with him?"

"I swear, I don't know."

Flint went at once to Buck's desk to look for the wire. It was not on the desk, so he looked through the drawers. With no luck, he decided Buck had taken it with him. Then as a last thought, Flint looked into the trash can and saw the crumpled-up telegram beside the empty whiskey bottle. Retrieving the telegram, he smoothed it out on the desk. It was from the U.S. marshal's office.

BE ADVISED PRISONER JESSIE SLOCUM
KILLED GUARD AND ESCAPED FROM
WORK DETAIL AUGUST EIGHT

That's all it said, but Flint knew why it'd been sent.

Flint had heard the story of Buck Jackson's face-off with the two Slocum brothers when they attempted to rob the Bank of Tinhorn. The bank had been built only a couple of years before the notorious Slocum brothers rode into town one Monday morning with the intention of cleaning out the cash. The incident occurred over five years ago, and it was the main reason Buck Jackson was assured the position of sheriff for as long as he wanted it.

Harvey Baxter, president of the bank, and now mayor of Tinhorn, would be forever grateful for Buck's fearless stand against the two outlaws. He was there to meet them when they came out of the bank, standing in the street with a .44 in each hand. He commanded them to drop their guns and surrender. Zack Slocum chose to resist, and Buck cut him down and waited for Jesse to make his move. Seeing his brother fall, Jesse raised his gun and pulled the trigger, but the pistol misfired. In a panic, he threw the gun down and raised his hands in surrender. Buck locked him up and held him until a deputy marshal came to transport him to the Huntsville Unit of the Texas State Prison.

As he climbed into the jail wagon, Jesse made Buck a promise. "The day I step outta that prison is the day you're dead."

"I better go find Buck," Flint told Ralph.

He didn't have to go far to find the sheriff. Walking into Jake's Place, he saw Buck seated at a table in the back of the room. He was facing the front door, but he gave no sign of recognition, even though he appeared to be looking directly at Flint. Ordinarily, Jake would be sitting at the table with Buck, drinking coffee and making small talk. But Jake was not sitting with Buck. He was standing at the end of the bar, talking to Rudy.

To Flint, this was not a good sign at all, and the expressions on both faces seemed to be calling for help as well as a show of relief upon seeing him.

"Flint," Jake reported anxiously, "somethin's eatin' at Buck. He ain't said more 'n two or three words since he walked in here and told me to bring him a bottle of whiskey. Rena cooked him some breakfast, but he ain't et the first speck of it."

"He's been workin' on that bottle, though," Rudy felt the need to offer. "Most of the time, he don't drink but a couple of shots after he eats his breakfast. Says it settles his stomach."

Jake took over the story again. "But this mornin', he was lit up pretty good when he walked in here."

"Did you talk to him?" Flint asked.

"I started to," Jake replied, "but he acted like he didn't wanna talk. Just told me to bring him a bottle and a glass, so I did. But he never used the glass. He just started takin' shots right outta the bottle. Rena brought him out a plate of food, so I figured I'd just let him eat and I came on over here to the bar."

"A little while ago, he looked like he was gonna eat somethin'," Rudy commented. "But then he stopped and just sat there starin' at the door, like he is now."

"I'll go talk to him." Knowing well what set Buck off, Flint walked back to the table expecting some show of recognition, but there was none.

Buck continued to stare at the front door, ignoring Flint's presence. A plate of bacon, eggs, and grits sat before him untouched except for the fork lying in the grits. Flint realized Buck had simply passed out, still sitting up, eyes wide open. Looking at the bottle on the table by his right hand, Flint had no idea if it was a full bottle when Jake brought it to him, but it was less than a quarter full now. On top of the half-full bottle he'd had in the office, Buck had downed whatever amount had been in the bottle on the table prior to what was left. On an empty stomach, little wonder he had passed out.

Figuring the best thing to do was just let Buck sleep it off, Flint realized he couldn't leave the sheriff passed out drunk in the saloon for the whole town to see. He tried to wake him. "Buck," he said sharply, trying to alert him. "Buck, wake up."

With no response from the sheriff, Flint could only think of one thing and went back to the bar. "Rudy, let me borrow that bucket you rinse the shot glasses in."

Rudy walked over to the center of the bar and picked up the bucket sitting on the shelf below it. "Want me to go dump the water out of it?"

"No, leave it in," Flint said and took the bucket from him.

Rudy frowned. "You ain't gonna—"

"You got a better idea?" Flint interrupted, pausing to hear it if he did, but Rudy and Jake both remained silent.

Flint took the bucket of cold water back to the table. "Buck," he barked sharply. "Wake up!"

Still no response from the sheriff. Flint reached over and pulled Buck's hat off his head, then waited to see if Buck would respond to that. He didn't, so Flint hung the hat on the back of a chair and flung the contents of the bucket on him. Three-quarters full, it was a heavy splash of cold water that caught Buck full in the face. The shock of it shook him from his near coma, but his natural reflexes caused him to react by trying to jump away from the assault. That resulted in sending him over backward in the chair to land on the floor.

Completely disoriented, Buck sprawled helplessly for only a few seconds before he reached for his six-gun. Anticipating that probability, Flint was already on the floor beside him and clamped his hand over Buck's, preventing the confused man from pulling the weapon.

"Buck, It's me, Flint. Everything's all right. You just got a little wet. We need to get you up and go on back to the jail."

Recognizing Flint then, Buck relaxed and looked around him as if searching for the source of the trouble. "What the hell?" he mumbled and rolled over to come up on one knee.

Then he took the hand offered to him by Flint and struggled to get to his feet. Once he was upright, he realized he was still a little wobbly. Hanging on to Flint when Rudy stepped up to hand him a bar towel, Buck wiped his face and his hair halfheartedly. Quietly to Flint, he said, "I need to get outside."

Flint recognized the urgency in his tone. "Right!" And with Buck hanging one arm on his shoulder for support, they headed immediately for the door.

Through sheer determination, Buck made it through the door and over to the side of the narrow porch before dropping to one knee and emptying the contents of his stomach. He remained there a few minutes while his stomach continued to heave the alcohol that was left, but nothing more came up.

After a minute or two, Flint said, "Come on. Let's go back to the jail. You musta ate something that didn't agree with you a-tall. You need to go to your room and get a couple hours' sleep. Then if you feel like it, we'll go to Clara's Kitchen and get you some solid food in your belly. Whaddaya say?"

Well aware of what drove Buck to the bottle, he decided to save that discussion until Buck was ready to address that particular threat. Flint also knew Buck would be mortified if he thought anyone knew what actually drove him to the bottle. He was just finding out how cumbersome a reputation like the one he had worn for years could come back to bite him when he grew a little older.

Buck looked at him and said, "I reckon I can make it across the street now. You're right. I musta et somethin' that weren't good for my belly. I'm sorry you had to bother with me, but maybe you're right. I think I'll lay down for a while before dinnertime."

"Weren't no trouble a-tall," Flint said. "You take a little nap and you'll be good as new. I'll keep an eye on the town, so don't worry about that."

"I know you will, Flint, and I appreciate it." Buck tried to make light of the incident then. "Wouldn't be too nice for the good folks of Tinhorn to see their sheriff on his knees, pukin' his guts out in front of the saloon, would it?"

"Reckon not," Flint replied and chuckled with him.

They walked back across the street and Buck went back to his room while Flint returned to the office to answer every one of Ralph's questions without telling him anything. Sorry he had reacted to the telegram with such concern in front of Ralph, he was going to have to erase an image of fear Ralph might have seen in the sheriff. Flint suspected fear had triggered Buck's drunken collapse. But Ralph wouldn't understand there are different kinds of fear.

Flint felt Buck might fear he would be inadequate in stopping Jesse Slocum in his intent to commit murder in Buck's town. Concerned Buck felt obligated to answer a challenge to a duel, aware that he had slowed down in all areas over the last four or five years, Flint said to himself, *I intend to make sure there ain't no duel between Buck Jackson and Jesse Slocum.*

"Is the sheriff all right?" Ralph asked as soon as Flint walked into the office.

"Yeah, he's fine," Flint replied. "He just ate something that riled his belly. I'm pretty sure it was a piece of that deer meat I brought back with Roy and Bart. He said he was hungry when he went back to his room this mornin' so he found a piece of that venison and ate it. It had already turned bad, I reckon, and when he realized it, he tried to kill it with whiskey. That just made it worse. Anyway, he decided he'd best give his belly a little more rest before dinnertime."

Flint figured, if you're gonna make up a story, make up a good one, and he thought that was good enough to satisfy Ralph.

He was mistaken. "I swear," Ralph said. "I thought he got into the bottle 'cause of that telegram he got. It said that feller busted outta prison. It'd been enough to make me wanna hide."

"That's where you're wrong," Flint told him. "If you'da seen Buck Jackson in Clara's Kitchen facin' down those four Wells Fargo robbers right by himself, you'd know there ain't no way in this world you could call him yellow."

"I reckon not," Ralph decided.

Chapter 19

"Hello the camp!"

The sudden call startled the two men sitting by the campfire on the creekbank. Both reached for their six-guns and rolled away from the fire's light.

"I didn't mean to spook you," the voice came again. "I've had a piece of bad luck and saw your smoke. If you can spare somethin' to eat, I'd sure appreciate it. I ain't et since yesterday."

"Show yourself," Arthur Wilson called out, "so we can see who we're talkin' to." Aside to his brother, he whispered, "Watch out behind us. He might not be alone."

Alvin shifted around so he could keep an eye on their horses behind them as a lone figure appeared, emerging from the tall bushes between the trees. Dressed in prison overalls, with his hands up to show them he held no weapon, he walked slowly toward them. "For God's sake, don't shoot," he called out. "I ain't a prisoner. I got jumped by one yesterday I reckon escaped from Huntsville Unit. He took my clothes, my horses, my guns, and left me his old prison rags." When they made no verbal response right away, he continued. "Don't blame you for bein' cautious.

If you can spare a little scrap of somethin' to eat, I'd surely appreciate it, then I'll leave you be."

"Sure, mister, come on in," Arthur called back. "You can eat your fill. We just killed a deer 'bout two hours ago." Aside to Alvin again, he said. "Watch him, brother. He might be wantin' more 'n just somethin' to eat."

"I'll watch him," Alvin replied.

Both watched the approaching stranger very carefully as he neared the fire, his hands still raised, palms out. Dressed as he was in prison issue, nothing seemed outstanding or unusual about him.

"You can use my cup if you want some coffee." Arthur tossed the empty cup to him when he came up to the fire. "Help yourself to them strips of meat roastin' on the fire."

"Much obliged." The stranger caught the cup, dropped to his knees in front of the fire, and poured from the coffeepot in the ashes. "I wanna thank you fellows for your kindness. After all the bad luck I had yesterday, I never expected to meet up with two Christian men like you today. I thought I heard a rifle shot a while back. Didn't know it was gonna be my signal to come to dinner, though." He pulled a strip of venison off a metal rod the Wilson brothers had fixed over the fire to roast the meat. The enthusiasm with which he attacked the deer meat was evidence enough to prove he wasn't lying about his hunger.

The brothers said nothing for a few minutes while they watched him devour strip after strip of venison. Finally he leaned back a little from the fire, appearing to be sated.

Alvin asked, "You say a prisoner jumped you yesterday and stole everything you had?"

"That's right," the stranger replied. "Cleaned me out."

"And he left you his prison issue?"

"That's a fact. I reckon I oughta be glad he left me any-thing at all. I didn't wanna put them on, but it was either that or start out walkin' in my long johns."

"You and him musta been the same size," Alvin commented. "Them prison clothes fit you pretty good."

The stranger laughed. "Yeah, they do, don't they? They make 'em outta some pretty tough material. I like the big ol' pockets they sewed on the back of the britches." As he said it, he reached behind him and pulled a revolver out of the back pocket. "Leaves your hands free to eat," he remarked as he pumped a round into Arthur's chest, then cocked the weapon fast enough to catch Alvin in the gut when he reached for his gun. He went around to the other side of the fire to check on his victims. Finding the older one dead, shot through the heart, he pulled his gun out of the holster just in case. "I don't wanna get shot by a dead man," he explained to the corpse. Checking on Alvin, he found him still alive, but in great pain from the shot in his gut. He bent over and poked him with his finger. "When you get to hell, tell 'em Jesse sent you and I'll send 'em another one soon as I get to Tinhorn."

"You son of a . . . ," was as far as Alvin got before the bullet to his head silenced him forever.

"Ha!" Jesse Slocum snorted in amusement. "I bet you two are brothers. You favor one another. Wonder if there's some little woman waitin' at home, sayin', 'I wonder if they had any luck?' Well, Honeybun, they had a lotta luck, but it was all bad. Today was Jesse's turn to have all the good luck. And if I knew where the hell home was, I'd come share some of that luck with you. The devil knows it's been over five years since I've given a woman the pleasure of my company." He started searching the bodies then. "Them boots you're wearin' look like they might be my size," he said, looking at Arthur's feet. "They'll suit me a whole lot better 'n these prison work shoes I'm wearin'. Reckon I'd better try on your britches first before I try to pull the boots on, though."

Thoroughly enjoying himself, Jesse stripped the two bodies of their clothes, trying on their shirts, trousers, and vests, until he came up with an outfit he was satisfied with. It was no contest picking the hat, for one of them wore a black hat with a wide silver band around the crown. A little snug, but he was determined to wear it.

Next, he inspected the weapons they were packing. Both carried a Colt Frontier Six-Shooter in good condition. Jesse could barely believe his good fortune. "That's more to my likin'," he uttered as he felt the heft of each pistol and broke the cylinders open to find them loaded with five cartridges and the hammers resting on an empty. He took a look at the .38 revolver he had taken from the prison guard, then tossed it into the creek.

With new duds and armed, he went down near the water's edge to judge the two horses he was now in possession of. He was drawn right away to the bay gelding the older brother, Arthur, had ridden primarily because the other horse was a paint, and he didn't care for paint horses. Paint horses were bad luck. His late brother, Zack rode a paint horse into Tinhorn that day when they'd hit the bank.

Since the two men he just killed didn't have a packhorse, Jesse figured they must live somewhere close. They carried supplies for only a couple of nights, things they could carry in bags tied onto their saddles. "Looks like I'm gonna have to sell one of those saddles to get some more supplies," he said, disappointed to find no money on either man. He looked at the paint and said, "I need a packhorse, and that's the only thing that's keepin' me from puttin' a bullet in your skull."

Once he was completely satisfied with his new outfit,

he decided it best not to linger any longer at the scene of the crime. With several hours of daylight left, he thought to put some miles between himself and the creek. His ultimate destination was Oklahoma Indian Territory after he made a stop in the little town of Tinhorn for a meeting with Sheriff Buck Jackson. That shouldn't take long, for Tinhorn was right on the way. But it was about ninety miles from where he stood. He was going to have to find some supplies somewhere along the way.

"I ain't gonna starve, though," Jesse declared with a chuckle as he looked at the freshly butchered venison laid out on the deer hide. Figuring it would be good for a couple of days before it turned, he would eat it until it did turn, then throw it away. He was not inclined to go to the trouble to smoke the meat and preserve it.

He packed up the horses, with the best saddle on the bay, and his deer hide bundle tied onto the paint's saddle. A sack with the coffeepot, cups, forks, plates, and a frying pan was hung on one side of the saddle, and another sack holding a small amount of flour, lard, and coffee was hung on the other side. Climbing up on the bay horse, he rode back along the creek to the road he had been walking on since early morning. It would continue to take him straight north, he hoped.

After riding for a couple of hours, he came to a sizable creek and decided to rest his newly acquired horses. The creek looked like a good spot to test his feel for the six-guns he had acquired, one of which was riding on his hip. Although identical guns, it didn't mean they didn't have a different feel. Before he was locked up he had prided himself in his ability to clear his weapon faster than most men and was anxious to find out just how much rust he had acquired over the years in prison.

He rode up the creek about fifty yards from the road.

While his horses drank from the creek and grazed on the long grass on its banks, Jesse tested his reflexes with his six-guns. After a short time practicing to draw and fire at a target, he was pleased to find the feeling was coming back to him quickly. By the time he was finished, he'd decided to call the sheriff out to face him man-to-man. And Buck Jackson would know why he was being killed and who killed him.

Flint waited to see if Buck was going to show up for dinner. Finally he had to go without him when it approached the end of dinnertime at Clara's. He considered going to Buck's room to check on him but decided it best not to and hurried to Clara's.

It was almost suppertime before Buck came into the office, looking pale, but sober. It was obvious he had shaved and cleaned up a little. And he was wearing a fresh shirt.

"You feelin' a little better?" Flint asked. "Did you ever figure out what you ate that tore your stomach up?" he asked in an effort to help Buck save face.

"Yeah, I figured it out," Buck replied gruffly. "It weren't nothin' I ate. It was too damn much whiskey." His frank declaration surprised Flint and Ralph, for he had always tried to hide his excessive drinking before.

Flint hoped it meant Buck had decided to do something about it. "You feel like you could eat some supper now? It's time for Clara to open up."

"Yep," Buck replied. "I feel like I can handle some solid food. One thing I'm sure of is my insides are empty. Anything in there came outta one end or the other. I know I'm hungry as hell, and I need some coffee. So, let's go."

"Right," Flint responded at once. He exchanged puzzled glances with Ralph, then followed Buck out the door.

The only words exchanged between them as they walked up to the dining room was when Buck asked if everything was running smoothly in the town, and Flint said they were. They went inside and sat down at Buck's usual table.

Then Flint asked, "When are we gonna talk about this business with the telegram?"

Buck waited until Bonnie set two cups of coffee on the table and went back to the kitchen before he answered. "There ain't nothin' to talk about that telegram. It's some personal business, and it ain't got nothin' to do with the town of Tinhorn."

"What?" Flint reacted at once. "I beg to differ. The hell it doesn't have something to do with the town," he insisted. "Maybe I misunderstood what you and the mayor and everybody else told me when I hired on as deputy. It was my understandin' all forms of gunplay are against the law in Tinhorn, and that includes duels." He couldn't believe Buck would actually accommodate Jesse Slocum's challenge. And like Buck, Flint expected there would be one.

"I 'preciate what you're tryin' to do, Flint, but I ain't never run from any outlaw, and at this late stage of my life, it's important to face up to these men who think they can come into town and call the sheriff out. Besides, that was five years ago when he said he would come after me if he ever got outta prison. If he's got any sense a-tall, he won't be showin' up here."

"Hello, Flint. Sheriff," Mindy greeted cheerfully as she brought two plates of food for them. "Sorry we didn't see you at dinner, Sheriff."

"Hey, Mindy," Flint replied without taking his eyes off the stubborn sheriff and continued his appeal to him. "If he comes into this town callin' anybody out, I'll lock his butt up so fast he'll know he can't do that in Tinhorn." So determined to talk some sense into Buck, he failed to notice Mindy's reaction to his indifferent return of her greeting.

"Well, excuse me," she said indignantly and turned away from the table. Walking past Bonnie in a huff, she informed her, "You can wait on them."

"No," Buck replied, "you just let me handle it. Jesse Slocum thinks he has a score to settle with me. I'll not back away from it."

"Pardon me for sayin' so," Flint said, "but that's crazy talk. In the first place, he ain't just somebody comin' into our town to call out the sheriff. You read the telegram. He's an escaped inmate of the state prison who killed a guard. We don't bargain with escaped convicts. We capture 'em and put 'em in jail. Ain't that right?"

"Ordinarily." Buck cut a sizable bite out of his pork chop and raked it through his mashed potatoes before thrusting it into his mouth. "But this ain't ordinary. You just let me handle it. You just worry about the drunks and the rowdy cowhands. I'll take care of Jesse Slocum."

"The hell I will," Flint declared, reaching a higher level of impatience with his hardheaded boss. "I'll do the job I told the mayor and the town council I'd do. And that's to uphold the law. I ain't about to let an escaped prisoner, who's a known gunman, come into our town and challenge the sheriff to face him in the middle of the street."

"Last time I talked to the mayor, I believe he said you work for me," Buck said. "Ain't that right?"

"Sure, that's right," Flint responded. "But I have to enforce the laws of the town and state even if I work for you."

"Even if I tell you not to?"

"Even so," Flint replied.

"Well, you don't give me a whole lotta choice, do ya?" Buck asked.

Flint shrugged helplessly.

"Then I reckon you don't work for me no more. You're fired."

Flint didn't respond immediately. At first, he thought Buck must be joking, but the solemn look on Buck's face was serious. He asked to be sure. "You're firin' me?"

"That's what I said," Buck replied.

A long empty silence fell upon the table as the two men sat staring at each other, one thinking surely a denial was forthcoming, the other determined not to rescind his order. It led to an awkwardness that gave Flint no choice but to pick up his plate and cup and move to another table, so both might finish their supper. Before he sat down, he took off his badge, walked back and placed it on Buck's table, then returned to his table.

Over by the front door, the three ladies who ran the dining room observed the curious relocation of Flint Moran to a table across the room.

"What the hell?" Bonnie drew out, turning to Mindy at once. "Go ask Flint what's goin' on."

"Why should I ask him?" Mindy replied, still a little pouty over what she felt was a rude snub. "You ask him."

"Go ask him, Mindy. He'll do anything for you," Clara told her.

"Turn on your charm, Mindy," Bonnie teased.

"Kiss my foot, Bonnie," Mindy replied, but she went over to the table where Flint was eating, his concentration seeming to be focused on his plate. "You need some more coffee?" she asked sweetly.

He looked up from his plate and smiled at her. "I guess I could use a little warmup, thanks."

She went at once to get the pot, paused briefly at the

table next to the kitchen door to fill Buck's cup, then made her way back to Flint. Thinking it best to approach it plain and simple, she asked, "Why did you move over here?"

He shrugged. "I thought Buck could use a little more room."

"Oh. He's always had enough room at that table before. Is something wrong?"

Flint smiled at her again. "I reckon you and everybody else will soon know, so you'll be the first person to get the news. I'm over here eatin' by myself because Buck fired me."

She gasped. "What? He can't fire you. What do you mean, he fired you? Buck can't make it in this town anymore without you."

Flint had to smile at that. "He must not think the same as you. Because he sure as the devil fired me."

"What are you gonna do?" She asked.

"Well, I'm gonna sit right here and finish eatin' this pork chop and all the fixin's with it. Then I'm gonna ask you if there's any kind of pie to finish off my coffee with."

"Margaret made up the last of those dried apples into a couple of pies. I'll go slice you a piece now, so you don't miss out on it. Why did he fire you? Surely, he didn't actually mean it."

"He sounded pretty convincin'. We had a little difference of opinion on something, and he's right, he is my boss. So he fired me." Flint was not inclined to tell her what the difference was about. No sense in creating a panic among the townsfolk. No telling when, or even *if*, Jesse Slocum might show up.

"What will you do if you're not the deputy sheriff anymore?" Mindy made no attempt to hide her concern. "Will you leave Tinhorn and go back to your family's farm?"

"Maybe." Then he said, "I don't know. I expect I'll hang

around town for a while till I make up my mind. My room at Hannah Green's house is paid up till the end of the month. I can even afford to eat here at Clara's once in a while if I want to."

She favored him with a worried look as she hoped for a more detailed explanation. Realizing he wasn't willing to share anything more, she said, "I'll go get your slice of pie."

When she returned, he thanked her for making sure he got a slice, knowing how fast they usually disappeared. He reminded her then to make sure Buck took a plate back to the jail for Ralph.

Flint was only half finished with his dessert when Buck got up and headed for the door, only to be stopped when Mindy called after him to take a plate back for Ralph.

"Right. I almost forgot it." Buck waited near the door. "I don't know where my mind is today," he commented to Clara.

"I think it's something going around right now," Clara said. "I've had a touch of it myself today." She waited for a few seconds to give him a chance to explain the weird behavior demonstrated by him and Flint. But he didn't offer any, so she asked, "Is everything all right?"

"What?" he replied as if surprised. "Oh, yeah, everything's all right. It was a fine supper."

At the end of her patience, Clara said, "I'm not talking about your supper. You know what I mean. What's going on with you and Flint? Why'd he move to another table?"

"We just needed some more room, that's all. Don't make a big thing outta somethin' that ain't nothin' at all." Then, leaving her no room to object, Buck said, "Here she is," and walked to meet Margaret when she walked out of the kitchen with Ralph's plate. "Thank you, ladies. Ol' Ralph would be upset with me if I showed up without his supper.

"See you tomorrow," he said as he passed by Clara at the door.

"Damn," she muttered to herself. "He didn't tell me a thing." She turned to look at Flint, who was getting up from the table.

He walked to the counter and paid Clara for his supper. "That was a fine supper," he said and started out the door.

"What's going on between you and Buck?" she asked.

He paused only long enough to say, "Ask Mindy. I told her." And he went out the door. Clara and Bonnie turned at once to look at Mindy.

"Buck fired him," she said. When Bonnie asked why, Mindy said, "I don't know." She thought back on the conversation. "He said they had a difference of opinion about something, but he didn't say what it was."

"Buck's gotta be crazy," Clara said. "I wonder what the mayor and the rest of the town council are gonna say about it."

"Who's gonna take care of the town after supper when ol' Buck's passed out drunk?" Bonnie was prompted to ask. "I reckon that'll be up to Ralph now," she japed.

Clara gave her a stern look and scolded her. "You ought not joke about Buck like that. Other people hear you talking like that about our sheriff, what would they think?"

"I know," Bonnie replied, "but it ain't like I'd be telling a secret. Hell, everybody in town knows about his problem."

"A lot of people say he's doing better since he hired Flint to help him," Mindy offered.

"That's why I think he's crazy to fire Flint," Clara said.

Chapter 20

"Where's Flint?" Ralph asked. "Ain't he comin' back to the office?"

"Reckon not." Buck handed the plate of food to him and then went over and sat down at his desk.

This was not good news to Ralph. He had been working in the jail long enough to have learned the primary reason Flint was hired as a deputy was to watch the town after Buck retired to his bed . . . and bottle . . . for the night. "If we lock up now, who's gonna take care of the town tonight?"

"I am," Buck replied. "Who'd you think?"

"Yeah, but—" Ralph caught himself before he blurted out what he was thinking. "Is Flint all right?"

"As far as I know," Buck answered. "Look, Flint ain't gonna be on the job for a while, but I'll be here all day and all night to handle any business needs to be took care of. All right?"

"Yes, sir, Sheriff. You're the boss." Ralph sat down on the bench where he usually ate. Out of one corner of his eye, however, he watched the sheriff, afraid he might start showing signs of repeating the prior night's breakdown. Ralph was sure of one thing—the drawer in the desk was empty. Buck had already finished all the whiskey usually in there.

As the clock ticked slowly on the wall, Buck could only sit idle for so long before the craving for alcohol began to gnaw away at his nerves. When it got to be too much, he got up from his chair and announced, "I'm gonna take a walk around the town. Lock the door if you go to bed before I get back." Then he walked out before Ralph had any time for questions.

Ralph got up from the bench and went to the window. "Well, at least he didn't head straight for Jake's Place. Maybe he is just gonna walk the street." Feeling somewhat better, he returned to the bench to finish his supper. "I wish to hell Flint was here, just in case Buck does jump into that bottle again."

If Ralph had remained at the window only a few minutes longer, he would have seen Buck had decided the town looked quiet enough up toward the hotel, crossed the street, and walked back in the direction of the saloon. *After all,* he told himself, *if there's any trouble in town, it'll most likely start at Jake's.*

"Well, howdy, Buck," Jake Rudolph greeted, a little surprised to see him after supper. Unless a meeting or something was going on in the saloon, it being the only place with enough chairs to seat everyone, Buck retired to his house. Thinking he must have forgotten a scheduled meeting, Jake turned to his bartender with a questioning look in his eye.

Rudy met his gaze with the same questioning look.

Turning quickly back toward Buck, Jake asked, "What can I do for you, Sheriff?"

"You can pour me a double shot of whiskey," Buck replied. "I just need to settle my supper down a little."

Rudy poured the whiskey and followed Buck and Jake

back to Buck's usual table. When they sat down, he placed the glass in front of Buck. Thinking of that morning when Buck completely lost control, he hesitated before asking, "You want the bottle?"

He and Jake were both relieved when Buck said no.

"Like I said, I just need a couple of shots to take the edge off."

Feeling somewhat lost in his new status of the unemployed, Flint walked next door to the hotel when he left Clara's. The front porch was empty, so he stepped up and settled himself in the rocking chair closest to one side where he had an unrestricted view of the street south of the hotel. Doc Beard's house was the last building north of the hotel, and didn't need watching. Flint couldn't help wondering why he hadn't ever sat on the porch before. His mind still in a state of flux after his unexpected firing, the porch seemed a quiet place to determine just where he stood. He felt no anger toward the sheriff for firing him. It was more a feeling of astonishment. And a sadness for what he believed was Buck's motive.

Flint was convinced it had taken many years of alcoholic abuse to reduce Buck to his present state of mind. While it seemed he and everybody else had come to accept his part-time guardianship of the town as just "Buck's way" of running the sheriff's office, that was not really the case. For Buck, the last years had been a time of lost pride in a career of keeping the peace. Instead of a lack of common sense, Buck saw the possibility of a challenge from Jesse Slocum as a chance to show his courage had never weakened.

Not if I can help it. Flint genuinely liked Buck Jackson,

and he wanted to save his friend from himself. More than that, Flint still held himself obligated to the citizens of Tinhorn to enforce their laws. They had trusted him to do that, so he intended to keep an eye on the town in his unofficial capacity until the threat from Jesse Slocum was over. *I owe them that much, but it would sure help if I knew for sure Slocum was going to show up here, and if so, when?* Flint remained on the porch for about half an hour before he decided to walk the street.

The town was peaceful enough, he thought as he walked past Jake's Place and the barbershop next to it before reaching the stable. He went inside to check on his horse.

"Evenin', Flint," Lon Blake greeted him. "I just put Buster in a stall for the night. Are you needin' him?"

"No, I ain't goin' anywhere. But I expect I'll take him out and exercise him a little tomorrow. I'm afraid he'll get lazy if I don't." Flint went inside Buster's stall, and the buckskin gelding came to him immediately to get his muzzle and face scratched. Flint spent a little more time checking the condition of his shoes. "I'm gonna make you work a bit in the mornin'," he told the buckskin. After that, he passed a little time talking to Lon before he said goodnight and walked back down the street.

Coming to Jake's Place, he intended to pass it by, but it had become so much a habit to check on the saloon every night he stepped inside to see any faces he had not seen before. He hadn't the slightest idea what Jesse Slocum looked like, but Flint had nothing better to do.

Pausing briefly, he saw no strange faces on the few customers but was surprised to see one familiar face, Buck Jackson's. Flint's first thought was to do an about-face and make an immediate exit, but then he told himsel he was just another patron. He no longer worked for the town of Tinhorn. So he walked over to the bar.

"Evenin', Flint," Rudy greeted him cheerfully. "You lookin' for Buck?"

"Nope," Flint replied. "I just thought I'd take a drink of likker before I hit the hay tonight."

Rudy hesitated before pouring. "You always said you didn't drink when you were workin'. What's the occasion?"

"I ain't workin' tonight," Flint said.

"Is that a fact? You mean Buck's workin' tonight?" When Flint nodded, Rudy said, "So that's why Buck came in after supper. I was wonderin' 'cause he never comes in after supper. After breakfast, but not after supper. You gonna take your drink back to the table with him and Jake?"

"No, I think I'll just stand here at the bar and talk to you. Maybe decide if I want another shot. I'm not gonna be long, anyway. I'm goin' to the house and go to bed." He tossed his whiskey back and set the glass back on the bar. "Boy, that burned pretty good. Better pour me another." He tossed the second one back, then said, "That'll do it for me. Good night, Rudy." Flint put the money on the bar and walked out the door, leaving a puzzled bartender.

Rudy, however, was not the only mystified witness to Flint's brief visit. "Well, now, ain't he actin' funny?" Jake wondered. "I thought he'd come back here. How come he didn't come set down with us."

"I reckon you'd have to ask him that," Buck said. "Maybe it's because he don't work for me no more."

"He quit?" Jake responded, surprised. "Flint Moran quit?"

"Not really," Buck answered stoically. "I fired him."

"Fired him?" Jake repeated. "For what?" He shook his

head, baffled. "You ain't likely to find another 'n can fill his boots."

Buck just shrugged. He agreed totally with Jake's assessment of Flint Moran, but felt he had no choice. With a last chance to prove his courage and maintain his reputation, Buck knew Flint stood in the way.

Jake was not satisfied with the simple declaration that Buck had fired Flint. "What the hell did he do?"

Again, Buck just shrugged.

"He musta done somethin' really big for you to fire him."

"He ain't done nothin' really wrong," Buck finally admitted. "We just had a misunderstandin' and agreed we wouldn't talk about it."

"Well, that sure is a sorry piece of news," Jake declared. "I like Flint. I've always thought he was a fine young man. But I reckon I didn't know him like I thought I did."

Buck felt he had to defend Flint. "Now, there ain't nothin' wrong with Flint Moran, Jake. He is a fine young man, but I told you, we just had a difference of opinion on how something oughta be handled."

"And you fired him for that?" Jake asked.

"I didn't come here to talk about the business of the sheriff's office," Buck finally blurted. "Pour me another shot. I've gotta get back to the jail."

As was his habit, Flint awoke early the next morning, but instead of going to the sheriff's office, he waited in his room until he heard sounds of Myrna bumping around in the kitchen. Then he went to offer his help with firing up the kitchen stove, startling the short, pleasant-looking woman as she bent over the wood box outside the kitchen door.

"I'm sorry, Myrna. Seems like I'm always sneakin' up on you, doesn't it? Here, let me get that wood." He took her elbow and helped her stand upright.

"Flint," she exclaimed. "I declare, I might have to nail some taps on your boots, so I can hear you coming. Whoever built this wood box made it too tall. Whenever I use up half the wood, the rest is so far down in this box I have to stand on my head to reach the pile."

"Let me get it," Flint said. "I'll get your fire started, then I'll go fill this box up to the top so you can reach more wood when you need it. It'll cost you, though. I'm gonna expect a cup of coffee when I finish."

She laughed, delighted. "All right. It's a deal. Are you having breakfast with us this morning?"

"Yes, ma'am, I surely am," he replied, following her into the kitchen with an armload of firewood. He laid it down then took kindling out of a small box by the kitchen door. "Looks like I better cut you some kindlin' too."

"You can just let John take care of that," she said, referring to Hannah's thirteen-year-old son. "That's his job."

Flint set the kindling, then laid some smaller pieces of the firewood over it. "Does that look like you like it?" She said it was perfect, so he struck a match and lit the kindling. Then he went out the back door to split more wood for the wood box. Since he was in no particular hurry, he took his time to split up the sawed portions of oak trunks into sticks of firewood until he had plenty to fill the wood box over the top. By the time he was finished, Myrna had a fresh cup of coffee waiting for him and her oven was hot enough to bake biscuits.

"Are you in a hurry to get up to the jail?" Myrna asked when she poured his coffee. "'Cause I can rustle you up some eggs and sausage, and let you get started while the biscuits are baking."

"No, ma'am. I'm in no hurry. You just go about your usual routine. This cup of coffee will do me just fine till you're ready with everybody's breakfast." Flint thought for a second, then said, "I would like to have one of those biscuits when they come right outta the oven."

She laughed and replied, "I might have one of 'em with you, soon as they're done." She went about the business of frying a generous quantity of sausage and putting on a kettle of grits. When the biscuits were done, she took them out of the oven and, except for the one she took for herself and the two she took for Flint, put them into her warmer oven. She broke three eggs into the pan she'd fried the sausage in and scrambled them for him. A couple of minutes later, she placed a plate before him with his breakfast on it. Only then did she sit down across the table from him with her coffee and biscuit.

"It's nice to have your company this morning," she told him. "How come you're not rushing off to the jail like usual?"

"To tell you the truth, Myrna, I've been fired." He opened his vest to show he was no longer wearing a badge. He had no reason to keep people from finding out, for they would soon realize it to be a fact. And it was definitely a fact.

His confession caught Myrna with her cup just an inch away from her mouth, and it remained in that position for several long moments before she was able to take a sip of coffee and replace the cup on the table. "When?" she asked, totally surprised. "Why?" she asked before he had time to answer her first question. Like most of the citizens of Tinhorn, she believed hiring Flint Moran was the smartest thing the town council ever did.

"Yesterday. As to why, Buck and I had a little difference of opinion on something, so he fired me."

She didn't know what to say. Finally she declared,

"Well, I don't believe that big ox knew what he was doing. When he thinks about it, he'll be wanting you back."

"Maybe so," Flint replied cheerfully. "Until he does, I'll be enjoyin' more breakfasts with you, like this."

That served to remind her of something she was going to warn him about. "I know I told you I would warn you if Hannah's niece, Nancy, was coming to visit. You've been coming home so late and leaving so early, I never got a chance to tell you till now."

"Yes, ma'am, I reckon that's so. When is she comin'?"

"Yesterday," Myrna said sheepishly.

Flint almost spilled his coffee. "She's here now?"

Myrna nodded and strained to smile.

"I expect I'd best get along outta everybody's way." Flint gulped down the last of his coffee and got to his feet. "Thanks for the breakfast, Myrna. If they ask about me, be sure and tell 'em I'm unemployed." He picked up his gun belt from the back of the chair and strapped it on as he went out the back door. Picking up his rifle propped against the porch railing, he went down the steps.

Although unsure how he was going to spend the whole day without colliding with Buck, he planned to spend the day in town. Flint had no intention of letting a vengeful escaped convict ride into town and shoot the sheriff. He didn't have to be a deputy to defend the town's sheriff.

He went around the boarding house to the front yard before crossing to the other side of the street and walking the short distance to the stables. He couldn't help a wry smile when he thought of Hannah Green's complaint—when the wind came from the northeast she was always reminded where the stables were located.

"Mornin', Flint," Lon Blake sang out. "You said you'd be early."

"Mornin', Lon. Yeah, I ain't goin' anywhere much. I

reckon I just wanna make sure Buster don't forget the weight of my fanny on his back." Flint took his time saddling the buckskin gelding, thinking how it was likely to be a long day. Remembering the vantage point from the night before, he couldn't think of a better spot to watch the street than the hotel porch, and decided to park himself in that rocking chair again. He climbed up into the saddle and slow walked Buster down the street.

By the time he reached the hotel, he had decided to make sure Gilbert Smith, the owner of the hotel, didn't object to his camping out on the porch all day. Flint left Buster loosely tied at the side of the hotel by the water trough and went inside. Fred Johnson had just taken over the front desk from the night clerk when Flint walked in.

"Flint," Fred exclaimed as if surprised to see him. "Good morning."

From Fred's reaction, Flint figured he already knew. "Clara told you?"

"Yeah," Fred replied, obviously uncomfortable about it. "I mean, I heard. Flint, what the hell?"

"Well, let me say it wasn't because of anything I did wrong. It was just that we didn't see eye to eye on a particular subject that's important to Buck. To settle the difference of opinion, he fired me. He's my boss. He can do that. Now the reason I came in here this mornin' was I wanted to see if you or Mr. Smith have any objection to me sittin' on your front porch. It's the best spot to keep an eye on the whole street without being too obvious."

"But you aren't a deputy anymore, are you?" Fred asked, confused.

"No, I'm not, but I am a concerned citizen of Tinhorn, and I think it would be a good idea to kinda help the sheriff out, if he needs it. Just keeping an eye on the town, pretty much like it was before I was fired. I just ain't gettin' paid for it."

Fred was more concerned than ever now. "Maybe I better wait till Mr. Smith gets up and let you talk to him. Do I need to be getting worried?"

"No, no," Flint quickly tried to calm him. "There ain't no danger to the hotel or the town. I just wanna make sure nobody causes Buck any trouble."

"But why do you think you need to guard the hotel?" Fred asked.

"I don't wanna guard the hotel," Flint insisted. "I just wanna sit on the porch 'cause it's the best place to watch the whole street. I ain't worried about any harm comin' to the hotel. Matter of fact, I won't be here all day. I'll be comin' and goin' a lot, I'm sure."

"I'll have to tell Mr. Smith," Fred said.

"Sure," Flint replied. "Just tell him I'd like to keep it quiet why I'm out there. 'Preciate it, Fred." Flint walked back out the front door and sat down in the rocking chair, wondering if it would have been better to not ask for permission to sit on the porch.

He settled back in his chair, and when he saw people going into Clara's Kitchen, he looked at his pocket watch. *Six o'clock,* he thought, *right on time.* She'll be open till eight.

He looked at his watch again when he saw Buck coming up the street. *Seven o'clock,* he noted to himself.

It was after eight when Buck left the dining room and walked past his office to Jake's Place.

Poor Ralph, Flint thought. B*uck sure took his time eating breakfast.* He shook his head impatiently. *And he ain't carryin' a plate for Ralph.* Since Buck was heading for the saloon, it appeared he had fallen back into his old routine of having a few drinks of whiskey right after his breakfast. He used to go to Jake's Place and Rena would cook him breakfast. Flint wondered why he went to Clara's instead, then figured it was because he had to get a plate for Ralph, a plate he obviously just forgot. Knowing Buck would be in the saloon for a while, Flint figured he had time to hustle a plate of breakfast down to the jail for Ralph.

Not bothering to take his horse, he walked next door to Clara's and tapped on the pane.

When Clara saw who it was, she opened the door at once. "Flint! You almost missed it. Come on in."

"No, thanks, Clara. I've already had breakfast. I just thought I'd check to see if you fixed up a plate for Ralph."

"Yes, we did. Then Buck walked right out without it. Mindy was going to carry it down there."

"She needn't bother. Just give it to me and I'll take it to Ralph."

She turned her head at once and called out, "Mindy, bring Ralph's plate! Flint's gonna take it." She turned her attention back to Flint then. "Are you back working with Buck?"

"No, I'm just doin' a favor for Ralph." His answer obviously disappointed her.

In a few seconds, Mindy was at the door with the plate of food. "Flint!" she exclaimed when she saw him. "I had to grab it out of Margaret's hand! She was just getting ready to dump it in with the scraps for the hogs. Did you have breakfast?"

"Yes, I did, and I'm glad you saved Ralph's. I'll tell him you saved it for him." He reached for the plate, but she didn't give it to him right away.

"I can carry it down there for you."

"That's awful nice of you, Mindy, but I think you'd best just let me take it to the jail." He was getting a little impatient to get to the sheriff's office before Buck came back from Jake's. "I figure I'll be back here for dinner," he said, remembering the niece Nancy was at Hannah's.

That brought a smile to her face. "Good. We were afraid we wouldn't see you here anymore."

"Buck just fired me as a deputy," Flint remarked. "He didn't run me outta town. I'll be back."

"And I'll continue to give you a discount on all your meals here," Clara volunteered. "That big ox is gonna realize he's made a mistake, and he'll be after you to put that badge back on. You'll see."

"Why, thank you, ma'am," Flint replied. "That's mighty nice of you to do that. I 'preciate it." He did appreciate it, but without a job, his money would soon be running out, discount or not.

Chapter 21

Flint walked into the sheriff's office to find Ralph sitting on his usual bench, his head hanging low, knowing Buck had forgotten his breakfast. When he heard the door open, he looked up, and when he saw who it was, he jumped to his feet.

"I got something here I thought you could use," Flint said, holding the plate out toward the startled man.

"Flint! What are you doin' here?"

"Bringin' you your breakfast. Figured Buck musta forgot it."

"Yeah, I saw him out the window, goin' to Jake's, and he weren't carryin' my breakfast. I won't tell him you brought it to me."

"I don't care whether you do or not," Flint said. "I was just doin' a friend a favor. Ain't no law against that. I expect I'd best go now and let you eat. He might not like it if he comes back and finds me here."

"He might not be right back," Ralph told him. "He said he was gonna ride up the river to check on somethin'." When Flint asked what Buck was going to check on, Ralph couldn't say. "He just said he was gonna check on somethin'." Ralph shook his head and gave Flint a worried look. "I wish you was back here, Flint. He don't act the same since you left."

"I'll be close by if you need me," Flint assured him. For a moment, he considered telling Ralph what was eating at Buck but decided it better he didn't. "He didn't say what he was gonna check on up the river, huh?"

Ralph shook his head slowly.

Unable to think of anything Buck might have been referring to, Flint was surprised to hear Buck was going to leave town at all, since he was so dead set on making himself available for Jesse Slocum's pleasure. "I'd best be on my way." He opened the door and paused to say, "Mindy was fixin' to bring you your breakfast when I went by there."

The simple expression on Ralph's face showed that possibility pleased him.

Flint glanced across the street toward Jake's Place but saw no sign of Buck. Walking back to his lookout post on the hotel porch, Flint still wondered what Buck was going to check on up the river. When it came to his responsibility, Buck's philosophy had always been a pretty firm lack of interest in anything that happened outside the city limits of Tinhorn, which just gave Flint one more thing to speculate upon. He settled once again in his rocking chair, glad none of the hotel's guests had the same idea.

It wasn't long before he heard the hotel door open behind him. Ignoring that, he continued to watch the saloon until he was startled by the appearance of a coffee cup before his eyes.

"I didn't mean to make you jump," she said. "It's a good thing I didn't spill it 'cause it's fresh hot out of a new pot."

He looked up to see Mindy's smiling face.

"Fred said you were sitting out here on the porch, so I thought you might like a cup of coffee."

"Why, yes, ma'am, I surely would," he responded. "That's mighty nice of you to go to the trouble of bringing it out here to me."

"It was no trouble," she insisted. "I hope you enjoy it. I'll wait while you drink it, so I can take the cup back." She giggled and confessed, "We're cleaning up the dining room and I said I was going to have a cup of coffee outside."

"You did? Well, I'll share it with you." He offered the cup.

Mindy shook her head. "No, thanks. I can't drink it black like that with no sugar."

"Well, it was mighty nice of you to bring me coffee. I'll go ahead and drink it down, so Clara won't think you're gone too long."

"You take your time."

Flint caught sight of Buck coming out of the saloon and heading for the stable. Evidently Ralph was right, Buck was going somewhere. Or maybe he just wanted to have his horse handy.

Realizing Mindy was wondering where his mind had gone to, he looked back at her and smiled. "I think I may have to go somewhere in a few minutes, myself." He gulped the rest of the coffee down and handed her the cup. "Thanks again, Mindy. That sure enough hit the spot."

"I'm glad," she said. "Are you coming to Clara's for dinner?"

"I'm definitely plannin' to," he replied as he got up from the rocker and held the door for her. He figured whatever Buck was going to check on wouldn't keep him from coming back for dinner.

She smiled up at him again as she went through the doorway. He closed the door behind her and went immediately back to the side of the porch. After a short amount of time, Buck walked out of the stable, leading his saddled horse behind him. Ralph was definitely right. Buck was going somewhere. Were it not for the fact he had the crazy notion of a duel, Flint wouldn't even think about following him, but he was curious enough he couldn't resist. He ran around to the side of the hotel and climbed onto his horse. While he watched from the edge of the porch, Buck climbed onto his horse, wheeled it around, and started toward the north end of town and the hotel.

Flint wheeled Buster around and rode back along the side of the hotel, past the watering trough to the back of the building, where he turned the buckskin around again and stopped at the corner. He waited there, and in a few seconds, he saw the sheriff ride by the hotel and continue out past Doc Beard's house on the road to Tyler.

"There ain't nothin' up that road till you get to Tyler," Flint said aloud.

Waiting until Buck disappeared around a bend in the road, Flint nudged Buster and followed. With so many tracks on the road he didn't even think about trying to track him. Holding Buster out of sight at the curve in the road, he waited for Buck to disappear again before continuing. Already he was telling himself following Buck farther was pointless.

When Flint reached a stretch of road that ran straight for over three-quarters of a mile, and there was no sign of Buck, he stopped. Certain Buck hadn't suddenly gained that much distance on him, he thought, *He must have turned off the road, and I just missed it . . . or he suspects somebody's following him and he's waiting in ambush up ahead.* As that thought came to mind, Flint definitely did not want Buck to know he was following him. Deciding he had nothing to gain, Flint turned Buster around and headed back toward Tinhorn.

He had not traveled fifty yards when he heard a gunshot, a pistol judging by the sound, from the direction of the river. A couple more shots sounded, then a lull in the shooting was followed by a barrage of shots. Figuring it was a gun battle on the riverbank, he had to find out what was going on, and if Buck needed help. Flint pressed Buster for more speed and the buckskin loped back the way they had come, traveling about one hundred yards before Flint saw the path where Buck had left the road. *Should have noticed it when I went by before,* Flint told himself.

He reined Buster back to a walk again and followed the path toward the river. As he neared a thicker growth of trees along the river, the shooting started up again. Close, he left Buster in the trees, drew his rifle from the saddle sling, and continued cautiously on foot.

Drawing closer, he realized a definite pattern to the shooting. Six shots, then a lull, then six shots again. And he suddenly understood what he was hearing. Immediately moving closer to the river he could see the sandy bank and the lone shooter. It struck him as a sad, almost pathetic sight. Buck Jackson going through the motions of a fast draw, then emptying his six-gun at a tree on a little island in the middle of the river.

The insanity of Buck's intention . . . and the stupidity of his quest . . . caused Flint to become angry. Even though Buck hit the defenseless tree most of the time, his *fast draw* could be timed by a sundial. Maybe in his younger years, Buck's draw was fluid and quick. Flint couldn't say, but seeing the jerky, cumbersome efforts he was witnessing, he wouldn't give Buck much chance against anyone. How much his addiction to whiskey contributed to the deterioration of his reflexes was hard to say, but it was safe to say it had not helped his condition.

Having seen all he needed to see, Flint stepped away

from the riverbank, picked up Buster's reins, and led him back to the road. Hearing another cylinder of .44 bullets emptied on the river, he climbed up into the saddle and headed to town, determined more than ever to prevent any showdown between Buck and Jesse Slocum.

Riding into Tinhorn, he walked Buster down to the stable and left him in Lon's corral. On the street everything looked the same as when he had left it a short time before. No horses were tied up in front of the saloon, so it was unlikely Jesse Slocum or any other stranger had come into town while Flint had followed Buck and seen the preparation for his moment of glory.

Taking his time walking up the street to reclaim his rocking chair on the hotel porch, Flint couldn't think of doing anything else that would be useful. He just planned to sit there and watch the people who showed up in town until time for the dining room to open.

Another hour had passed when he caught sight of Buck returning to town. Watching as he rode past, it appeared Buck failed to notice Flint sitting on the porch. Buck hadn't looked toward the hotel but seemed to be looking at the post office across the street. Flint wondered if the big man had had any change of mind after his practice session by the river. He was probably counting a great deal on the fact that Jesse Slocum had spent the last five years in prison and had not had a gun in his hand. No doubt he would be rusty.

Even so, as Flint recalled the picture of Buck practicing on the riverbank, he was willing to put his money on anyone facing him in a fast draw competition. As those thoughts laid heavily on his mind, he realized it was time for the dining room to open. He had seen no sign of Buck in the street since he'd left his horse at the stable and gone into his office.

Good, Flint thought, *I'll get in the dining room and sit down as far away from his table as I can.*

"Good afternoon, Flint," Clara greeted him cordially when he walked into the dining room. "We missed you this morning at breakfast. I'm glad you haven't stopped coming to eat with us." She appeared very conscious of the manner in which she received him.

To Flint she seemed almost uncertain if she was supposed to pick a side, his or Buck's. Then it occurred to him what that was all about. He unbuckled his gun belt, took it over to the designated table, and left it there. Clara looked relieved at once.

"Why would I stop comin' here?" he asked. "This is the best place in town to eat. If you're worried about me and Buck, there ain't gonna be any trouble between us. I like to think we're still friends. Hope he feels the same way. But to make it easy on you, I'll sit at that last table in the corner." He pointed to the opposite the side of the room from Buck's usual table.

"You sit where you like. Mindy will be right with you."

As he went to the table he had indicated, Mindy was there with a cup of coffee before he sat down. Far from dense, he knew the reason Bonnie never seemed to wait on him. He was Mindy's customer, and was sure it was by her choice. Actually he wanted no one but her to wait on him but was careful never to open that door, not even ajar, because he could not support a family on a deputy's salary. And now, he didn't even have that.

He believed that if he truly cared for her, he would hope

she'd meet some young man who could support her and take her out of the business of waiting on tables. He never figured himself as a man short on courage, but knew he didn't have the grit to tell Mindy they had no future together, nor the confidence to tell her they did.

"What are you concentrating so hard on?"

He startled at her question.

"That's the second time today I've made you jump." She placed a plate of beef stew on the table and gave him a big smile. "What were you thinking just now?"

"I was thinkin' I oughta get a cowbell and hang it around your neck, so I can hear you comin'."

"You really know how to flatter a girl," she came back, pretending to be hurt.

"I'm still tryin' to learn to keep my mouth shut," he confessed.

Before she came back with a response to that, Buck walked in the door, which caused her to inhale sharply. Mindy, like Clara and Bonnie, could only speculate on the real cause of Flint's firing, for they were all agreed that neither Flint nor Buck had told the true story behind it. Buck exchanged a few words with Clara, then walked back to his regular table.

From across the room he nodded in Flint's direction. "Flint."

Flint nodded and returned the acknowledgment. "Buck."

From that point on, throughout the dinner hour, no more words passed between them, which served to frustrate the women no end. Buck seemed to be at his neighborly best with all the other regulars who came in to eat. To Flint, it seemed if he didn't know better, he would have thought the big bear of a man was running for political office.

Feeling no need to linger in the dining room, Flint told Mindy he'd had more than enough coffee and he got up to leave. "Maybe," he said in answer to her question if he was going to be back for supper. "I'm not sure right now." He went to the register, paid Clara for his dinner, then went over to the table to pick up his weapon. While he was strapping it on, Bonnie walked up and handed him a covered plate of food.

"What's this?"

"It's Ralph's dinner," Bonnie said, looking at him as if he should know. "Buck said to give it to you to take back. And he said for you to wait there. He's got some things to talk over." She handed him a smaller plate then, also covered with a cloth. "And he said don't eat all the biscuits."

Flint turned and found Buck looking at him. When their eyes met, Buck nodded and grinned, then turned his attention to the stew on his plate. Not quite sure what to make of the strange change in Buck's behavior, Flint figured at least Ralph would get his dinner today. Carrying the two plates, he went out the door.

Once again, Ralph was happy to see him when he showed up at the office bearing food.

Flint couldn't help but wonder what good could come of waiting for Buck. Then he remembered Buck had also said, "Don't eat all the biscuits." So he removed the cloth over the biscuits and saw only two biscuits on the plate. The third lump was his deputy's badge.

"Looks like you're back on the job," Ralph commented happily.

"Looks like," Flint agreed. "I don't know, though. This badge was on your biscuit plate. Maybe you're his new deputy. Yeah, and Bonnie told me Buck said for me not to eat the biscuits. Maybe they're all for you, Deputy Cox," Flint japed.

"Oh, Lordy, I hope not," Ralph groaned. "I can't be no lawman. My daddy and my granddaddy would be turning over in their graves. My whole family would be shamed."

The simple man seemed truly upset, so Flint told him he was just japing. For whatever reason, Buck was reinstating him as deputy.

"Go ahead and enjoy that stew. You're still an outlaw, even though you're a reformed one."

It wasn't a long wait until Buck showed up and sent Ralph into the cell room to finish his dinner.

"I 'preciate you waitin' for me, Flint. I see you found your badge. I'm hopin' you'll pin it on after you hear what I wanna say. First off, you're the best damn deputy any sheriff could have. My mind was messed up, probably from all the likker I drank. I don't know. But the dang-fool idea in my head was all wrong. You kept telling me what my responsibility was—to uphold the law and arrest Jesse Slocum if he shows up in this town. It wasn't for me to contribute to the lawlessness. So, I'm offerin' you my apology. I was wrong to fire you. Even though I don't think I meant it for good, I was wrong to do it and I want you back on the job. We'll throw Mr. Jesse Slocum in jail if he comes in our town." Buck paused to watch Flint pin his badge on silently.

The sheriff extended his hand then, and Flint shook it.

All smiles, Buck confessed. "I took my .44 up on the river to see how fast I could draw and fire." He shook his head and chuckled. "I wonder if I was ever really as fast as I thought when I was a young man. Either way, it sure has got old with the rest of me. Hell, one time this mornin', I damn near shot myself in the leg."

"Buck, I knew you'd do the right thing when the time came. You know, it'd be a pretty big thing if the little town of Tinhorn was to capture an escaped killer like Jesse Slocum and return him to prison. That would sure add a lot to your reputation as a lawman."

"I reckon it would at that," Buck replied. "We'll keep a sharp eye out for Mr. Slocum and give him a real Tinhorn welcome, if he shows up here."

Their conversation was interrupted as Harvey Baxter walked into the office. He seemed startled seeing the sheriff and his deputy talking.

"Mr. Mayor," Buck greeted him. "What can I do for you?"

Baxter hesitated before answering, obviously not sure what to say. "To tell you the truth," he finally said, "I wasn't expecting to find both of you here."

"Why is that, Mr. Mayer?" Buck asked, deciding to bluff it.

"I was told by Gilbert Smith you had fired Flint, and we no longer had a deputy sheriff. Naturally, I was concerned. Thought I'd come by, see if we've got any kind of trouble the town council needs to talk about."

"I shoulda known one of 'em would tell Mr. Smith about it, since he owns the hotel," Buck replied immediately. "I'm sorry it caused you to worry, Harvey. I reckon I didn't know that little joke could get outta hand. Flint and I were just havin' a little fun with the women in the dinin' room. Tell you the truth, I've been havin' some trouble with my innards the last couple of days, and it was causin' me some big discomfort. Well, Flint was japin' me about it, said he was gonna set at a different table when we went to eat dinner, picked up his plate, and moved across the room.

"'Course the gals in the dinin' room wanted to know why, and I told 'em I fired him. Flint didn't tell 'em no different. I shoulda squashed it right then, shoulda known they'd tell everybody I fired Flint. They shoulda known we was japin' 'cause Flint didn't go nowhere."

He paused and looked over at Flint. "'Course, it didn't help none when Flint came in the dinin' room today and took his gun off before he sat down." Buck shook his head and apologized. "I'm dang sorry if we caused you to worry about it."

"You two oughta be ashamed of yourselves. Those ladies were truly upset," Baxter said. Then he shook his head and laughed, relieved to find no sign of trouble from his law enforcement department. "Everything's running smoothly, right?"

"Like a brand-new railroad watch," Buck told him.

When the mayor went out the door, Buck looked at Flint and grinned.

"I've gotta give you credit," Flint said. "You came up with one helluva story."

Although they didn't express it, both men were glad Baxter had accepted Buck's story. The dining room wasn't the only place either lawman had told someone about the firing.

Chapter 22

The object of Buck and Flint's concern was about one day shy of Tinhorn.

Leading the paint behind him, Jesse Slocum turned up the path to a frame farmhouse and barn, just off the road to Crockett, Texas, and rode up to the back door of the house. As he stepped down from the saddle, the kitchen door opened.

A middle-aged woman stepped partially outside. "How do," she said, not recognizing the stranger. "You lookin' for Dewey?"

"That's right," Jesse answered. "Is he here?"

"Him and Calvin are workin' in the cornfield down by the creek," Rose Welch replied. "What is it you're wantin' with him?"

"Well, it don't have to be him, I reckon. Is somebody else here I can talk to?"

"There ain't nobody else here. What is it you're wantin' to talk about?"

"I got some deer meat that's gonna turn bad in a day or so, and I'd like for somebody to look at it and tell me if it's still all right. If it is, I'm hopin' to trade some of it for some flour and coffee."

"Who in the world told you to come to see Dewey about it?" Rose asked, thinking the man a bit touched in the head. "You ain't that far from town. You need to take it to the store in Crockett. We ain't got stuff to trade for deer meat. You'd best take it into town. They'll help you there."

"Yes, ma'am," Jesse said politely. "I'll take it to town. Can you tell if the meat's still good or not?"

"Yes, I can tell if it's spoiled," she said, thinking anything to send him on his way. She went down the steps to the deer hide bundle tied to the saddle on the paint horse. Quickly pulling up a corner of the hide, she sniffed the bundle. "It's on the way, but it'll be all right long as you cook it tonight." She turned to face him only to catch the full force of his fist against her jaw, knocking her to the ground.

He reached down, grabbed her blouse, and picked her up on to her feet. Shocked and dazed by the blow, she could stand only because he supported her.

"Do you wanna die?" His mouth touched her ear. "If you wanna live, you take me to where Dewey keeps his money. If you don't, I'll choke the life outta you till you're dead. Get me the money and I'll let you live. I just want the money. The sooner you get it for me, the sooner I'll be gone. But you better hurry. If Dewey and Calvin come back to the house before I'm gone, I'll shoot both of 'em. Then I'll take care of you."

She gasped desperately, finally regaining sense enough to think. "In the parlor."

Supporting her with one arm wrapped tightly under her arm, Jesse dragged her into the house and to the parlor.

She pointed to the sideboard. "In the drawer. I'll get it." And she started to reach for the drawer.

"The hell you will," he said, tightening his arm until

she couldn't breathe. He released her then to collapse on the floor, gasping for air. He opened the drawer. "Well lookee here. Was you gonna use this on me?" He held up the single-action Army Model Colt, tucked it into his belt, and opened the metal box the gun had been resting on. "You folks ain't saved a helluva lot." He made a quick count. "About fifty-five dollars, ain't hardly like robbin' the bank, is it?"

He stood over her for a long moment. "What to do with you now," he mused aloud. "I believe you woulda tried to use that gun on me."

She just gazed up helplessly at him.

"You been so nice about helpin' me out, I don't reckon I'll kill you. But I'm gonna have to tie you up, so you don't go runnin' to get your husband. Come on, get up from there." He grabbed the back of her blouse, picked her up off the floor, and walked her into the bedroom then shoved her into a chair beside the bed. Finding several belts in the dresser, he used them to tie her hands behind her back. Next, he threw the quilt back and ripped the sheet off the bed, twisted it into a rope, and tied her to the chair. He saw no need for a gag, figuring she could scream until she was too hoarse to make a sound, and no one would hear her.

Finished, he said, "I expect you're liable to get a good whuppin' for not havin' supper ready when ol' Dewey comes in. I believe in bein' fair about it so I'm gonna leave you about half of that deer meat out there. Won't take a long time to roast it over a fire."

He paused at the kitchen door to take a good look out at the barnyard to make sure Dewey and Calvin hadn't quit work early. Satisfied they hadn't, he stepped down into the yard, climbed into the saddle, and trotted down the path to the road to Crockett. He did turn toward town but didn't stay on the road very long. Leaving it several miles short of Crockett, his intention was to ride around it. He would take no chance of Dewey showing up to catch him in town. Although anxious to buy a drink with the money Dewey left for him, he would wait to buy it in the town of Tinhorn.

Although Buck was the only one who could identify Jesse Slocum, both lawmen knew five years in prison could change a man's appearance quite a bit. Buck wasn't ready to guarantee recognition on sight, which left Flint to speculate on any stranger who showed up. Fortunately, no strangers showed up in town for a few days, meaning things were almost back to the normal peace usually enjoyed in Tinhorn.

The lawmen were still catching some grief from the ladies in Clara's for what they considered a cruel joke, but Ralph, having been on the verge of a nervous breakdown, was happy again. The folks at Hannah's boarding house were undecided if it had been a joke on the town or not.

Maintaining she never believed Buck would fire Flint under any circumstances, Hannah finally nailed Flint down for Sunday dinner before her niece was set to return to Fort Worth, and asked him to take Nancy to the train station Monday morning.

The Sunday dinner was not something he looked forward to, but having dodged Hannah's plans so often, he decided he owed it to her.

Not surprising, Hannah had arranged the chairs so he and Nancy sat next to each other, but Flint *was* surprised to find Nancy quite cheerful and charming. Adding to her good points, she was a very attractive woman. By the time he went to bed Sunday night, he held quite a different opinion of the young lady.

Monday morning, he hitched up Hannah's buggy and drove niece Nancy to the train station, getting to know her better. Away from the gang at the boarding house, she was more inclined to talk about her personal life.

By the time they pulled up at the station, he knew most of Nancy's private thoughts. He knew she was desperately in love with a young lawyer in Fort Worth who would be at the station to meet her. She had kept that a secret from Hannah because her aunt hated lawyers.

"She thinks they are all schemers, out to swindle you out of your life savings," Nancy said.

Flint laughed. "I reckon there's a lot of 'em that are. Sounds like you've found one that ain't."

"I was going to tell Aunt Hannah while I was here but lost my nerve," Nancy confessed. "She's so worried because I'm seventeen and haven't married yet. I guess I'll take the coward's way and tell her in a letter." She opened her purse, took out a ring, and slipped it onto her finger. Then she held it up for Flint to admire. "He asked, 'Will you,' and I said, 'Hell, yes.' We've already set the date."

"Well, let me be the first in this part of the territory to wish you the best of everything."

He waited with her until the train pulled in, then wished her a safe journey home.

"I've enjoyed talking to you, Flint," she said as she stepped up on the train. "I wish I had been able to spend more time with you. It would have made the trip more fun."

"Glad you think so," he replied. "I enjoyed gettin' to know you, too. I think that lawyer fiancé of yours has got himself a real prize."

"Thank you, kind sir," she said sweetly, then went in to find a seat.

After parking Hannah's buggy in the barn and leaving her horse in the corral, Flint went inside the house to find Hannah.

She was waiting for him and asked, "Did you take the opportunity to get to know Nancy?"

"Yes, ma'am, I sure did," he answered.

"Isn't she a real sweetheart?"

"Yes, ma'am, she sure is."

"She's the kind of girl who will make a young man happy."

"I reckon so. I wouldn't be surprised if you hear she's found one she wants, any day now. Yes, ma'am, it was a pleasure meetin' her. Now, I expect I'd best get myself to the jail before Buck thinks I've quit."

As he walked out of the yard, he thought, *I wonder if it would help if I told her what the deputy sheriff of Tinhorn's salary is?*

"I was wonderin' what happened to you this mornin'," Buck said when Flint walked into the office.

"I had to take Hannah's niece to the train this mornin'," Flint said.

"Ralph said he saw you and a woman drive by the office in a buggy. I thought he was just out of his head, but I reckon he ain't as crazy as I thought." Buck chuckled. "I hope Mindy didn't see you drive by the hotel with that gal in the buggy."

"If she had, I doubt she'da given two cents' worth of thought about it. About the same as Hannah's niece." Flint changed the subject. "Don't reckon you've seen any strangers in town this mornin'."

"Nope, but the day's still early," Buck said. "That telegram said he killed a guard and escaped a work detail. Didn't say anything about anybody else helped him escape. I expect it was just Jesse on his own, but maybe he ain't as hot about gettin' even with me as he was when I shot his brother, and he ain't thinkin' about comin' to settle with me first. You'd think he wouldn't go where everybody is expectin' him to show up. More likely, he's workin' on not gettin' caught and sent back to prison. He'd head for Injun Territory where most of the outlaws hide out. Don't make no difference if he comes here or hightails it for the Oklahoma line. He's gonna have to get himself a horse and supplies and that might take him a little time."

It might have taken Jesse Slocum a greater amount of time before he was ready to ride into Tinhorn, had he not been fortunate to happen upon the Wilson brothers. Thanks to them, he'd picked up two good horses as well as the answer to his immediate needs for food. Next on his path, he picked up a little pocket money from the dresser drawer in Dewey Welch's bedroom, thanks to his wife's cooperation. It was not a great deal of money but was enough to buy him a few drinks and something to eat before he proceeded to finish the job he and Zack gone to Tinhorn five years ago to accomplish—rob the Tinhorn Bank. They'd also planned to shoot down Sheriff Buck Jackson when he came to prevent the robbery.

Luck had been with Jackson on that day.

Facing the big lawman at point-blank range, Jesse's gun had misfired. He was arrested and sent to prison. The odds of that happening again were astronomical, but he was carrying both six-guns that had belonged to the Wilson brothers, just in case. Only one thing worried him—whether or not Buck Jackson was still the sheriff of Tinhorn. And that was on his mind when he rode into the town.

He wasn't sure what time it was when he rode past the stable on the south end of the street, but daylight was already failing, and the owner of the stable was transferring horses from the corral to the stalls inside. He remembered a dining room next to the hotel, but he figured it was too late for that. His best bet would be a saloon. Heading to Jake's Place, diagonally across the street from the sheriff's office, he thought of the possibility of Buck Jackson walking in for a drink.

If that happened, Jesse was not at all undecided about what he would do. He would shoot him. Perhaps without warning, although he preferred to have the sheriff know who his executioner was. If that happened, it would cancel his plan to rob the bank. But he felt the bank owed him money for the time he had spent in prison simply because of a misfire. First he wanted to know if Buck was still the sheriff. If he wasn't, Jesse needed to know where to look for him.

He pulled the bay up to the hitching rail in front of the saloon and stepped down. A thought suddenly crossed his mind. Some folks in town who had witnessed his arrest five years ago might recognize him. Knowing he looked a lot different from how he looked back then, he discarded that as unlikely. His hair was longer, down to his shoulders, and he was wearing Arthur Welch's clothes and his hat with the fancy silver band around the crown. So, feeling fairly confident, he tied his horses at the rail and walked into the saloon and up to the bar.

"Whaddle it be?" Rudy asked.

"I ain't had a drink of rye whiskey in a while," Jesse replied, "and I need somethin' to eat. Looks like I got here too late to get supper in that place by the hotel."

"You must be a stranger here if you didn't know you can always get somethin' to eat in Jake's Place. Rena's always got somethin' cooked up for when some of our customers get to drinkin' too much on an empty belly." Rudy poured him a shot of whiskey. "This your first time to visit Tinhorn?"

Jesse tossed his whiskey back and motioned for another. "I was here once before, but it was several years back. Looks like it's growed a little."

"Little by little, more folks are finding us. You want me to tell Rena to fix you a plate?"

"Yeah, tell her I'm hungry. What is it tonight?"

"I don't know," Rudy said. "It's early yet, so ain't nobody ordered supper so far. It'll be fit to eat, whatever it is. That's the thing, supper here is chuckwagon style. You don't get no choices. She just fixes one thing, but it'll be good and it don't cost you but a quarter."

"It'll be all right," Jesse said, "long as it ain't deer meat. That's all I've et for the last couple of days."

"Set yourself down at a table if you want. I'll go tell Rena to bring you some supper. You want some coffee with it, or you want another shot of rye?"

"Both," Jesse said.

Rudy poured him another shot, then went to the kitchen door to tell Rena she had a customer while Jesse carried his drink to a table against the far wall.

He cocked his chair a little to make it easier to look over the patrons then sat down. Wondering if Buck had changed much in the five-year period, Jesse scanned the room and felt sure the big lawman was not there. In a moment, Rudy came from the kitchen carrying a cup of coffee and placed it on the table.

Before he could return to the bar Jesse asked him a question. "Say, is Buck Jackson still the sheriff here?"

"He sure is," Rudy replied. "Do you know Buck?"

"No, I've just heard of him, that's all."

"If he was in here, I'd point him out to you, but he ain't here. He don't come in much at night unless there's some trouble." Rudy stepped to the side so Rena could see the coffee cup, and she went straight to the table and placed a plate before Jesse. Without comment of any kind, she turned around and went back to her kitchen.

Rudy called out after her, "Rena! What is it?"

"Beef!" she yelled back, still without looking at them.

Jesse speared a sizable chunk of it and thrust it into his mouth. "It'll do just fine," he told Rudy as he chewed. He was thinking it looked a lot like some of the food he had been eating during the last five years at Huntsville. But he had to admit the taste was a hell of a lot better than what he got at the prison.

He took his time eating, and when finished remained at the table, watching the customers come and go, enjoying his recent freedom and the lusty noise of a saloon cranking up for the night. Even though it was tempting to hang around for a day or two to enjoy the atmosphere of a busy saloon, he knew that would be a little too risky. There would soon be Texas Rangers, U.S. marshals, or both, in the town looking for him. He decided it was time to find a spot to camp. With the money he took from Dewey's drawer, he had enough to stable his horses and sleep in the hotel, but thought it a better idea to make a camp and sleep with his horses. No sense in making his face familiar to any more witnesses than necessary.

At that moment, however, Lucy Tucker came down-stairs to work the evening crowd.

Looking the room over, she saw only one customer who was a stranger, and decided to check him out first. "Well, don't you look like the lonely one?" she asked, walking up to Jesse's table. "What's the matter? Won't nobody talk to you?" From the thoughtless expression on his face, she at first thought him too drunk to respond.

He surprised her when he rolled his eyes up at her as if considering another biscuit. "How much?" he asked with no change of expression.

Suddenly sensing an animal-like bearing in his dull blank face, she answered, "Five dollars," thinking it best to inflate her usual price in his case. As soon as she quoted it, she had a feeling she should have doubled it.

"All right," he said simply and got up from the chair. He had never been approached by a woman before, prostitute or otherwise. Since he usually had to make the proposition, he quickly accepted.

"Come on, darlin'," she said gamely, thinking she might have made a big mistake as she took his hand, a hand hard and rough from working on prison chain gangs. She glanced toward the bar and happened to catch Rudy shaking his head and grinning at her as she led Jesse toward the stairs.

Rudy walked over, picked up the empty plate and coffee cup from the table, and took them back to the kitchen. "Your customer's gone upstairs with Lucy," he said, handing the dirty dishes to Rena. "He ain't paid me yet. Soon as he does, I'll give you yours." He chuckled and added, "If I'da talked to Lucy first, I believe I'da told her not to approach that fellow. He's got a look about him like he ain't been house-broke before."

It wasn't long before Jesse appeared at the top of the stairs and came on down to the saloon again. Seeing his table had been cleared, he went to the bar where Rudy was waiting. "I paid her upstairs," he told the bartender.

"Right," Rudy replied. "That business is between you and her. All you owe me for is the whiskey and the supper." He told him the total figure and Jesse promptly paid without questioning the number of drinks he had been charged for. "Come back to see us," Rudy said as he took the money. "Was everything all right?"

"Yeah," Jesse said and walked out the door.

Quite a while passed with no sign of Lucy. When Rudy realized it had been almost half an hour since Jesse had left, he began to worry she might be in trouble. He started to leave the bar when she suddenly appeared at the top of the stairs.

She paused there a few minutes before walking down the steps and going straight to the bar. "I need a drink of whiskey," she announced desperately. "I know what it's like to be mauled by a grizzly. If he ever comes back, I need a great big ragdoll to let him play with, and I'll go down to the stable and wallow around with the horses."

Rudy tried to keep from laughing but found it hard to do. "I swear, I don't mean to laugh, but if I coulda talked to you before you talked to him, I woulda told you that fellow acted like he'd been livin' under a rock most of his life. Did he hurt you?"

"Not on purpose," Lucy admitted. "He just thought I was a ragdoll or something to play with. When he finally wore out, he told me he had a good time. Said this was his first time in a long time. Said his brother used to visit with the ladies a lot, but his brother's dead now." She shook her head and remarked, "If his brother treated women like he treated me, I can guess what killed him."

"What was his name?" Rudy asked.

"I don't know," Lucy replied. "He never told me."

"Did he say he was stayin' in town, or just passin' through?"

"He didn't say one way or the other," Lucy complained. "He wasn't much for conversation about anything."

Chapter 23

Jesse Slocum rode out of Tinhorn and followed the river north of the town for a distance of approximately a mile and a half, close to the place where Buck had practiced his fast draw. He watered his two horses then hobbled them for the night before gathering wood for a fire in the morning. He had already eaten a big supper at Jake's Place and didn't need a fire for warmth, since the nights weren't really chilly. The two bedrolls he'd gained from killing Arthur and Alvin Wilson provided a comfortable bed.

Satisfied he'd had an enjoyable day, he crawled into the top bedroll. Thinking for only a few minutes about what he was going to do in the morning, he assured himself Zack would be proud of him. With his head empty of all other thoughts, he drifted off to sleep right away.

It was still early in the evening at Jake's Place when Flint walked in.

"Howdy, Flint," Rudy greeted him. "Can I get you somethin'?" He wasn't sure if Flint was on duty or just dropping by before he went home for the night. Flint usually did not drink if he was watching the town.

For the last couple of nights Rudy had seen more of the deputy and the sheriff than usual. For no particular reason, according to them. Rudy suspected something was going on they weren't talking about. They always asked him if he had seen any strangers in the saloon, so there must have been a notice sent out about somebody on the loose. Often a stranger drifted through town, usually somebody on their way to Tyler, or somebody coming from Tyler. The lawmen didn't seem particularly interested in those.

Tonight was different.

Rudy waited for Flint to ask the question, but he didn't right away. Impatient, Rudy asked it. "Ain't you gonna ask me if I've seen any strangers in the saloon tonight?"

"I don't know," Flint responded, making an effort to sound casual. "Have you?"

"I'll say I did. We had us a dilly. I oughta call Lucy over here to help me tell you about him. Ain't nobody you and Buck might be on the lookout for, but he was a strange one." Rudy went on to describe Jesse, then told him how he acted like he had been out of the world for a long time.

Remembering how Lucy had described her exposure to the stranger, Rudy declared, "I swear, I couldn't keep from laughin'. She said he claimed she was his first woman in a long time. Said his brother was big with the ladies, but he was dead now."

That comment triggered an alert in Flint's mind.

"He said his brother is dead?" Flint asked.

"That's right. He said his brother's dead," Rudy confirmed.

"Did he say what killed his brother?"

Rudy shook his head.

"Did he tell you his name?"

"No, he didn't. I asked Lucy, but she didn't know,"

Rudy answered, suddenly aware Flint was more than a little interested in the stranger.

"Did he say where he was headin'?" Flint asked.

Rudy shook his head again.

"Do you know if he was plannin' to stay in Tinhorn tonight?"

"I swear, I'm sorry, Flint, but I don't know any of that. I never thought about askin'."

"That's all right, Rudy. I wouldn't have expected you to have asked him all those questions. I was just askin' in case you did. I reckon I'd best finish my rounds. I'll most likely see you later tonight." With that, Flint turned to leave but paused to ask one more question. "Did he act like he was light on cash?"

"No, he didn't seem to care what anything cost. He had money to pay for it."

"And he's wearin' a black hat with a wide silver band around the crown?" Flint asked, then thanked him and went straight for the door.

Lucy walked up in time to see Flint disappear through the batwing doors. "I was gonna say hello to our young deputy. You musta said something to scare him away. Either that, or he saw me coming."

"I was tellin' him about your grizzly bear customer," Rudy said. "I don't want you to get your heart broken, but Flint 'pears to be more interested in him than you are."

Flint was definitely interested in the stranger wearing the fancy hat. He knew Buck would be as well. But Buck had gone to his room when it appeared it was going to be another typical night in Tinhorn.

If the stranger turned out to be Jesse Slocum, it might be better if Buck were not along. Slocum might shoot on sight. He didn't know Flint, which made things even, because Flint didn't know him.

It sounded as if this stranger might be able to afford spending the night at the hotel. Flint hurried up the street, knowing it was about the time J.C. White took over the desk from Fred Johnson. If Jesse Slocum had checked in earlier, J.C. might not have seen him. Flint was in luck, however, for when he went into the hotel, he found Fred and J.C. talking at the check-in desk. Both spoke to Flint when he walked up.

"Pardon my interruptin', but I need to know about a stranger that mighta checked into the hotel. It's important." Flint got their immediate attention, so he continued. "This fellow would be easy to identify. A little bigger than average, the thing that sets him off is his hat. It's a black, wide brim hat with a fancy silver band around the crown. And he's got long stringy hair down to his shoulders." He watched anxiously for their response.

Both clerks shook their heads.

"I believe I would have remembered somebody like that," Fred replied. "I haven't checked any new guests in today but a man and his wife from White Creek, who are catching the train to Tyler tomorrow. And J.C. is just getting ready to take over the desk, so he hasn't checked anybody in yet."

"No chance he mighta checked in yesterday?" Flint asked, just to be sure.

Again, both clerks shook their heads.

"Somebody like you just described hasn't checked into the hotel, period," Fred declared. "I think somebody would have seen him if he was around. And yesterday, I checked in a couple of men who stop here routinely on their way back and forth to Fort Worth. They were the only new guests I checked in."

"Thank you very much," Flint said. "Sorry to interrupt."

His next stop was back the way he had just come, to the stable at the other end of the street. He received his usual "Howdy" from Lon Blake when he went into the barn to find him.

"Lon, are you boarding any horses for a stranger tonight?" Flint thought it was a possibility this stranger might be sleeping in a stall with his horses.

"No, sir," Lon replied. "I ain't got any strangers with their horses here tonight. "Who you lookin' for?"

"Well, I thought I might be lookin' for some fellow on a wanted poster we got in the mail," Flint lied. "A fellow in Jake's tonight sounded like the one on the poster, but I reckon he moved on out of town after he ate some supper. I was just makin' sure he wasn't still in town."

Lon took good care of all the horses left in his care, but while he was there, Flint took a look at Buster to make sure he was all right, even though he had no reason to suspect the buckskin needed anything. Actually, he was just killing time while deciding whether to go tell Buck about the stranger in the fancy hat. For two reasons Flint was reluctant to bother Buck after he had retired for the night—Buck was still battling his demons from the whiskey bottle, and if Buck was asleep, Flint hated to wake him.

Anyway, it appeared the stranger had already left town. Flint told himself he was overreacting. Jesse Slocum had only one purpose in coming to Tinhorn, and that was to kill Buck. The outlaw would most likely come, seeking to find him, instead of eating supper at the saloon and going upstairs with Lucy Tucker.

Flint returned to the office, unlocked the door, and went inside.

Ralph had locked the door, figuring Flint gone for the night. "You don't usually stay much later than this, if everything's peaceful. I was fixin' to turn in, myself."

"You go ahead and go to bed," Flint told him. "Everything seems all right in town. I'm gonna sit here at the desk for a little while. I'll lock the door when I leave." He'd take one more look around town before he went to his room at Hannah's.

Flint awakened early the next morning, happy to see it had been a peaceful night in Tinhorn.

Already in the office when Flint got there, Buck decided they would go to breakfast as soon as Clara opened. The first to arrive at the dining room, they received the attention of both Bonnie and Mindy. Buck was in a good mood. He had slept very well for a change.

Bonnie commented on it. "How come you're so cheerful this morning? It usually takes a couple of cups of coffee before you're ready to talk."

Buck responded by saying he had a good night's sleep and felt good enough to put up with her nonsense that morning. The conversation continued, light and cheerful. It had the feeling of a nice day to be in the town of Tinhorn. When some of the regular customers started showing up, the girls had to share their attention. Flint and Buck decided they had lingered long enough, took the plate Margaret fixed for Ralph, and departed.

The morning had gone so well Flint couldn't resist asking Buck, "Are you goin' to Jake's?"

"No, I don't think so," Buck answered. Then he japed,

"I don't want those boys over there to see me sober. Might make 'em uneasy."

"Might at that," Flint remarked, and they both laughed.

It was only recently Buck could joke about his drinking problem. Flint saw that as a sign that the big lawman was on the road to recovery. That suited Flint. He wasn't anxious to replace Buck as the sheriff of Tinhorn.

"No, I don't think I'll go to Jake's this mornin'," Buck repeated. "I'm gonna walk up to the post office. I ain't looked in our box for a couple of days. We mighta got some flyers on our boy, Jesse Slocum."

Flint nodded his agreement. "I'm gonna stay here long enough to help Ralph empty that coffeepot, then I'll take a walk around town."

According to the watch Jesse had found in Arthur Wilson's pants pocket, it was almost nine o'clock, time for the bank to open. *Time for my withdrawal,* he thought. *It'll be the first one in five years.* The thought brought a wicked smile to his face. He hoped they resisted. He was anxious to shoot someone, for he pictured the scene in his mind as it had unfolded five years before. The shots would bring Sheriff Buck Jackson running to the bank to stop him, just as he did then. Only this time, there would be no misfire. Jesse's guns were ready and so was he.

Walking into the bank, he turned the CLOSED sign around behind him. Two teller windows were open with five customers lined up—two at one window, three at the other. None of them looked likely to cause him any trouble. He walked across the lobby to the president's office, where he found Harvey Baxter seated at his desk.

Startled by the sight of the strange man suddenly in his

doorway, Baxter responded, "Can I help you?" Seeing the six-gun aimed at him, he froze in shock.

"Get up from there," Jesse ordered. "You give me one little bit of trouble and I'll put a hole in your head." He motioned for him to come out of the office. "Damn you! Move!" he barked when Baxter didn't jump to his command.

Terrified, Baxter hurried into the lobby. Aware what was taking place, one of the customers, a middle-aged woman, screamed.

"You shut your mouth, or I'll blow your head open," Jessie threatened her.

She sank back against the man standing next to her.

Holding Baxter by the back of his collar, Jesse walked him over in front of the tellers' windows, his other hand holding his gun against the back of the banker's head. "This is a holdup," he announced to the terrified group of people. "Anybody tries to stop me, Mr. Big Shot, here, gets shot in the head. You two in them cages, get out here, and bring them cash drawers with you. I know you got some canvas sacks under that counter. Dump the money in those bags." He was going by his memory of the robbery attempt five years before when they found the bags under the counter.

Robert Page and Eugene Bannerman, the two tellers, did as he ordered and moved out of their cages, bringing the money with them.

"All right, set yourself down on the floor. Not you," he nodded at Bannerman, the smaller of the tellers. "You're gonna take another one of them bags to the safe and fill it up. First wrong move I see and Mr. Big Shot, here, gets an airhole in his head."

"I can't open the safe," Bannerman said. "It's on a time-lock. Nobody can open it till noon."

"You're lyin'," Jesse threatened. "You go fill that sack up, or I'm gonna blow your head off."

"He's not lying," Baxter said. "The safe is on a time-lock. You'll have to wait till noon."

"Then maybe we'll just do that," Jesse said. "You folks over there, come over here and set down on the floor."

Thinking they had no choice, all but one started over toward him. Paul Roper, who worked for Harper's Feed and Supply, moved slowly behind the others, as if he were going to follow. When Jesse pulled Baxter out of the way, Paul suddenly made a dash for the door, reaching it before Jesse could swing his gun around to fire. Just as Paul was going out the door, Jesse managed to fire, hitting him behind the shoulder.

It wasn't enough to stop Paul from bursting out of the door, yelling, "Robbery! He's robbin' the bank!" Stumbling, he fell into the street, but rolled over to get to his feet again, still yelling at the top of his voice as he ran into Harper's store, next to the bank.

Furious, Jesse had to forget about the money in the safe but was sure the second part of his plan would still be successful. For Buck Jackson would surely answer the call, just as he did when he killed Zack. *And I'll shoot him down like a mad dog,* he thought.

He shoved Baxter hard enough to knock him to the floor, then he picked up the two sacks of money in one hand while he still held his gun ready to shoot with the other. "If you wanna get shot, stick your nose out that door," he told the folks sitting on the floor.

As fate would have it, Buck was across the street at the post office when he heard the shot and Roper's cry of warning. He and Louis Wheeler, the postmaster, ran to the window to see Jesse come out of the bank, his six-gun still in hand. People along the street stopped to gawk at the bank and continued to stare stupidly as Jesse hooked his sacks onto his saddle horn.

"Oh, My Lord in Heaven!" Louis blurted.

Buck did not hesitate. Gun in hand, he was out the door in seconds. In the heat of the moment, it didn't occur to him the bank robber had time to jump into the saddle and race away between the bank and the feed store. To the contrary, the robber stood by his horse long enough for Buck to confront him.

"All right," Buck commanded. "That's as far as you're goin'. Drop that weapon, or I'll cut you down." He was not prepared for the culprit's reaction.

"Sheriff Buck Jackson," Jesse mocked, still holding his gun. "You drop that weapon, or I'll cut *you* down." His lips parted to form an evil grin. "Looks like we've got us a stand-off, don't it? Last time we had one of these, you came out on top because my gun misfired. Reckon you could be that lucky again?"

Jesse Slocum! It struck Buck like the blow from a cold hammer. Even though he'd expected him, he had not recognized him after his years in prison. Knowing who he was, Buck could identify the same cruel face he had sent to prison five years ago. "I'm gonna tell you again, Jesse, drop that gun. You're under arrest. Ain't no sense gettin' yourself killed."

Jesse smiled at him again. "I'm right glad to see you recognize me, but you don't seem to understand, Sheriff. One of us, or both of us is gonna die. Don't matter if you shoot me or not, I'm gonna put a bullet in you. The only chance you've got to stay alive is if you've got the guts to face me man to man, guns in the holsters. If you ain't got the guts, I guarantee you will die, whether you kill me or not."

In a fix he hadn't seen coming, Buck realized Jesse was

in control of the situation. He obviously didn't seem to care whether he lived or died. Either that, or he was lightning fast on the draw. Buck thought about Flint's insisting he should arrest Slocum, and not face him in a fast-draw contest. *Well, I tried it, Flint, so much for that,* he thought while the two of them stood in the street with guns pointed at each other.

Buck knew he was stalemated. In the brief seconds he had to think, one thought flashed through his mind offering little encouragement—how clumsy he had become when he'd practiced his fast draw down by the river. His only other option was to back away and permit Jesse to get on his horse and ride away with the bank's money.

Not even considering the second option, Buck said, "All right, Jesse. I'll face you man to man, if that's what you want, but it's gotta be a fair draw."

Jesse's smile widened. "It'll be fair. We'll lower our guns at the same time and drop 'em in the holster. You ready?"

Buck nodded.

"Drop 'em," Jesse said.

Both men, with their eyes glued on their opponent, slowly lowered their weapons and dropped them into their holsters.

The spectators who had gathered stood as still as the two duelists, captivated by the drama unfolding on their street. No one offered help to their sheriff. Jesse stepped away from his horse and Buck took a couple of steps backward. Then they faced each other, poised to strike.

"Whenever you feel lucky," Jesse said, still smiling.

It happened in a split second, but seemed to Buck it was all in slow motion. He saw Jesse go for his gun, and he grabbed for his. It seemed heavy and uncooperative as he tried to level it, already seeing Jesse's gun barrel rising to aim at him.

Then Jesse jerked backward and sank to his knees, his face a mask of disbelief, a bullet hole in the center of his chest. He remained that way until Buck came to his senses, walked toward him, then shoved him to the ground. Not sure what had happened, he stood over the body, trying to remember exactly when he pulled the trigger.

His thoughts were interrupted when he heard Flint running up the street, yelling, "Buck! You all right?"

Then Buck heard the noise from the spectators gathering around him and the body.

"You got him, Buck!" Louis Wheeler exclaimed as he ran out from the post office.

"You okay, Buck?" Flint asked again when he got to him. He was carrying his rifle and had run all the way from the jail. "I couldn't get here any sooner. I was sittin' in the office when I heard somebody yellin' that the bank was bein' robbed."

"Yeah, that was Paul Roper," Louis interrupted. "He got shot in the shoulder."

"And I grabbed my rifle and started runnin'," Flint continued. "But it looks like you've got everything taken care of." He looked down at the body. "Is that Jesse Slocum?"

"Yep, that's him, all right," Buck answered, seeming still in somewhat of a daze, which prompted Flint to ask him for the third time if he was all right.

"Yeah, I'm okay," Buck replied. "I'm still standin'."

"I reckon that finally closes that chapter," Flint said. "Reckon it also kinda takes care of that other thing that was botherin' you."

"Right," Buck replied, "reckon so. Lemme see your rifle for a second." Instead of waiting, he reached over, took Flint's rifle, and cranked the lever ejecting a spent shell. "You always leave a spent cartridge in your rifle?"

"I musta been in a hurry the last time I fired it," Flint said, taking his rifle out of Buck's hands. Anxious to change the subject, he asked, "Reckon the bank wants their money back? I better take it inside. That's a nice-lookin' bay horse he was ridin', too. Wonder who he stole that from? I'll take that down to the stable. I expect he might have another horse tied up somewhere. Maybe we can find it."

Buck didn't say anything, just let him keep talking while he continued to fix on him with a suspicious grin on his face.

Flint took the two sacks off the bay's saddle and carried them inside the bank, wondering what his chances were of lying his way out of his successful attempt to save Buck's life. Unsure what Buck's feelings might be about what he did, Flint saw himself as having no other choice. He had even hesitated till the last second to make sure.

Hearing the shot fired inside the bank, he had immediately grabbed his rifle and cranked a cartridge into the cylinder. Out the door he went, knowing Buck was at the post office, which meant Flint had little chance of arriving at the bank first. He got no farther than the harness shop when he saw Buck and Jesse facing each other, both with weapons drawn. He started to continue on but stopped short when he saw them both holster their weapons.

It struck him they had agreed to make it a contest. *Not with what I saw of Buck's draw,* he had thought. Immediately, Flint had dropped to a kneeling shooting position and took dead aim at Jesse's chest. It was no more than forty yards, so he was confident of the shot. He watched, could see they were set to draw, and hesitated.

It took but an instant to see Buck was going to come

in second. Flint squeezed the trigger and dropped Jesse Slocum. The impact of the bullet must have caused Jesse to pull his trigger, sending his shot into the ground. The shots sounded so close together Flint thought it a good possibility no one was aware the kill shot had come from down the street. And judging by Buck's confused state after the shooting, he didn't know whether he had shot Jesse or not.

The fact Buck had checked Flint's rifle was not a good sign, however.

After Flint returned the money to the bank, Harvey Baxter had recovered enough to go outside to view the corpse.

Louis Wheeler, who was still standing with the other gawkers, greeted Baxter with the announcement, "Sheriff Jackson gunned him down, Mayor!"

"Damn good job, Buck," Baxter told him. "Flint said this is one of the two men who tried to rob the bank five years ago, that he had broken out of prison a few days ago. I declare, I didn't recognize him."

"I shot his brother the first time they tried to rob you," Buck informed him. "I hope there ain't nobody else in the family that's wantin' to rob your bank."

Walt Doolin walked up to take a look at the body. "Ready for me to take him, Buck?"

"Yep. He's all yours. His name's Jesse Slocum, if you need it for your records."

"Slocum," Walt repeated. "Weren't that the name of that other 'n a while back?"

Buck said it was his brother.

"Want me to display him?" Walt asked.

"Nope. The sooner we forget about him the better," Buck told him, but he was looking at Flint when he said it.

Flint had a notion it wouldn't be a good idea to get into a deep discussion about the shooting until Buck had a chance to think about it for a while. "Since I ain't got nothin' better to do right now, I think I'll saddle Buster and do a little scoutin'. I'll bet Jesse left another horse tied up real close around here somewhere, and it might be where it can't get to water or grass."

"That's a good idea," Buck said. "He sure ain't carryin' nothin' to camp with on this bay."

Flint started to lead Jesse's horse away then stopped when he saw Paul Roper walk out of Harper's Feed and Supply with his arm out of one sleeve and a wad of cloth tied around his shoulders.

Right behind him, John Harper asked Paul, "Are you sure you don't need any help?"

"Yes, sir, I can make it all right," Paul answered.

Flint was naturally interested. "What happened, Paul? Looks like you hurt your shoulder."

"Gunshot," Paul answered proudly.

When Flint was obviously surprised, John Harper informed him. "I told him I didn't expect that outta him. I sent him to the bank with my deposit. He was in there when the holdup started. And when he got a chance, he made a run for it, and that fellow shot him when he went out the door. He's goin' to see Doc Beard right now, but I told him that deposit wasn't worth risking his life for. He's the one you musta heard yelling that the bank was being robbed."

"It ain't that bad," Paul protested modestly. "I expect Flint knows about gunshot wounds."

"Yeah, I know about 'em. They're all bad."

Chapter 24

It was the only topic of conversation in the town of Tinhorn for the rest of that day. The bank had been struck again, and just like the last time, Sheriff Buck Jackson prevented it from being robbed.

"I hope any potential bank robbers out there will pay attention and be advised to take their outlaw ways someplace other than Tinhorn," Mayor Harvey Baxter stated to the small crowd who had gathered outside the bank.

As he led Jesse's horse down to the stable, Flint heard a cheer go up in response to Baxter's statement.

"Howdy, Flint," Lon Blake greeted him. "Helluva thing, weren't it? Buck and that outlaw decidin' to settle it with their guns?"

"Sure was. Buck said Slocum didn't give him any choice. He had to do it that way. I reckon Slocum took the chance 'cause he figured gettin' killed was better than goin' back to prison."

"You know, when I heard all the ruckus, I ran out to see what was goin' on," Lon said. "I saw you when you ran outta the sheriff's office and started up the street. Then you dropped down and brought your rifle up like you was gonna shoot, but I couldn't tell if you did or not."

Flint hesitated a moment before answering. Then he said, "Yeah, I wanted to get up there to help Buck, but saw I wasn't gonna make it. So, I just dropped down and tried to line up a shot, but I couldn't take a chance on hittin' Buck. Turned out he didn't need me a-tall."

"I figured that musta been what happened," Lon said. "Like I said, I couldn't tell if you pulled the trigger or not. The two shots were so close together, they sounded like one shot."

His comments bothered Flint a little, striking him as being a little skeptical of the way the shooting went down, but willing to accept Flint's version of it.

"That the bank robber's horse?"

"Yep, you know what to do with him. He's not a bad-lookin' horse."

"You fixin' to saddle your horse?" Lon asked.

"Yep, I figure I'll bring you another horse to keep for us, if I can find where Jesse left it," Flint replied. "If you'll take care of this one, I'll saddle Buster."

When he rode Buster out of the stable, he turned up the street, assuming Jesse would have left his packhorse close to where the bank was located. Riding out past the doctor's house, he cut over to the bank of the river, thinking that the best place to look. He didn't have to ride far before he came upon a paint horse tied to a willow tree near the water's edge. The horse was carrying a regular riding saddle, but it was obviously being used as a packhorse.

Flint didn't bother to dismount but rode up to the willow, reached over to the limb, and untied the paint's reins. Seeing ashes from a small fire, he guessed Jesse had spent the night there. He led the horse out to the road and back to the stable.

"I'll leave this one with you, too," he told Lon. "You

can take a look through those sacks. I doubt if there's anything but food in 'em, maybe something you can use." He took Buster's saddle off him and turned him out in the corral.

"Buck said come on to Clara's when you get back," Ralph told him when he walked into the office. "Said he needs to talk to ya."

"What about?" Flint asked.

"He didn't say. Just said he needs to talk to ya."

Flint could well imagine what Buck wanted to talk about, and why he didn't want to discuss it with Ralph hanging around them. Flint also knew there was no way he could avoid the discussion, no matter how much he'd try to persuade Buck to just leave the situation like it was.

He walked on up to the dining room where he was cheerfully welcomed to a dinner honoring Tinhorn's sheriff. "Margaret baked Buck's favorite cake," Clara said. "Come on. He's waiting for you to show up."

"I ain't gonna sit with you unless I get a guarantee I get a big slice of that cake," Flint joked as he pulled back a chair at Buck's table and made an effort to join in the general mood of Clara's staff.

"Set down, Flint. Then maybe they'll let us have some dinner." Buck paused while Mindy poured a cup of coffee for Flint, then refilled his. "Did you find another horse?"

"Sure did. Another fine-lookin' horse, a paint. You gotta hand it to Jesse. He stole good horses."

Buck offered his opinion. "Most likely the first horses he came across, and the owners are layin' dead in a ditch somewhere. I expect it was the same place he got his fancy hat with the silver hatband."

It was a little while before the girls became too busy to

spend all their time over the table of the two lawmen and let them eat.

"There's somethin' I need to tell you about that shootin' this mornin'," Buck finally got a chance to say.

Before he went any further, Flint cut him off. "There ain't nothin' you need to tell me about that shootin'. I wasn't close enough to help you make the arrest, but I saw the shootin'. Everybody did. You beat him fair and square. He didn't give you no choice, so you gave him what he wanted, a showdown. Now, eat those beans before they get cold."

"Doggone it, Flint. I'm tryin' to tell you, you saved my life today," Buck insisted on confessing. "When that man went down, I couldn't even remember when I pulled the trigger, or even *if* I pulled the trigger."

"Well, you must have," Flint insisted. "'Cause he sure as hell went down."

Buck continued to stare at him for a few moments before he continued. "I'll tell you, partner, I ain't ever been one to believe in coincidence. What happened to me this mornin' was either one helluva coincidence or some evil force workin' on me.

"When I went back to the office, I pulled my gun out and checked it. That bullet never went off. I had a misfire. I could see where the firin' pin struck the cartridge, but it never went off. I remember now when I pulled the trigger. I pulled it before I even got my gun raised because he was ahead of me. And he woulda killed me sure as hell if you hadn't cut him down."

He nodded solemnly and said, "Five years ago, when I killed his brother, he mighta killed me, but his gun misfired. Now you can talk all you want about coincidence, but if this ain't the handiwork of somebody tellin' me it's time to hang up my badge, I don't know what is."

"Ah, Buck, you don't mean that," Flint was quick to insist. He didn't want Buck to be thinking about quitting. He was afraid it would be the end of the man. "This town needs you in that sheriff's office."

"This town's lucky," Buck replied. "It's got you in that sheriff's office. I think it's time they realized that." When Flint started to protest, Buck cut him off. "You know damn well you've been doin' most of the heavy liftin' for the past year, and you ain't gettin' the pay for it. I know you think this thing this mornin' is makin' me talk like I am right now. But that ain't entirely the truth. I've been thinkin' about it for a while now. I've gotten old and slow, and I can't seem to lick my damn whiskey problem. That ain't a good combination for a sheriff with my reputation."

Flint tried again to interrupt, but Buck held his hand up to silence him. "Just let me say what I've gotta say. It took me long enough to make up my mind to tell you. Oh, I can still talk big and throw my weight around a little to take care of the drunks and rowdy cowboys. But my reaction time has got too slow for situations like the one this mornin'." He looked at Flint, who was just sitting there shaking his head as if in disagreement. "I trust you, Flint. Like I ain't never trusted a man before. On account of that, I'm willin' to tell you I'm ready to quit. I don't want the pressure of the sheriff's job no more."

Flint hesitated a moment, not sure if Buck was going to let him comment. When Buck seemed to turn his attention back to his dinner, Flint spoke. "I appreciate your faith in me, and I'll never knowingly let you down. We'll just keep this between you and me. There ain't no need for anybody else to know. I'll try to take on more of the responsibility of the job."

"Hell, Flint, you're already doin' that," Buck declared. "You don't understand. I ain't aimin' to hide it from anybody. I'm just ready to quit. I've already told the mayor I need to talk to him, and he told me to come into the bank about two o'clock. I want you to go with me."

"Damn, Buck." Flint hesitated, not sure what to say. He took a deep breath and asked, "Are you sure about this?"

"I'm more sure since this mornin' at the bank than I was before," Buck answered. "If you hadn't got there with that rifle when you did, you'da been the new sheriff, anyway." He couldn't prevent a little chuckle. "I like it better this way."

Flint wasn't quite sure he liked the way the transition was coming about. Content to back up Buck, he had harbored no thoughts about taking over the job as sheriff. As he recalled, it had not been that long ago Buck had to convince the town council Flint was not too young to take the job of deputy. He had since proven his qualifications on numerous occasions but was still a young man and not sure he could present the image of control Buck had.

The rest of their meal was finished in almost absolute silence as both parties thought about the meeting coming up at two. It was so unusual Mindy had to ask Flint if anything was wrong.

"Nope. We're just enjoyin' this fine dinner Margaret fixed up for Buck."

Unable to resist teasing Mindy, Buck said, "Me and Flint was just havin' a serious conversation about somethin' important to both of us."

"I doubt if Mindy's interested in anything we were

talkin' about," Flint quickly interrupted, "Bonnie, either. They don't care anything about that."

"Why, I think they surely ought to," Buck replied, tickled he had hooked Flint on the line as well. He looked back at Mindy "We were talking about how good this dinner was and wonderin' if Margaret ever took the time to teach you two young girls how to cook to please a man."

To Buck's delight, Mindy bit right away. She looked straight at Flint and declared, "I beg to differ. I certainly do care about cooking. I helped my mama in the kitchen since I was knee high to a grasshopper, and I'll match my cooking against anybody's."

Buck chuckled. "There you go, Flint You can mark that off, or maybe you oughta call her bluff on it."

Realizing Buck had tricked her into a boastful claim, Mindy spun around and retreated to the kitchen.

They finished eating and when they got up to leave, Flint let Buck lead the way to the door, and he hung back until Mindy came out of the kitchen to clear the table.

"Don't pay Buck no mind," he said to her. "He just likes to tease. We weren't talkin' about yours or Bonnie's cookin'."

"Thanks, Flint. I really am a pretty good cook, though."

"I woulda bet on it," he replied. "I'll see you later."

"Supper?"

"I expect so." Pausing at the door to pay for his dinner, Flint then hurried to catch up with Buck.

"You won't have to do that anymore," Buck said as they walked back to the office.

"Do what?" Flint asked.

"Pay for your dinner. When you're the sheriff."

"You know, they may not accept your resignation," Flint suggested. "A couple of years ago they didn't wanna hire me as a deputy. They might wanna hire a more experienced man for your job."

At two o'clock they went to the bank for Buck's meeting. Baxter was surprised to see Flint too, but he graciously invited both into his office.

Fully expecting the meeting to be a request for a raise, Baxter said, "I thought it was just gonna be Buck. Let me get another chair."

Flint beat him to it and fetched a side chair from a big table on one side of the lobby.

Baxter closed the door and sat down behind his desk. "Before we get started, I'd like to express my appreciation to you for stopping that holdup this morning, and how glad I am you came through it with no scars. I have a suspicion of what this meeting is about, and I don't blame you for picking this time to petition for a raise. But I have to remind you all matters of this nature have to be approved by the city council."

"Well, I hope I ain't gonna disappoint you, Mr. Mayor," Buck said, "but I didn't come here to ask for a raise. I came to submit my resignation."

Sitting in the side chair, Flint saw Baxter's face freeze with mouth and eyes wide open.

Buck calmly continued. "I've known it was time for me to quit for some time now, and this mornin' showed me I almost waited too long."

Baxter was truly shocked. Like everyone else in Tinhorn, he thought Buck Jackson was an entity that would always be. And like all but Flint and perhaps Lon Blake, who'd witnessed Flint's actions in the street short of the bank, Baxter was certain he saw Buck gun Jesse Slocum down, man to man. "You can't be serious," he finally uttered.

"I'm dead serious and I'll tell you why." Buck went through the whole confession he had given earlier, ending it by saying he couldn't risk the protection of the town in unsteady hands. Finished, he pointed to Flint. "There's the best man you can find anywhere to take my place, and that's the reason I brought him with me. He's ready. I'll guarantee you that, and this town would make a big mistake if they don't make him the new sheriff."

"Like I said," Baxter repeated, "the decision isn't one hundred percent mine. The town council will have to vote on it. But I'll sure as hell back your candidate. Nobody can say Flint hasn't done a first-class job as a deputy. But what are you gonna do? This town owes you a helluva lot."

"Don't worry about me. I'll get by," Buck said. "I've saved up most of my salary over the last five years. I'll find somethin' to do."

After sitting through Buck's whole confession and the mayor's reaction to it, Flint spoke up for the first time. "I'd like to make a suggestion if I could."

Both Baxter and Buck turned to hear what he wanted to say.

"I was just as surprised as you are, Mr. Mayor. I 'preciate Buck's confidence in me, and if I was given the job of sheriff, I'd be doin' all I could not let you or Buck down. I'm not assumin' the town will go along with Buck's recommendation. But if it did, I could use Buck to help me protect the town. I've learned an awful lot from him in the last couple of years, but I know there's an awful lot more I could get from him. And you'd be gettin' a helluva lot more for your money, instead of hiring another deputy."

"I like the sound of that," Baxter said. "That's what I'll pitch to the town council tomorrow night at our regular meeting."

"There's one more thing," Flint said. "As sheriff, I

expect my salary to be in the neighborhood of what you've been payin' Buck. If there's a problem between the council and what Buck's new salary should be, I suggest you shave a percentage of what you pay me and add it onto Buck's salary."

Things in Tinhorn rotated around a peaceful and normal existence the next day.

In the evening, the town council met in Jake's Place for their regular meeting. Harvey Baxter had sent a message they would be voting on a matter of utmost importance so all the members were present.

The sheriff was not in attendance, which was not unusual. The members were accustomed to his absence at any meeting after supper. Deputy Moran was seen walking the streets, but he didn't attend the meeting either. The members soon learned the reason why.

The meeting ran later than usual, with almost everyone having a say. Certain of what he had witnessed the morning of the bank robbery, Lon Blake declared his support for Flint Moran right from the beginning, no matter how young he was. Lon didn't confess what he had seen, however. He didn't want to destroy the image the others had of Buck Jackson gunning down Jesse Slocum as his final act as sheriff.

Flint and Buck learned of their new positions when they went to breakfast the following morning. They were unofficially notified of their new titles by the women in Clara's Kitchen. They'd gotten the word from J.C. White, who had been told by Gilbert Smith, the owner of the hotel.

Flint and Buck were summoned to the mayor's office to be officially sworn in and get all the details of their employment. What it all boiled down to was Flint's income was raised considerably, plus he received many gratuities, such as free meals at Clara's and free stable care for his horse. In their gratitude for the years of service from Buck, the council voted to let him retain all his gratuities as well as his room in the jailhouse building. They differentiated between Buck and a regular deputy, as Flint had been, by naming Buck a special consultant to the sheriff.

That distinction suited Flint and Buck just fine.

TURN THE PAGE FOR AN EXCITING PREVIEW!

**JOHNSTONE COUNTRY.
TRAVEL AT YOUR OWN RISK.**

Some call it the most dangerous stagecoach in the West. But the hard-driving owners of the Frontier Overland Company will get you where you want to go— if you don't mind a detour through hell . . .

The Civil War is over. But Wyoming Territory is still a battleground for the native tribes who live there. Most folks avoid the area altogether. But not former Texas Ranger Butch Keeler and his saloon fight buddy Tucker Cobb. They figured Wyoming would be the perfect place to launch the Frontier Overland Company— a rough-and-ready stagecoach operation that dares to go where others fear to tread. Butch and Cobb don't scare easily. But their next stagecoach trip could change all that. And it just might be their last . . .

The passengers are good people: Colonel McBride, who's delivering much-needed supplies to Fort Washington, and his lovely niece, who wants to visit her dying father. Even though the road to get there is overrun with armed Lakota, Cheyenne, and other threats, Butch and Cobb are happy to help an old friend. Problem is, their worst enemy—a power-hungry business rival and self-described "King"—is out there. Waiting for them. Laying a trap to destroy their operation. And plotting to burn everything to the ground. *Over Butch and Cobb's dead bodies . . .*

Nationally Bestselling Authors
William W. Johnstone
and J.A. Johnstone

FRONTIER OVERLAND COMPANY
DRY ROAD TO NOWHERE

On sale now, wherever Pinnacle Books Are Sold

Chapter 1

Tucker Cobb could feel the whiskey was starting to get to him and did not mind one bit. "I told you before and I'll say it again, Butch. I'll leave when I'm good and ready to leave, Butch, and not a moment sooner."

His partner, Butch Keeling, stood beside him at the bar. He had pushed his empty glass away from him half an hour before and had not allowed Cobb to refill it since. "Our coachline hasn't been exactly thriving since Hagen put the word against us. I hate seeing you throw away what little we have on a woman who doesn't want to see you anymore. Jane's moved on and so should you before you drive yourself crazier than you already are."

Cobb closed his eyes. *Jane Duprey.* Just thinking about her gave him some small measure of comfort. He had not known how much she had come to mean to him until she shut him out of her heart. He had been a bachelor his entire life—content to roaming the open country without any real aim or purpose—until he had met her.

He had once prided himself in the fact that he had made it past forty without allowing a woman to get her hooks into him, but Jane had him hooked good and deep.

He had been a fool to allow her association with "King"

Charles Hagen to come between them. He knew that now, but feared it was too late to remedy the situation. He had seen whatever affection die in her eyes that night when they quarreled in front of the hotel all those weeks ago. She had gone on to open the Longacre House since then and, by all accounts, it had been a success.

But no matter how much time Cobb spent waiting for her to come down to see him, she never did.

"We've got bigger concerns at the moment," Butch went on. "We need to keep our wits about us if we have any hope of fighting off Hagen."

Cobb's mood darkened as he thought of Charles Hagen. The king of the Wyoming Territory. The industry titan's hatred of them had spread far beyond Cobb's love life. It had been several weeks since Cobb and Butch had refused Hagen's offer to buy their Frontier Overland Company.

Business had been rough ever since. Hagen had already purchased or controlled most of the stagecoach lines in the territory. Cobb and Butch were among the last of the holdouts and were paying a heavy price for their independence. None of the respectable hotels in their part of the territory would recommend their stagecoach line to their guests. They pushed them to ride on Hagen-owned lines instead. Some even went as far as refusing to allow them to rent rooms while they were in towns along their route. The two men had been forced to stay in the haylofts of the same liveries where they kept their team of horses. Lately, some liveries had even begun to refuse their business out of fear of reprisals from Hagen. Cobb expected that number would only increase as Hagen's vendetta against them spread.

Cobb tried not to think much about it, for when he did, he felt like he was on the edge of a high, steep cliff.

"Sometimes I think we just should've sold out to him like everyone else."

"Now I know you're drunk." Butch took the glass from Cobb's hand and placed it on the bar. "We didn't start this business because we liked working for other people. We started it because we wanted to be our own men, and we can't live like that under Hagen's thumb."

"I'd say we're already under his thumb," Cobb said. "Look at the kind of trade we've got now. We're lucky if we roll only half full and that's on a good run. All we get are widows and drunks who can barely pay their fare. I've lost count of how many times we've had to wash down the inside of that coach in the past few months."

Butch was not so easily persuaded. "That'll get better in time. Besides, we've managed to keep ourselves going by running freight, haven't we? That's helped some."

"Barely." Despite his present drunkenness, Cobb had not lost his head for business. "But there's only so much our rig can hold. It's only a matter of time before Hagen finds out what we've been doing and puts the stop to that, too."

"Hagen might be a powerful man, but he ain't God, Cobb. He'll lose interest in us soon enough and things will get better." Butch tried to ease his friend away from the bar. "Hell, they already are. We've got that big meeting with Colonel McBride in the morning, don't we? He's never been one who looked kindly on drunkenness. You'll need your rest if you hope to be at your best for it. He's trying to help us, and I think he will if we let him. He's always done good by us and vice versa."

But Cobb would not be moved. At six feet tall, he was bigger than Butch and weighed a solid thirty pounds heavier. He could easily see over the heads of the men drinking around them while scantily dressed women acted like they were hanging on their every word.

Cobb eyed the ornate wooden staircase in the middle of the place and the plush red carpet secured to the stairs by gleaming brass fittings. It was a staircase worthy of a queen. Worthy of a woman like Jane Duprey.

"She's got to come down here sometime," Cobb said, "and I aim to be standing right here when she does."

Butch did not take his hand away from his partner's arm. "Leave it alone, Cobb. You're killing yourself over a train that's already left the station. And no amount of whiskey or heartache will be enough to make it come back."

It had not been too long ago that Cobb had been obsessed with concerns like time and reputation. About drumming up new business for their stagecoach line and keeping schedules. But all of that seemed silly to him now that he felt like he had a hole right through the middle of him. A hole that could only be filled one way and not by whiskey.

"Why won't she see me, Butch? Why won't she give me only a few minutes of her time? She has to know how much it would mean to me."

Butch sighed as he pushed his hat further back on his head. "Which is probably why she won't give it to you. Jane's still mighty sore about you not trusting her like you should have and she's making you pay for it. Some women get mad. Some yell and throw things. I've known one or two that liked to throw a punch when they were angry. You should count your blessings that Jane's not that sort of gal."

"She won't even let me apologize. She won't let me tell her how sorry I am."

"Just give it time, Cobb. That's the only thing that'll

work right now. Time and sleep." He pulled on his partner's arm. "Let's go."

Cobb remembered something his partner had told him when they had first returned to Laramie. "You said you saw her. What did she say?"

Butch pulled him away from the bar. "I already told it to you. Repeating it won't do you any good, but I'll do it if you start moving."

Cobb let his partner pull him along, but was desperate for any attachment to her. Even a second-hand story he had heard a hundred times was better than being ignored like this. "Tell it to me again."

Butch began to lead him through the men and sporting ladies toward the door. "She had me come upstairs to talk to her in her rooms. The place still smelled of drying paint and wallpaper paste. It's done up in red velvet and fancy furnishings. I practically begged her to let you see her for a few minutes, even if it was down here with her customers, but she refused. She said your lack of faith in her wounded her deeply, and it's best if you both forgot about each other. She said she's got a new enterprise here and won't change it on account of you or any other man living or dead."

Cobb had heard all that before but hoped, with each retelling of it, that he might find some nugget of hope he could cling to in these darkest of times. "Did she sound angry when she said it?"

Butch politely pushed through a group of men in evening clothes as he said, "She sounded hurt more than anything. She doesn't hate you, Cobb. She just doesn't want to see you anymore, and you've got no choice but to take her at her word. You've been down here pining for her every night in the week since we got back, but she won't come down to see you. That ought to tell you everything you need to know even though it's not what you want to hear. It's best if you do what you do best. Move on and leave the past behind you."

But Cobb could not move on, not from her, which had been the devil of it. He had spent his life being careful to not allow himself to feel much in this world. Besides Butch, he had never bothered having many friends, much less business partners. The world was tough enough without the burden of being tied down to one person or place.

Butch had been different. They had formed a friendship somewhere along the many miles of cow trails between Texas and Nebraska. Jane had just been another pretty lady who had bought a ticket on their stagecoach to take her from North Branch to Laramie. He had not been looking for a woman to love then but had grown to love her anyway. He had not realized how much until he had been foolish enough to question her loyalty to him over "King" Charles Hagen.

Cobb glanced at the staircase again as Butch led him toward the exit, hoping he might catch a glimpse of her. But all he saw was one of her hostesses bringing a drunken customer up to one of the rooms above. His eyes filled with tears, and he looked away.

"We'll be back in a week," Butch assured him, as they cleared the crowd. "A week can be a long time when it comes to a woman's temperament. Hanging around here won't do you any good, but a few hours of sleep will. The colonel wants to see us bright and early in the morning, remember? And from the sounds of it, we might be looking at a decent payday for our troubles."

But Cobb did not care about Colonel Louis McBride or paydays or reputation. He only cared about getting back in Jane's good graces.

"Maybe you're right," Cobb said, though he didn't believe it.

"Now you're talking sense." Butch pulled Cobb past him and gave him a hearty slap on the back. "Once we're back on the road, you'll be as good as new. I'm bound to think of another way I can talk Jane into seeing you again. You know I can be mighty persuasive when I put my mind to it."

As the passed through the red drapes on their way to the front parlor, Cobb saw the doorman step out in front of them. He was a skinny man with bad skin and longish hair already going gray, though Cobb doubted he was much older than thirty yet. He had narrow, quick eyes that never settled on any one thing for long but did not miss much.

"Hold on, you two," the doorman said, when they got closer. "I want to have a word with you."

Butch urged Cobb to keep going. "We've had more than enough words for our liking for one night, mister. We've paid for our drinks and now we'll be going on our way."

But the doorman held his ground. "I told you to wait, so you'll wait."

Cobb tried the door, but it was locked. The emotion he had barely been able to tamp down began to rise within him. "Open this door."

But the skinny man with bad skin did not. "Not until we get something straight. You two have been coming in here every night for the past week."

"And paid for our drinks every time," Butch said. "We didn't even complain about how expensive they were, either."

The man opened his hands as if revealing the parlor for the first time. "A place like this costs money and it doesn't run on selling whiskey alone."

"Whiskey's all we were in the market for," Cobb said. "Now open this door and leave us be."

But the man made no effort to look for the key. "You leaving things be is why we're having this conversation right now. You haven't been too friendly to our hostesses. Haven't shown them the least bit of interest. That hurts their feelings."

"Not to mention your pocket," Butch said. "We know what this place is and what you are. We don't come here for that, so you'll just have to take what we buy in whiskey."

"Lots of places in town serve whiskey," the man said. "So, if that's all you're here for, you can find that anywhere else in town. I can even recommend one or two saloons for you. But if that's all you want, don't come back in here. This here is what you might call a quality establishment, and I don't like a couple of trail rats like you taking up valuable space that a couple of sporting men could put to better use."

Butch tried to intervene, but Cobb squared up to the man. "This is your last chance to open that door before I start looking for the key."

The doorman's lips drew into a sneer. "You really don't know who you're talking to, do you, mister? I'm Lucien Clay and I run this place for Miss Jane." He offered a slight shrug. "Well, Miss Jane's true employer, anyway."

Cobb's left hand shot out and snatched Clay by the throat. He pushed the smaller man against the wall as he grabbed hold of the breast pocket of his jacket and tore it away. As a handkerchief fell to the floor, Cobb pulled off the pockets of the jacket. He had ruined the second pocket when a key dropped out.

Cobb kept squeezing Clay's throat as he tried in vain to

break the coachman's grip. "Pick up that key, Butch, and let's get out of here. Looks like we've worn out our welcome with Mr. Clay."

Butch picked up the key, opened the lock, and threw the door open. "You'd best let him go now, Cobb."

Cobb pulled Clay off the wall and hurled him out into the street. The doorman stumbled off the boardwalk and fell into the thoroughfare on his backside. Passersby gasped and moved back at the sight of the man splayed in the mud and mess on the ground.

Cobb moved outside and pointed down at Clay. "Let that be a lesson to you, boy. I come and go in here as I please. The next time you raise a hand to me, you'd better have some friends around who can back your play."

Clay's small eyes grew even smaller. "Next time? There won't be a next time."

In one swift motion, Clay rocked up onto a knee and pulled a knife from his boot before launching himself at his attacker.

But Cobb saw him coming and threw a roundhouse right that connected flush with Clay's jaw while the smaller man was still in the air. He was unconscious before he landed on the floorboards of the boardwalk. His knife clattered away and into the street.

Cobb stood over the fallen man. "I have half a mind to stay here until he wakes up so I can be sure he got the message."

Butch looked down at Clay. "Judging by how hard you hit him, I'd wager we might be waiting a long time for him to wake up. We'd better get out of here while we still can."

"No one's going anywhere," a man called out from behind them.

Cobb turned, fists up and ready to swing, but lowered them when he saw it was Rob Moran, sheriff of Laramie. He was fast approaching with one of his deputies close behind.

Cobb had learned through bitter experience that it was best to stay away from lawmen when he could, but Sheriff Moran was a different sort. He liked and respected the man.

As was his custom, Butch stepped forward and did the talking for both of them. "It was a fair fight, Sheriff. That fella pulled a knife on old Cobb here, and he had no choice but to defend himself."

"Was that before or after you threw him into the street?" Moran asked. "Clay's the doorman of this place. He had a right to ask you to leave if that's what this was about."

"We were leaving, anyway," Butch said, "but he locked the door on us and refused to let us go. Wouldn't let us leave until he spoke his mind. That's got to be against some kind of law, don't it, Sheriff?"

Moran motioned for his deputy to tend to Clay as he said, "Only Butch Keeling would try quoting the law as he's leaving a whorehouse." He surprised them by taking Cobb's arm. "Let's go, Tucker. I'm locking you up for the night until you dry out."

Cobb was too surprised to be taken in hand to resist. "But I'm not hardly drunk."

"Drunk enough to start a fight," Moran said. "And dumb enough to have spent every night this week in there mooning over a woman who doesn't want anything to do with you." He pulled Cobb closer. "You don't think people talk about this? You think you're the first man to be thrown over by a woman? Especially *that* woman? Her kind break hearts in there every night of the week."

Cobb balled his hand into a fist, but the cold look in Moran's eye made him stop.

"I've seen this play out hundreds of times, Cobb," Moran said. "Tonight, it was Lucien. The next time it could be the bartender or one of the customers or worse. You'll never get Jane back by turning into a drunk, and I'm not going to waste my time worrying about you every time you pull into town. A night in a cell will do you some good. Probably more than you know. Now get moving. I'd hate to have to force you."

It was only then that Cobb noticed all of the people on the street who had stopped to look at him. He had not realized he had raised that much of a ruckus. He looked back inside the Longacre House in the hope that all the trouble he had caused might have been enough to bring Jane down from her room to see what had happened. Just a glimpse of her would have made all of this worth it.

But all he saw were potential male customers peeking outside with drinks in their hands and cigars in their mouths. A couple of sporting ladies were fussing over Lucien Clay as Moran's deputy tried to get him back on his feet.

Cobb felt all of the fight go out of him. He felt ashamed. For what he had done and for what Moran said he might do because, deep down, he knew he was right. "I won't fight you, Sheriff."

Moran kept hold of Cobb's arm as he led him out into the street.

Butch trailed after them. "How long are you fixing to keep him locked up, Sheriff? We've got a meeting with Colonel McBride tomorrow morning, and I'd hate to have to explain Cobb's absence."

"If he behaves himself," Moran said, "I'll let him go around sunup. But if he so much as looks at me or one of my men sideways, I'll keep him in jail for a week until he cools off."

Cobb's shame only grew worse as he heard Butch stop following them. He took a final glance back at the house of ill repute and could have sworn he saw a curtain on the second-floor drop back into place. He liked to think it had been Jane looking out at him. It was not much of a hope, but it was all the hope Tucker Cobb had at the moment.

Chapter 2

The next morning, as he sat across from Cobb at Colonel McBride's dining room table, Butch could see his partner was in a bad way. The dark circles under his reddened eyes were almost the size of saddlebags and his skin bore a yellowish tinge to it. He looked like he had not slept a wink in jail, and Butch imagined alcohol was only partly to blame for his sleepless night. His sorrow over losing Jane's favor and his violent run-in with Lucien Clay had likely played a part in keeping him awake. He knew Cobb was a man of great pride who was capable of feeling great shame on those rare occasions when he allowed his emotions to get the better of him.

But although Cobb looked the worse for wear, he managed to remain attentive to what Colonel McBride had begun to tell them.

"I've asked you gentlemen here this morning to discuss a matter of grave importance and urgency," the colonel explained. "I'm asking you to help not only me, but your country."

Butch had been expecting McBride to hire them for a private charter, not this, but said, "We'll help if we can.

You know Cobb and me owe you for getting us out of that scrape with Hagen a few weeks back."

"Doing a decent deed is its own reward," the retired colonel said, "and doesn't require gratitude. If you agree to do this, I'll be the one in your debt and so will the army."

Butch did not know Colonel Louis McBride well, and he had not known him long, but he knew McBride was not given to exaggerating. The former army man was about sixty with iron-gray mutton chops that did little to hide how jowly his face was becoming. His suit was expensive and had been tailored to fit his roundish frame. But although age was beginning to gain the advantage on him, his deep-set eyes were as clear as they were intense.

"Sounds serious, Colonel," Cobb pointed out. "Might as well lay it out for us so we can give our answer."

McBride cleared his throat. "The matter concerns Fort Washington, which is only an hour's ride from here. I take it you're familiar with its location."

"We've ridden past it a few times," Butch said, "but we've never had call to go inside yet."

"Colonel John Carlyle is the commanding officer of the fort. He was an artillery officer who served under me during the War between the States. He was only a major then, but received a battlefield promotion that was made permanent after the war. I'm sure I don't have to tell you that almost every such promotion was rescinded after the hostilities ended. John kept his rank. That should give you some idea of his merit as an officer."

Cobb said, "I can't imagine an army colonel like that would have much use for a couple of mule skinners like me and Butch."

"Unique problems call for unique solutions," McBride explained. "Jack is a sick man. His doctors believe he is suffering from a cancer that has spread to most of his innards.

They don't believe he has much longer to live. The colonel sent for his daughter as he would like to see her one final time before he passes on. In fact, she's upstairs sleeping right now. Her name is Eustice, but she goes by Tess for short."

Butch saw Cobb bring his hand to his mouth as his empty stomach growled and cramped. His body was beginning to make him pay for his excesses from the night before.

Butch spoke quickly to cover his friend's obvious discomfort. "We're sorry to hear about your friend, but Cobb was right earlier. I don't see why he can't send some of his men to fetch her and bring her to him."

"Under normal circumstances," McBride said, "that's exactly what he would do. Unfortunately, these aren't normal circumstances because Fort Washington is currently under attack."

The colonel spoke over their expressions of surprise. "I only learned of the attack last night when a rider from the fort managed to escape under cover of darkness and bring word to me here. A band of Lakota and Cheyenne warriors have laid siege to the place. They attacked a supply wagon train more than a week ago, and when Colonel Carlyle sent a patrol to find them, the warriors attacked them, too. The fort has been cut off from the outside world ever since and is in desperate need of supplies."

"A siege?" Cobb said. "I've never known a tribe to attack a working fort. They like to hit and run in the open ground."

"I fought a different sort of enemy in the war," McBride said, "but this time they seem intent on using the army's foolishness about fixed fortifications against them. Those soldiers have been trapped behind their own walls for the past week and are running mighty low on provisions.

That's why I'll need your help. Not only to bring Tess to her father, but to get those soldiers the supplies they so desperately need."

Cobb's mouth dropped open. "You mean you want us to run a stagecoach laden down with supplies and a woman through a band of hostile Indians on the warpath?"

McBride nodded. "That's exactly what I want you to do, Mr. Cobb. And, what's more, it needs to be done this morning. Without delay. Both Colonel Carlyle's condition and the condition of his men demand it."

Butch knew there had to be a better way. "Did you send word to one of the other forts? The army's better able to take on Lakota and Cheyenne warriors than we could."

"The young private who brought word to me here also sent a telegram to all the forts in the territory," McBride explained. "The tribes planned their attack well. The closest forts are short on men as they've already sent out their regular patrol. Fort Laramie should be able to send men within a couple of days, but those men in Fort Washington don't have that much time, hence the urgency. I hate to say it, but Colonel Carlyle's desire to see his daughter before he dies has become an afterthought."

Cobb sank back in his chair. "What you're asking is suicide, Colonel."

McBride arched an eyebrow. "Having seen the extent of your valor back at Delaware Station, I'm disappointed in your hesitation."

When Butch saw Cobb's face redden, he spoke up before his partner's mouth got them in trouble. "Valor's one thing, but keeping our hair is another. Cobb's right. We can't outrun those warriors, and there's not enough of us to fight them off. Do you even know how many are out there?"

McBride shifted in his chair. "At least twenty, but likely more."

"Words like 'likely' don't do much against Lakota or Cheyenne," Cobb said. "Butch and me have ridden by that fort plenty of times, and what you're asking us to do won't be easy. There's a thick band of trees that circle the fort at a distance. There's a narrow clearing in one place, but we're as good as dead if we try to use it."

McBride frowned as he was clearly growing frustrated. "I'm quite familiar with the land, Mr. Cobb. Colonel Carlyle is an old artillery man. That tree line is exactly one thousand yards away from the fort. The rest is open ground. John insisted on that distance because he keeps a couple of twelve-pound howitzers hidden behind the walls. The Cheyenne and Lakota may think it provides cover for their warriors. They don't know they're sitting in a tinderbox. One exploding shell in the heart of those trees will be enough to set the whole place alight."

Butch wondered when the army would realize that fighting Indians was not like fighting soldiers. "But he ain't used them yet, has he? Probably because he knows they'd just scatter as soon as they caught sight of that cannon. And I'd bet my last cent that they already know he's got them. Besides, cannons won't do us much good."

Cobb picked up where Butch left off. "Since we can't use that gap in the trees, we'll have to ride through the trees before we even catch sight of the fort. The roots and overgrowth will threaten to flip us over every step of the way. Even if we make the clear ground, which will take a miracle, a heavy coach has no chance of outrunning braves on horseback."

"I didn't say it would be easy, and I'm not asking either of you to do anything I'm not willing to do myself," McBride said. "I'll be putting myself in harm's way right beside you. I plan on accompanying both of you to Fort Washington." He held up a hand to stop any attempt to talk him out of it. "My leg may forbid me from moving around as well as I used to, but I don't need my legs to work a rifle from inside the coach. I intend on helping you boys repel any of the attackers who are certain to descend on us once we reach open ground. And the trees will provide as much of an obstacle to the warriors as they will to us. I've fought in heavily wooded areas before and it's a great equalizer. I know it can be done because I've done it. The messenger assured me that the men at the fort are awaiting us. They'll ride out to help us as soon as they see us."

Cobb ran a hand over his mouth as he thought it over. Butch imagined his partner had the same empty feeling in his stomach. Only in Butch's case, it was not due to too much whiskey the night before.

Colonel McBride cleared his throat again. "To put a finer point on it, I wouldn't have asked you to do this if I wasn't confident that you're the right men for the job. And I assure you, I'll personally see to it that you're well compensated for the trouble."

Cobb slowly lowered his hand. "We can't spend money if we're dead."

Butch added, "And we've heard what the Lakota like to do to their captives. They won't make it quick if they catch us, and it'll be even worse for the woman."

"It's certainly a possibility," McBride admitted, "but I ask you to take Private House's accomplishment into account. He found a way to escape the fort and ride here to Laramie right under the noses of the warriors. I've spoken to him, and he's quite sure he can get us to the fort safely. I have every confidence that he can do it, too."

Cobb glanced at Butch before saying, "This Private

House tell you how many other messengers tried to escape the fort and failed?"

McBride frowned. "Three."

Cobb frowned, too. "That's what I thought. I know what you did in the war, Colonel, but you've never gone up against the likes of these men before. I've faced them a time or two, and Butch here has had plenty of scrapes with the Apache and Comanches down in Texas. They don't fight like you're used to fighting, and the only reason why your Private House escaped is because they let him escape. I wouldn't be surprised if that was their aim all along. To draw the cavalry into some kind of trap. They're not the mindless savages that folks back east think they are. They're smart and ruthless and they're not afraid to dic."

Butch had not known Colonel McBride for long but could tell he was disappointed to the point of being insulted. "I've forgotten more about war than either of you could ever hope to know. I didn't expect you to relish the idea of this request, but I certainly thought you'd show more backbone than this."

Butch knew Cobb was still raw from the night before and feared he might lose his temper but was glad when his partner showed restraint. "You might be right if it was just our scalps I was worried about. But you want us to take a girl right smack dab in the middle of a siege."

"I'm not a girl, Mr. Cobb," a woman said from the hallway.

Cobb and Butch got to their feet as Mrs. McBride escorted a tall woman into the dining room. She had straight black hair pulled back into a tight bun and wore a plain floral dress devoid of lace. She had a longish face with high cheekbones, dark eyes, and a thin line for a mouth. Butch supposed some men might have called her ugly or plain, but there was a certain quality to her countenance that he found appealing.

"Gentlemen," Colonel McBride said, "this is Eustice Carlyle, the colonel's daughter. She also happens to be my godchild. You already know Mrs. McBride."

Cobb and Butch bid the ladies a good morning as Mrs. McBride gestured for them to sit down. "No need to stand on our account, boys. We've just finished packing Tess's things and decided it was time for some coffee."

But Tess was not as pleasant as her hostess. "We managed to hear some of your concerns as we were coming down the stairs just now, Mr. Cobb."

Cobb blushed, which was the first hint of color Butch had seen in his partner in a week. "I didn't know you'd be listening, ma'am, or I'd have chosen better words."

"Plain speaking is important in times like these," Tess said, "especially when you happen to be right. One of the sacrifices of being a soldier's daughter is that we aren't often spared from the dangers our fathers face in this part of the country. I have no misconceptions about what those warriors might do to me if our plan fails, but I'm willing to take the risk. But the burden of seeing my father before he passes is mine, not yours. Don't let my Uncle Louis here bully you into risking your lives on my account. I'll just have to return to the fort with Private House on horseback later this morning. We'll just have to make other arrangements regarding the supplies. The private and I will carry as much as our horses can bear."

Butch spoke over Cobb's objection. "You can't do that, miss. That private was lucky he got out of there in the dark. Riding to the fort in daylight is just plain crazy."

"Then I suppose I'm quite mad." Tess smiled. "Others have said as much about me before. But my father's condition does not allow for delay. He needs me, and I intend on being there for him to help ease his passing. Each one of my siblings would do the same if they were here, but as they're not, the task falls to me. You needn't trouble yourselves about the matter any further. It's settled. Private House and I will go alone. I bid you both a good day."

Cobb and Butch began to rise as the women left the dining room, but Tess gestured for them to remain seated.

There was something solemn and resigned in that simple gesture that struck Butch at his core. He found her bravery touching and felt ashamed of his lack of it until now.

The colonel rested his hands on the armrests of his chair. "Well, gentlemen, it seems that the matter is, indeed, settled. As you can see, my niece is a headstrong woman who speaks her mind. She's much like her father in that regard. I'm sorry for having wasted your morning. We'll have to find another course of action."

But although the colonel began to stand, Cobb and Butch remained seated.

Butch watched Cobb begin to turn over the prospect of the matter in his mind. It was clear that Tess had succeeded in shaming him into considering it, too.

"A stagecoach won't move as fast as free horses on open land," Cobb said. "It'll be louder, too. They'll hear us coming and they'll see us approach from a long ways off."

McBride cocked an eyebrow. "True, but the hostiles would be facing five guns instead of just one. Tess is more than a fair hand with a rifle and pistol. Her father made sure all of his children knew how to fight."

Butch felt the burden of his own doubts begin to lift. "It *is* mighty flat land, though. After those trees, I mean. And our coach runs better than most its size. With me and my rifle up on the roof, I might be able to bring down a few of them up front." He looked at McBride. "With you and Tess shooting out from inside, it might be enough to slow them up some until those horse soldiers ride out to meet us."

"And ride out they will." McBride's eyes were bright with pride. "You can rest assured of that much."

"Rest and assurances don't play much of a part in this," Butch said. "Do you have a rifle of your own or do you need us to get one for you?"

"I have my pistol from the army," McBride said, "but I won't be able to take it with me. I haven't told my wife of my plans to join you, and I want to keep it from her until the last possible moment. And yes, gentlemen, I'm more afraid of crossing Mrs. McBride than I am a band of warriors."

Butch admired the older man's grit. "We'll get one you can use and plenty of bullets to go with it."

Cobb asked, "You still want to head out this morning?"

"Before noon, if possible," McBride said. "I took the liberty of purchasing provisions for the fort. There is a pile of goods waiting for you to pick up at the general store. We can put them inside the coach to help center it while weighing it down. It won't make for comfortable accommodations inside the coach, but this isn't a pleasure ride. My niece and I will gladly suffer it."

Cobb stood, followed by Butch. "Looks like we've got a lot of work ahead of us, Colonel. We'd better get to it. And if you change your mind about coming with us, we'll understand."

McBride leaned on his walking stick as he stood, too. "I'll be ready to travel, gentlemen. And so will Private House and my niece. We'll give a good accounting of ourselves."

Butch did not doubt it as he followed his partner out of the McBride home.

Once they were out on the boardwalk, Cobb asked his partner, "What did we get ourselves into just now?"

Butch was beginning to wonder that himself. "Hopefully a good story we'll live long enough to tell one day."

As they loaded up the goods from the general store in the stagecoach, Butch decided it might be a good time to tease his partner a little. "Judging by how you're moving all this stuff, I guess what they say is true."

Cobb slid a sack of flour into the coach. "And what do they say?"

"That there's nothing quite like the prospect of losing your hair to cure a hangover."

Cobb grinned as he grabbed another sack of flour. "I think I'd prefer the hangover, but since I've already got one, it doesn't matter."

Butch took the last box of McBride's provisions and slid it inside the coach. The volume of supplies reached from the floor of the coach to the roof, with just enough space for Tess Carlyle on one side of the bench and for Colonel McBride on the other. "That niece of the colonel's shamed us into doing this, you know."

"Yeah, I know," Cobb admitted, "but she was right. I wouldn't have been able to live with myself if we let her and that private ride out there alone. Would've been like Delaware Station all over again, only this time, we wouldn't be able to double back and help them. Besides, it sounds like those soldier boys need all this stuff."

Butch knew they did, but he was bothered by one question he could not quite shake. "I didn't know the Lakota and the Cheyenne were on the warpath again. I'd have thought we would've heard about it before now if they were. This sort of thing doesn't just happen overnight. There are usually rumblings about it before it starts."

"Everything's got to start somewhere at some time, I guess." Cobb shut the door of the coach. "We've found ourselves on the beginning end of it is all."

Butch had seen enough brawls and skirmishes in his life to know it did not take much to set men against each other. White, black, red, or yellow did not make much of a difference when it came to violence.

But of all the tribes he had encountered in Texas and in the years since, he never saw a warrior do something without a good reason. Getting members of two different tribes like the Lakota and Cheyenne to ride together—even against the army—did not just happen. These were not a couple of braves who got themselves worked up over something a loudmouth said over a cookfire. There was more to this than that. And he had a feeling McBride knew what that was but doubted he would tell them. He did not think it would make a difference if he did. Cobb had already made up his mind and that was the end of it.

"Let's just hope that Private House the colonel mentioned has enough sand to ride against them Indians a second time around."

Cobb shut the coach door, climbed up on the running board, and used his weight to try to test the balance of the coach. "If he was brave enough to reach safety and go back, I'm sure we can count on him to do his share of the fighting." Cobb stepped onto the loading bay of the general store and put all his weight against the coach. "She'll ride a lot heavier than normal. We'll have to move slow over those trees if we don't want to risk cracking an axel."

Butch knew the coach faced another, even greater difficulty. "Hauling so much weight will mean the team will be near played out by the time we get there. But they've had a good long rest here in town this past week, so we ought to be able to squeeze enough speed out of them when we need it most."

Cobb jumped down from the loading dock. "Getting there's only half of it. Getting out again will be harder."

Butch did not think so. "I figure we'll be safe enough if we just stay behind them high walls they've got around the place. Keep our heads down until those horse soldiers arrive from Fort Laramie. The colonel said they ought to be there in a couple of days at most."

"You know how the army is," Cobb said, as he climbed up into the wagon box. "Two days is just as likely to turn into a week. They'll want to save their men, sure, but the Lakota and Cheyenne will have something to say about how fast they get here."

Butch climbed up next to his partner and took his Henry rifle from the bench before sitting down. He always kept the rifle in fine working condition, and it had never let him down yet. He hoped this time would not be an exception.

"Did you think to get some cartridges for that shotgun of yours?" Butch asked his partner.

"Two boxes worth." He released the hand brake and snapped the reins, sending the team into motion. "We'd best go pick up the colonel and his niece. I just hope that soldier boy who brought that message is ready to ride. The more I think about this, the less I like our chances."

For one of the few times in their friendship, Butch found himself with nothing to say, for Tucker Cobb had just said it all.

Visit our website at
KensingtonBooks.com
to sign up for our newsletters, read
more from your favorite authors, see
books by series, view reading group
guides, and more!

BOOK CLUB
BETWEEN THE CHAPTERS

Become a Part of Our
Between the Chapters Book Club
Community and Join the Conversation

Betweenthechapters.net